# BY MY HANDS

29645

A NOVEL BY

## ALTON GANSKY

**Chariot VICTOR**
**PUBLISHING**
A DIVISION OF COOK COMMUNICATIONS

Victor Books is an imprint of ChariotVictor Publishing,
a division of Cook Communications, Colorado Springs, Colorado 80918
Cook Communications, Paris, Ontario
Kingsway Communications, Eastbourne, England

Editors: Sarah Peterson and Carole Streeter
Design: Andrea Boven
Cover Photo: Uniphoto

Library of Congress Cataloging-in-Publication Data

Gansky, Alton.
    By my hands / by Alton Gansky.
        p.  cm.
    ISBN 1-56476-534-2
    1. Hospitals—Fiction.  I. Title
PS3557.A5195B9  1996
813'.54—dc20
                                                    96-4915
                                                       CIP

2 3 4 5 6 7 8 9 10 Printing/Year 00 99 98 97 96

For information write
VICTOR BOOKS
4050 Lee Vance View
Colorado Springs, Colorado 80918

# Acknowledgments

Many writers unashamedly admit that their work is the direct result of not only the author's efforts but also the contributions of many others. I number myself among those who willingly offer thanks to the many people who made the task of writing enjoyable and considerably easier.

To my wife, Becky, my teenage children, Crystal, Chaundel, and Aaron for their patience, encouragement, and willingness to let me leave this world and enter the domain of my characters.

To Pat Henson for her excellent proofreading and her profound ability to point out my literary errors without exploding into laughter.

To Dave Horton and the staff of Victor Books for seeing something of value in my work.

To Jack Cavanaugh, fellow writer, adviser, mentor, and most of all friend, for his timely and firm push. Thanks, Jack, I needed that.

And to the various technical advisers from the Coast Guard, FBI, surgeons, nurses, and news staff who struggled to keep me close to the realm of accuracy.

# One

## Sunday, March 1; 1:30 A.M.

Lois Langford shifted her body in the hospital chair and fixed her gaze again on the small red light indicating each drop of fluid that passed from the suspended plastic IV bag through the electronic IVAC unit. Its rhythmic pulsating had helped her drift off to sleep when reading or watching television had failed. Sleep was a rare commodity in a hospital; even after midnight the Kingston Memorial Hospital could be a busy and noisy place.

Lois allowed her eyes to trace the frail form on the bed before her. Even under the bed sheet she could tell that her husband's body was too thin. Bill had always been so robust and active. Preferring outdoor activities to staying around the house, he had given up his civil service job to take employment with Cal-Trans, maintaining the landscape along San Diego County's freeways.

Now he hardly seemed the same man. His deep tan had faded to a vague yellow hue. The once muscular body was now atrophied; his bright eyes lacked their former luster. Now they were merely mirrors of the slow death that pirated a little more life away from Bill with every passing hour.

5

The family had tried to get her to go home and rest, but how could she? Not after the doctors had told her that he could die at any time. There was great doubt that he would live through the night. She had spent thirty-seven years with Bill: sharing his food, his home, and his bed. She would not leave him now.

Four months ago they had been planning a vacation. Bill had wanted to drive to Custer, South Dakota for some camping and fishing with his brother. A few days before they were to leave, he had begun to experience lower abdominal pain and had difficulty keeping food down.

Lois had insisted that he see Dr. Lewis, their family physician. At first, Bill was reluctant, but she put her foot down, "No doctor— no trip."

He had studied her for a few moments then weakly nodded his head and said, "Okay, Sarge, whatever you say." He called her that when he thought she was being too bossy. She hated the name, but now she would give anything if he would open his eyes and say, "Hi, Sarge."

After examining Bill and running some tests, Dr. Lewis informed them that gallbladder surgery was needed. "Probably nothing to worry about," Dr. Lewis had said optimistically. "Pretty routine surgery, but you'll have to postpone that vacation. Don't worry, I'm sure Mt. Rushmore will wait for you."

Bill resisted at first, but sensing the doctor's concern he reluctantly consented. Surgery was scheduled for the following afternoon.

That was four months ago, before the verdict of cancer that had spread to the kidneys and liver. For four months Lois had sat by Bill's bedside waiting . . . watching. . . .

The dim light made it difficult to focus on the wall clock opposite her chair. Three o'clock in the morning? Lois realized she had fallen asleep. She looked toward Bill's bed. Was he still alive? Everything seemed in place: the IV unit . . . and the doctor? She hadn't heard him come in. He didn't usually visit this early.

"Is everything all right?" Lois asked apprehensively and started to rise from her chair.

Without looking up, the man in the white lab coat raised a finger to his lips. He stood at the side of the bed gazing down at the form before him. Then he raised his hand and brought it to rest on

Bill's chest. Slowly, almost imperceptibly, his hand began to glow a pale blue in the dark room. Lois stared unbelieving. She started to say something, but thought better of it. She sat motionless and watched the unbelievable, and then inexplicably dozed off again.

When she awoke, she saw Bill, sitting up in bed, and looking healthy and full of life. The yellow pallor and gaunt appearance had been replaced by the rugged complexion of the man she had known for nearly four decades.

"Looks like it's going to be a fine, sunny day," he said. A wry smile stretched across his face. "Do you suppose they'll let me out of here for a little walk?"

Tears filled Lois' eyes.

## Sunday, March 1; 7 A.M.

Dr. Rachel Tremaine had opted to take breakfast in the hospital cafeteria. Taking her food to a table near a window, she opened the latest edition of the *American Medical Journal*. The need for constant education was just one of the many stresses associated with her profession. Frivolous malpractice lawsuits, the need to face death and disease daily, and the ever-present fear of making a life-altering decision took its toll. Many doctors simply gave up trying and moved into general practice in the suburban areas of the city. Some even left the profession. She had vowed never to do that.

She was only a few paragraphs into an article on anesthesia-induced comas when two nurses sat down at a nearby table. One nurse had shoulder-length blond hair, the other dark olive skin. Rachel had little fondness for nurses. They were, admittedly, a necessary part of medicine, but to her they were also a chronic annoyance. She found them resentful of her position and authority.

She glanced at the nurses over her magazine but they were oblivious to her. Their conversation began with complaints about the first shift supervisor on the third floor, west, and the pregnancy of a mutual friend. But then it took a different turn. Something unusual had happened on the fourth floor medical wing last night. Rachel intensified her eavesdropping.

"Have you heard all the chatter from the fourth floor?" the dark one asked.

"No. What happened?" the blond replied.

"You know Beth Greensberg, don't you?"

The blond shook her head.

"Well, she works the graveyard shift in the medical wing. We rode down the elevator together this morning, and she said the weirdest thing happened last night. It seems the patient in room 402 has terminal cancer, stomach and liver, I think, and the doctors expected him to kick off last night. Instead, this morning they find this guy sitting straight up in bed chatting with his wife like he was sitting on his front porch. His skin color was normal, and so were his vitals. He had even gained weight. Sure has the doctors puzzled."

"That's not too difficult to do," the blond said giggling. "So what happened?"

"I don't know and Beth didn't either. They called in several doctors and kept everyone else out. But Beth saw the man and he looked different this morning than he did last night."

"What are the doctors saying?"

"They won't talk about it, but her shift supervisor was pretty shook up."

"It is kinda' shocking when someone gets well around here, isn't it?" Both women laughed.

Rachel studied them for a moment and considered saying something but decided against it. Gossip and rumor were part of hospital life and making a scene would achieve nothing. She would just consider this overheard conversation for what it truly was: a flight of fancy by bored nurses. If anything of such magnitude had happened, then she would hear of it through proper channels.

## Sunday, March 1; 7 A.M.

Music slowly worked its way into the sleep-shrouded mind of Adam Bridger, gently urging him awake. Adam begrudgingly opened one eye and peered over his pillow at the red numbers on his alarm clock. Seven o'clock and his stomach hurt. His anxiety was always punctual. He turned off the alarm and rolled onto his back, trying to rationalize away his nagging insecurity.

How often had he done this? Three times every week for fifteen years. Twice on Sundays, once on Wednesday nights for fifty weeks each year came to 150 times each year. Multiplying by fifteen years equaled a grand total of 2,250. "Two thousand two hundred and fifty times," he said aloud. "And each time I fight this battle. It should all be cut and dried by now."

He began the morning's routine that had been polished over the last fifteen years. Each Sunday morning after he showered and shaved, he would review his sermon notes over breakfast: a bowl of cereal, a cup of coffee, and orange juice. Then he dressed and drove to the Maple Street Community Church where he had served as pastor for the past nine years. In his office he would review his notes again. By the time he stood in the pulpit at 11 that morning, the anxiety would be gone and he would find himself enjoying the exhilarating act of preaching.

This morning, however, Adam noticed that his stomach hurt more than usual.

## Sunday, March 1; 11 A.M.

He would have considered it an exceptional morning if it hadn't been for the persistent pain in his abdomen. Earlier he had attributed the pain to his usual Sunday anxiety, but his anxiety was always gone by the time the worship service started. Even Melba Watson, president of the Woman's Missionary Fellowship and the church's "official" busybody, had commented that he appeared a little pale. Perhaps he was coming down with the flu. That had happened to him once before and to keep from becoming ill in the pulpit he had to cut his sermon short and exit through a side door that led to a courtyard between the sanctuary and the Sunday School building. He dreaded the thought of having to do that again.

The worship service was unusually full. The church had nearly 500 members of which about 300 attended each Sunday. This Sunday, however, there were at least 400 people sitting in the church's aging pews. Adam looked over the sea of faces, noticing the regular attendees and several people he had not seen before. New faces always pleased ministers and Adam was no different. He would make sure that he shook hands with them before they left.

The service opened as it always did with Adam giving the announcements first, followed by the congregation standing and shaking hands with those around them. As the service progressed, Adam knew that it was going well. He also knew that he felt far from well. *No doubt about it*, he thought, *I've got the flu. Maybe I shouldn't do any handshaking today.*

As the soloist sang, "Cast Your Bread upon the Waters," Adam reviewed his opening illustration and rehearsed the sermon's three points. He also debated whether to start with a joke or move directly into the message. When Adam first came to Maple Street Community Church, he had used a lot of humor which quickly endeared him to the congregation. It wasn't long, however, before people began to expect their Sunday morning jokes, commenting if Adam preached a message without them. Fearing that his sermons would soon degenerate into a stand-up routine, Adam became very judicious in his use of jokes, saving them for sermons that were weighty or might otherwise be uncomfortable.

Deciding to dispense with the joke, Adam stood and made his way to the white oak pulpit centered on the rostrum. As he did, he was seized with a sudden stab of abdominal pain. He clutched at his stomach and grimaced. He paused for a moment behind the pulpit, aware of 400 pairs of anxious eyes fixed on him. He needed to say something.

"Perhaps it's time I stopped eating my own cooking." His voice was shaky, not the usual "pulpit" voice he had cultivated over the years. The pain subsided and he began his message by announcing the text: "This morning we will begin by looking at one of the most exciting passages in the New Testament." Adam was attempting to sound confident and relaxed, but he doubted his success. He felt feverish, weak, and nauseated, but reminded himself that the message would last only thirty minutes; surely he could endure that long. "The passage is at the very heart of the Christian faith. Turn with me now to 1 Corinthians, chapter 15." He paused for a moment and listened to the rustling of pages as people turned to the passage.

"First Corinthians, chapter 15," he repeated. "Our morning's message is entitled, 'Resurrected to Reign.'" Adam was pleased that his pulpit voice was returning. "Now that you've found the passage, we'll begin by reading verses..."

Suddenly the pain returned with a vengeful force. Adam let out a little moan despite himself. He clutched at his stomach with both hands. His whole insides felt as if they were on fire. He felt his legs give way as he fell to his knees behind the pulpit. Wave upon wave of nausea passed over him.

"Please, God," he prayed, "don't let me be sick here. At least let me get outside."

Adam was aware that he was surrounded by several people. He knew they had come to help, but he wished they would go away. His pain was compounded by embarrassment.

"Pastor, are you all right?" It was the voice of Dick Slay, the chairman of the deacons. "Do you want us to call an ambulance?"

Adam responded by vomiting on the floor.

# Two

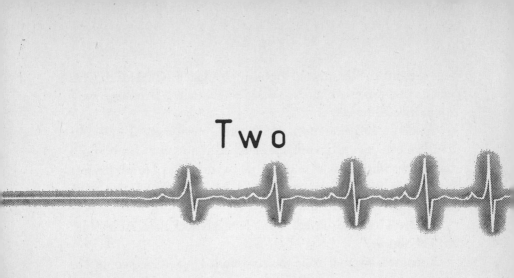

## Sunday, March 1; 8:15 P.M.

Adam's mouth was dry and his throat raw. His unfamiliar surroundings confused him. He was in a room with lights that seemed entirely too bright. There was something he was trying to remember—but what was it? As his eyes adjusted to the bright light, he noticed Dick Slay sitting next to his bed.

"I always thought that when I died, I would wake up in heaven." Adam was surprised by the raspy sound of his own voice. "But it looks like I was wrong."

"Cute." Dick loved to engage in witty repartee with his pastor. "How ya' feelin'?"

"Lousy. I assume it's all over?"

"Yep. You're now minus one inflamed appendix. It was a close call. The nurse told me that your appendix came very close to bustin', and that would have caused all kinds of trouble."

Adam thought about that for a moment and then took inventory of his room. To his left was a large window through which he could see a steady stream of headlights moving along Interstate 805. Across the room was a shelf filled with flowers sent from church members. Suspended over the shelf was a color television. An empty hospital bed was to his right. A small table with a green plastic pitcher of water and a telephone was next to his bed. Adam had seen all this before. During his ministry he had made hundreds of visits to hospitalized church members.

"How long have you been here?" he asked, turning his attention to Dick again.

"Awhile."

Adam knew that meant that Dick had been in his room for some time. "We need to get a speaker for tonight's service."

Dick smiled. "I'm afraid your timing is a little off. Tonight's service was over an hour ago. And I don't want you to worry about the church. We have the next four weeks covered. You won't have to do anythin'."

"I think I'll be able to be back to work before the end of four weeks." Adam tried to swallow, but his mouth was too dry. He reached for the pitcher of water.

"Oh, no you don't." Dick stood, took the pitcher, and poured the water into a paper cup. "When you come back we want you at your best. You're going to be taking the next four weeks off, whether you like it or not. Besides, we need to hear some decent preachin' for a change."

Dick Slay was a balding, solidly built man whom many considered intimidating and overbearing. Adam attributed this to his upbringing. Dick spent his early years on a central California farm with three older brothers. After a four-year hitch in the Navy, he had started a small trucking company. Dealing with rough and no-nonsense truckers over the years had caused him to develop an uninhibited, forceful manner. There was never any doubt about where Dick stood on an issue. His abrupt manner alienated a few of the more sensitive church members, but Adam knew that there wasn't a more loving or giving man in the congregation. There had been several occasions when Adam had been called to help a family in crisis only to find Dick had arrived before him. He was a man who could be counted on for help at any hour of the day or night.

Although Adam had been out of the recovery room for hours, he was still struggling to clear his mind of the anesthesia-induced fog when a nurse entered the room.

"So, we've decided to wake up, have we?" she said in a cheerful Jamaican accent.

"Do they teach all nurses to speak in the third-person plural?" The water had helped Adam's voice.

"Just the good-looking ones," she replied with a wink.

Adam couldn't help noticing that her remark, flippant as it was, was certainly true—she was striking. Her ebony skin was highlighted by strong facial features: high cheekbones, a well-defined jaw-line, piercing dark eyes, and bright teeth that provided a stark contrast to her dark skin.

"Are you comfortable?" she asked, her eyes fixed on the plastic IV bags suspended over his head.

"Actually, I've felt much better." As he finished the sentence, the nurse slipped a sterile covering over the electronic thermometer and placed it under his tongue. A few moments later the device beeped and revealed Adam's temperature in red numbers: ninety-nine degrees.

"A little above normal, but nothing to be concerned about," the nurse said as she recorded the statistic on Adam's chart. Quickly and smoothly she finished her examination: blood pressure, pulse, and general appearance were checked and the proper notations made on the chart. It was obvious that she had done hundreds of such routine postoperative exams. Adam read her name tag—Ramona, R.N.

"While you're at it," Dick said, "why don't you check his oil too?"

"I'm sure it would be a quart low." The woman never missed a beat. She was the kind, Adam decided, who liked to tease and be teased. He would remember that whenever he needed cheering up.

"Ramona," Adam said as she was leaving the room.

She turned to face him. "Yes?"

He wanted to say something witty in return, but his mind was still too sluggish, so he said, "Thanks." She responded with a smile and a wink, then disappeared into the outer hall.

## Sunday, March 1; 11 P.M.

"Mr. Bridger." The voice seemed distant. "Mr. Bridger." Adam felt a hand on his arm. He struggled, willing himself awake. Slowly he opened his eyes. The lights seemed dimmer than before. It was still dark outside. He wondered how long he had been asleep. Focusing his eyes on the clock on the opposite wall, he saw that it was almost 11. He had been asleep for two hours. Adam realized that he must have fallen asleep while talking to Dick. Patients had done the same to him on many occasions.

"Mr. Bridger, I'm Dr. Tremaine, your surgeon."

Adam shifted his gaze to the figure standing next to him, a woman in a white smock.

"I had planned to be here earlier, but an emergency kept me away." Adam thought he detected impatience in her voice. "I want to ask you some questions." She began a series of general questions about his medical history, followed by questions about his present condition. She kept her eyes fixed on Adam's chart throughout the questioning, never making eye contact. The only time she looked up from the chart was to examine the three-inch-long incision on his lower abdomen.

Adam had not been in the ministry very long before he developed an ability to identify those who were intrinsically unhappy. Dr. Tremaine was a classic example.

"What were you doing when you had your attack?" She spit out her words quickly as though she were late for a meeting. Adam felt as if he were detaining her.

"I was in the pulpit." Adam began shifting his position in the bed, but a stab of pain curtailed the action.

"Pulpit?" She sounded shocked.

"Yes. I'm the pastor of Maple Street Community Church."

"I see," she said. The disdain was obvious in her voice.

"Well, Mr. Bridger, or should I call you Reverend Bridger?" She emphasized the word Reverend.

"Actually, I prefer Adam."

"Well then, didn't you sense something was wrong prior to stepping behind the pulpit? Didn't you have earlier discomfort? Or fever? Appendix problems don't occur instantly, you know; they develop over a period of time. Surely you had earlier abdominal trouble today?"

"I always have stomach discomfort on Sunday morning: nerves—it goes with the job." Adam could not understand the purpose of her questions, and was beginning to feel guilty for his illness. Taking a closer look at her, he saw a woman of less than average height, no taller than five-foot-one. Her hair was black and very short. She wore no makeup.

"I thought clergy feared no evil. 'Thy rod, Thy staff' and all that." Her antagonism puzzled him.

"Not fear, Doctor," he explained patiently. "Just a little anxiety. Keeps me humble."

"Have you vomited since coming out of surgery?" she asked.

"No. Just some soreness."

"Your chart shows that you've had no trouble relieving yourself. Is that true?"

"Uh," Adam flushed with embarrassment. He knew there was no reason for abashment, but he felt his face become warm anyway. "I've gone to the bathroom once."

"Is there anyone at home to take care of you?"

"No, I live alone."

"You should have some help at home. I don't want you ripping sutures out trying to get out of bed alone."

"I appreciate your concern, but I think I can manage." Adam forced a smile.

"It's more caution than concern, Reverend. Be sure you get some help for a couple of days. Can you do that?"

"I think I can," Adam replied quietly. Then he said firmly, "I'm sorry."

"Sorry?" Dr. Tremaine said. "Sorry for what?"

"For inconveniencing you with my illness," Adam said, making direct eye contact.

This time she blushed. "If I seem curt, it's because I've had a rather frustrating day. I should've been home four hours ago."

"I understand," Adam said with a wry smile. "My day has been rather annoying too. At least you didn't toss your breakfast in front of 400 people, surrender an internal organ, and find yourself confined to bed."

An awkward silence hung in the room. Adam could see his doctor's discomfort and felt a little guilty for causing it, but he knew that she needed to see beyond her own inconveniences.

Dr. Tremaine started to say something when her pager sounded. Without another word she turned and left the room. Adam watched as she strode purposefully away. "Saved by the bell," he said, and then closed his eyes and searched for sleep.

## Monday, March 2; 4 A.M.

There are few wards of a hospital more emotionally grueling than the one in which Lisa Halley had spent the last two weeks. The burn ward at Kingston Memorial Hospital was considered one of the top three in the United States. Yet, despite its reputation, it was a horrible place to work, and an even more horrible place in which to stay. Burn ward nurses were considered the most dedicated and loving, yet as many as 50 percent of the staff left every two years. Burn patients faced far more than the usual discomfort of illness. Their pain was beyond description. Their burned skin left nerve endings exposed and raw. The halls were often filled with the groans of patients whose flesh had been rendered stiff and black. The odor of scorched flesh overpowered the usual antiseptic smells associated with hospitals. Only those with the strongest stomachs and the highest level of dedication chose to work here.

Lisa was alive—barely. The emergency room doctors had described her injuries as extensive; 60 percent of her body was covered with the blackened flesh of third-degree burns.

Lisa had been expected to die within one or two days, but so far she had endured twelve days of physical and mental anguish. Now that it appeared that she might live, there were baths of silver nitrate, long periods in a hyperbaric chamber, and huge quantities of fluid to receive: blood, plasma, and saline intravenously introduced into her body. At the end of each day, she was taken to a bed with no covering, for even a soft bed sheet on her exposed nerves caused excruciating pain.

The accident was still fresh in her mind. It was all so unfair, so patently unfair. She had been returning home from a study session with a friend. Lisa was enjoying her senior year at Madison High School. A grade point average of 3.8 had allowed her the luxury of choices in colleges and universities. There was little that could make her life better, but many things that could make it worse.

One such thing was a drunk driver on Interstate 15. The MG Midget Lisa's father had bought for her eighteenth birthday offered little protection against the three-quarter-ton pickup truck as it crossed over the center divider and crashed headlong into her. Her last-second maneuvering had kept her from being killed instantly, but it could not keep the gas tank from rupturing. The ensuing flames engulfed her. The image of uncontrolled flames rising around her was etched deeply into her memory. The flames had not only scarred her body, but scarred her mind, searing an image of hell into her brain.

She relived that night every time she fell asleep. The ending was always the same—she lived. Why had she not died and saved herself and her family this ordeal? If she had died, she would be buried and her family would be going on with their lives. But now, every day they came, dressed in the green sterile clothing that all visitors wore, to see her grotesquely charred body.

The accident had burned all of Lisa's hair from her head, as well as her eyebrows and lashes. Both legs were deeply burned and, if she continued to live, they would be amputated. The swollen and charred skin had made her unrecognizable to family and friends. Bill Payne, the high school's first-string quarterback and Lisa's steady boyfriend, had come by to visit the day after the accident; he had not been back since. They had secretly made plans to be married after their first year of college, but Lisa knew that dream was over.

John Halley, Lisa's father, had said good-bye to his red-haired daughter at 6 o'clock that tragic evening. When he arrived at the hospital four hours later, he found the strange figure the doctors told him was Lisa. They had also told him it was a miracle she had lived. John wasn't so sure.

Morphine quieted the noisier patients that evening. For a few hours they were oblivious to their environment and their pain. The hall lights had been dimmed and the nurses of station B-West had settled into their heroic yet dismal watch.

No one noticed the nondescript man in a white smock emerge from behind the stairwell door. He moved down the dim hall and into room 015 only to exit a few moments later. The unknown visitor made his way up the stairs and withdrew into the cool moonlit night. His task for the evening was finished.

## Monday, March 2; 6:30 A.M.

Word circulated quickly through the hospital. With each telling of the story, the details were slightly altered, but the truth of the tale remained the same. Somehow, the horribly burned and disfigured body of Lisa Halley had been changed. Skin, soft and pink, had replaced the scorched black flesh. The morning duty nurse, accustomed to seeing the worst that fate could deliver, lost her composure as she stepped into Lisa's room. Her scream echoed through the burn ward. The nurses and doctors rushing to her aid were greeted by a perfectly healthy Lisa, who met each outburst of disbelief with an immense smile.

After gathering his composure, one doctor suggested that a camera be brought to the room to record the event. A nurse, sensitive to feelings that many miss, returned to her station and pulled a mirror from her purse and, making her way through the crowded doorway, slowly raised it so that Lisa could see what she had not been allowed to see for the last two weeks—her face.

## Monday, March 2; 11 A.M.

"Because I need the challenge." Priscilla Simms spoke the words slowly, enunciating each syllable. Irwin Baker, the station's news director, leaned back in his leather chair and stared at the woman across the desk. She was the epitome of the television anchor woman—strong, distinctive features and a full head of red hair. Even without the special makeup and television lights, she was stunning. During the two years she had anchored the evening news on KGOT-TV, the ratings had steadily climbed until they were the number one station in San Diego.

"Priscilla, you knew that anchoring the evening news had both pluses and minuses," Baker said firmly. "Investigative reporting has more challenges; anchoring has more money and prestige; you chose the latter."

"I'm not asking to be an investigative reporter again. All I want is an occasional assignment that has some meat to it."

"Like what?"

"I don't know. Anything would be more challenging than reading a teleprompter every night like some mechanical mannequin."

"You provide a valuable service. Hundreds of women . . ."

" . . . would love to have my job. The sad thing is that any one of them could do it. Irwin, I have a master's degree in journalism. I need a greater challenge. Give me something I can chew on, something that lets me use my talents."

Irwin turned his chair slightly, just enough to gaze out the window, and ran a hand over his balding head. "Who will do your job while you're out poking in the bushes and looking under rocks for your Pulitzer Prize?"

"I will." Priscilla stood and leaned over Baker's desk. "I'm not asking for every story, just one challenging enough to keep my skills sharp. I'm just as subject to the laws of physics as you. I'm getting older, and the time will come when your employers and mine will decide, in their infinite wisdom, that I'm not appealing enough to the viewers. Then I'll be out looking for work."

Baker said nothing. He knew that what she was saying was true. It was not unusual for news stations to reassign or outright fire news anchors because age had taken away some of their sex appeal. Several stations had been sued for age and sex discrimination with only limited success for the plaintiffs.

"I've spent years honing my skills as a journalist," Priscilla said pointedly, "and I don't want to lose them."

Baker had difficulty believing that Priscilla could be anything less than beautiful. She was a prize catch for any man, and many men had tried to claim her; but her indomitable spirit had left their

20

egos bruised and battered. Even he had thought of asking her out, but had trouble mustering the courage. She was strong-willed and opinionated and had left several men shell-shocked.

"I don't own the station, you know," Irwin said, swiveling his chair back to face Priscilla.

"No, but you've worked here for a long time and you're the only person who can get away with murder. No one will second-guess your decision."

That was true enough. Irwin had come to KGOT-TV as a journalistic intern while still taking classes at San Diego State University. After graduation he was hired as an assistant news writer. His way with words and his ability to uncover facts from overlooked sources led to speedy advancement including several award-winning years at a large San Francisco station. Over the years he had developed a reputation as a solid newsman and a more than competent executive. The parent organization, Prime Television Group out of Phoenix, kept Irwin on staff with praise, frequent raises, and substantial bonuses. Other companies, including large market stations in Los Angeles, Chicago, and Houston, had tried to woo him away, but he stayed where he was. Irwin was nothing now if not loyal.

Irwin looked at her and smiled. "I'm waiting."

"Waiting for what?" Priscilla asked suspiciously. A moment later she tightened her jaw and said, "If you think I'm going to break down and cry, or beg, or offer some sexual bribe then ..."

"No, no. Nothing like that," Irwin said, holding up his hands. "I know you're too professional for that. I'm waiting for the part where you say, 'If I don't get this assignment, then I'll just have to take the job offer from XYZ-TV.'"

"Well, it's not like I don't get offers, you know. And the money in L.A. is a lot better than what I get here."

"And?"

"Oh, come on, Irwin," Priscilla was exasperated. "You know I don't want to go anywhere, and you also know that I can do this."

"Yeah," Irwin said with a sigh. "I know that you can. The question is, *should* you be doing it?"

"Dan Rather does it. Tom Brokaw does it. Why can't I?"

"Because Rather and Brokaw have a bigger staff than I do, not to mention much bigger budgets. Besides, Rather and Brokaw don't do investigative reporting."

"Maybe not technically, but they've been known to travel all over the world to report on special events. Besides, this won't cost the company more money. I'm not asking for a raise. I'm asking to do some investigative work like I used to do. What could that hurt?"

The conversation lapsed into silence with Priscilla standing in front of Irwin's desk and Irwin seated in his chair rubbing his forehead.

"Well?" Priscilla asked a moment later.

"I'll see what I can do." Baker felt defeated.

"Great!"

"I didn't say I'd do it, just that I would see what I could do."

"I understand fully," Priscilla said, grinning for the first time since she entered the office. "I'm not trying to pressure you."

"Oh, right. Then why do I feel beat up?" Irwin asked.

"You just work too hard, that's all."

"Well, speaking of work, we better get to it. After all, we still have a news program to put together."

Priscilla took her cue and walked to the door. As she was leaving, she turned to Irwin and offered a genuine smile. "Irwin, you're the best."

"That's what I keep telling you."

Irwin looked at the news schedule on his desk, but his mind was far away. Priscilla had left his office forty-five minutes ago, but he was still thinking about her. He considered her brash, arrogant, and the loveliest woman he had ever known. She could simultaneously enrage him with a self-centered comment and dissolve him into a stammering suitor with a smile.

He couldn't blame her for wanting to get out of the studio and on the streets. In fact, he felt the same way. A day didn't pass that Irwin didn't wish he could leave his office and pursue just one more story. Just one story of substance. But he knew those days were past. It wasn't his age or his appearance that prevented his journalistic enterprises. At forty-six, Irwin still looked professional enough to be on camera. Granted, he didn't match the image of the handsome news anchor, but he was pleasant enough not to frighten children or alarm little old ladies. No, it wasn't his appearance that kept him off the streets and off the screen—it was his past.

Irwin gazed around his office: it was spartan in size and content. He sat in a cheap swivel chair behind a cheap metal desk. The walls were adorned with inexpensive art purchased at an office furniture outlet. The wall behind him was dressed in the only thing that revealed Irwin's past and character: awards, certificates, and letters of appreciation hung in silent testimony of a previous life when he was San Francisco's star journalist, admired by viewers and peers alike. But that was more than a decade ago.

Irwin did his best to never look at the plaques and certificates. Their presence pierced him, but he could not take them down. Those papers in frames and those brass plaques on wood were him, Irwin Baker: notable journalist, investigative reporter, and prominent social figure. Now he was Irwin Baker: the middle-management-paper-shuffling baby-sitter of egomaniacal personalities.

He sighed. He knew he was being unfair. The people he worked with were highly experienced professionals who were every bit as good as he. Bitterness brewed a vile and vindictive attitude that threatened to poison his personality just as alcohol had poisoned his judgment. Envy was the real problem. He wanted to be out there like they were out there. He wanted to be before the camera like they were before the camera. He wanted that more than anything else in the world; that and to have his daughter close by and to have Priscilla as his wife—none of which would come true. He had made his purgatory; now he had to live in it.

Irwin wanted one other thing, a drink, but that's how it all began: A drink here, a drink there, a string of drinks together; each day a new string of drinks. His wife complained; he ignored her. She complained again, and then again, and he ignored her again and again. One day she stopped complaining; she simply left, and took the only thing he loved more than his work—their twelve-year-old daughter.

Loneliness is a compelling emotion, and it compelled Irwin to drink even more. Three months after his wife left, his news director asked—actually demanded—that Irwin seek help or get another job. At the time Irwin thought it was nothing more than professional jealousy that had prompted the reprimand. All he needed was an exciting news story, something with which he could scoop the competition, something to put him back in the good graces of his employers and his public. Unfortunately for Irwin, important news stories came and went at their own whim. So, in a Chivas Regal haze he decided to cheat fate and create his own story.

The story brought him notoriety and fame, but not the kind he wanted. The plan seemed so simple to Irwin. How could he get caught? After all, he was an experienced journalist with a history of groundbreaking stories.

All he needed was a reliable source who insisted on remaining anonymous; he could create that person. He also needed a public official to serve as the accused. Since the informant could not be questioned by others (and Irwin would appear the pillar of journalistic ethics for refusing to reveal his source), any charges brought against the politician would soon pass and everything would be back to normal, except that Irwin would have made national news. Sure, the politician would suffer some inconvenience, but that's why politicians existed. If you couldn't attack your local representative, then who could you attack?

After an evening of planning that was lubricated by a steady flow of Scotch, Irwin decided to undertake his mission to fame. His target was the newly elected U.S. Senator from California, Bob Hollingsworth. Irwin's plan called for a simple implication of duplicity. He would accuse Senator Hollingsworth of selling secrets to the Chinese government on a recent junket there. He would cite his unnamed source as one who traveled on the trip and had personal knowledge of the illegal transaction of information. The nonexistent informant would remain secret and therefore unimpeachable. Since there were still five years until the Senator ran for reelection, the whole issue would blow over, and no one would get hurt.

It all made sense to Irwin, but then he had been living in an alcohol-induced fog for months. Irwin broke the story on a Tuesday evening broadcast; by Friday the scam had been uncovered. Irwin had overlooked the details necessary for a believable lie. He had also underestimated the Senator. By noon Wednesday Hollingsworth knew all there was to know about Irwin and his story. By Thursday morning, with the help of his staff and the most expensive private detective in the Bay area, he had been able to prove Irwin's report a lie. By Friday morning a phalanx of attorneys descended on Irwin and the station. Within two weeks, both the station and Irwin were being sued. Once convinced that Irwin was the duplicitous one, the station was compelled to fire him.

Friendship is what saved him. George Jenkins, Irwin's roommate in college and fellow journalist, was a partner in the Prime Television Group, owners of radio and television stations around the country. Two months after "Irwingate," Jenkins phoned Irwin. He offered him a job; not a great job—those days were gone—but a chance to start over as Jenkins' assistant. The position was a low-level executive role, but Irwin knew it was the only job he could get.

Irwin quickly accepted the position even though it meant moving to Phoenix. A new city might be just what he needed. The job came with a price: Jenkins insisted that Irwin get professional help for his alcohol problem. It was a tough commitment, but with the help of Jenkins, an expensive psychiatrist, and a determination to make amends for his moral failings, Irwin overcame his addiction, proved to be as outstanding an administrator as a journalist, and quickly rose through the ranks until the board of Prime Television Group gave him the reins of struggling KGOT-TV in San Diego.

Leaning back in his chair, Irwin pulled open the large file drawer of his desk. Reaching into the drawer, he removed the lone item and stared at it as he did each day. It was a gift from Jenkins when he came to work in Phoenix. He remembered Jenkins' words; "Irwin, you've come a long way. You're a valuable member of the team and, most of all, you're my best friend. I'm giving this to you so that you will never go back to the hell you came from. I wouldn't blame you if you hopped up and hit me with your chair, but I'm hoping that you'll understand why I'm doing this." Jenkins then set a shoe box on the desk.

It had taken a moment for Irwin to gather the courage to open the unwrapped box. When he did, he found the bottle that he now held—a bottle filled with a golden-brown fluid that looked like Scotch.

Floating in the liquid was a photograph of Irwin, his wife, and daughter at an awards banquet. Taped to the bottle was a piece of paper with the hand-lettered words, "That was then; this is now."

# Three

## Monday, March 2; 7 P.M.

Rachel leisurely strolled along the shoreline. She was alone, very alone and very happy. She paused to take in the deep azure sea with its wisps of lacy foam and the pure, white sand. The water was warm as it lapped at her feet. Above her, a lone sea gull cried and rode effortlessly upon the air currents. Terns dove headlong into the ocean in their search for food. The wind, full of the smell of the sea, caressed her face and ran its invisible fingers through her short black hair. There was peace here. No phones, no operating rooms, no life and death decisions, just peace. She wanted to stay here forever. Everything was at her command. If she wanted to turn the sea red, she could. If she wanted an eagle overhead instead of the sea gull, it would be so. This was her private world....

"Dr. Tremaine, two-two," a voice filtered its way into her mind. "Dr. Tremaine, two-two."

Rachel was suddenly back in the surgeon's lounge. She looked at her watch; reality had allowed her only ten minutes of solitude. Uninterrupted sleep was a rare commodity for her. Even after surgeries and rounds were over, her mind would be reeling from the pres-

27

sures of her occupation. To relieve the stress, Rachel had developed several mental exercises—fantasies actually. Closing her eyes, she would slow her breathing, counting every inhalation. After a few moments, she would imagine herself in any number of different places. Her favorite was an imaginary deserted beach. No hospitals, no phones, no people—just the silky white sands, the lukewarm, azure water lapping at her bare feet. She loved her fantasies. They were the things that were truly hers. No one could deprive her of them. She could travel anywhere, do anything, be anyone.

"Dr. Tremaine, two-two. Dr. Tremaine, two-two."

Rachel stared for a moment at the audio speaker recessed in the ceiling, then went to the yellow phone on the wall and dialed extension twenty-two.

"Second floor west, Ann Jacobs speaking." Rachel knew Ann was a capable nurse, always doing her work without complaint. If there was any fault to be found in her, it was that she was chronically chipper.

"This is Dr. Tremaine." Rachel's voice betrayed her irritation.

"Oh, good. We have a situation with one of your patients."

A situation. That meant a problem, something serious. "Go on."

"It's Mr. Lorayne; he's comatose, and we have been unable to revive him." Ann continued with his vital signs and other pertinent data.

"I'm on my way," Rachel replied curtly and hung up. Numb with fatigue and longing for solitude, she made her way to second floor west.

## Monday, March 2, 7:10 P.M.

Even to a trained eye David Lorayne appeared to be sleeping. His chest rose rhythmically with each breath as it had for forty-six years. His color was normal, as was his pulse and blood pressure. If it were not for the monitors, IV bags, and nurses, someone might simply have thought that David was resting in his bed at home.

Rachel studied the patient's chart intently, searching for the elusive clue that would explain why an otherwise healthy male would slip into a coma shortly after routine surgery. She looked up from the chart and glanced at Ann Jacobs who awaited direction.

Rachel was confused. She had been taught in medical school that every doctor would eventually encounter an event that defies explanation. Knowing this did not make the situation any easier. Lorayne's surgery had been routine; he had been admitted with bleeding ulcers and Rachel had removed a small portion of his stomach. A serious condition, but one that Rachel had dealt with many times. The coma simply did not fit.

"I want a full workup—blood gases, EEG," Rachel said curtly. "Tell the lab I will be waiting for the results." She turned and exited the room before her face betrayed her confusion and anxiety.

## Tuesday, March 3, 10 A.M.

Priscilla Simms made her way from the kitchen to the balcony of her fourth-story condominium in Mission Valley. She sat in a high-backed rattan chair and opened the morning paper. Since she anchored the 6 o'clock and 11 o'clock news, she was not required to be in the newsroom until after lunch. She spent her mornings drinking coffee and reading several newspapers. On San Diego's frequent sunny mornings she would sit on her balcony overlooking the heavily traveled Friars Road and watch the morning rush-hour traffic or retirees playing golf on the nearby golf course.

This morning she was frustrated. The last few days had been slow. If only something newsworthy would happen. She felt a twinge of guilt at that thought. She had never been able to reconcile the conflicting emotions with which many news people struggled. A good news day was filled with the shocking: murders, wars, and political problems. To hope for a spectacular news day was to hope for someone's personal disaster. Since she was unable to reconcile the irony, she had been content merely to ignore it.

The papers were filled with the usual fare. Priscilla drained the last of the coffee from her cup and decided to go to the kitchen and pour another. She knew she drank too much coffee. Someday she would cut back, but not today.

Coming from the kitchen, she glanced around at the place she called home. She had lived here for five years. Her decorative skills had given the 1,200-square-foot condominium an air of elegance.

There was no doubt that she had expensive tastes. But so what? She worked hard for everything she had. Since she earned it, she felt free to spend it. Priscilla tended toward the extravagant, buying without compunction items that were beyond most people's budget, including the white leather sofa and love seat she had had custom-made, the Persian rug, and the engraved glass coffee table. Most of all she loved the art. She knew she had an eye for well-crafted paintings and sculptures. There was not a room in her home that didn't have several pieces of art. At one time she thought that she would like to be an artist, but the lack of patience and talent ended that little dream.

Priscilla was jarred from her thoughts by the phone.

"Yes." Her voice was curt.

"Is that any way to treat your admiring news director?"

She recognized Irwin Baker's voice. She glanced at her watch— 10. She was not due at the station until 1:00. "You're not going to ask me to do the noon news are you? If you are, then I have a headache."

"Have I ever asked you to do the 12 o'clock?"

"Yes. Twice."

"Well, I'm not going to today. In fact, if you're not nice to me, I may be inclined to give this story to someone a little more respectful. Say, Judy Moore."

"She's an opportunist who reads like a third-grader."

"That's not what the ratings show."

"It's not her journalistic skills they're watching."

"Now, let's not be nasty." She could almost see him grinning over the phone.

"Is there a point to this call?"

"Indeed there is. The last time we talked, you had said that you might like to do a little investigative reporting; remember?"

"Just get to the point, Irwin."

"If you don't mind starting to work earlier today, you may want to stroll over to Kingston Memorial Hospital. Word has it that some unusual things are happening over there."

"Like what?"

"People are being healed."

"Cute, Irwin." Priscilla's mood was getting worse.

"You don't understand. People are getting healed without the doctors."

"Go on, I'm listening."

"I got the call this morning. A woman—she wouldn't leave her name—said that a young girl had been healed in the burn ward. The girl, Lisa Halley, had been in a car accident and burned over most of her body. They thought she was going to die, but she hung on. Sometime before 4 this morning the girl was well."

"What do you mean, well?" Priscilla asked suspiciously.

"Just that. Her burns are all gone and she looks absolutely normal."

"Irwin, have you ever been in a burn ward?"

"No, but I've seen plenty of people burned, and I know it's not a pretty sight."

"Then you know that burns don't just go away. They scar the person for life. Someone must be pulling your chain."

"I don't think so."

"Why? You said she wouldn't give her name."

"True enough, but I know she made the call from the hospital. I heard the paging system in the background, and I heard a man address someone as 'nurse.'"

"Okay. Maybe she made the call from the hospital, but that doesn't mean that charred skin can be healed."

"Come on, Priscilla, give me some journalistic credit, will ya'? I called the hospital back and asked if they had a patient by the name of Lisa Halley. They did. I asked if I could speak to her and they said no, but they would connect me with the nursing station in the burn ward. The nurse who answered the phone was the same person who called me."

Priscilla said nothing as she weighed what she had just heard.

"You said you wanted a story to investigate," Irwin said. "Here's your chance."

"I'll take it," she said and hung up. Twenty-two minutes later Priscilla Simms was in her red BMW 320I weaving her way through traffic.

# Tuesday, March 3; 1:15 P.M.

"You sure you don't want some of this?" Adam offered, pointing to the plate of bland food in front of him.

"You've got to be kidding," Dick Slay replied, holding his hands up in mock resistance. "I thought I was your friend."

Adam considered the food on his plate, the first solid food he'd had since Sunday's breakfast: a small fillet of fish in a watery, brown sauce, dry mashed potatoes, and creamed corn.

"They say that stuff is good for you," Slay said. "It'll make you big and strong." He laughed loudly as Adam twisted his face in disgust. "Maybe tomorrow it'll look better."

"If it doesn't, I'm going to order a pizza."

"Better not tell your doctor." Slay pulled up a chair. "Who is your doctor, anyway?"

"The surgeon was Dr. Rachel Tremaine."

"A woman?" Dick asked incredulously.

"They *can* do more than clean house, you know."

"Yeah, but cut you open with a knife and . . ." Slay stopped mid-sentence realizing his indiscretion. "Sorry."

"That's all right," Adam replied. "She's really a live wire. Came in late Sunday night and grilled me about my illness. I felt guilty for being sick. Then when she found out I was a minister, she began to act like I was some kind of witch doctor." Adam pushed the control button that lowered the head of his bed. He was still sore and weak. "I don't think she holds the clergy in high regard."

"Ah, a woman of discriminating tastes," Slay said jovially.

"Careful," Adam said as he shifted his position in bed. "I may never come back."

"Who you trying to kid? If this hospital bed had a motor, you'd drive it into your office."

"Speaking of the office, how is everything at the church?"

"What's the matter, afraid we'll change locks on ya'?"

"No. Just wanting to know what's going on."

"Well, everything is being handled just fine. Fannie is watching the office, George Kellerman is preaching, and I'm taking the hospital visits."

"Fannie has been church secretary long enough that she runs the office anyway," Adam said. "And George has filled in for me several times. We were fortunate to get him on the deacon board."

"I told you not to worry. All you have to do is get better."

"How come you got the easy job?"

"Easy?"

"Sure, I'm the only church member in the hospital, and I'm a pleasure to visit."

Slay laughed. "Wrong on both counts, Pastor. It just so happens that as soon as I'm done cheering up your life, I've got another church member to visit in this very hospital."

"One of our members is in this hospital?" Adam's voice betrayed his surprise. "Why didn't you tell me?"

Dick lowered his head and sighed. "Because I knew you'd do just what you're doing right now: getting all excited when you should be resting."

"Well, the least you can do is tell me who it is." Adam was insistent.

Slay said nothing while he debated whether or not to reveal the information. "You promise not to do anything stupid?"

"Of course."

"It's David Lorayne," Slay said reluctantly. "He had surgery yesterday."

For a moment Adam felt angry that he had not been informed, but his anger did not last; after all, his church was just trying to protect him. "How's he doing?"

Slay sat stone-faced wondering how to answer his pastor.

"What's wrong?" Adam asked, reading his deacon's face. "Tell me everything."

Resigning himself to defeat, Slay explained, "No one knew that he was coming in to surgery. You know how David is. He never wants to bother anyone. Anyway, like I said, he came in yesterday to have surgery on an ulcer. The surgery went fine, or so everyone thought until last night."

"What happened?"

"He slipped into a coma. No one seems to know why. He just won't wake up."

Reaching for the bed controls, Adam slowly brought the head of the bed up until he was in the sitting position and then gently swung his feet over the edge of the bed and stood up. He wobbled slightly and wondered if Slay had noticed.

"What are you doing?" Slay said, leaping to his feet. "You promised that you wouldn't do anything stupid."

"This isn't stupid," Adam said defensively. "I'm supposed to walk every day anyway. If I don't, the nurses beat me. Hand me my robe, please. It would tarnish my image to be seen walking around the hospital bare-bottomed."

"I'm not sure you should be doing this," Slay objected.

"I'm fine, Dick, really. Now are you going to hand me my robe or not?"

Opening the small closet in the corner of the room Slay reluctantly pulled out a green bathrobe and handed it to Adam.

"What room?" Adam asked firmly.

"223."

"Good, that's the same floor we're on. Let's go."

A few moments later the two men stood just inside the door of Lorayne's hospital room.

"Ann," Adam said softly.

"Oh, Pastor." The woman who had been sitting next to the bed dabbed a tissue at her red eyes, stood up, and walked toward him.

"I hope you'll excuse my appearance. I've just recently found out about David. I got here as soon as I could."

"You shouldn't be here," she said softly. "You've got to take care of yourself."

"I'm doing fine, Ann. No need to worry about me. Besides, I was in the area." Adam put his arm around her, walked over to the side of the bed and gazed down at the sleeping figure. Slay stood silently near the door. "How's David doing?" Adam asked.

"Fine, I . . . I guess." Ann Lorayne was a handsome woman of forty-five years. Her genteel manner and bright personality had made her one of the most popular people in the church, especially with the fifth-grade Sunday School class she faithfully taught. "He just won't wake up." She began to sob quietly.

"What do the doctors say?" He held her a little tighter.

"They don't know what happened. They're running some tests, but they seem as confused as I am. Oh, Pastor, I don't know what to do." She turned to him, buried her face in his shoulder, and began to weep.

"What you'll do is take one step at a time." Adam's voice was gentle, yet firm. "You'll cry when you need to, feel angry when you need to, and make decisions when you need to. I'll be here with you any time you need me. Have you talked to the rest of the family?"

"Yes. My son is driving down from Los Angeles now. He should be here soon. Larry, David's brother, is already here." She turned and looked at her husband.

Adam dropped his arm from around her shoulders and took her hand. He wished he could say something worthwhile, something to ease her anxiety; but as was often the case, no words came to mind. Adam stood watching in grim silence.

## Tuesday, March 3; 10:40 A.M.

Priscilla's red BMW moved slowly along Interstate 8, a departure from her normal rash driving style. Her deliberate driving wasn't grounded in caution but in her need to gather her thoughts and formulate a plan. In a few moments she would be at Kingston Memorial Hospital seeking information on the healing. Whom should she speak to first? Administrators? Doctors? Nurses? The approach she chose would be crucial; one wrong step could mean the difference between an attention-getting dramatic story and a mediocre one.

It was less than a twenty-minute drive from her condominium to the hospital, and she wanted to make use of each minute. Methodically she envisioned the various scenarios. She could take the diplomatic approach and speak to the hospital's public relations department. If they were hesitant to provide information to the media—and hospitals often were if they thought it could adversely affect their public image—they would stonewall, leaving Priscilla without a story or, at best, a story without any real meat to it.

No, it would be better to start with the rank and file, but who? If the nurse who called Irwin was on shift when the healing took place, then she would probably have already gone home. Maybe the woman was just coming on duty, discovered the incident, and decided to call the station. That would be a stroke of luck, but then Priscilla always considered herself a lucky person.

Irwin had said the woman was reluctant to answer questions and wouldn't give her name. *Why so secretive? The administration must be putting a lid on it*, she thought. If so, then her decision to start at the bottom before approaching the administrators was correct.

When she arrived at the hospital, her plan was secure in her mind, replete with contingency strategies. She drove into the front parking lot and found an open stall. A sign at the head of the stall read: "Clergy parking."

Knowing that an affectation of confidence was seldom challenged, she briskly walked into the hospital lobby, checking the display on the pager in her hand. Priscilla quickly marched through the lobby and turned left down the first hall she saw, looking every bit the busy executive or doctor.

Priscilla's luck held: the hall she had turned down led to a bank of elevators. One of the doors was opening and several people exited. Quickly she stepped into the empty compartment and then realized that she didn't know where the burn ward was located. *Well*, she thought, *the best way to find the top is to start at the bottom*. She pushed the button marked B.

The elevator groaned as its hydraulic piston slowly lowered the compartment. A moment later the doors opened, and Priscilla stepped out of the lift. She was standing in a wide hall with pale green walls and a large placard with the words RECORD STORAGE and an arrow pointing to her left, and two other lines: MORGUE and BURN WARD with arrows pointing to her right. The first line and arrow were printed in green, the morgue in blue and the words BURN WARD in yellow. Looking at the floor she saw three lines painted each in its own color: green, blue, and yellow.

"At least I won't need a compass," Priscilla said to herself. As she followed the yellow line on the highly polished floor, her footsteps echoed off the plaster walls making her feel uncomfortable. She felt as though she were walking down hallowed halls forbidden to the uninitiated.

The corridor led to a T intersection and Priscilla followed the yellow line to the left, into a new corridor filled with office doors that bore engraved signs: Dr. J. Mendoza, Dr. R.S. Ailes, Shift Nurse, Lounge. It was, however, the double doors at the end of the hall that interested Priscilla. They were painted a yellow that matched the line on the floor and had a sign with a red background and white letters: ADMITTANCE RESTRICTED. ALL GUESTS MUST DIAL 011 TO SPEAK TO NURSE. On the wall next to the doors was a white phone.

Priscilla's luck was running out. She had hoped to be able to walk in, find Lisa Halley and, if the story was verified, call for a camera crew. She was counting on the element of surprise. Now she was left with a decision: She could call the nursing station and ask for permission to speak to Lisa, or simply walk in. Maybe if she just strolled in with an air of confidence, no one would pay attention to her. If she asked permission first, they might not only refuse her admission, but might also refuse to speak to her. That would force her to go through administration and, if they were keeping a wrap on the story, she would be left empty-handed. *I'm not going back to Irwin without a story, not after the fuss I made*, she thought.

Just then one of the doors swung open and a young man in a white lab coat walked through, his head down and his gaze fixed on the clipboard he held. Priscilla quickly reached for the phone and averted her eyes. She didn't want to answer questions, not yet. She needn't have worried; if the man saw her, he gave no indication of it. Priscilla watched as he walked down the hall and entered one of the office doors.

It was then that she decided to act. Before the door could close, she stepped through.

The room was large and, unlike the corridor outside, was painted in cheerful colors of blue, yellow, and green. In the center of the room was the nursing station, marked off by a counter that formed a circle in the middle of the room. Two nurses sat behind the counter. Around the perimeter of the room were cubicles with glass fronts through which Priscilla could see people lying in bed. Instead of doors, each little room had curtains, all of which had been drawn back. Priscilla estimated that there were about ten cubicles; only four had patients, and Priscilla could see them clearly. One was a little boy about ten years old whose left arm was heavily bandaged. The patient in the next cubicle was under a sheet that was suspended over supports so that it didn't touch the skin. The occupant of the third cubicle was in a crib. In the fourth occupied cubicle, a young woman in a hospital gown was smiling and chatting with a man and a woman in hospital greens. The young woman wore no visible bandages, didn't seem to be scarred, and showed no signs of pain. In fact, Priscilla noticed that the she looked overjoyed.

"Hey," a strong female voice said.

Priscilla's attention turned to the source of the exclamation— a squat, dark-haired, dark-skinned, rotund woman in a green nurse's uniform, with green paper head covering and shoe covers.

"Hi," Priscilla said smiling, "I'm Priscilla Sim ..."

"You can't be here," the nurse said forcefully.

"But I ..." The nurse grabbed Priscilla by the arm and turned her toward the doors that led to the corridor. Priscilla noticed that the nurse was wearing rubber gloves and wondered what those gloves had been touching a few moments before.

"You'll have to leave."

"Wait a minute," Priscilla objected. "I only wanted ..."

"Outside. Now."

A moment later Priscilla found herself in the corridor, this time face to face with the angry nurse.

"Now just a minute," Priscilla said, hoping not to reveal how rattled she felt.

"You have no business in that ward without permission," the nurse said forcefully. "Our patients are very susceptible to infection. Your presence endangers them."

"I didn't know. I only wanted ..."

"You didn't know because you ignored the sign on the door that told you to call the nursing station first. And we all know what you want, Ms. Simms. You want a story."

"So you know who I am?"

"Yes, I know who you are, and until this moment I had a lot of respect for you."

"Look, something has happened here, something newsworthy." Priscilla looked at the plastic name tag on the nurse's uniform. "Care to tell me about it, Nurse Hobbs?"

"Come with me," the nurse said sternly and then marched down the corridor and stopped abruptly in front of one of the office doors. Without knocking she opened the door and strode into the room. Priscilla dutifully followed behind her.

The man Priscilla had seen exiting the burn ward was seated behind a metal desk. On the desk was the clipboard, a half-eaten onion bagel, and a Diet Coke. He looked up, irritated at the abrupt entrance, and started to speak but was cut short by the nurse. "Doctor, this is Priscilla Simms from the television station. She was just in the ward."

He looked at Priscilla for a moment. "Who saw her?"

"A couple other nurses, maybe all of them."

"Did anyone else speak to her?"

"No. I took the initiative and dragged her out."

"That's good. We have to be careful." The doctor took a sip of the soft drink. He was a baby-faced man who looked younger than his thirty-two years. Small wrinkles around his eyes heightened his weary appearance. His amber hair was in need of a trim.

As Priscilla watched them, she could sense their tension. They shared a secret that held repercussions. "Look," she said, "I'm sorry if I did something wrong. I don't know much about hospitals and I didn't think it would hurt to talk to . . ."

"The fault is mine," the doctor said. "I'm Dr. Robert Ailes, the chief resident. I'm the one responsible for your being here."

"How so?" Priscilla asked.

"I asked Nurse Hobbs to call your station." Priscilla looked at the woman next to her.

"Not me," the nurse said, "my sister. She works the night shift. I didn't come on duty until 7 this morning."

"Your sister called? Where is she now?" Priscilla asked.

"Home probably. She was pretty shook up."

"Would she talk to me?"

"That depends," Ailes said.

"On what?"

"On how you handle what we're about to tell you."

Priscilla shook her head. "I'm confused. I thought I was about to get chewed out for walking in uninvited."

Ailes chortled. "Actually you deserve to be chewed out, but we'll skip all that if you promise not to go charging into any more restricted areas. As it is, we don't have the time to give you a proper tongue-lashing."

"Let's get to it," Hobbs said. "I don't want to be out of the ward too long."

"Agreed," Ailes said. Motioning to a chair next to his desk he said to Priscilla, "Please sit down." As she did so, he continued, "I have only a few minutes before the head of every department comes down here. If they find out we've been talking to you, there'll be a huge price to pay and I, for one, am not willing to pay it. So listen fast." Ailes leaned over the desk and lowered his voice. "Since you're here, I assume that you have a basic idea of what's happened."

"Someone was healed in a strange manner."

"Strange is a good word. Amazing might even be better." Ailes pulled the clipboard in front of him. "I'll not bore you with all the details, but here it is in a nutshell: Lisa Halley, an eighteen-year-old female in good health, was in an auto accident. The gas tank of her car ruptured and the gas ignited. She was trapped inside. When she arrived at the hospital, her vitals were tenuous. She had third-degree burns over 60 percent of her body, second-degree burns over the remaining 40 percent. Her trachea was burned and swelling shut. The emergency room staff did an amazing job keeping her alive. To everyone's surprise she lived through the night and for several days after. Despite her tenacity the medical staff agreed that she would die soon. She was beyond hope."

"Until last . . ." Priscilla said.

"Until the early hours of yesterday," Ailes said. "About 6 that morning one of our nurses checked in on Ms. Halley. What she saw was . . . unbelievable. Lisa Halley was whole. Fully, completely, and utterly whole. No burns, no scars, just pink flesh."

"And you've never seen anything like this before?" Priscilla asked.

Ailes and Hobbs looked at each other. Hobbs spoke, "Do you know what a third-degree burn is, Ms. Simms? It is the destruction of all the layers of skin and often the tissue beneath the skin. This means that the skin is utterly destroyed and must be replaced by skin grafts. Lisa's skin is whole. In short, we don't know where it came from."

"It?"

"The skin, Ms. Simms," Ailes said. "Where did the new skin come from? For that matter, where did the charred flesh go?"

Priscilla could see the confusion in Ailes' eyes. He was truly puzzled, maybe even frightened. "Would I be able to speak to one of the nurses from that night's shift?"

"Absolutely not," Hobbs said pointedly. "We shouldn't be talking to you. The hospital is clamping down on this. They want to keep it secret, and I half agree with them."

"Then why are you talking to me now? Why did you have your sister call the station?"

The doctor and nurse looked at each other for a moment.

"Honestly, Ms. Simms," Ailes said leaning back in his chair, "I don't know. Keeping it secret just didn't seem right."

"Can I talk to the family?" Priscilla asked. "Will you let me speak to Lisa?"

"No. This is as far as I go, and it's probably too far."

"How's the family responding?"

"They're ecstatic, of course," Hobbs said. "It's taken every bit of persuasion we could muster to keep Lisa here for tests."

"Tests?"

"It's what doctors do," Ailes said. "We're a curious bunch. We don't like surprises and we hate mysteries. They mock us."

"Any guesses as to what the tests will reveal?"

"Normal. They'll all come back normal." Ailes took a sip of soda.

"How do you know that?" Priscilla pressed.

"I don't know. You asked for a guess."

"Dr. Ailes, what do you think happened?"

Ailes rubbed his eyes. He looked tired. More than that he looked shaken. His orderly world had been challenged, leaving him not only without understanding, but without even rudimentary speculation. "I truly don't know."

Carl Fuller didn't sit, nor did he offer a seat to Priscilla. He stood in front of his desk with his arms crossed over his barrel chest rumpling his yellow Yves St. Laurent tie. "There's nothing I can tell you, Ms. Simms. There really is nothing newsworthy here." His voice was deep and resonant.

"I have reason to believe that something unusual has happened here." Priscilla was careful to sound confident, but not insolent. She needed a statement from someone in administration, and after talking to a receptionist and two secretaries, she found herself standing in the office of Carl Fuller, the hospital's public relations man. Both Dr. Ailes and Nurse Hobbs had expressed concern when she told them of her intent to question administration. It took her several minutes to convince them that she would not use their names.

"If anything newsworthy had happened here, I would be the first to know; it's part of my job."

"I'm sure you're very good at your job, but I have reason to believe that a significant event occurred here sometime yesterday."

"I'm not sure who has been telling you stories, but you can rest assured that nothing of consequence is going on. If it were, I would be happy to help you."

"So nothing happened in the burn ward?"

"Many things happened in the burn ward, Ms. Simms. Many things happened in the coronary unit too. This is a hospital where something is going on all the time. All those things, however, are routine and not worthy of the attention of your viewers."

"What does the name Lisa Halley mean to you?"

"Nothing."

"She's a patient here," Priscilla said matter-of-factly.

"She may well be, but we have 600 beds in this hospital, most of which are occupied."

"She's in your burn ward. She was healed of her injuries."

Fuller sighed. "Did you speak to this patient?"

"No, but..."

"Did you talk to family members?"

"Well, no."

"Did one of our staff tell you that this healing actually occurred?"

Priscilla was ready for the question. She didn't want to directly lie, and she certainly didn't want to compromise her sources. "Mr. Fuller, I don't see what all this has to do with my questions."

"Simply this, Ms. Simms. A hospital is like a small village. Close friends are made here as well as enemies. Like all small towns, hospitals are subject to their fair share of rumors and gossip. What you've heard is the result of a practical joke or unsubstantiated rumor that has grown out of proportion. I'm sorry if you've been inconvenienced by all this."

Priscilla smiled. "Thanks for your concern, but I don't feel inconvenienced at all. In fact, I feel confident enough to go forward with the story."

Fuller's countenance darkened. "That wouldn't be wise."

"Not wise? Is that a threat?"

"Threat?" Fuller smiled. "Oh, no. I was merely concerned about your professional reputation."

"So you refuse to confirm the incident?"

"There's nothing to confirm."

## Tuesday, March 3; 1 P.M.

"You're not going to believe it." Unlike her deliberate drive to the hospital, Priscilla was weaving through traffic, car phone pressed to her ear. "The hospital's administrators were close-mouthed, but I was able to find a nurse and one doctor willing to spill their guts. This tale is straight out of *Amazing Stories*."

"When can you have the story ready?" Irwin Baker's voice sounded mechanical and fuzzy through the receiver.

"I want to run it on tonight's broadcast."

"That's not much time. I don't think . . ."

"I can do it." Priscilla was adamant. "I'll need a camera crew as soon as possible. Oh yeah, see what you can do about getting me the home address of Lisa Halley."

"Do you know how many Halleys there are in San Diego?"

"Lots, but only one who has a daughter nearly burned to death in an auto accident. We ran a story on it a few weeks ago. You can start by checking the files."

"In case you've forgotten, I'm the news director." The irritation in Baker's voice was evident.

"Then get someone else to do it for you, but whatever you do, save three minutes for me on tonight's program." Priscilla set her handset back in its rack.

# Four

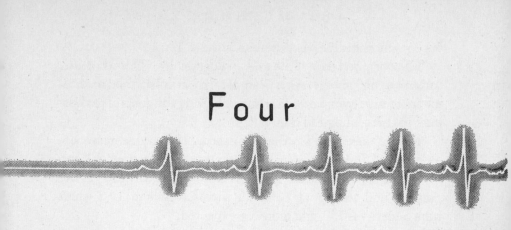

## Wednesday, March 4; 10 A.M.

Dr. Evan Morgan popped two antacids into his mouth, returned to the window, and gazed down at the massing crowds eight floors below. The whole scene was too surrealistic for him—the gathering crowds, the wheelchairs, people on crutches. It seemed that all the infirm of San Diego were on the doorstep of his hospital.

"Dr. Morgan?" Mary Rivers said, stepping into the office.

"Where have they come from, Mary?" Morgan asked without turning from the window. "Why are they here?"

"I imagine they're here because of last night's news report."

"Of course they're here because of the news report," he snapped. "My question was purely rhetorical."

"I'm sorry," she replied timidly. "I didn't mean to offend."

Morgan turned from the window to face Mary. She was an attractive woman with an appealing smile. Her brown hair and brown eyes reminded him of his twenty-two-year-old daughter. Perhaps that's why he had hired her. Since his daughter's marriage two years ago and her subsequent relocation to Houston, he had felt lonely. His wife provided all the companionship any man could ask for, but somehow his life was different without Terri.

"Of course you didn't," he said apologetically. "This whole situation has me on edge. After years of study in college and medical school to save lives, I now find myself barring the doors of my hospital to those who need it most."

"But, sir, there is no way the hospital could admit that many people at once." She walked over to the window. "It is an amazing sight. I understand people are checking out of hospitals as far away as Los Angeles and attempting to admit themselves here. Last count from Security is 150, and more are expected."

Morgan didn't reply, he simply gazed vacantly out the window.

Realizing that no response was forthcoming, Mary continued. "There have been quite a few requests from the media to talk to you."

"Refer them to Carl Fuller in Public Relations; it's his job anyway."

"I've tried, but they insist on speaking with the hospital administrator."

"Maggots." Morgan spat the word out angrily. "They wait with their camcorders for some crime or disaster so they can crawl all over the scene and report every gory detail. Who do they think they are to make demands of me? I don't work for them, and I won't answer to them."

Mary allowed a few moments of silence to pass before speaking. "The board wants you to hold a news conference, don't they?"

Morgan turned and silently stared at his administrative assistant. A grin slowly spread across his face. "You know me pretty well, don't you?"

"After two years, I like to think so," she responded, returning his grin.

"Well, you're right." His grin disappeared. "I want you to schedule a news conference for 3:30 today. No, wait. Make that 6:30. I don't want the conference to air on the evening news. It's bad enough that it will be on the 11 o'clock."

"It might also keep Priscilla Simms from attending," Mary said.

Morgan was grinning again. "You're right. It was her snooping that started all this. Any word on the staff members who talked to her?"

Mary shook her head.

"I want to know as soon as personnel finds out. Also, I need someone to head up an in-house investigation. It needs to be a medical person—say, Dr. Freedman."

"I think he left on vacation last Thursday. He won't be back from the Bahamas for another three weeks."

"Well, who's running his department while he's gone?" Morgan's voice revealed his irritation.

Mary walked over to Morgan's desk and opened a blue-tabbed file marked Department Personnel. "Here it is, Dr. Rachel Tremaine."

"Yes, I know her. She's a very able doctor. Tell her I want to see her this afternoon, before 3 if her schedule will allow, and tell Carl Fuller I want to see him right away. We've got to get this press conference pulled together."

Without another word Mary turned and left the office. Morgan returned his gaze to the scene below his window. As he watched, another van with a large microwave dish antenna and the call letters of a local television news station pulled into the parking lot.

"Maggots," he said with disgust.

## Wednesday, March 4; 10:15 A.M.

Rachel was nearly finished with her morning rounds when she heard her name paged over the hospital's public address system. Leaving a patient's room on third floor west, she went to the nursing station, picked up the handset on the phone, punched two-two, and then waited for the switchboard operator to answer. After receiving her message, she dialed Dr. Morgan's number.

"Administration."

"This is Dr. Tremaine."

"One moment please, I'll connect you with Dr. Morgan's administrative assistant."

Rachel could hear the connection being made.

"Dr. Morgan's office, Mary Rivers speaking." Mary's voice was pleasant and cheerful.

"This is Dr. Tremaine," Rachel said dryly.

"Oh, good, Dr. Tremaine. Dr. Morgan would like to see you as soon as your schedule allows. For what time should I schedule you?"

Rachel wondered what would happen if she said that her schedule didn't allow for an unplanned meeting.

Before Rachel could respond, Mary added, "I've checked with surgery and noticed that you have nothing scheduled for this afternoon."

Rachel felt a twinge of anger at having her schedule "investigated," but she knew that antagonizing her employer wouldn't be wise. "I have two more patients to see on my rounds. That will take about forty minutes. I could be there at 12:15."

"Just a moment, please." Rachel was put on hold. She realized that it was useless to feel irritated at being made to wait. After all, waiting was a part of life—certainly the medical life; nonetheless, the irritation was there.

"Dr. Morgan says he will not be free until 1," the voice came back. "Will that be convenient?"

"One o'clock will be fine," Rachel said, concealing her frustration.

"We'll see you then," Mary said, and promptly hung up.

Rachel stared at the disconnected phone for a moment, feeling angry that she had been hung up on. She knew that there was nothing else to be said; yet, she somehow felt slighted. After a few moments reflection she decided that Mary Rivers wasn't worth her concern.

## Wednesday, March 4; 12:57 P.M.

At three minutes to 1 Rachel stepped from the staff elevator that opened into a large reception area. A large pair of doors directly behind the receptionist bore the name, "Dr. Evan Morgan, M.D."

The receptionist looked at Rachel as she stepped from the elevator. "Good afternoon. How may I help you?"

"I'm Dr. Tremaine."

"Of course, you have a 1 o'clock appointment. Dr. Morgan's office is through that door. Miss Rivers will help you from there."

Turning the handle, Rachel crossed the threshold and closed the door behind her. Although she had met Dr. Morgan on several occasions, usually at staff meetings, she had never been in his office. The plush surroundings astounded her. Seated behind a large oak desk was a woman with shoulder-length brown hair and dark, penetrating eyes. Her complexion was light and contrasted with the darkness of her hair. She wore just enough makeup to highlight her features. She was gorgeous. This appraisal was maintained when the woman rose from her chair. Her body, clad in a red knit dress with a broad, black waist belt, would have pleased any fashion photographer.

"I'm Mary Rivers, Dr. Tremaine. Won't you please sit down? Dr. Morgan shouldn't be a moment." With that Mary turned and disappeared behind another door.

While she waited, Rachel took in the room. The walls were covered with teak paneling. The plush carpet and furnishings were all in earth tones. A computer terminal had been installed next to the desk. Classical music gently filled the room. Rachel couldn't help but think of her spartan office on the fourth floor. The incongruity that an administrative assistant should warrant an office of greater comfort than a highly trained physician angered Rachel.

Mary reappeared with a smile. "Dr. Morgan will see you now." As Rachel nodded and crossed the threshold into the hospital administrator's office, she was immediately struck by the difference in interiors. Mary's office was like a warm den in a large home; a place where one would drink herb teas and read the classics. Dr. Morgan's office was a cavernous high-tech room that looked like something out of the future. The walls were painted with a high-gloss white enamel. All the furnishings, couches, chairs, and a large conference table, were stark black. The thick pile carpet was white with thin, black, intersecting lines that made Rachel feel like she was standing on graph paper.

"Thank you for coming, Dr. Tremaine." The cheerful voice came from a distinguished-looking man seated behind a large, glass-topped desk. As he stood to greet her, Rachel was reminded of how tall he was. Six-foot-three, she judged. He was slim, lacking the usual paunch that middle-aged men develop. His hair was absolutely white and his smile was impeccable.

"Please, Doctor, sit down." He motioned to the black leather chair opposite his desk. "I appreciate your coming on such short notice. I know your schedule must be terribly busy. May I offer you some coffee or tea?"

"No, thank you," she responded. Rachel was out of her element, and the comfort of the chair did nothing to dispel her anxiety. She

felt like a child called from class to the principal's office without knowing why.

"Mary, if you are ready, we'll begin." Turning to Rachel he said,
"Mary takes notes on all my meetings. I assume that you are aware
of the unusual happenings of late." Rachel remained silent. "What
I mean is the sudden, shall we say, symptomatic reversals."

"The healings," Rachel said matter-of-factly.

"Exactly." Dr. Morgan leaned forward, placing both elbows on
the desk and folding his hands. "Unfortunately, word got out
before we could do any meaningful investigation. The sick are arriving from all over the city, and there appears to be no letup."

"I'm afraid that I'm not very good at admission problems."

Morgan laughed, filling the room with his sonorous tones. "You
misunderstand me. I'm not asking you to help in the admitting department." Morgan picked up a brown folder and handed it to Rachel.
"That folder holds the medical records of both patients who have
been involved in these incidents."

Taking the folder from Morgan's hand, Rachel wondered at his
consistent redefining of the healings, preferring terms like "incidents"
and "unusual happenings."

"I want you to be this hospital's investigating physician. You'll
have free run of the hospital and labs—within reason, of course. You'll
also help with the press."

"Dr. Morgan," interrupted Rachel, "I'm not sure that my schedule will allow me ..."

"I'm not finished." Morgan's tone became authoritative. "This
task is very important. Our board of directors wants some answers
as does this hospital's medical board, and I've chosen you to help
find those answers. Your patients will be assigned to other staff for
the remainder of the investigation."

"But, sir ..."

"Of course, you may oversee their care, but I want you to give
this your utmost attention." Morgan stood, signaling the end of the
discussion. "I have every confidence in your abilities. Your record
here is spotless. You will report directly to me or to Mary and—please
hear this carefully—to no one else."

"Dr. Morgan." Rachel knew Morgan was issuing a command and

not requesting help. "Perhaps someone else would do a better...."

"No. You are my choice." Morgan walked over to the door and Mary followed. Rachel knew the meeting had ended. She rose from the chair and turned to leave. "You begin immediately. Mary has already reassigned your patients. Thank you for coming." Morgan closed the door behind Rachel.

Alone inside the elevator Rachel could contain her outrage no longer—she kicked the elevator's metal doors. "The unmitigated gall of that man! Summoning me without explanation, assigning me a task that takes me away from my work, and having my patients summarily assigned to others!" Although she knew her outburst was useless, she could not contain her anger. She kicked the door again, this time shooting stabs of pain up her leg.

Calming herself, Rachel paused to evaluate her options. She could walk back into Morgan's office and flatly refuse to accept the assignment, but the best that would do is get her dismissed. A poor recommendation from the hospital's chief administrator would be a difficult blot to remove from her record. The hospital was owned and operated by a large medical group that paid her salary and consequently held sway over her. In other hospitals she might have more freedom and greater control over actions, but not at Kingston Memorial. Here she was an employee. Rachel knew that her only option was to accept the task, do it quickly and efficiently, and then get back to the practice of medicine.

# Five

### Wednesday, March 4; 3:10 P.M.

"You're not going to like this," Irwin Baker said as he set his coffee cup on his desk.

"I've been disappointed before," Priscilla stated. "Whatever it is, let's get to it. I have calls to make."

Irwin stared at Priscilla for a moment. There was no doubt that he was attracted to her, but not like most men. It was true that he found her beauty captivating, but he was also attracted to her for reasons he had trouble defining. At times he felt fatherly toward her, even though he was only three years her senior; but most of the time he just felt a longing for her that made him ache. It puzzled him, for she could be an irritating person and easily gave offense. She could be short-tempered, curt, and even rude. But she was quick, and she laughed easily. Irwin Baker wondered if he loved her. He would like to take her in his arms and....

"Earth to Irwin."

Her words snapped him back to reality. "I'm sorry, I let myself get distracted."

"So what's this news I'm not supposed to like?"

52

"Dr. Evan Morgan has called a news conference; that's the good news." Irwin paused for effect. "The bad news is that it's scheduled right in the middle of tonight's broadcast."

Priscilla sat silently for a moment and then slowly began to smile.

"I must admit, you're taking it well." Irwin picked up a piece of paper and glanced over a list of names. "I think we can send Bob Parker. He has no live reports tonight and . . ."

"I'm going." Priscilla stood as if to leave.

"Oh no you don't! You've got a program to anchor."

"Get Judy Moore to do it."

"You don't like Judy Moore. Remember?" Irwin stood up. "You said she read like a third-grader."

"I know. This way I'll know that my job will be safe." Priscilla quickly exited the office.

"Priscilla!" Irwin shouted and jumped to his feet. He considered chasing her into the open office area but decided that the effort was useless and would only embarrass him before the reporters and writers. She was a good reporter, the best Irwin had ever worked with. She was also pompous and bullheaded. He ought to fire her; none of his supervisors would blame him; she was as obnoxious with them as she was with him. He would fire her—someday; but right now she was too hot a property to lose. The station would drop several rating points the minute the news was out that she was gone. There was nothing to do now but tolerate her behavior and wish that things— many things—were different.

## Wednesday, March 4; 6:30 P.M.

The hospital conference room was filled with cables, lights on stands, and microphones. Thirty members of the press were seated on metal folding chairs. Cameramen with their insta-cams fixed to their shoulders were situated behind the seating area. Newspaper photographers stood near the white walls.

Dr. Morgan entered the room through a side door, followed closely by Rachel. Morgan was dressed in a dark blue Caraceni suit and a yellow silk tie and looked as if he'd just stepped from the pages of *Fortune*. His white hair dazzled under the camera's lights as he took his place behind the podium. Rachel took a seat just to his right. Morgan stood silently until he was sure he had the full attention of those gathered. "I wish to thank the members of the press for their courteous response to our invitation. I will make a short statement and then allow a few moments for questions."

"As you know," Morgan continued, "certain anomalies have occurred in this hospital. Much of what you have heard has been exaggerated. It is our hope that those of you whose responsibility it is to keep the public informed will exercise discretion in reporting these events. We have no secrets from you; however, we are obligated by certain professional restraints and ethics not to divulge information that will disrupt or disturb our patients. Being professionals yourselves, I'm sure you understand our concerns."

Morgan's glibness and easy delivery impressed Rachel. He could hold his own with any politician. He had an ease and confident charisma that most found endearing. Rachel felt drawn to him. Yet, despite the attraction, she was still furious at him for presuming to volunteer her for such a ridiculous task. She was here because she was commanded to be and for no other reason. Morgan had insisted that the press be introduced to the "investigating physician."

Morgan's speech continued for another ten minutes. He gave a brief account of Bill Langford's unexpected recovery from cancer and Lisa Halley's remarkable change. The gathered crowd sat in disciplined silence, perhaps a little intimidated by Morgan's strong projection of self-assurance.

"Before we take a moment or two for questions, I would like to introduce Dr. Rachel Tremaine, a surgeon on staff here. She will be heading up our in-house evaluation of the recent events. Dr. Tremaine, please come and stand with me."

Rachel shuddered inside. As a rule she was self-confident, but speaking to a large group of people terrified her. Even her high school speech class had proved a living hell. As a doctor she dealt only with a few people at a time—never a gathering. Swallowing hard, she rose and stood on Morgan's right. With any luck the questions would be asked of Morgan.

"All right, ladies and gentlemen, who has the first question?"

Several hands went up at once. Morgan recognized a man in a

red vested sweater. "Dr. Morgan, Bill Challee from the *Daily Report*. To what or to whom do you attribute these miraculous healings?"

Morgan stood silently for a moment sizing up the reporter. "As individuals involved in scientific pursuits," Rachel noticed that Morgan was now using plural pronouns, "we are most careful in the use of terms such as *miraculous* and *healings*. To answer your question, however, it is too early for us to attribute the recent events to any single agent. That is why we have asked Dr. Tremaine to pursue a detailed inquiry."

"Dr. Morgan." A woman whom Rachel judged to be in her fifties had leaped to her feet and had begun speaking before he could call on another. "Dr. Morgan, Judith Lew of KSST radio news. Could you tell us if any other 'anomalies,' as you call them, have occurred?"

"No, madam, there have been no other occurrences. Also . . ."

"Do you expect any more occurrences?" she interjected.

"That, madam," Morgan said condescendingly, "would depend on the still undetermined cause."

The woman began to interject another question when Morgan quickly turned and pointed at a dapper man with dark hair and graying temples. "Mr. Lynol Jefferies of PBS news hour has a question. We are honored, sir. Please ask your question."

"Thank you, Dr. Morgan." Jefferies was a celebrity of sorts in San Diego. As anchor of the hour-long Public Broadcasting News, he had elevated the viewership by nearly 30 percent in two years. Although highly intelligent with impressive degrees from notable universities, he was received by television audiences as the man next door. Doctors and dock workers turned to him daily for the news. One television critic wrote, "Lynol Jefferies is to broadcast news what Willie Nelson is to country music."

"Dr. Morgan," he began. "I think we can all appreciate your delicate situation here, just as I'm sure you can appreciate our desire to report this matter to our patrons who depend on us for information. Sir, to pick up the previously unanswered question; do you expect any further occurrences? Also, it is known to all that the lobby of this hospital is rapidly filling with the sick and dying. How do you plan to deal with those increasing crowds?"

"Well, Mr. Jeffries, I am not a prognosticator by any means; my expertise is in medicine and hospital administration. But I can say that I would be very much surprised should another event of this sort occur. As to the crowds attempting to check into our hospital, they will be dealt with courteously. We are referring them to their personal physicians. If their doctors wish to admit them, then we will take as many as we can properly handle."

Before Morgan had finished his sentence, Priscilla Simms was on her feet calling his name. He stared at her for a moment. Why wasn't she doing her evening broadcast? She was the one who had caused all the trouble. Because of her sensationalized broadcast, hundreds of the ill were camping on his hospital's doorstep. He wondered how he might bypass her question. He couldn't ignore her; all the other reporters had relinquished this moment to her. Even though he had not called on her, the rest of the press had ceased vying for his attention. He had to call on her, but perhaps he could have a little fun.

"Yes, Mrs. Primm, you have a question," Morgan said with an affable smile.

"Simms, Dr. Morgan, Priscilla Simms of KGOT-TV." Priscilla was unshaken.

"My apologies. I'm afraid I never catch your show." Snickers rippled through the room.

Priscilla ignored Morgan's comments, deciding that a verbal battle with him would be unprofessional and counterproductive.

"Dr. Morgan, how do you account for a patient who is terminally ill with cancer, and not expected to live through the night, suddenly finding himself completely free of cancer? And how do you account for a burn victim who awakens one morning without scars and scorched flesh? Is your hospital doing some hidden research of which the public should be aware?"

"We are conducting no special research," Morgan said with a disarming smile. "We are not a research hospital; we are a privately owned health maintenance organization. We hire our own physicians to maintain the highest quality of health care. Our reputation is spotless and national in scope. We do not conduct experiments on the patients who have placed their unwavering trust in us.

"As to how I account for these recent events, I can only refer you to the previous answers. I do not account for them. That is why Dr. Tremaine is investigating. Unlike many professions, we in the medical field prefer facts, not sensational speculation."

There wasn't a person in the meeting who missed the verbal jab at Priscilla.

"You acknowledge then, Doctor, that you have events happening in your hospital over which you lack both knowledge and control?"

"Your phrasing of the question is obviously meant to cast aspersions on . . ."

"A simple yes or no answer would be most helpful, Doctor."

Morgan felt anger surge through his body. She was trying to manipulate him. Morgan's voice barely concealed his wrath. "May I remind you, Ms. Simms, that this is a news conference and not a court of law; that you are a reporter and not a trial lawyer; and further, that I am not on trial." Morgan's voice had elevated in volume. "I will answer as briefly or copiously as I choose. If that is not agreeable with you, you are perfectly free to leave."

Silence covered the room. Priscilla sat down grinning. She had accomplished what she wanted. She had made Dr. Morgan pay for attempting to shut her out of the news conference.

Morgan was embarrassed and felt the need to escape. Deftly, so that none would see, Morgan slipped his hand to his side and flicked the test button on his pager. A shrill beep echoed through the room. Morgan feigned surprise and frustration.

"Ladies and gentlemen," Morgan continued, his voice returning to its previous pleasant tone, "I must excuse myself to attend to some other important matters, but Dr. Tremaine will be glad to answer any further questions." Morgan turned and quickly exited the room.

Rachel felt her stomach tighten as she watched, what seemed to her, a hundred pairs of eyes staring, prying and piercing her very soul. *Why do I have to be so insecure before crowds? I can cut open a human body without a second thought; why do I feel like running from the room?* Standing up, Rachel took her place behind the lectern.

"Who will be next?" she said softly. Her throat was dry. She knew she had a classic case of stage fright. She also knew that Morgan had abandoned her. She had nothing to offer these people. She had received the assignment only a few hours before. All she had time to do was read the medical charts of the two patients involved, and she had been warned by Morgan not to disclose any details contained in them. "It might cause certain legal complications," he had said.

The next thirty minutes were filled with a repeat of the questions asked of Morgan and inquiries about her task. "Why were you selected? What do you think happened? How long before any information will be released? Do you believe in miracles?" Rachel fielded the questions as best she could, telling the reporters that they would have to be patient, that it was too early to make definitive statements. She then thanked them for their attentiveness and dismissed herself.

# Six

Wednesday, March 4; 7:45 P.M.

Priscilla did not return directly to the station. Before attending the news conference, Irwin had handed her the addresses of Bill and Lois Langford and Lisa Halley. The Halleys lived on Charger Boulevard in the community of East Clairmont. The Langfords lived in Linda Vista. Since the East Clairmont address was closer, Priscilla decided to make that her first stop.

It took less than ten minutes for Priscilla to navigate her red BMW through traffic on Interstate 805 to Clairmont Mesa Boulevard and over the surface streets to the Halleys' home. The house was a relatively new two-story home with a wood and stucco exterior. With the increasing cost of housing in San Diego, Priscilla knew that this house could easily sell for over a quarter million dollars.

Priscilla parked her car curbside and walked up to the front door. She listened carefully for a moment for any indication that the occupants were at home. Hearing nothing, she rang the bell. No one answered. Turning to what she assumed was the window to the front room, Priscilla looked in. It seemed to be a formal living room; perhaps the house had a family room in the back. If so, it was possible that the Halleys had not heard the bell. Stepping back to the front door she again rang the bell and waited. Again nothing. She was glad that she hadn't brought the camera crew.

Looking at her watch, Priscilla saw that it was almost 7:45. Maybe the neighbors would know where the Halleys were. She walked across the lawn to the next house. When she rang the doorbell, she was greeted with noise. A small girl answered the door accompanied by two Pomeranians that yapped constantly. The girl was no more than three years old, with tangled blond hair and two dirty fingers placed firmly in her mouth.

"Is your mother home?" Priscilla asked, raising her voice over the barking of the dogs.

"Yes," the child responded, but remained stationed by the door.

"May I speak with her, please?" Priscilla pleasantly persisted.

"I don't care." The little girl was now hanging from the doorknob with one hand like a tiny chimpanzee.

"Would you go and tell her I'm here, please?"

"Okay." With that the toddler ran to the back of the house screaming loudly, "Mommy, mommy, some lady wants to talk to you." The dogs remained behind, barking incessantly. Priscilla wished she had gone to another house.

A few moments later a perspiration-soaked woman appeared dressed in a bright red jogging suit. "I'm sorry," she said, "I was doing aerobics in the den." She turned quickly and addressed the child who was now in front of the television set. "Ashley, turn that down. Mommy can't hear herself think." Ashley ignored her. The mother repeated the command with the same effect. Excusing herself she walked over and turned the volume down. This brought tears to the eyes of the child and then a wailing cry. The little girl jumped up and disappeared into the back of the house. Priscilla heard a door slam.

"Kids!" The woman returned to the door. "This maternal instinct isn't all it's cracked up to be. Now, what can I do for …" The woman paused mid-sentence. "Wait. Aren't you that newswoman on television?"

"Yes." Priscilla still enjoyed the notoriety that went with her job. At times it was a nuisance, but for the most part she reveled in it.

"I wonder if you could answer a few questions."

"Wait, let me get a pen and paper. I must have your autograph." The woman disappeared and returned in a moment. "You don't mind, do you? If I don't have your autograph, my husband won't believe that I've really met you. He's in sales, travels a lot."

She opened the screen door and handed the paper and ballpoint pen to Priscilla. Then suddenly realizing her faux pas she said, "Oh, where are my manners? Won't you come in please?"

Priscilla stepped into the house.

"Just have a seat anywhere."

"I wonder if I might ask you some questions," Priscilla said while signing her autograph.

"I guess so."

"Well, Mrs...."

"Mifflin." The woman interjected. "Judith Mifflin. Everyone calls me Judy."

"All right, Judy it is then. And please, call me Priscilla." The woman smiled, feeling special about being on a first-name basis with a television personality. "I'm trying to get in touch with your neighbors, the Halleys. Do you know when they might be home?"

Judy paused and eyed Priscilla suspiciously. "Are they in some kind of trouble?"

"No, nothing like that." Priscilla had to phrase this so as not to appear to be prying. "As you may know, something special has happened in their lives, and I wanted to talk with them about it."

"Special?"

"Yes. I tried to get hold of them yesterday but never made contact. I really would like to speak to them." Judy looked puzzled. "Did you see my evening broadcast last night?"

Judy's puzzled expression was replaced with an embarrassed one. "Well, actually no," she said softly. "I don't watch much news on television. I find it depressing. I recognized you because my husband watches your show when he's home."

"So you are unaware of what happened to them yesterday?"

"Yesterday?" The puzzled look returned.

"Yes. At the hospital."

"I know their daughter is in the hospital. Is that what you mean?"

Judy's eyes widened as a thought occurred to her. "She didn't . . . I mean, she's not. . . ."

"Dead? No. On the contrary, she's very much alive. That's why I must speak to them." Priscilla spent the next ten minutes explaining the events in the burn ward. Judy sat speechless, spellbound by Priscilla's rehearsal of the unexplained events.

"As you can see," Priscilla continued, "I really would like to speak with them."

"I find this all so hard to believe." Judy paused, reflecting on what she had just been told. "I'm afraid I can't help you. I haven't seen them for at least two days."

"Have you seen their car, or maybe lights on at night?"

"No, I don't think they've been home since yesterday morning."

"Why do you say that?"

"Because I usually see Lea when she gets her newspaper."

"Lea?"

"Yes. Lea Halley, Lisa's mother. You see, the newspaper comes about the same time every day—about 4 o'clock. I hear the paper land on our porch where the delivery boy throws it. Then I go out to get it and Lea is picking hers up from their porch. She always waves at me. Seems like a real nice person."

"Seems? Then you don't know her very well?"

"Only talked to her once. That was when we first moved here— about three months ago. Can I get you some coffee or a soft drink?"

"No, thank you." Priscilla thought for a moment. "You say the paper comes about the same time every day, yet you haven't seen Lea pick up the paper. Have you seen anyone else pick it up?"

"No, no one."

"Perhaps they've had the paper stopped."

"No, I don't think so. I saw the paper there today and yesterday too."

"But, there was no paper when I was there a few moments ago."

"Perhaps they've gone on a trip and someone is picking it up for them."

"Perhaps." Priscilla couldn't say why, but something didn't seem right. It made perfect sense for them to leave with their recently healed daughter—probably to get away from the onslaught of reporters who would descend after yesterday's report. Or, maybe to get away from doctors who would want to run more tests. It made sense, yet Priscilla's reporter instincts said there was a story here.

Priscilla repeated the scene with the other neighbors, but with the same results—no one had seen or heard from the Halleys since yesterday morning, and no one knew them well enough to suggest where they might be.

Priscilla walked back to her car and pulled away from the curb. If she hurried, she could be at the Langfords in fifteen minutes. Maybe they would have some answers to the questions that were percolating in her mind.

Priscilla made it to the Langfords' street in thirteen minutes. As she slowed and looked for the address, a black and white car caught her eye. On the door were painted the words, "To Protect and to Serve." She parked behind the San Diego Police car and quickly walked up to the officer standing on the doorstep of the Langfords' home.

# Seven

## Wednesday, March 4; 8:15 P.M.

"I'm sorry," the policeman said with polite firmness, "but this is a crime scene, and only authorized personnel are allowed in. You'll have to remain outside the barricade." The officer was so young that she guessed he was fresh out of the academy. The barricade he spoke of was a three-inch-wide yellow plastic ribbon with the initials SDPD printed in large, black letters. The ribbon enclosed the entire front and side yards.

"I'm Priscilla Simms of KGOT-TV," Priscilla said, attempting to sound authoritative. "I'm here to cover the story."

"I'm sorry, ma'am, but I can't help you."

"You don't understand, I've just used my car phone to call for a camera crew. They'll be here any minute. I would really appreciate some information and a chance to film inside the house."

"I still can't help you, ma'am." The young officer was resolute. Priscilla would have to take a different approach.

"What exactly are your orders, officer?"

"To keep individuals away who might disrupt this investigation."

"You may not know that that doesn't include the press."

"Until I am told otherwise it does."

Priscilla's anger was growing. As she considered what to do next, another officer appeared through the door. He was a short, heavy-set man with close-cropped hair.

"Is there some problem here, Officer Gerrick?" The man directed his question to the young officer.

"This woman has identified herself as the press. She insists on entering the building."

Priscilla noticed the officer had three stripes on the sleeve of his khaki-colored uniform. "Sergeant, I'm Priscilla..."

"Simms," interjected the officer. "I know very well who you are. I watch your show when I can." In an easy, gallant move he gently placed his hand on her elbow and walked with her away from the house to the street.

"Sergeant..." Priscilla paused to look at the name plate on his uniform. It bore the name T. Reedly. "Sergeant Reedly, I wonder if you could tell me what is going on here."

"Not much to tell actually." His voice was pleasant, and his manner disarming. At first glance Priscilla thought he would be harsh, impatient, and gruff. Although he had the appearance of the stereotypical Marine drill sergeant, he spoke and acted like an ivy league gentleman. "We are still conducting our investigation."

"Investigation of what?"

"Those questions are best asked of the investigating detective. I'm merely the officer in charge of the scene. My job is to secure the crime scene until the detectives from the proper department can arrive."

"Can you tell me if the Langfords are hurt?"

"Do you know the Langfords?" he asked glibly.

"No, not really."

"Did you have some reason for meeting them today?"

Priscilla was infuriated with herself. Without her knowing it, he had switched roles with her. She was the investigative reporter— she was supposed to be asking the questions. She had to admit that Reedly was smooth.

"I'll make a deal with you," Priscilla said. "I'll tell you all I know, if you will tell me what went on in that house."

Reedly was smiling. "How do I know that this will be an equitable trade?"

"I'm with the press; you can trust me."

Reedly's laughter could be heard three houses away. A moment later he said, "Forgive me. I'm afraid my dealings with the press have been less than pleasant. I love to read my quotes in the paper to see what I've said. They usually bear little resemblance to my original comments."

Priscilla said nothing, but stared hopefully at Reedly.

"All right, I'll trust you. About an hour ago we received a call from one of the neighbors. She had just returned home from work when she saw a car leaving the Langford house. According to her it left rather quickly. There were two people in the back seat. They may have been the Langfords. That, however, was not what caused her to call the police. As she drove past the house, she noticed that the front door had been left open. No one in this community would leave their house unlocked, not to mention leaving the door standing open. She became suspicious and called us."

Priscilla looked around the neighborhood. The houses had been built after the second world war to accommodate the returning Navy personnel who had decided to settle in San Diego. At one time it was a pleasant community, but now it had gone the way of many such neighborhoods: as the newer subdivisions were built, more affluent homeowners moved out. The families who moved in were too cash poor to maintain the houses they had rented or bought. The area was known for its ever-increasing crime rate and deteriorating property values.

"So what's in the house?"

"Not much. There are signs of a struggle."

"Anything else?"

"No, that's about it. Now, it's your turn."

Priscilla lived up to her promise. She told Reedly about the mysterious healings and her visit to the Halleys. She informed him that her reason for being there was to gather background material for tonight's 11 o'clock broadcast. Now she had a little more than expected.

"So it's your intention to broadcast this tonight?"

"Absolutely. Do you have a problem with that?"

"Not if you promise not to quote me," he said smiling. "We have a P.R. officer for such things."

"I promise. How about if I refer to you as 'an officer at the scene'?"

"That will be fine."

A van with the initials KGOT-TV parked across the street just as an unmarked sedan pulled up to the curb.

"Well," said Reedly, "it looks like it's time for both of us to get back to work. I do have one other question for you."

"Shoot."

"Don't ever say that to a policeman." Reedly laughed. "My question is, would you consider having dinner with me sometime?"

Priscilla was taken aback. On a purely physical basis, she had no interest in Reedly. Yet, there was something about him—a charisma that attracted her. She could think of no reason to refuse, so she simply said, "I think I would like that."

"Wonderful." His grin was enormous. "I'll call you at the studio later this week." With that he turned and walked toward the two detectives who were approaching him.

Priscilla turned her attention to the cameraman and soundman who asked, "Where do we set up?"

## Wednesday, March 4; 11:35 P.M.

Irwin Baker stepped onto the news set after the 11 o'clock broadcast.

"Priscilla, you can be a royal pain, but I'll be the first to admit that you're doing a superb job with this hospital story. That videotaped remote about the missing Langsfords was sheer genius. If you were a man, I'd offer you a cigar."

"Keep the cigar and buy me a drink instead."

"It's a deal, but I'll make mine coffee." Irwin knew that this was a purely platonic gesture on Priscilla's part, but it was as close as he ever got to dating her. He would have to be content with this occasional gesture.

They left the station together in Irwin's white Mercedes 240 SL. It was not a new car, but one that Irwin had spent many hours restoring. Priscilla had been in it twice before; both times she was amazed at its immaculate condition. The floor of her car was always covered with maps and portions of newspapers she had meant to read.

"Where to?" Irwin asked.

"Johnny's is close."

"So be it."

Irwin directed the car down Balboa Avenue and turned north on Genesse Avenue. Johnny's was a small, intimate bar in East Clairmont that catered to the Yuppie crowd. It was also close to the Halleys' house.

"Listen," Priscilla said, "do you have any objection to taking a little detour?"

"Your place or mine?" Irwin asked, grinning.

Priscilla smiled, "Neither."

"I thought so." Irwin feigned hurt. "Don't tell me, let me use my Sherlock Holmes deductive powers to determine where you want to go. . . .You want to drive by the Halleys' house, don't you?"

"An amazing deduction, Sherlock. How ever did you guess?"

"Elementary, my dear Priscilla. A true detective must always know one's enemies and one's friends; and I know you."

"Which am I? Friend or enemy?"

"Friend, usually." Irwin paused for a moment. "And hopefully more someday."

An uneasy quiet filled the car. Priscilla had long known of Irwin's interest in her. Unfortunately, the interest was not reciprocal. There was nothing wrong with Irwin. He was handsome enough, and he was certainly intelligent. But there had never been time in her life for Irwin, or for any man. She dated occasionally, but usually found such outings boring. Most men were intimidated by her or had ulterior motives.

Irwin broke the silence. "What street was that on?"

"Charger Boulevard," she said, grateful for the change in subject. "Take Clairmont Mesa Boulevard to Doliva Street. Doliva dead-ends into Charger. Turn left at the intersection. The house is about two blocks from there. It will be on our right."

"Got it." Both settled back into silence.

Since it was nearly midnight, few cars were on the road. Within ten minutes Irwin was parking in front of the Halleys' house. "Looks like a nice place."

"All the lights are out."

"It's nearly midnight, Priscilla. What did you expect?"

"I was hoping they were home."

"How do you know they're not?"

"I don't know for sure, but I doubt it. Their curtains aren't drawn."

"So?"

"So, do you leave your curtains open at night?"

Irwin thought for a moment. "Now that you mention it, I don't."

"Very few people do. Most people like privacy at night; closing the curtains provides that. It also provides a certain psychological security."

"Is there no end to your talent?"

"What's that?" Priscilla asked excitedly.

"What's what?"

"I thought I saw a light."

Irwin leaned over, trying to see around Priscilla and out the passenger window.

"There it is again."

"You're right. It looks like someone playing with a flashlight."

"They're being burglarized." Priscilla's heart was racing. "Get on your car phone and call the police."

Irwin reached down and pulled the handset of his car phone from its cradle and dialed 911. The emergency operator answered, "Operator 32."

"Operator, this is Irwin Baker. I'm calling from my car phone. I believe there is a burglary in progress at . . ." A light came on inside the car, startling Irwin. At first he was confused why the dome light in his car would come on by itself. Then he realized that Priscilla was opening her door. "Hey, where do you think you're going?" It was too late; she had already slipped out of the car.

Irwin was flustered. He could hear the operator calling him as he watched Priscilla approach the house in a crouched position. Irwin quickly gave the Halleys' address and demanded that a patrol car be sent immediately. He slammed down the receiver and exited the car.

"Have you lost your mind?" Irwin said in a hushed voice, as he crouched next to Priscilla who was now near the front window that she had peeked in earlier that day. "If the burglar doesn't kill us, the police probably will."

Priscilla placed a finger to her lips motioning Irwin to be quiet. "I want to see who is in there."

"Did it occur to you that if you can see him, he can see you?" Irwin was furious.

"What makes you think that the intruder is a he?"

"Can we carry on this conversation in the car?"

"No." Priscilla slowly raised herself up enough to look through the window. A nearby streetlight dimly illumined the room. The once clean and orderly house was now a shambles. Cushions were strewn around the floor. The sofa had been turned over and its stuffing was scattered throughout the room. In a corner a dark figure with a flashlight was looking in a drawer.

"What do you see?" Irwin asked apprehensively.

Priscilla shook her head. Suddenly the intruder turned, his flashlight beam sweeping the room. The beam moved quickly across the walls and came to rest on the window, fully illuminating Priscilla's face. Startled by the sudden exposure, she remained motionless. Irwin, seeing the light strike Priscilla's face, reacted.

"That's it," he said, grabbing Priscilla by the arm. "We're out of here."

Before they could run, the front door opened explosively. Irwin turned at the sound of the door, slamming against the wall. Standing before him was a man garbed completely in black, his face covered by a ski mask. The intruder brought up his right hand and crouched in the typical police shooting position. Instinctively, Irwin stepped between Priscilla and the assailant. Then he heard an unrecognizable noise and felt something impact his chest. The impact was followed by a burning that raged through his body. Irwin knew he had been shot.

Stumbling back he felt two arms grab his shoulders. His legs felt rubbery under his weight. He wanted to do something, anything—

run, scream, strike back—but he could do nothing. Blue and red lights filled the neighborhood. Irwin felt himself slowly losing consciousness. He fell backward landing on something soft. Darkness flooded his eyes. He heard a noise—no, a voice, a distant, beckoning voice.

Priscilla landed hard on the damp grass; pain raced up her leg. Everything seemed in slow motion; the yellow streetlights cast a surrealistic amber glow. Irwin had let out a gasp and clutched at his chest. A moment later he had fallen backward, landing on top of her. Although she heard no retort, she knew that Irwin had been shot. All that remained now was for the black-clad assailant to shoot her.

She watched as the attacker slowly positioned himself for a clear shot at her. She struggled to get out from under Irwin's limp body, but his dead weight was too much. Then an unexpected calm descended on her. *If I am to die*, she thought, *I am going to do it with dignity*. She stopped struggling and looked directly into the dark eyes of the masked assassin.

Suddenly the neighborhood was flooded with blue and red lights. A police patrol car pulled up in front of the house, its front wheels jumping the curb. The doors of the car swung open and two officers crouched behind them, police revolvers drawn.

"Police! Don't move!" The voice was familiar.

The gunman lowered his weapon and appeared to resign himself to capture. Then, bolting toward the street, he raised his weapon and fired a round. The patrol car's windshield shattered. Priscilla screamed and covered her head with her arms. The two policemen returned fire, each firing twice. All four bullets found their mark. The gunman reeled and dropped to the ground.

Mustering all her strength, Priscilla rolled Irwin off her body and knelt beside him. In the glow of streetlights made brighter by the headlights from the police car, Priscilla could see a crimson circle emanating from Irwin's chest.

"Oh, Irwin, I'm sorry. I'm so sorry." Priscilla began to sob uncontrollably. "What have I done? What have I done?"

Looking up from Irwin's limp body she watched as the policemen, one with his revolver pressed against the burglar's head, checked for other weapons and then for a pulse. She saw one officer shake his head, and she knew the man in the black mask was dead.

"Help!" Priscilla cried. "Help me, he's been shot." Turning her attention to Irwin, she saw him slowly open his eyes. He smiled and blood trickled from the corner of his mouth.

"Sorry," he said in a voice barely audible. "Sorry about the drinks."

"Hang on, Irwin," she said, tears streaming down her face. "We'll get you well, and then we'll have lots of drinks."

"Make mine cof . . ." Irwin convulsed, closed his eyes, and let out his last breath. Priscilla heard the deep rattle in his lungs that only the dying make.

"No, Irwin, don't leave me! I'm sorry. I'll make it all up to you, just don't leave me."

Irwin did not respond.

A strong hand touched her on the shoulder. She looked up into the face of Sergeant Reedly.

# Eight

## Sunday, March 5; 10 A.M.

"I'll tell you what I want," Adam said forcefully. "I want out of this place."

Dick Slay simulated shock. "Why? You have lovely women waiting on you hand and foot, meals brought to your bedside, cable television for entertainment, and lovable people like me to engage you in meaningful conversation."

"I don't deserve such fortune," Adam replied, with a barely perceptible grin. "I should be forced to return to work immediately, instead of lying in bed and walking hallways I've walked a dozen times. I want my bed, my home, and the inalienable right to fix my own meals."

The two men sat in silence for a moment, then Adam continued, "Besides, the nurses on the night shift aren't all that cute."

"Lechery is not a pretty sight in a pastor," Dick said laughing.

"It's not lechery, it's frustration. I want to go home."

"Just one more night, Pastor. You can endure that."

"Of course I can, but why should I? I feel great."

"Great?"

"Okay, maybe not great, but I feel well enough to take care of myself."

73

"The nurse said that the doctor will release you tomorrow if your fever doesn't come back. Besides, there's no one at the house to take care of you."

"I'm smart enough to come back if my fever returns, and I can take care of myself. They should release me now."

"Adam, if you were sitting in this chair talking to me lying in that bed, and I said I wanted to go home before the doctors released me, what would you say?" Dick leaned back in his chair and waited.

At first Adam said nothing. He was remembering the times when he had conversations just like this one and had insisted that the person do as the doctor instructed. A few times he even pulled rank—"I'm your pastor, and I'm telling you that you need to stay." Now he realized that it was easier to give advice than take it.

"Well?" Dick asked, with eyebrows raised.

"All right, you win. I make a lousy patient."

"That's what the nurses say."

"Okay, so I tend to be a little testy."

"Did you really kick a nurse out of your room?" Dick was wearing a Cheshire grin.

"Well, she wanted to weigh me."

"So?"

"It was 5 in the morning. I told to her come back at 7 and assured her that I would weigh the same."

Both men laughed, but Adam's laughter was cut short by a stabbing pain. "It only hurts when I laugh."

"I thought that was just an old saying."

Adam shook his head, "I wish it were."

"You know, Pastor," Dick said, "I'm really glad you're all right."

Adam nodded, "Thanks, Dick. You've been a big help."

The two fell into an awkward silence that men experience when expressing emotions to one another. Adam knew it was silly, but he was as much a product of his upbringing and environment as any male. Dick Slay was the closest thing to a best friend that he had. Despite his profession, Adam spent a great deal of time alone, partly by choice and partly by the circumstance of his personality.

As a child, Adam had been a loner. With no brothers or sisters, he spent many hours alone while both parents worked hard to keep their home and put food on the table. Both his mother and father worked for General Dynamics near Lindberg Field in downtown San Diego, his father as a machinist and his mother as a secretary. Coming home to an empty house didn't bother Adam; in fact, he learned to enjoy it. He would watch cartoons, play with his toys, or play fetch with their collie, Sparky.

The loner habits Adam developed as a child carried over into adult life. He relished times at home by himself, although he occasionally missed Sparky. Yet, he had not allowed his love of being alone to interfere with his normal social development. He was an entertaining host, a fine pastor and, according to his few close friends, a great confidant.

Most of the friends Adam had made came from college and seminary. Unfortunately, all had moved to churches outside the area. He occasionally saw them at conventions, but most contact was reduced to the occasional phone call.

Adam's limited number of friends was also by design. If asked, he would say that every one of his congregation was his friend; but deep and abiding friendship required the ability to confide in others. As a pastor, he felt comfortable being confided in, but uncomfortable confiding in others. So Adam had surrounded himself with an invisible shield through which he could reach out, but no one else could reach in—no one except Dick Slay.

No two men could have been more different than Dick Slay and Adam Bridger. Adam was tall with dark hair and thick glasses, a highly educated scholar, and (except when confined to a hospital) had the patience of Job. Dick was short, squat, and blunt. While he had developed a better than average vocabulary which grew from his love of mystery novels, he lacked the refined knowledge that came from a fine college education. Yet, no one ever thought of Dick as slow. His mind was quick, and his ability to comprehend new facts was amazing.

Despite his abruptness, Dick was filled with an abundance of love. He liked people, liked laughter, and loved his pastor. The two had become fast friends. In many ways, Dick became the brother that Adam never had.

"You the one giving me a ride home?" Adam asked, breaking the hush.

"I'm your chauffeur. I've been thinking about bringing one of my big rigs. It'd do you good to be bounced around in the cab of an eighteen-wheeler."

The thought made Adam wince. "You're not serious, are you?"

"Nah. My wife said I could bring the minivan."

"That's a relief."

"When should I be here?"

"They'll probably spring me around noon."

"I'll be here with bells on."

"Could I ask one other favor?" Adam said. "Would you please make sure the church doesn't make a big fuss over me. All I need is a couple days of quiet."

"Are you kidding? They haven't even noticed you're gone."

"How's the church doing?"

"We burned it down, didn't you hear?" Dick shook his head. "Stop worrying, Adam. Everything and everyone is fine."

"What about David?"

Dick frowned. "No change, but then you know that. You've been making the nurses give you reports."

"I can't believe they wouldn't let me visit him."

"It's their job to make sure you take care of yourself. You can visit him tomorrow."

"I wish there was more we could do besides wait."

Silence once again shrouded the two men. Dick chose to change the subject. "You sure you won't stay with Chloe and me?"

"Thanks, but I'll be fine."

The condo seemed colder than normal as Priscilla entered and locked the door behind her. The gunman was dead, the police had told her that; yet, she was apprehensive. Perhaps this was normal for one who had narrowly escaped being shot. Perhaps this was how one felt when one watched a friend die. Except the one was Priscilla, a hard-as-nails journalist who couldn't stop sobbing or shaking.

Shedding her coat on the floor she slowly made her way to the bathroom. As she went, she kicked her shoes off and dropped her purse. She was in emotional shock. Scenes from the night's violence randomly popped into her head like images of slides being flashed on the screen of her mind.

In the bathroom she looked in the mirror and saw that the carefully styled red hair, her trademark, was mussed with several pieces of grass clinging to her curls. Her eyes were dark and her cheeks streaked black with mascara; her nose was red and irritated from repeated blowing. Priscilla took in the sight that was her image. She had seen others with this look, others who had watched family die or a house burn, others she had interviewed for broadcast. Now she understood the look. Now she could comprehend the storm of personal anguish that raged inside. She would have to be more sensitive.

"All right, young lady," she said to the face in the mirror, "it's time to pull yourself together. After all, you have an image to protect. You're strong and you can deal with this." She gazed at the reflection for a moment and then watched as it burst into tears, sobs erupting from a wounded soul.

Time no longer had meaning. She wasn't sure if she had cried for a moment or an hour. She just slowly became aware that she was sitting on the floor of the bathroom, knees pulled to her chest in a fetal position; rocking back and forth.

"I've got to get a grip on myself," she said aloud. "Maybe a drink would help." She thought about the Scotch she kept in the kitchen. She thought about pouring a large glass and drinking it as fast as she could. Perhaps the alcohol would numb her mind and blur the images of the night. Shaking her head, she dismissed the idea. "That's all I need right now—mass consumption of a depressant. No, I've got to stay clearheaded."

Pulling herself up from the floor she opened the shower door, leaned in, and turned on the water. She finished undressing and stepped into the steaming compartment. She let the hot water run over her head and down her body. In an odd way she envied the water: it was mindless, without feeling, and simply following nature's course. She wished she could melt and flow down the drain into nonexistence, but the images came back in clear, crisp, and vivid detail. Each scene was reenacted in slow motion and with the greatest detail. She could see the flashlight beam as it shone through the window and onto her face; she could hear the door of the house smash against the wall, she could hear Irwin groan as the bullet pierced his chest, she could feel the fiery pain from her twisted knee; she could feel the damp grass where she landed with Irwin on top of her; and most of all she could see the hateful eyes of her assailant.

Her mind shifted to other scenes: the policemen administering CPR; the ride to the hospital with the paramedics still pumping Irwin's chest; even the cracking of his bones as the force of the CPR flailed his rib cage. Then there was the official announcement of what she already knew: Irwin was dead. The bullet had pierced his aorta causing internal bleeding.

An emergency room doctor had wrapped her knee and suggested that she keep ice on it. The wrapping now lay in a heap next to the shower. She barely noticed the pain in her knee; a greater pain ruled the moment.

The police had been gentle and kind. Apparently Sergeant Reedly was running interference for her. She had expected to be grilled about her actions that led to Irwin's death, but a police lieutenant asked just the most basic questions. She was released and Sergeant Reedly drove her home.

It was over now. There would be more questions by the police but no trial, since the gunman had been killed. The police would file reports, and the news media would tell the story. The news media ...she was the news media. What would she do now? For the first time in her professional life she didn't want to report a story. Perhaps that was because for the first time in her life she *was* the story. But the story would be reported by every newspaper and news show in the area including her own.

It was odd that no one had contacted her. The station had a radio scanner that monitored all frequencies used by police and fire departments. Surely someone had heard about the shooting. They may have shown up at the scene, but she left in the ambulance with Irwin and would have been gone when they arrived. Still, someone would have tried to contact her.

There would be messages on the answering machine. She considered stopping the shower to retrieve her messages, but chose instead to remain in the warm blanket of water. The truth was that she didn't want to speak to anyone. She had always thought the story was the most important thing, but now isolation seemed far more valuable. There would be time later to talk, but now was the time to search for oblivion; mindless, emotionless oblivion.

## Thursday, March 5; 6:45 A.M.

"Good morning, Reverend Bridger."

Adam turned to see a tall, lanky young man wearing a white doctor's smock enter his room.

"That depends," Adam said, offering a cautious smile.

"Don't tell me," the young man said. "It depends on whether you get to go home today. Right?"

"On the money."

"Well, be nice to me then because I'm the one who gets to make that decision." He smiled as he read Adam's chart. "Let's see, you've been off antibiotics for a while and still maintained a normal temperature; that's good, considering that little infection you had."

"Little infection? It kept me several days longer than I wanted."

"Yes, little infection. Occasionally, people whose appendixes burst spend time in ICU. At least you were spared that. Your chart looks good. How do you feel?"

"Fine, actually. Some tenderness, and my back hurts from spending too much time in bed."

"The tenderness is normal. After all, we did cut you open to get that mess cleaned up."

"Excuse me for asking, but who are you?"

"Oh, I'm sorry. I'm Doctor Fredrickson, an intern here. Normally, Dr. Tremaine would do this, but she's been reassigned to some special duties."

"Special duties?" Adam felt some relief at not having to match wits with his surgeon.

"I can't be sure. I'm just an intern. But my guess is that it has something to do with that." He pointed at the television mounted on the wall opposite Adam. The screen showed the front of the hospital with a massive crowd gathered around the entrance. Police were stationed across the front of the building.

"What's going on?" Adam asked.

"You haven't been watching the news?" Dr. Fredrickson asked.

"No."

"Strange things, my friend, strange things." Fredrickson paused, as if weighing the ethical implications of discussing hospital matters with a layman. "I'll let the media fill you in. In the meantime, let me have one last look at that incision, and then I'll start the discharge papers."

"Great."

"Do you need to call someone to take you home?" he asked as he pulled the dressing back.

"A friend is picking me up later today."

Fredrickson replaced the bandage, stood straight and said, "You can go home today."

"That's what I wanted to hear."

The intern chuckled, "I thought as much. The nurses will be in to change the dressing again and give you some literature to read. They will also schedule you for a follow-up visit."

"Will Dr. Tremaine be doing the follow-up?"

Fredrickson shrugged his shoulders and left the room.


"You about ready, Partner?" Dick Slay was standing behind Adam's wheelchair.

"I've been ready for a couple of days." Adam was dressed in a loose-fitting jogging suit and leaning forward.

"Are you sure you don't want me to do that?" The discharge nurse asked.

"Nope," Dick replied with a grin. "I've been waiting to push him around for a long time. This isn't what I had in mind, but it'll have to do."

"Well, I'll see you to the car," the nurse said.

"Home, James," Adam said, "and don't spare the horses."

"Lucky for you we're going out the back way," Dick said. "At least you won't have to deal with the crowds."

"Somebody needs to explain that to me," Adam said. "I feel a little out of touch."

"I'll explain it on the way home, Pastor." Dick said. "Unless our nurse here would like to tell us what we're not hearing on the news."

"All I know is what I watch on television," the nurse said.

It took less than ten minutes for Adam to be ushered out of the hospital and into the back seat of the blue Chrysler minivan.

"Hi, Pastor," Chloe said from her front passenger seat. "Is there something I can do to make you comfortable?"

"No, I'm fine, Chloe. Thanks anyway."

"Do you want to lie down on the seat back there?" she asked. "I brought some pillows, to . . ."

"Leave the poor man alone," Dick said. "If you're not careful, you'll mother him to death."

"I'm only trying to help," Chloe said.

"And I deeply appreciate it," Adam replied, as he slid over to the middle of the seat. "You're one in a million. Dick doesn't deserve you."

"That's what I keep telling him." Chloe smiled at Dick. The two had been happily married for twenty-seven years. Outsiders might misread their quips and brusque manner, but their friends knew that no two people were more married or more in love.

The small van pulled from its curbside spot and drove through the parking lot, through a temporary gate and out toward the frontage street. Adam looked out his window as they passed the front entrance. Uniformed guards were stationed along the curb to keep the crowd of people off the macadam parking area. Several hundred people milled around on the grass in front of the hospital. Adam guessed that a few dozen more were inside the lobby.

"What's going on?" Adam asked.

"It's been all over the news and you haven't heard?" Dick said.

"No. I didn't watch television or read a paper. I did see some of the images on the news this morning, but I was being examined by a doctor so I didn't hear the story. I guess I'm out of touch."

"Healings," Dick replied. "Strange healings."

"Healings? What do you mean 'healings'?"

"So far two people, a girl with third-degree burns and a man with terminal cancer. Both expected to die."

"You mean, they're going to make it?"

"Oh, no, Pastor," Chloe said. "They were healed. No more burns and no more cancer."

Adam studied Chloe for a moment. She was a large woman stand-ing three inches taller than Adam and weighing a good thirty pounds more. Her premature gray hair, something she blamed on living with Dick and rearing three boys, gave her a soft, matronly look. Her mind was sharp and her wit keen. She could give and take good-natured barbs with the best of them. She was the epitome of good nature and was helpful to those in need. One thing to which she wasn't prone was exaggeration.

"Let me get this right. One person was healed of a terminal dis-ease and the other—a burn victim—is no longer burned?"

"That's right," Dick said. "But I think it was the other way around."

"No," Chloe said, "it was the man with cancer, then the girl with the burns."

"Nah," Dick said, "ya' got it backwards."

"I'm sure I'm right."

Adam shook his head and said, "It doesn't matter. All those peo-ple standing outside are there because they think they might be healed?"

"That's right," Dick said.

"Incredible."

"What? You don't believe in miracles, Pastor?"

"Of course I believe in miracles. It just seems ... unusual."

"It's certainly that," Dick replied.

The drive to his apartment passed quickly for Adam; his mind was engaged in what he had been told. He had never seen or expe-rienced a miracle, but that didn't shake his belief. In fact, he *had* to believe in miracles, not because he was told to, but because of his belief in God. By definition God was both omnipotent and omni-scient, which meant that He possessed both the power and the knowl-edge to perform miracles. The Bible, of course, was filled with mir-acles executed by God, Old Testament prophets, Christ, and the apostles. Despite his intellectual belief, Adam felt a sense of dis-quiet about what he had been told. Would God perform miracles in secret, leaving a mystery behind? Would He send His emissary stealthily to walk the halls of a hospital? No, God always performed miracles to draw attention to the message-giver; and since, at least so far, there was no message, then these events must have some rational explanation instead of supernatural.

"We're here," Chloe said jovially.

"I hope you kept your promise," Adam said to Dick.

"What promise is that?"

"The one where you agreed not to make a big fuss," Adam said sternly.

"Hmm. I don't recall a promise like that," Dick said, pretending to look puzzled.

"They're not going to yell 'Surprise' when I walk in, are they?"

"What 'they'?" Dick exited the vehicle and jogged around to open Adam's door. "I think you worry too much."

"They teach us to worry in seminary. They teach us to be especially worried about devious deacons."

"Well, it's a good thing you don't have any of those."

"I'm not so sure."

Chloe said nothing, but kept her silence masked behind a smirk.

"You're part of this, aren't you, Chloe?"

"I'm just a simple housewife, Pastor."

"Chloe, I know you to be many things, but simple isn't one of them."

Together the three walked to Adam's apartment. The walk proved to be a challenge for Adam; he winded easily and each step caused his tender abdomen to ache. At the door, he pulled his keys from his pocket, opened the door, and braced himself for the "Welcome home" cheer from the church members in his apartment.

When the door opened, he was greeted with silence. There were no cheers, no "Welcome home," and no hidden church members. To his surprise, Adam felt a twinge of disappointment. "So you did keep your promise, then," Adam said, making his way across the living room.

"Well, sorta," Dick replied. Then, facing the kitchen area he yelled, "Ladies, look who's home."

Rounding the wall that separated the kitchen from the dining nook came Adam's secretary, Fannie Meyers, and the president of the Ladies Mission Auxiliary, Mrs. Bachelder. Fannie, a cheerful, slightly rotund woman in her fifties, rounded the corner at a near trot, her face beaming.

Mrs. Beatrice Bachelder was the antithesis of Fannie. Tall, her hair pulled back into a tight bun, she was a serious woman who viewed her role in life and in the church with the gravity of an overworked undertaker. Where Fannie was quick to laugh, Mrs. Bachelder rarely smiled.

"Oh, Pastor," Fannie said jubilantly, "I can't tell you how good it is to see you. We've missed you at the church."

"Thanks, Fannie. I missed you too." Adam leaned over and gave her a kiss on the cheek. "And I even missed the office. I hope you brought me some work."

"There'll be none of that now," Mrs. Bachelder said. "Deacon Slay said that you should have your rest and I agree wholeheartedly. You are our pastor, and it's our job to take care of you."

"I only meant . . ." Adam started.

"No, I'll not hear of it," Mrs. Bachelder crossed her arms as though preparing for a fight. Even at seventy Adam felt that she could take on half the church and not even scrape a knuckle.

"Well, maybe just the mail . . ."

"That's all been taken care of," Mrs. Bachelder said. "We have everything under control. You won't have to do anything but rest for the next two weeks."

"I'm sure I'll be able to function long before . . ."

"We insist on you resting. We want you back in tiptop shape. The pastor's role is a demanding one, you know."

Adam looked at Dick who merely offered a wry grin and shrug.

"Now to make sure you rest," Mrs. Bachelder continued, "we of the Ladies Mission Auxiliary have stocked your pantry and refrigerator with sufficient staples for breakfast and lunch. We have been careful to choose foods that require a minimum of preparation. Then for dinner one of our ladies will bring you a hot, nutritious meal."

"Thank you, Mrs. Bachelder, but there's no need . . ."

"Oh, of course there is. It's our Christian duty. You wouldn't deprive us of that, now would you?"

"No, of course not, Mrs. Bachelder, I only meant . . ."

"Well, it's settled then," she said, taking two steps back in a restrained victory dance. "And someone will be by each day to tidy up."

Adam started to object but he knew it would be a useless effort, and he had grown tired of standing. "I think I'll sit down now," he said, and gingerly eased into an overstuffed chair.

"Very wise," Mrs. Bachelder said. "I'll just finish straightening up the pantry." As she turned to go to the kitchen, she added, "You should take more care of your pantry, Pastor. If you're not careful, you'll attract mice."

"Just what you need, Adam," Dick said in a hushed tone. "Another pest."

Chloe smacked her husband's shoulder. "Dick, that was horrible." She looked at Adam and saw that he was biting his lip. "Do you have a pain, Pastor?"

Adam glanced over his shoulder at the kitchen and then looked at Dick. A moment later both men erupted in laughter.

"Ow!" Adam said, holding his abdomen. "Oh, that hurts."

"It serves you right," Chloe said smiling and with mock outrage. "You two ought to be ashamed of yourselves."

"I can't be held accountable, Chloe," Adam said, still grimacing from the pain. "I've been sick."

"Well, it is good to see you laugh," Fannie piped in. "I brought you a get-well present." Walking over to the television she picked up a brown paper bag and handed it to Adam.

"What's this?" Adam asked.

"Open it," Fannie said.

Adam reached inside and pulled out an old, leather-bound book. The book's worn edges did not detract from its beauty and craftsmanship. The front of the book bore an ornate embossed border with the initials T.R. in each corner. A larger set of the same raised initials was prominently displayed in the center.

"This couldn't be what I think it is," Adam said quietly. Holding the book reverently he turned it so that he could read the spine. At the top were the gold-lettered words: *Theodore Roosevelt, an Autobiography*. At the bottom of the spine was one word, also in gold, Scribners.

"I found this in an old bookstore in Ojai," Fannie said, as she nervously chewed her lower lip. "I know how much you like to read about Teddy Roosevelt."

Gently Adam opened the book. Its pages were yellow with age and brittle to the touch. He turned past the first few blank pages and came to the reproduction of the Laszio painting of Theodore Roosevelt when he was president.

"It was published in 1922," Fannie said. "He wrote it in 1913, but you probably know that. I know it's not a first edition, but it's the first edition Scribners printed."

"It's magnificent," Adam said in hushed tones. "This is really too much. You shouldn't have."

"I couldn't pass it up," Fannie replied. "I was going to save it for your birthday, but since you're going to have some time on your hands, I thought you might appreciate it now."

"Thank you," Adam said sincerely. "I don't know what to say except I love it and will enjoy reading every word."

"Well," Dick said, "if you like that, then you're going to love this." He handed him a glossy, multicolored piece of paper.

"A baseball schedule?"

"Yup. I know how much you like baseball, so I took the liberty of subscribing to all the cable telecasts. You can sit here, watch the Padres play, and read your new book between innings."

"The season doesn't start until next month," Adam said.

"I know that. This nifty package includes preseason games—well, at least some of them."

Adam chuckled, "If I had known I would get such great treatment, I would have blown an appendix earlier. I might just get used to this."

"You can't be serious," a voice said behind him. Turning he saw Mrs. Bachelder enter the room again.

"No, Mrs. Bachelder, I'm not."

"We should be going," she said authoritatively. "You need to rest. Now promise me you'll go right to bed after we leave."

"Soon, Mrs. Bachelder," Adam said, starting to get up from the easy chair. They each tried to object to his rising, but he waved them off. "I have to get my strength back. Sitting in a chair all day isn't going to help. I need to move about."

"But not too much," Fannie said.

"I'll be careful."

They said their good-byes and began to file out of the apartment. The last to leave was Mrs. Bachelder. She paused at the door, turned, and faced Adam: "It really is good to see you doing so well."

Adam sensed her sincerity. For a moment, just a moment, she was lowering her guard and letting a genuine emotion escape. He walked over to her, leaned forward and kissed her on the forehead. "Thank you, Mrs. Bachelder. Thank you for everything. It means a great deal to me." Despite her apparent brusqueness, Adam had come to treasure her as a unique member of the church. Without her, both he and the church would be diminished.

Slowly she touched the spot where Adam had kissed her. Her eyes moistened. "It is I who should thank you."

A moment later, Adam was alone.

# Nine

## Monday, March 9; 2 P.M.

A late winter storm slowly moved overhead, pushing its bruised and swollen clouds further south on its journey that originated in the far reaches of Alaska and would end somewhere south of Baja, California. The storm had dropped nearly two inches of rain in Los Angeles and was supposed to do the same that evening in San Diego. The water-gorged clouds seemed to consume the normally vibrant colors of El Camino Memorial Park.

The weather matched Priscilla's emotions; the ashen clouds reflected her deep contrition. She did not feel the cool March breeze or take notice of the mist. She was too filled with anxiety to be bothered with physical sensations. In the turmoil of competing thoughts and emotions, she struggled to not think or feel at all, but there were too many reminders to snap her back to real time and place.

Most of the people stood in clumps of three or four making small talk and masking their discomfort. Some, however, stood numbly watching, lost in their thoughts or wondering when the graveside service would begin. Some of those gathered sat on brown folding chairs positioned in rows under a beige canvas canopy. The front row had been reserved for family, but only three people sat there, none of whom Priscilla had met before.

She knew that Irwin had a daughter and had seen a picture of her on Irwin's desk. The young woman who sat gazing vacantly at the cherry wood casket had the same straight blond hair and hazel eyes. She had to be Irwin's daughter. Seated to her right was a gaunt man with hollow cheeks and a ruddy complexion. His thin brown hair fluttered in the moist breeze. He wore a blue blazer that had passed from fashion a decade before; his shoes were scuffed, and he coughed frequently. He had an air of poverty and illness about him. Priscilla felt sorry for him and knew that the weather must be causing him great discomfort. He coughed, pulled a handkerchief from his coat pocket, and wiped his mouth.

To the left of the daughter sat a man in an expensive double-breasted pinstripe suit and red tie. He was as dapper as the other man was tattered. He held her hand in his and whispered in her ear. Priscilla knew who he was because he had delivered the eulogy during the memorial service in the chapel. George Jenkins was a close friend of Irwin's and one of the partners of the media group that owned KGOT-TV. She could only wonder what he thought of her.

Priscilla wondered if she should approach the woman and offer her condolences but was uncertain about the response she would receive. Will she blame me for her father's death? Priscilla didn't know and didn't want to find out in such an open forum.

The breeze increased and Priscilla put a hand on her black, broad-brimmed hat. She, like many people present, was wearing black. In her case a medium-length black skirt, a powder-blue blouse, and black coat. It was her desire to be as inconspicuous as possible. She was uncomfortable, not just because of the funeral, but because she believed that her coworkers credited her with Irwin's death. In more rational moments, she knew her fear was fabricated from the emotional debris left over from the attack. Still, she thought she saw them looking at her askance. No one had said anything, but she couldn't shake the belief that she was responsible and that others knew it.

"How are you holding up?" a voice on her right asked. Turning she saw Pham Ho, the assistant news director.

"Okay, I guess," Priscilla said as she broke eye contact.

"I've never been very good at funerals," Pham said. "It seems as though there's something I'm supposed to say, but I never know what it is. So I end up standing around saying nothing."

"I've been to only one other funeral; my grandmother died about ten years ago." Priscilla paused and looked at the crowd of Irwin's friends and coworkers. "This is different."

"Yeah. A lot different."

An uneasy silence settled between them; Priscilla stared off into the distance, and Pham looked at the ground.

"Camera crew gone?" Priscilla asked a few moments later.

"Yeah. We didn't think it was right to shoot this part of the service, although Irwin would probably have insisted." Pham had assigned a crew to tape part of the memorial service. It was his plan to play a portion of it at the end of the evening newscasts. "We wanted to be sensitive to the family's needs. Have you met them?" he asked, nodding at the three people in front row.

"No."

"The woman is Irwin's daughter, Irene. The man in the sport coat is Irwin's older brother. He lives on a farm in central California—McFarland, I think. The other man is George Jenkins, an old friend of Irwin's. He's also one of the owners of the station. I hadn't known that Irwin was so well connected."

"How are things at the station?" Priscilla asked quietly.

"Different. It's not the same without Irwin. He was one of the great ones." Pham turned and looked at Priscilla. "I might also add that it's not the same without you. We miss you."

"It's only been a few days, Pham." Priscilla had not gone to the studio since Irwin's death but had spoken to Pham over the phone, giving him the details needed to telecast the story. Other than that she had isolated herself in her home, not even returning phone calls from friends or other reporters. "I'll be back soon."

"I'm not trying to rush you. You take as much time as you need. We just miss you, that's all."

"I know," Priscilla said softly. "I just need a little time to sort things out."

"There's something you should know." Pham turned to face Priscilla and, after a moment of hesitation, reached out and put his hands on her shoulders forcing her to face him. "No one blames you, Priscilla. I mean *no one*. Irwin was an experienced newshound, and he knew the danger. I'm no psychologist, but I think you're afraid that we're sitting around accusing you of killing Irwin. We're not. Irwin's not the first to lose his life pursuing a story, and he won't be the last."

"But it was *my* story, not his. He was killed because I ..."

"Absolutely not! Irwin was the news director. Every story was his. You are not responsible for his death. The burglar killed him, you didn't."

"But he died protecting me."

"That's the kind of man Irwin was. He reacted on instinct. Sometimes his instinct got him in trouble, but most of the time it served him well. What happened to Irwin was a tragic accident. You're not culpable. And no one blames you. Everyone wants you to know that."

The two stared at each other and then he embraced her. Priscilla fought to bridle her tears but could not.

The minister, a short, bald man in a black suit and gray tie, stepped to the head of the casket. He was from a local church whose name Priscilla could not remember. He seemed pleasant, friendly, and genuinely concerned for the grieving. He had delivered the memorial service message, mixing words of comfort with the promise of a future life. Priscilla heard little of his message then and even less now. Her mind was flooded with images of a dark night, the glimmer of a flashlight beam, a masked man, and Irwin's bloody chest.

Despite Pham's assurances that her coworkers held no animosity, Priscilla felt uneasy as she walked into the studio. She had unpleasant fantasies that people would avoid her or, worse yet, accost her with a volcanic eruption of emotion. Nothing of the kind occurred. The studio was emptier than normal because many of the people who attended Irwin's funeral had not returned. The few people who were there greeted her more with sympathy than antipathy.

Even though she had been off work only a few days, the studio felt strange. It seemed years since she had walked its carpeted floors, negotiated her way around the many desks of newswriters, producers, researchers, and other employees. She had come to the studio because after the funeral Pham Ho said he needed to speak with her about schedules and upcoming stories. Priscilla wondered if she would ever feel comfortable in the studio again.

"You made it," said a cheerful voice. "I was hoping you would stop by." Pham was substantially more upbeat now that the funeral was over.

"You said you wanted to see me."

Pham nodded. "I do. I know I told you I wanted to discuss schedules, but that was only part of the reason."

"What's the rest of it?"

Before answering, Pham paused and studied Priscilla. Even depressed she was gorgeous, but something was missing.

"Let's meet in here," Pham said, motioning toward the office next to his.

"Couldn't we just meet in your office?" Priscilla asked. If memories haunted these halls, then they would converge in Irwin's office.

"No," Pham said simply and walked through the door. Reluctantly, Priscilla followed after him.

Everything in the office was the same. She remembered that last time, arguing with Irwin about her role as an investigative journalist as well as news anchor. She was filled with sorrow, for she had won the argument and lost Irwin.

"Have a seat," Pham said, nodding toward a chair in front of the desk.

"No, thank you," she said curtly. "Let's just get on with this."

"Ah, it's still there," Pham beamed.

"What?"

"Chutzpah," Pham said grinning. "I noticed it was missing at the funeral and feared you were losing it here." Pham pointed at his chest.

Priscilla looked at Pham with confusion. It seemed incongruous to hear the Yiddish word uttered by such an Asian face. "Chutzpah? What do you mean?"

"You know. Brashness. Boldness. Confidence."

"I know what the word means, but what does it have to do with me?"

Pham sat on the edge of the desk. "You're the epitome of chutzpah, almost to a fault. But I was afraid that it had been killed along with Irwin."

"Don't make light of Irwin's death," she snapped.

"I don't make light of anyone's death, and I certainly wouldn't do so of Irwin's. I valued him for his skill, professionalism, and his friendship. As far as I'm concerned, they can turn this office into a shrine."

"Then why are we here?"

"Because I'm doing what Irwin would do, and would want me to do."

"And that is?"

"And that is to get you back on track." Pham got up and paced the room. "You're one of the finest reporters and news anchors in the business. I don't know how Irwin kept you from skipping town to go to a larger market like L.A. I know you've had offers. I may not know why you've stayed, but I'm glad you did, and I want to make sure it stays that way."

"What makes you think it would be any different now?" Priscilla's tone softened.

"Because events like you've experienced can sap the strength from you. I've seen it before. You begin to blame yourself, and then you assume everyone else is blaming you. Then you simply drop out."

Priscilla stood in the middle of the room and watched Pham pace.

"Let me ask you something," he continued. "When you walked in here, how did you feel?"

"I don't see what that has to do with any of this," Priscilla said.

"Just tell me," Pham was just short of shouting.

"I felt lousy, scared, guilty, responsible, uncomfortable. I felt like I don't belong."

"Exactly right about what you felt, and exactly wrong about the truth. You do belong."

"No, I don't. You don't know what it's like to watch someone die like that. To be that close to death, and to have it be your fault."

Pham stopped pacing and stared at her. Priscilla knew immediately that she had said the wrong thing. As a thirteen-year-old refugee from Vietnam, he and his parents fled the country after it fell to the communists. He and 160 other frightened nationals escaped in a leaky wooden boat. North Vietnamese pirates stole what meager possessions they had, and then, for the "sport of it" indiscriminately killed many of the defenseless refugees, including Pham's parents. The corpses had to be dumped at sea. Pham had watched in horror as sharks shredded the bodies of his mother and father. Fourteen years later, through hard work and the help of a foster family, Pham had graduated from San Diego State with a degree in journalism. He was a natural behind-the-scenes man, never appearing on camera. Those in the know considered him an administrative genius. He had spent the last year as Irwin Baker's assistant. Now that Irwin was gone ... Priscilla didn't want to think about that.

Priscilla threw up her hands, "All right, I guess you do know."

"Better than anyone I know. And I'll tell you what else I know— that a painful past doesn't mean a painful future; injustice doesn't mean no justice; and fear doesn't mean the absence of courage. You belong here, Priscilla. If anyone was custom-made for this job, it's you. Don't let your fear and guilt, wrongly placed as it is, kill your future like that burglar killed Irwin. Call on the strength you're famous for, and seize life."

"I just need a little time off."

"This isn't about time off. Of course, you need time off. Anyone would. But if you let sorrow and fear steal your heart, then the time you take off will become permanent."

Priscilla lowered her head. It was true: fear and guilt had almost taken control. She had nearly surrendered the rest of her life without a struggle. Pham was saying exactly what Irwin would have said.

"You take as much time off as you need," Pham said in a soft voice. Then in a firm, authoritative tone he stated, "But you *will* be back to work, and you *will* do a wonderful job."

Lifting her head, Priscilla nodded. "Monday," she said. "I will be back Monday."

"Now the hard question. Do you want to continue covering the Healer story?"

After a brief meditative pause, she replied, "Absolutely."

Pham slapped his hands together and grinned. "Chutzpah!" he shouted.

"Chutzpah," she echoed and grinned for the first time in days.

# Ten

## Sunday, March 22; 8:45 P.M.

Adam prepared a no-frills sandwich—two pieces of bologna with mustard on wheat bread—and plopped down on the sofa. He turned on the television and watched a National Geographic special on the Bengal tiger.

It had been a disappointing Sunday. His alarm didn't go off, which led to a hectic morning of preparation. He had to do without his usual sermon review time. Both Sunday School and morning worship attendance had been down. This often happened on long weekends, but occasionally, as this Sunday, it happened without conspicuous reason.

The smaller group, coupled with an overcast day, made for slow services. By the time Adam stood in the pulpit, he was uncertain if he were in a worship service or a funeral service.

The evening service had been no better. The congregation was sparse, making it difficult for Adam to preach. He had often maintained that he would much rather preach to 5,000 than 50; not for vanity's sake, but because of the human dynamics between audience and speaker.

The phone jarred Adam from his silent complaining. It was Ann Lorayne. Her message was short and delivered between bitter sobs, "David...is...dying."

## Sunday, March 22; 9:45 P.M.

Adam's stomach hurt again. He hated these calls. In all probability he would sit with a woman who would become a widow. There was so little that could be said, and less still that could be done. The only ministry option available to him was to simply be there. Although he had done this task many times, he had never reached an emotional balance with it. No matter how often he had watched people die, he could never grow used to the grief left behind.

The doctors and nurses would do all they could, then express their sorrow and leave. Although it was probably unfair, he often envied them. Their work was over, and his was just beginning.

Having parked at the far end of the hospital's parking lot, Adam walked, head down and lost in thought, toward the glass doors that led to the lobby. As he entered, he was greeted with a staggering vision: the large room was filled with people in wheelchairs and lying on stretchers. There before him were the lame with atrophied limbs; the weak with nasal tubes carrying oxygen from green tanks to ailing lungs; the blind with their red-tipped white canes; the uncontrolled bodies of those with cerebral palsy, their head and limbs jerking from one position to another. But worst of all were the children, some bald from repeated exposure to radiation and the infusion of chemotherapy. One mother gazed vacantly at the cyanotic infant she held in her arms, and quietly hummed a lullaby.

There was a strange quiet in the room, and with it an unmistakable air of expectation. As he entered, everyone looked his way. The sudden confrontation as well as the magnitude of human suffering jolted Adam. He had seen the crowds when he was released, but didn't realize that the sick and lame were still at the hospital. *What are they waiting for?* he wondered.

Adam was so lost in his thoughts that he did not immediately notice the crooked little figure at his feet. Looking down he saw a boy, maybe ten years old, whose body was twisted. His spine was curved so severely that it was nearly impossible for him to look up.

"Mister, are you the Healer?" The tiny voice that came from the frail form shook Adam's very soul. Simultaneously feeling compassion and repulsion, Adam knelt down to look into the boy's eyes. He saw an incomprehensible sadness and yet, a brief but discernible spark of hope. Adam could say nothing; he simply gazed at the tragically deformed boy.

"Mister, are you the Healer?" the boy asked again. "Have you come to heal me?"

The incongruities in the boy's voice impacted Adam's mind like a meteor crashing into the earth. It was a voice of hopeful sadness.

Confusion numbed Adam's mind. Healer? Was he waiting for a doctor or some new treatment? "What do you mean, son?"

"Are you the Healer? I want to be healed." There was mournful sadness in the boy's voice, a melancholy rooted in a hope that teetered on the edge of despair. In his eyes, Adam saw something possessed by children, but lost to adults: a simple willingness to believe, to cling to hope no matter how unreasonable the situation. That expectancy glistened in the boy's bright blue eyes—eyes that had never looked directly forward. Something in those eyes touched Adam with a searing hot intensity that branded the boy's image on his soul.

Not knowing what else to say, Adam slowly shook his head and replied softly, "I wish to God I was, son. I really wish I was."

Adam stood and quickly made his way to the elevator leaving the boy behind. At the elevators he was stopped by a large, uniformed guard with heavy eyebrows, a broad nose, and narrowly spaced eyes. May I help you, sir?" he asked firmly.

Adam was nonplussed. He had been to this hospital many times to visit ailing members and had always simply walked wherever he wanted.

"I beg your pardon," Adam said, adjusting his glasses.

"Do you have business in the hospital?" the guard asked intently.

"Yes, I do," Adam replied coolly. "I'm Reverend Adam Bridger, and I've been called to the bedside of one of my members."

"What is the name of the person you are visiting?" The guard clipped his words as he spoke.

"I'm afraid I don't understand," Adam said. "I've been in this hos-

pital hundreds of times over the last few years, and not once has anyone stopped me from …"

"I'm just doing my job, sir. Look," he continued, "you just
walked through the lobby, didn't you?"

Adam nodded.

"And you saw all those people, didn't you?"

Adam nodded again.

"Well, they come by the hundreds and sit there. Most of them
wait quietly. Others wander around the halls, often disturbing the
patients. For a few days, the hospital almost shut down. So unless
you show me that you have legitimate reason for going upstairs, this
is as far as you get."

Gazing back at the lobby, Adam considered what he had just heard.
He had trouble believing that he had been so sequestered as not to
have read or heard about all of this beyond the initial information
provided by Dick Slay.

"I understand," Adam said. "I'm sorry if I seemed a little gruff.
I'm afraid I've been out of touch the last few weeks, and I guess I
was overwhelmed by the people in the lobby. I'm here to see Mr.
David Lorayne in ICU."

The guard checked his clipboard list and then nodded. As
Adam rode the elevators to the fifth floor, his mind was filled with
the image of the crooked little boy. The meek and hopeful appeal
echoed in his ears, "Are you the Healer?" Adam was surprised to
discover tears in his eyes.

After identifying himself to the ICU nurses through an intercom,
Adam was granted permission to enter. David Lorayne's room was
just inside the door. Ann stood by her husband's bed. Her face was
drawn and her eyes red. She stood stooped over the dying figure.
David Lorayne lay motionless, an oxygen mask covering his face.
A plastic bag with clear solution was suspended on an IV stand. Above
his head was a heart monitor that showed his heart rhythm and gave
a digital readout of his pulse rate.

Adam took his place beside Ann and, placing his arm around her
shoulders, began to silently pray. Due to his own recuperation
and overwhelming schedule, Adam had not visited the Loraynes
in the hospital—Ann had insisted on it. Normally, he would visit

the hospital several times a week, but his own condition had forced him to visit only by phone.

Fifteen minutes later Adam spoke. "How long have you been up here?"

"They brought David up two hours ago." Her voice was shallow and raspy from crying. "They say he could go at any minute or linger for hours. I just don't understand. They said that it was a routine operation and assured us that very little could go wrong."

"Do they offer no hope?"

"None." Tears trickled down her face and fell onto the bare arm of her husband; Ann gently wiped them off. "The doctors say that David may have had a negative reaction to the anesthesia; that the blood vessels in his brain constricted causing his brain to slowly shut down." Adam had heard all this before in their phone conversations, but allowed her to explain it again. It was Ann's way of coping. "They want to know if I want them to do things if David stops breathing."

"Things?" Adam was puzzled for a moment. "Heroic efforts?"

"Yes. That's what they called it—heroic efforts." Ann reached for a tissue from a box on the nightstand. "I don't know what to tell them. I can't say let him die, but I don't want him to be hooked up to all the machines either."

"Is the rest of the family here at the hospital?"

"Yes. They went to the cafeteria for some coffee. Michael is . . . do you remember Michael?"

"I met him last Easter at the church. He's a civil engineer, isn't he?"

"Yes, in Los Angeles. What I started to say was that he's having trouble dealing with this. He won't show it or say it, but I know he's afraid."

"That's normal. In fact, it's good. His fear is an indication of love, not unmanliness."

"Pastor, what do I tell the doctors when they ask me to sign those papers to let David die?"

Adam stood silently. There was no clear answer. Being an optimist he always had hope, and he wanted to believe that David might wake up someday if they kept him alive. But his experience also forced him to be a realist. If the doctors were suggesting that the family sign release papers that would free the hospital from the responsibility of maintaining a life with extraordinary means, then they probably had good reason for doing so.

"I think it's best that we discuss it with the rest of the family," Adam finally said.

"I don't feel right leaving David."

"Ann," Adam said softly, "there's nothing you can do here. David may linger on for hours, maybe even days. It is unreasonable to expect yourself to stand here hour after hour. You have an important decision to make, one that should be made with the rest of the family."

"I still don't know."

"Ann, you're exhausted. At least come down to the cafeteria for a cup of coffee."

She said nothing.

"Ann, if the situation were reversed and it was you on the bed and David standing where you are, what would you tell him?"

After a moment of silence Ann reached for her purse. "You're right. But only for a few minutes."

Adam found the family huddled around a table in the center of the cafeteria. As he and Ann approached, a man he recognized as Michael stood up. Even at a distance, Adam could see the fear in his eyes.

Adam spoke quickly. "There's no change in your father's condition." Adam thought he detected a sigh. *Humans are wonderful creatures*, Adam thought. *Even when no hope is available, they cling to it.*

Ann introduced Adam to the others around the table. In addition to Michael there was Larry, David's older brother, and his wife, Eva.

"I know that this is a very difficult time for you all," Adam began. "I honestly wish there were words that would make this time easier, but there are none. All that remains for you is to face the situation and your emotions honestly. I also want you to know the whole church is praying for you. We will do anything we can to help."

After a moment of silence, Eva said, "Thanks." Adam had never met her before, but he had met her husband once at a church softball game. Larry was the antithesis of David. Where David was tall and thin, Larry was squat and heavy with a dark beard that shadowed his face.

Michael was Ann and David's only son. He appeared to Adam to be the spitting image of his father—blond hair, deep-set hazel eyes, and a preponderance of freckles.

"Ann tells me that the doctors have asked you to sign an agreement releasing the hospital from taking heroic efforts with David. Would you like to talk about it?"

"We haven't signed anything yet," Michael said. "The hospital chaplain explained everything to us, but we haven't signed the papers."

"It doesn't seem right," Larry said bitterly. "They're asking us to sign David off—to simply give up." Adam noticed tears in Larry's eyes. "We're not deciding whether to put a dog to sleep here; we're talking about my brother—my only brother."

Adam watched as the hard exterior of Larry broke. Times like these were often harder on men, for they were ill-equipped to deal with pain and heartache. It was something that Adam blamed on society. Too many men grew up with John Wayne and Clint Eastwood as heroes—men who were too tough to cry. A lifetime of repressing strong emotions could be powerful and frightening.

"You are absolutely right, Larry." Adam spoke softly, yet firmly. "However, it is a decision that must be made. Not making a decision is, in effect, making a decision. This hospital could take extraordinary means to sustain David's life—even if there is no hope for life. Theoretically, they could artificially sustain David indefinitely. Once they do that, it becomes a very difficult thing to have David removed from life-support devices."

"Are you suggesting we sign the papers?" Larry asked.

"No. But I'm not suggesting that you don't either."

"Then what do you suggest?" This time it was Eva who spoke.

"I'm suggesting that you, as a family, talk this through."

A worker in the cafeteria moved past their table picking up empty cups. The group remained silent until she passed. Adam was thankful, for it gave them time to think.

Michael broke the silence. "I'm not very knowledgeable about religious matters, Pastor. Is there any reason why we should not sign the papers? I mean any reason from the Bible?"

Adam had wrestled with this question before. Yet, even though he had previously thought through all the arguments, he still felt a sense of confusion. It was never easy for a pastor to say, "Let him die."

Adam began softly. "The Scriptures teach that all life is from God. They also teach that man is made in the image of God. By that I mean that man is a spiritual creature with a soul that exists eternally. Because of this and other reasons, life is always to be held sacred. But we must also understand what we mean by life and what we mean by death. There has been much discussion about when death occurs. Some say that a person has died when the heart can no longer beat. Others insist that death occurs when the brain no longer functions. It's hard to be dogmatic, but I agree with the latter."

Adam paused reflectively and then continued. "Michael, your father's brain is shutting down. There will come a time when it will no longer be able to tell his lungs to breathe and his heart to beat. When that time comes, the doctors can artificially, through machines, do those functions for him. Then the question will be, 'Is your father still alive?' If there is hope that he might regain the use of those vital functions, the answer is obvious—keep him alive. But if there is no hope for recovery—if the brain is dead— then all the doctors can do is keep the shell alive."

"I'm not sure I understand," Eva said.

"Let me see if I can make it clearer." Adam leaned forward over the table. "You and I are not machines. Our bodies function somewhat like a machine. Just as a machine requires fuel, our bodies require food. Just as machines run down, our bodies run down. But we are also very different from machines. We have within us a spark of life. Actually, more than a spark; more like life itself. The Bible calls that immaterial aspect the soul. As a Christian minister, it is my belief that the body is really a structure that houses the soul. While the body may die, the soul will continue to live. When a person dies, the body and soul are separated. That's what death is—the separation of the material from the immaterial. What you have to decide is whether or not to let the doctors keep the house functioning when the tenant has gone."

"That makes no sense!" Larry's tone was sharp and angry.

"Larry!" Eva said.

"I'm sorry," Larry continued with a softer tone, "but this is my brother we're talking about here."

"And my husband." Ann's voice was firm, but not angry. "And I know what the pastor is saying, and I believe it."

"What's your point, Pastor?" Michael asked.

"My point is that you have no need to feel guilty about asking the doctors not to take heroic methods. If they tell you there's a chance for any degree of recovery, you would, of course, do all that you could. But, there comes a time when the best course of action is to let go. The decision is yours, of course, but please make sure that your decision is not made because of guilt. The solution is not easy. However, most doctors would tell you that life ceases when the brain ceases to function."

The family looked at each other. "Pastor," Ann said, "I think we would like to talk it over."

"I understand," he replied, somewhat relieved to have an excuse to leave. "I want to check on David again. Before I go, let's pray together." They bowed their heads and Adam led them in a short prayer, asking for peace and wisdom for the family and comfort for David. Then, as was his custom, he asked that God would lay His "healing hands" on David. When he had finished, he looked up and saw tears in the eyes of each family member. "If you need me for anything," Adam said softly, "I'll be in ICU."

Adam excused himself and made his way from the cafeteria through the pale green halls to the ICU. He wondered if he had advised the family correctly. In seminary he had been taught to use nondirective counseling, a form of counseling that offered no opinions but sought to bring the counseled to a self-realized catharsis; but to Adam that approach seemed not to be counseling at all. His doubts were based in his knowledge that he was not a professional counselor.

When Adam came to the ICU, he entered without using the intercom to ask permission. Walking through the door, he entered the tiny cubicle that served as David's room. What he saw made his heart pound.

"Hi, Pastor," said a smiling David Lorayne. "Have you seen my wife? Are you all right, Pastor?" David asked. "You don't look so good."

"Blessed Jesus," Adam said in prayerfully hushed tones. He was bent over, holding his stomach and panting, gasping for precious breath. A moment later he righted himself, looked at David, and said, "Oh, blessed Jesus," bent over and started gasping for air again.

"You sure look pale, Pastor," David said, concern evident in his words. "Should I call one of the nurses?"

Adam held up his hand, shook his head and said, "No, no." Then Adam began to laugh. He laughed, wheezed, laughed, gasped, laughed, and clutched at his stomach. He laughed, because of the irony: a man, who moments ago was on the verge of brain death, a man comatose with no hope of recovery, was asking if he should get a nurse for Adam. The incongruity was more than his shocked mind could take.

"Pastor?" David got out of bed and walked effortlessly to Adam. Adam's eyes widened as if he had seen a specter from the grave. "Let me get you a chair." A moment later Adam was seated in a large, high-backed, padded chair.

David went back to the bed and sat on it. He gazed with concern at his pastor and friend. "Are you sure you're okay?"

Adam nodded, finally caught his breath, and stared at David. A broad smile graced the face that had been so drawn minutes before. His rubicund complexion belied the physical ordeal he had endured over the past twenty days. His eyes were clear and bright, and Adam could swear that he had gained weight.

"David, uh, David . . ." Adam's voice seemed unresponsive. "I don't, uh . . . I mean to say . . ."

"I don't think I've ever seen you speechless," David said.

"You're a miracle,"

"Well, I like you too."

"No, a genuine miracle." Exasperated at his inability to communicate, Adam rose from the chair, walked over to David, and hugged him. Confused, David returned the hug and patted Adam on the back.

They embraced for a long moment.

"What are you doing to him?" a loud voice said from the doorway. "He's in no condition to be moved. How dare you . . ." The nurse's words were cut off by the sight before her.

Adam stepped back and David turned, slightly embarrassed, to face the nurse. "Will my surgery be soon?" he asked her. She said nothing. She just leaned back against the metal door jamb and stared slack-jawed.

"Will somebody tell me what's going on?" David was becoming exasperated. "Does anyone know where my wife is?"

Adam's eyes widened. "Ann," he nearly shouted. "I've got to tell Ann." Adam bolted from the room, edging his way by the stunned and still staring nurse. A moment later he poked his head back in the ICU cubicle, "I'll be right back. Don't go away."

"Where would I go?" David replied, shrugging his sholders.

Not wanting to wait for the elevators, Adam raced down the stairwell, oblivious to his recently healed incision. Adam sprinted down the corridor that led to the cafeteria, slowed only to turn through the door, and slid on the highly polished flooring into the cafeteria. The Loraynes were still talking, Larry waving his hands about animatedly, Eva quietly covering her mouth with a handkerchief, while Michael sat close to his mother and held her hand. They didn't see Adam's explosive entry.

"Ann!" Adam said loudly as he moved quickly to their table. "Ann, come quick...the rest of you too." They looked at Adam as if he'd lost his mind. "Something good. Come now. Come quick. Something great has happened."

They rose in unison and dashed toward the elevators. "What's happened?" Larry asked urgently.

"I'll show you," Adam said. "Just trust me."

The elevator ride seemed interminably long and every eye was affixed to the overhead display that indicated the floors they were passing. When they arrived at David's floor, Adam led the family into the ICU room. All the nurses were standing near David's bed; one was crying, and all looked stunned.

Adam motioned them back. Ann, closely followed by Michael, Larry, and Eva, crept into the room, not knowing what to expect.

"There you are," David said joyfully. "I thought you'd run off with a rich doctor."

Ann noisily sucked in air and covered her mouth. She said nothing, but stood at the foot of the bed and gazed at her husband through unbelieving eyes.

"Why is everyone staring at me?" David asked, his voice tinted with irritation.

"Oh, Honey," Ann said, stepping forward and embracing him. She hugged him tight, not wanting to let go. She wept, openly and unashamedly, as did everyone in the room.

# Eleven

## Sunday, March 22; 10:45 P.M.

Dr. Evan Morgan leaned back in his favorite easy chair and reflected on his love for Sundays. After years of keeping a doctor's schedule, he now enjoyed having a regular work week. As an administrator, his workday was seldom longer than ten hours, and he almost never went to the office on weekends. Instead, he played golf with the doctors from his former practice. After the game he would come home to his luxury downtown condominium on the twenty-sixth floor of the Lyman Building. Once home, he would leisurely read through the Sunday editions of the *Los Angeles Times* and the *San Diego Union*. With his wife visiting her sister in Bakersfield, the condominium was especially quiet. For Morgan nothing could be better.

Actually, Evan was feeling a sense of euphoria. Things at the hospital had quieted since Lisa Halley's unusual event. Oh, there were still the crowds in the lobby, but he was sure that they would start thinning down any day now. He looked around his home and felt a rush of pride and pleasure. The carpet was a rich, deep-blue pile that contrasted with the light hues of the wall coverings.

Unlike the contemporary decor of his office, his home was more sedate—a concession he made for his wife. If she had had her way, the entire house would be filled with antiques, but Morgan had no desire to live in a museum. The compromise resulted in a plush, traditional decor. His eyes paused on one of the many watercolors that he collected. It was a portrait of his daughter that he had commissioned. It hung in the most conspicuous place in the living room, over the mantle of the fireplace.

The remote telephone on the coffee table sounded its familiar beep. Morgan eyed it suspiciously before placing aside his strong desire to ignore the call.

"Doctor Morgan, this is Aretha Miller. I'm the head nurse in ICU. Something has happened here that I think you need to know about."

"How did you get my number?"

"Switchboard dialed it, sir."

"Okay, what's the problem?"

The voice on the other end of the line hesitated and then blurted out the message, "There has been another incident similar to the one that happened to the girl in the burn ward and the man on the second floor."

"I see," Morgan said in a quiet voice that concealed his shock and dismay. Looking at his watch he saw that it was 10:45. That meant the swing shift nurse would be there for a few more hours. "Here's what you must do." Morgan's voice was firm and decisive. "No one, and I mean no one but doctors and other essential personnel, is to enter ICU. Tell your nurses that they are to talk to no one and they are not to leave—not for lunches, not for breaks, not for any reason. I'll be there shortly. Is that understood?"

"Yes, sir!" the nurse snapped back with military precision.

"Good. I want this contained." He paused for a moment then continued, "One more thing. I want you to call Dr. Rachel Tremaine and tell her to meet me as soon as possible in ICU."

"Yes, sir. I'll do that."

His voice softened. He could tell that the woman was upset by what she had seen. "Aretha," he said gently, "you've done just the right thing. You are to be commended."

After switching off the phone, he slammed it to the floor and gazed silently at the plastic and electronic pieces scattered over the rug. This was not the way he wanted his Sunday to end.

## Sunday, March 22; 10:55 P.M.

"Sir, I'll have to ask you to leave now." Adam turned to see who was speaking. It was a short, stout nurse; her name tag read Aretha Miller.

"It's all right, nurse; I'm the family's minister." Adam recognized her as the one who stood frozen with shock in the doorway when she first saw David.

"You'll still have to leave."

"Why?" Adam asked, simply sensing that something wasn't right. There was an indefinable quality in her manner that made Adam suspicious. He had been asked to step out of hospital rooms before, but only if a doctor or nurse were about to perform an examination or treat a patient. The minister's access to ill members of his church had always been respected by the health care community and held sacrosanct.

"Rules, Reverend, rules." The nurse was resolute. "Now if you don't mind..."

"But I do mind." It was not Adam's intent to be obstinate or rude, but every one of his ministerial instincts warned him something was amiss. "I don't wish to be difficult, but something unusual has happened here, and as this family's minister, I believe I have a right to remain."

David spoke for the first time. "It's all right, Pastor. I feel great, and I'm not going anywhere right away. The truth is I'm a little tired. Maybe we can talk tomorrow."

"We do have other patients, Reverend," the nurse persisted. Then turning to the members of the family who had gathered in the small cubicle she said, "It would be best if you all left so that Mr. Lorayne could get some rest. The doctor will be here later, and I'm sure she'll answer all your questions after she's had a chance to run some tests."

"Perhaps she's right," Adam said, despite his desire to stay. There was no use in pushing the issue. The nurse was clearly upset, and Adam sensed that she felt pressured by the sudden well-being of one of her patients. To push the issue would only lead to an argument and upset the family. If he needed to take the matter up with the hospital administrators later, he could. For now, retreat was the best choice. "Tomorrow's a big day for you all. A good night's rest would be good."

David encouraged them all to go home to rest. Ann leaned over and kissed her husband; a kiss that said welcome back instead of goodbye. Her eyes were filled with tears again—tears of joy.

"Miracles are probably old hat to you, Pastor," David said, "but isn't this a hoot?"

"It certainly is. It certainly is."

As Adam and the family left, he noticed that the other ICU nurses had huddled together and were whispering feverishly. Adam knew they had a lot to talk about.

## Sunday, March 22; 11:15 P.M.

Thirty minutes after Morgan had received the phone call, he was standing in ICU reading David Lorayne's medical chart. Aretha stood next to him.

"Has his doctor been notified?" Morgan asked, his words short and explosive.

"Yes, sir," Aretha replied. "His physician is Dr. Tremaine."

Morgan made no attempt to conceal his scowl, "Where's Dr. Tremaine now?"

"I called her as you asked, and she's on her way in. She lives in the Mission Valley area so she should be here soon."

As if fulfilling the nurse's prophesy, Rachel came through the door. Her eyes were red and puffy, her hair disheveled.

"What happened to you?" Morgan asked coldly. "You look like death warmed over."

"I was asleep when the call came."

"At 10 o'clock?"

Rachel bitterly wondered what business it was of his. "I've just finished eight hours in surgery."

"I thought I made it clear that you were to work only on the project I assigned you." Morgan's words were curt. He was obviously upset, and he didn't care if the staff knew it.

"There were several cases that couldn't be rescheduled," Rachel replied coolly.

"I can only hope that you are a better researcher than you are an administrator."

Rachel was furious. To berate a fellow doctor before hospital staff was at best unprofessional. *Maybe that's the problem*, she thought. *Maybe he doesn't see me as a fellow professional. To him I'm just a woman playing doctor.*

"I assume you've called me here for a reason," Rachel said as calmly as she could.

"Here, read this," he said, thrusting the metal clipboard holding David's medical chart at her. "And follow me."

Dr. Morgan's chameleonlike change astounded Rachel. The moment they entered the tiny cubicle of David's room, he was cheerful and kind. "Mr. Lorayne," he began, "I'm Dr. Morgan. You know Dr. Tremaine. I understand you've had quite a night."

"I'm afraid I don't remember much," David said smiling. "I was pretty much out of it."

Rachel looked up from the chart she was reading and gazed at the latest miracle—her patient. What she had expected was a pale, comatose man—that's what he looked like yesterday when she, despite Morgan's orders to reassign her patients, checked on him during rounds. What she saw was a healthy-looking, middle-aged man.

"Your chart says that you were admitted for surgery," Morgan said.

"Ulcers. I'm afraid I don't deal with stress very well."

"Do you remember anything after the surgery?"

"No," David said slowly shaking his head. "To be honest, I don't even remember having the surgery."

"Do you remember dreaming, or hearing the conversations of nurses?"

"No. The last thing I remember is the anesthesia mask being placed over my nose and mouth. After that, nothing."

"How about tonight? Do you remember anything that happened?" Morgan was persistent.

"No." David paused, then, "Wait a minute. I do recall something when I woke up, but it's not very clear. In fact, it may only be a dream."

"I'd like to hear about it," Morgan said in a bedside manner that had been cultivated over the years.

"Well, like I say it may only be a dream, and it isn't much."

"I'd still very much like to hear it."

"Okay. All I remember is opening my eyes, but I couldn't see too much. I saw the ceiling first and then the light coming in through the door. The strange thing was the light."

"The light from the hallway?" Morgan was puzzled.

"No. The blue light. There was a blue light all over the room and all over the doctor."

"What doctor?"

"The doctor standing next to me."

"Was it Dr. Tremaine?" Morgan hesitated, then looked at Rachel judging her response. She had her eyes fixed on David and was clearly having trouble believing what she was seeing.

David thought for a moment and then said with a slightly embarrassed grin, "No. Believe me, I'd remember if it were Dr. Tremaine. Actually, I couldn't see him very well. As I said, he was covered in this pale blue light."

"How do you know he was a doctor?" Morgan inquired.

"Well, I don't really. He was dressed like a doctor. You know, in the white coat you guys usually wear."

"What did he look like?"

"Just a guy in a white coat. I didn't get a look at his face."

"Did he say anything?" Morgan was beginning to sound like a police inquisitor.

"No. But he did shush me."

"Shushed you?"

"Yeah. You know. He put his finger to his lips and went 'shush.'"

Morgan was exasperated. "Let me make sure I have this right. All you remember is waking up, seeing a blue light and this man in a white lab coat. Is that correct? Is that all?"

"I'm afraid so." David was apologetic. "I wish I could tell you more. Say, there's no problem, is there? I mean the guy is a doctor here, isn't he?"

"There's nothing to worry about. We're just glad you're doing so well." Morgan's sweet disposition had returned. "Dr. Tremaine, do you have any questions?"

"No, but with Mr. Lorayne's permission I would like to examine his incision." David looked puzzled. "It's just routine, Mr. Lorayne. It will only take a moment."

David nodded his approval. Rachel slowly pulled the sheet back and away from David's abdomen. Morgan leaned forward and gazed intently.

Aretha gasped and covered her mouth with her hands. Both Rachel and Morgan flushed.

"Incredible," Morgan said. "Utterly incredible."

They stared at David's abdomen. Where a surgical scar should have been was only healthy skin. It was as though David Lorayne had never had surgery.

"Hey," David said, "can someone tell me what's going on?"

Outside in the hall that led to the ICU, Drs. Evan Morgan, Rachel Tremaine, and Nurse Aretha Miller spoke in hushed tones.

"This is unbelievable," Morgan said, struggling to keep his voice subdued. "Are you sure this man had surgery?"

"Yes, I'm sure," Rachel said evenly. "I removed part of his stomach."

"Are you sure you got the right man's stomach?"

Aretha jumped in, "He definitely had surgery, sir. I changed his dressing myself when he was first admitted to ICU. The incision had healed normally and looked like a three-week-old scar."

"Well, this can't be happening," Morgan said, squeezing the bridge of his nose with his fingers. "Things like this just don't happen."

The three stood in silence.

"What about the man in the lab coat?" Morgan asked. "Did anyone else see him?"

Aretha shook her head. "After I spoke with you, I asked all the ICU visitors to leave, and then I quizzed the other nurses about what they saw or heard. And I, of course, gave them your message. None of them saw or heard anything, but then the ICU is full, and we were all pretty busy."

"Great!" Morgan said forcefully. "So that leaves us with a wide-awake coma victim with a vanishing scar and no eyewitnesses." Turning to Rachel he asked, "What have you found out about the other mystery cases?"

Without thinking, Rachel lowered her head. "Nothing. I've amassed the medical charts and have started interviewing . . ."

"I want answers, Dr. Tremaine, and I want them fast. Tomorrow you will reassign all your patients and devote full time to this investigation. No excuses. If we're not careful, these events could bring down this whole hospital." Then to Aretha he said, jabbing his finger in the air, "I want a lid put on this. You go back in there and talk to your girls and tell them that if word of this slips out to the media, heads will roll. Have I made myself clear?"

"Very clear," Aretha said. Rachel noticed that she looked shell-shocked.

Morgan spun on his heels, leaving the two women alone. They looked at each other a moment, then parted without speaking.

## Monday, March 23; 12:30 A.M.

Adam spent a restless night. His mind rehashed the day's events through surrealistic reenactments. A grotesque little boy with a twisted body chased him through the hallways of the church. The faster Adam tried to run, the slower he went. Around every corner and behind every pew were the mournful faces and twisted bodies of people screaming in pain and crying, "Help us, Pastor. Help us. Don't leave us alone."

When Adam awoke, he was sitting straight up in bed, his breathing labored, and his body coated with sweat.

# Twelve

## Monday, March 23; 6:30 A.M.

Monday was Adam's usual day off. He liked to sleep in, catch up on household chores, watch old movies, and read. This Monday, however, was different; the haunting dreams had plagued him all night. He was restless, his mind racing, unable to pause even for a moment. What had happened to David Lorayne? It was wonderful that he had suddenly—"miraculously?"—come out of the coma, but was it truly a miracle? If so, how could he know? Why was the nursing staff acting so strangely? And why were the pitiful people still in the lobby? Adam had exited with the family through the front doors, and the mass of ill were still there, looking hopefully at him and everyone who traversed the lobby. They left to a chorus of cries, "Are you the Healer?"

It took Adam a long time to get ready for the day. Each step of preparation, from selecting the clothes he would wear that day to showering, was interrupted by thought.

What occurred to David Lorayne was indeed remarkable, but surely others had come out of comas before. Why would the nurses be so amazed? And why did they all but push him and the family out

115

the door? If Adam understood anything, he understood people, and the nurses were acting like soldiers who had been given specific and urgent orders. No, Adam decided, there was more here than met the eye.

The Healer aspect must be related. But how? Adam closed his eyes. He had a keen and highly disciplined mind that could concentrate on a single issue for hours if necessary. When he concentrated, the world dissolved around him. He had been known, while in a high state of deliberation, not to hear the telephone ringing. Slowly, Adam's mind severed the bonds of distraction and centered on last night's events.

*What do I know?* Adam asked himself. *I know that David should be in a coma, but he's not. Thank God. I know that the nurses seemed more than surprised, they seemed astounded. I know that a variety of desperate people are looking for someone they call the Healer. But that's all I know.*

Things might have been easier for Adam had he not been emotionally involved. If it hadn't been one of his members so close to death and now so full of life, and if that bent little boy had not reached in and left his fingerprints on Adam's soul, then he might be able to look at the matter more analytically. That was not the case, however. He showered until the water ran cold trying to unsort the churning cauldron of his emotions. The child's face haunted him. Who was the Healer, and did he have anything to do with David Lorayne?

"Priscilla?" The electronic voice asked.

"What?" The curt reply was muffled by the feather pillow over her head.

"Wake up, will ya'?"

"Who is this, and why are you calling me at . . ." She opened one eye and looked at the red numerals on her radio alarm ". . . at 6:30 in the morning?"

"It's Pham Ho. Now cart it out of bed."

"Are you insane?" Priscilla asked abruptly.

"There's been another healing."

Priscilla suddenly sat up. "When? Where? Who?"

"Are you awake yet?"

"Don't toy with me, Pham. Just let me have the info." She snatched a pencil and a pad of paper from the drawer of her nightstand.

"Last night at Kingston Memorial Hospital, a guy named David Lorayne came out of an anesthesia-induced coma. Word has it that the guy's incision is gone too."

"What do you mean *gone?*"

"Gone. Disappeared. Just as if he had never had surgery."

"How did you find out about this?"

"One of the nurses in ICU is a big fan of yours." He laughed. "I promised her you'd take her to dinner."

"Okay, but the station is going to pay for it." She struggled to hold the phone to her ear and write on the pad while still reclined in bed. "What's her name?"

"She said she'd let us know later. She's afraid for her job."

"Understandable. I don't think that Morgan would think twice about canning her if he finds out. Anything else?"

"A camera crew will be there in an hour. So go and make yourself pretty."

Priscilla hung up without comment.

## Monday, March 23; 12 P.M.

The report made the noon news. Those watching saw Priscilla, every red hair perfectly in place, standing by a hospital bed quizzing David Lorayne. What they did not see was a nurse attempting frantically to prevent their entry. Nor did they see the nurse calling for security. The total interview lasted less than five minutes before an elderly man in a blue security uniform appeared. He emptied the room quickly with the simple announcement, "The police will be here in five minutes."

Although dramatic, the report lacked substance and that frustrated Priscilla. David Lorayne remembered nothing. She had hoped for more. A phone call to Dr. Morgan for comment gained only the expected threat of a lawsuit. Priscilla had the satisfaction of ending the report with several soul-shaking shots of the crowds of sick and dying in the lobby.

But what was going on? Could the hospital be doing some form of bizarre experiment? Or was there really someone or something performing miracles? One thing was for sure, the reporter who found out could win an Emmy.

## Monday, March 23; 12:30 P.M.

"Isn't it wonderful, Pastor?" Ann's joy was easily transmitted over the phone. "All our prayers have been answered."

"Have they said when David can go home?"

"Today," she said gleefully. "Michael and I were just about to leave when you called."

"Would you mind if I met you there? I would very much like to see David again."

"Of course, Pastor. If it weren't for your prayers, David would still be in ICU."

Adam disliked such comments. There were always those in the church who thought that a pastor's prayers were more potent. That somehow he had been given a special dispensation of grace that required God to listen a little more closely, and act a little more quickly. He referred to this as the "witch-doctor syndrome." The pastor was viewed as the ancient witch doctor who healed with magic words and potions.

"I think you're giving me too much credit. God can heal without me."

"You're too modest, Pastor. We'll see you at the hospital. Don't be late. I want to get David home just as soon as possible."

## Monday, March 23; 1:30 P.M.

The noon news report sent another wave of ill crashing in on the hospital. The massive crowd of infirm had spilled out of the lobby and onto the concrete plaza. They sat on lacquered wood benches and concrete planters. Some reclined on the small grass areas that decorated the hospital grounds. Those sentenced to life in wheelchairs had gathered together under the shade of a large tree. Children who should have been full of vitality sat motionless. Some leaned against weary mothers and fathers.

Adam moved quickly through the crowd. His desire to avoid their pain shamed him, but nothing, not his ministry, not seminary, not graduate school, had prepared him for such an exposure to suffering. Such scenes had always been confined to the pages of news magazines.

"Are you the Healer?" someone cried.

Adam moved quickly to the entry door and then stopped. Leaning against a concrete block wall was a young woman with long, blond hair. In her lap was "the boy," his twisted body motionless as he slept. A deep well of emotion stirred within Adam. He turned and walked through the lobby doors.

The elevator took him to the fifth floor where he found the Lorayne family gathered in the hall outside ICU. David was dressed in jeans and a sport shirt and was sitting comfortably in a wheelchair. Michael stood behind the chair, a nurse next to him. Adam did not recognize her. She was not one of the ICU nurses he had seen the night before, but then he realized that they would have gone home hours ago. A woman dressed in a doctor's smock had her back to him and was speaking with the family.

"Pastor," David exclaimed, "you didn't have to come down here."

"It is my pleasure, David. How are you feeling?"

"Great. I don't think I could stand it if I felt any better."

Although Adam had known David for years, he had never known him to exhibit such energy. He bubbled.

"Pastor," Ann said, "I would like you to meet . . ."

"Dr. Rachel Tremaine," Adam interjected as he extended his hand in greeting. "It's good to see you again."

Rachel shook his hand. "Reverend Bridger," she said dryly.

"Oh, I see you two have met," Ann said.

"Dr. Tremaine was the surgeon who did my appendectomy." Then he spoke to Rachel, "I didn't know you were the one who operated on David."

Rachel said nothing.

"She's doing some kind of research," David said. "You know, about my healing. Listen, how long are we going to stand around here? I want to go home."

"Since your doctor has released you," Rachel said, "you can go home anytime. I only wish I could persuade you to let me run some more tests."

"Not a chance, Doc." David was emphatic. "I feel great. I've been healed, and I've had all I can take of hospitals. You've poked, prodded, and X-rayed. Now I'm ready to go home."

Rachel was insistent. "Perhaps your pastor could influence you?"

"No way," David replied before Adam could speak. "Don't get me wrong. I think the world of him, but I want out of this place. I want to be with my family."

Adam looked at Rachel and shrugged. "If I thought it would do any good, Doctor, I'd try, but it looks as if his mind is made up. Is there any danger in his going home?"

"If there were," she said surely, "we would not have released him." Rachel's disappointment was obvious. "If I can't persuade you to remain, perhaps I can impose on Reverend Bridger. I would like to ask him a few questions."

"It would be my pleasure."

"Can we go now?" David asked. "I want to get out of this wheel-chair."

"They won't let him walk out." Michael said. "Afraid he'll fall down or something."

"I'll check in on you later, David." Adam patted him on the shoulder. Michael began pushing his father toward the elevator, followed by Ann and the nurse.

"Would you follow me, Reverend?" Rachel turned and made her way down the corridor. Adam obediently followed.

Rachel led Adam to the staff elevators and punched the button. In the elevator Adam took a moment to examine his guide. She had changed little from the last time he had seen her a few weeks ago. Her diminutive size seemed incongruous with her disposition. Although he would not call her beautiful, she was attractive. Her cream complexion was handsomely augmented by her short, coal-black hair. She wore no makeup. Her clothing was plain—simple tan slacks and white blouse.

The elevator doors opened at the second floor and Rachel led Adam down another hall and through a door to the doctors' lounge.

"Please sit down," Rachel said, motioning to one of the easy chairs. "Would you like some coffee?"

"No, thank you."

Rachel poured herself a cup, took a sip, and set it on the table. "I would like to ask you some questions."

"I have some questions, also. So perhaps we can help each other."

"Agreed. My first question, Reverend, is this: How long have you known . . ."

"Just a minute please." Adam raised his hands halting her mid-sentence. "First things first. If we are to continue, you must agree to call me Adam, or if you must insist on a formal title, then call me Pastor, but Reverend has to go."

"I prefer to keep this on a professional level." Her words had a coolness about them.

"I do too. I'm simply saying that I would be more comfortable without the adjectival title."

"I don't understand."

"*Reverend* is more a description than a title. It is a social contrivance meant to identify a person as a religious leader. Although, like you, I have an earned doctorate, neither Doctor nor Reverend describes what I do and, therefore, I prefer not to use them. The term *pastor*, which means "shepherd," does describe what I do. Formal titles are usually unnecessary and sometimes get in the way."

"I wasn't aware that your profession required doctoral-level work."

"It doesn't. In fact, some pastors have little or no college. In the early days of our country that was necessary, especially in pioneer areas. It was difficult to get trained clergy in the frontier. So the churches selected men from within their ranks who showed unusual biblical insight to be their pastors. Today, however, most ministers attend college and seminary. In fact, in terms of hours of education, I have spent more hours in school than many medical doctors."

Rachel seemed to take offense. "You are aware that our education extends three years beyond college and then there's specialized training."

"I am aware of that. And I do not mean to diminish that work. But many doctors think of ministers as ignorant shamans. In reality, the average minister has the traditional four years of college, followed by three years of graduate-level work in seminary. But whereas your three years of medical school led to a doctoral degree, the three years of seminary leads to a master's degree—a Master of Divinity, to be exact. The Ph.D., or for some schools a Th.D.—that is, Doctor of Theology—is about three years of graduate work beyond that."

"But what of the level of work?"

"Having never been to medical school, I could never compare the two. I personally have great respect for those of your profession. Only a small percentage could endure the grueling schedule of a medical education. But by the same token, a theological education is not a cakewalk. Most ministers with doctorates have a working knowledge of Hebrew, the language of the Old Testament, Koine Greek, the language of the New Testament, and at least one modern language, such as German."

"What's your point?"

"I want you to call me Adam."

"Okay. Now may I ask my questions?"

"Shoot."

"First, how long have you known the Loraynes?"

"Let's see. I became pastor of Maple Street Community Church nine years ago and they were members then, so I'd have to say nine years."

"What happened last night?"

"Not much to tell. I got a call at home from Ann. She said David was dying and asked me to come over. I found her in ICU. She mentioned that she was struggling with the decision about heroic efforts. She didn't know whether to sign the release or not, so we went down to the cafeteria and met with the rest of the family. After some discussion I left them alone to talk it over and went back up to ICU. When I went into David's cubicle, he was sitting up in bed."

"How long were you in the cafeteria?"

"I don't know. Maybe forty minutes or so."

"When you went to ICU, did you ask permission to enter from the nurses?"

Adam flushed for a moment. She must have talked to the ICU staff. They would have given her this information. "No."

"You are aware that no one, not even clergy, is allowed into ICU without permission from the nursing staff?"

Feeling like a scolded child, Adam replied, "I know that. You see, I had just been to see David a short time before, and being in hospitals as much as I am, I just took it upon myself to enter. I knew the family was in the cafeteria, and if the nurses were working with David, I'd just slip back out again."

"Did Mr. Lorayne say anything to you?"

"Yes, he asked for his wife."

"Why did you go back to ICU?"

"To pray."

Rachel grimaced slightly. "After he asked for his wife, what happened?"

"Well, as you can imagine, I was astounded. I didn't know what to say, so I hugged him. Then the nurse came in."

"What did she do?"

"You'd probably get a better answer from her."

"I'd like to hear it from your perspective," she said firmly.

"Well, when I entered ICU, I didn't see anyone. The nursing station was empty, so I assumed they were tending patients. A few moments after I entered David's room the nurse came in ..."

"What did she do when she entered Mr. Lorayne's cubicle and saw him sitting up?"

"She gasped."

"Gasped?"

"Loudly." Adam allowed himself to grin slightly. "So loudly the other nurses heard it and rushed over. They gasped too."

"One last question. How do you explain all of this?"

"All of what?"

"Mr. Lorayne's sudden awaking from his coma and the disappearance of his surgical scar."

"Surgical scar?" Adam was nonplussed.

"You didn't know?"

"No. I only thought he had come out of the coma. Do you mean to tell me that his incision is gone?"

Rachel paused, then decided it was too late to conceal it. Besides, the Loraynes would tell him anyway. "That's right. Just as if it had never been there."

"Dr. Tremaine, two-two." Rachel was being paged over the hospital intercom system. "Dr. Tremaine, two-two."

Rachel left Adam to his thoughts and went to a phone. "I'm on my way," she said into the receiver. Turning to Adam she said, "I've got to go now."

"Wait a minute," Adam protested. "We had a deal. I answer your questions, and you answer mine."

"Can't be helped. I'm expected in a meeting." Rachel made her way to the door.

"Is this the action of a professional?" Adam tried to look hurt.

His comment stopped Rachel as she opened the door. Somehow he knew the one thing that would make her reconsider; her professionalism. "What do you want me to do? I can't very well tell the hospital administrator to reschedule the meeting."

"Then meet me later to finish this. All right?"

"Okay. How about the coffee shop across from the hospital at 8 this evening?"

"I'll be there."

# Thirteen

## Monday, March 23; 2 P.M.

"I don't think I've ever seen the sky so blue," Ann Lorayne said, as she looked out the car window. David Lorayne smiled, placed his arm around her, and pulled her close. They gazed at each other for a moment and then kissed.

"All right, you two," Michael said from the driver's seat, glancing back through the rearview mirror.

"You just keep your eyes on the road," David said good naturedly. "You don't want us all back at the hospital, do you?"

"No. Visiting was bad enough. Just stop steaming up my windows."

They were ten minutes from Kingston Memorial Hospital and traveling north on Interstate 805. In ten more minutes they would be home.

"Larry and Eva are at their place fixing things up for you," Ann said as she laid her head on her husband's shoulder. "Since the doctor said you could eat anything you want, Larry decided to barbecue some ribs."

"Sounds great." David kissed Ann on top of the head. "This whole thing is unbelievable. Was I really in a coma for twenty days?"

"Twenty days. Twenty eternally long days." Tears formed in

Ann's eyes. "I really thought I was going to lose you."

"Hey, don't go getting all weepy on me. I'm fine; couldn't feel better."

"I know. It's just that I don't know what I'd do without you." Ann wiped a tear away with the back of her hand.

"Well, now, thanks to God, you won't have to find out."

"Hey," Mike said, "did anyone think to invite Pastor Bridger to the celebration?"

Ann looked puzzled. "I thought you were going to do that."

"If I was, then I forgot in all the excitement."

"He must think us horrible ingrates," Ann said somberly.

"No sweat," David said. "This is his day off. We'll call him at home and insist he join us. I've never known him to turn down a good meal."

Michael directed the car up the ramp that led to their University City home. The red Volvo station wagon weaved its way over the surface streets, its occupants happily looking forward to a time of family fellowship. Michael, his mind euphoric with joy, noticed too late the dark blue sedan that suddenly backed into the street in front of them. Instinctively, he plunged the brake pedal as far as it would go. The squeal of tires echoed down the residential street. The Loraynes' car stopped inches from the sedan. A man, tall with a ruddy complexion and a black goatee, exited from the driver's seat. Another man sat in the front.

"Are you nuts?" Michael exclaimed through his now open window. "I almost hit you."

The driver stooped over and peered at Michael and smiled. "Aren't you the Lorayne family?"

"Yes," David said leaning forward. "And just who are you?"

"I would like you to follow me, please." The man was still smiling—an unnatural smile that revealed crooked yellow teeth.

"Follow you? Why should we?" Michael was still looking to vent his anger.

From his coat pocket the man removed a small gray lump with a black box the size of a transistor radio attached to it and placed it on the hood of the car less than an inch from the windshield. The package made a distinct magnetic click when it touched the car's metal body.

"Hey, what's that?" Michael asked. "You'll scratch the paint."

"It's a gift," the man said. His insincere smile increased in intensity. "It's a very special gift. Do you recognize it?"

"No." Michael was suddenly apprehensive. The man frightened him, but he didn't know why. "It looks like modeling clay."

"It's similar to modeling clay, except that this clay explodes. You see, this tidy little bundle contains a plastic explosive and a radio receiver. My partner in the car over there has his finger on a transmitter. If you don't follow us, he will touch a button and you will all die. The rest of your family will get to bury whatever remains of your charred bodies. You wouldn't want that, now would you?"

The blood drained from Michael's face. They were being kidnapped in broad daylight, and there wasn't a thing he could do about it. He turned to see his parents in the backseat. They were sitting quietly, his father's arm wrapped around his mother. Turning back to his kidnapper he said, "If it's me you want, then I'll go, but leave my parents alone. My dad's been ill, and ..."

"I want you all. You will now follow me." Turning, he quickly walked back to his car and pulled away. Michael obediently followed.

## Monday, March 23; 2:30 P.M.

"I want to know what's going on and I want to know now." Dr. Evan Morgan was livid. He paced back and forth in front of the large teak conference table that dominated the room. His face was red and he gestured as he spoke. "At last count I have over 150 sick people sleeping in my lobby asking every Tom, Dick, and Harry if they're the Healer. My staff tells me that I can expect another 150 by this time tomorrow. What am I going to do with them?"

Those around the table nervously looked at one another. They had never seen the hospital administrator so out of control.

Morgan continued his diatribe, "I can't admit them. The hospital is full. I can't evict them because the news media would have a field day. I can see it now—'Hospital Administrator Kicks Ill and Dying into the Streets.'"

Pulling a pipe from his pocket, Morgan went through a pipe smoker's routine: placing tobacco in the bowl, tamping it down with a silver tamp, then slowly lighting it. Blue smoke formed a cloud around his head. The act calmed him.

He silently looked at those in the meeting. Carl Fuller, the hospital's public relations officer, didn't look up from the papers before him. His job had become overpowering in the last few weeks. Formerly, he worked an eight-hour day and then went home. The only previous excitement that his office dealt with was when a local movie star had been admitted for injuries sustained in a drunk-driving accident. Now his days were extended to fourteen hours, and his office was logging nearly 100 calls a day from all over the country.

Next to him was the head of security, Bill Sanchez, a retired San Diego police detective who had left the force after being injured while arresting a violent drug dealer. The dealer resisted by firing at the police officers who came to his door. One round struck Bill in the left elbow, shattering the bone. The elbow had been knit together with various metal pins that left his arm with little mobility.

Rachel sat opposite the two men, rereading the notes she had taken in her discussion with Adam Bridger.

Morgan walked over to a window that overlooked the east parking lot and puffed furiously on his pipe. "All right, let's hear what you've got," he said, without turning from the window. "Let's start with you, Sanchez."

Sanchez cleared his throat. "We have interviewed everyone who could have possibly seen someone entering or leaving ICU. Unfortunately no one knows much. We quizzed Aretha Miller, the head nurse of ICU for swing shift. She didn't see anyone enter or leave. I've got to admit that I find that a little difficult to believe."

He reached into his suit coat and pulled out a silver cigarette case with an unusual emblem engraved on its face. Rachel strained to see the image. It was an etching of a police badge. She grimaced as he lit the cigarette and carelessly blew smoke in her direction. The very thought of breathing something that had only moments before been in someone else's lungs repulsed her.

"What do you find difficult to believe, Mr. Sanchez?" Rachel asked fanning the smoke from her face.

"That Aretha Miller didn't see anything. I mean, there is only one way into ICU, right? And the nursing station is smack-dab in the middle of everything. Anyone walking through the door would have to be seen by her or one of the other girls."

"How often have you been in an ICU ward?" Rachel made no effort to conceal her irritation.

"A couple of times. Why?"

"The I in ICU stands for Intensive. Isn't it possible that she and her *girls* were busy with patients in the other rooms? Do you know how many cubicles there are in the ICU?"

"Not exactly, but . . ."

"Fifteen, Mr. Sanchez, fifteen, and every one filled. How many nurses were on duty that night?"

"That one I know: five. They said they were one short that night."

"So then, there are five nurses caring for fifteen patients who require around-the-clock supervision. Simple math would indicate that each nurse would be caring for three critical patients." Rachel paused for effect. "It seems a simple step of logic to assume that all five nurses could be tied up tending patients, which, by the way, is their job."

Morgan thought it best to break up the polemics. "Did anyone else see anything?"

"No, nothing. And who would with all those people camping in the lobby and parking lots?" Sanchez said.

"In other words," Morgan stated coldly, "you really have nothing for us."

"No, sir."

Rachel noticed the admission both embarrassed and angered Sanchez.

Morgan turned from the window. "How are things going with you, Carl?"

"It's a madhouse, sir." Carl's appearance bore out the statement. His white shirt was rumpled, and his tie hung limply from his unbuttoned collar. He had the appearance of a man who had worked all night. "The switchboards are tied up with calls from the news media. To make things worse, the story's gone national. I've received calls from every major television network, both AP and UPI, and six of the nation's largest newspapers. I even got a call from the BBC in London."

"What are you telling them?" Morgan asked.

Rachel detected a sympathetic tone in Morgan's voice.

"Not much. Just that the reports of unexplained events are being researched, but as yet there is nothing to report."

"Sounds general enough," Morgan replied.

"The real problem is Priscilla Simms. She's becoming a real pain. Apparently she's made this her journalistic crusade."

"So how do we deal with her?" Morgan puffed on his pipe faster, sending a chain of small clouds rising toward the ceiling.

"I don't know, but I think she has an inside source—someone who is informing her of every occurrence. That source needs to be stopped."

"Who would betray this hospital?" Morgan asked.

Rachel wondered at the word *betray*. She had previously noticed that Morgan often referred to the hospital as "his" hospital, but had always written it off as a convention of speech. Could he really view the hospital as his personal kingdom?

"Anyone," Fuller said matter-of-factly, "doctors, nurses, orderlies. You see, many people view these reporters as stars. To actually talk to them gives them a thrill. You know, they have a few friends over to the house and then they say, 'Oh, I know what you mean. When I was talking to Priscilla Simms—you know, of the "Evening News"—well, she and I were talking and. . . .' You get the idea."

"Still, it could be more than one person." Morgan turned back to the window. "So how do we locate the source or sources?"

"Let me see if I can run that one down," Sanchez said.

"Okay," Morgan said, "but do it quickly. I don't want any more leaks. I want the pipeline to Simms shut down." Turning from the window, he asked, "Did your interview with the Loraynes' minister help us any?"

"Not really," Rachel said nonchalantly. "He assumed that Lorayne had only come out of the coma. He didn't know about the . . ." Rachel struggled for an acceptable term. "About the physical alteration."

"Where was he when the event happened?" Morgan asked.

"In the cafeteria with the family."

"He just left them there to go up to the ICU?"

"They were struggling with whether to sign the heroic efforts release papers. He left to give them some privacy."

"And when he walked into Lorayne's cubicle, what did he see?" Morgan persisted.

"The patient sitting up in bed."

Even with Morgan's back turned to her, she could tell he was puffing on his pipe more. A stream of smoke rose to the ceiling. "I wonder," he said quietly.

"Excuse me," Rachel said, unsure of what she heard.

"I was just wondering if he could be our man." Morgan turned and walked to the conference table. "After all, no one saw him come in. He knows the family. The nurses were tied up with other patients." Turning to Sanchez he asked, "Bill, what kind of evidence do the police look for at a crime? I mean if you already have a suspect."

"Just like what you see on television." Sanchez sat up as he spoke. "We look for evidence that shows motive, means, and opportunity."

Morgan paused thoughtfully. "Well, this preacher had motive, he's a friend of the family; he had opportunity when he was in Lorayne's room alone. The only thing we don't know is if he has the means." Turning to Rachel he asked, "What do you think? Could he be our man?"

Rachel thought for a moment then asked, "What about the other events?"

"He was a patient of yours, wasn't he?" Morgan turned to face her.

"He has his own physician, but I performed the emergency appendectomy."

"When was he admitted?" Sanchez asked.

"Sunday, a few weeks ago," Rachel said then paused to mentally calculate the date. "That would be March 1st. He came in a little before noon. We operated soon after that."

Sanchez rolled the cigarette back and forth between his fingers. "That's the day of the first heal . . . occurrence. The second event happened the next day."

"Interesting," Morgan said.

"Wait a minute," Rachel remarked. "The first healing took place in the predawn hours of March 1st, Bridger wasn't admitted until hours later."

"Does Bridger live in the city?" Sanchez asked.

"Yes."

"Then what's to stop him from taking a little late-night drive down here?"

"This doesn't make sense to me," Rachel exclaimed. "Why would a person who can heal others need to be admitted to the hospital for surgery?"

"Maybe things aren't what they seem." Sanchez looked up.

"His appendix was real," Rachel said. "I held it in my hands, and I cleaned up the mess it left. His attack was real. It still doesn't make sense."

"And what, Dr. Tremaine," Sanchez said calmly, "does make sense about any of this? A terminal cancer patient with no cancer, a burn victim with no burns, and a surgery patient with no scar. This makes as much sense as anything I've seen so far."

Rachel sat quietly. She knew Sanchez was right; nothing made sense anymore.

"Perhaps," Morgan said, taking his seat for the first time since the meeting began, "just perhaps this deserves a little more scrutiny."

# Fourteen

## Monday, March 23; 12:30 P.M.

An interior decorator would have considered the office uninspired. The large room was filled with a hodgepodge of furniture and memorabilia scattered throughout the room. On the walls were photos of the famous and influential shaking hands with a short, stout man with deep-set, piercing gray eyes.

It was the same short, stout man who leaned back in his executive chair and punched a button on the TV remote that turned off the set in a floor-to-ceiling bookcase opposite his desk. Then he drummed his fingers on the arm of his chair, lost in thought.

A moment later he punched the telephone's intercom button.

"Yes, Reverend?" A sweet, high-pitched voice came over the speaker. It instantly brought its owner's face to his mind. Of his 230 employees, Christie Harper was the prettiest. Beauty was a job requirement for each of his personal secretaries.

"Christie, honey," he said smoothly, "call R.G. for me and tell him that I need to see him in my office as soon as possible."

"Yes, sir."

The man with the piercing eyes smiled as he enjoyed the thrill of a new idea. Within the next few weeks, the name of Reverend Paul Isaiah would be on the lips of every person in the nation, maybe even the world.

Adam had not driven straight home. Instead, he spent several hours sitting alone on a park bench overlooking the azure waters of La Jolla Cove. It was one of his favorite places in the city. Although towers of expensive condominiums had sprung up around the beach area, he could still come here and lose himself watching people snorkeling in the legally protected underwater park or the children playing in the sand. He felt a strong compulsion to swim with the skin divers and swimmers, with their faces under the cool March water and their fins slapping the surface. Unfortunately his swimsuit was at home.

This was the place he came when troubled; its serene setting freed his cluttered mind. He often prayed as he strolled the winding concrete walk that paralleled the shore. Other times he simply sat, letting his mind roam. Today he was sorting the many questions that were plaguing him. What had happened to David Lorayne? It was one thing to "wake up" from a coma, but it was another thing to have an incision completely disappear. Theologically this didn't bother him, but experientially it did. Why? He had always taught that miracles were a present-day possibility. There was no biblical reason to discount them. But on the other hand, he had never truly seen a miracle, certainly not one of this nature. Other questions swirled in his mind. Why did those people in the hospital lobby make him so uncomfortable? Could there really be a person with the power not only to make people well, but also to reverse the effects of their illness, removing even scars? There were plenty of biblical examples: the lame walking, lepers given healthy skin, the paralyzed made mobile, and even the blind being made to see. Still it was almost too much to believe.

Adam walked along the cove past Alligator Point and continued on to the Children's Cove. He stopped and leaned against the rusting metal rail that separated the sidewalk from the cliffs that bordered the shore. He gazed down the thirty-foot drop and watched as the white-laced waves crashed on shore. He listened to the gulls overhead and took a deep breath of salt air. It was then that Adam learned something about himself—that he was a skeptic, hesitant to believe that a man or woman could walk into a hospital and facilitate a dramatic healing. Yet, if anyone should believe such things, it should be he. After all, he was a man of faith, one who preached faith.

Suddenly the matter took on new and greater dimensions. It was no longer about the good news of David's remarkable recovery but about Adam's faith. Not his salvation—that was secure, and not about his belief in God—of that he had no doubt. What he now realized was he didn't know if he believed in the miraculous or, at least, in contemporary miracles. This was something he needed to know. And to know, he needed knowledge; information about the previous healings and more facts about David.

Adam decided a trip to the library was in order.

## Monday, March 23; 12:45 P.M.

R.G. was twenty-eight years old and considered a genius by those who worked with him. A rail-thin man with dark, curly hair and a distinctive Southern drawl, he had made a name for himself as a master statistician. He had earned a Ph.D. in statistical analysis from MIT, but being bored with the world of academia he chose a different career and spent three years working for network television in New York, formulating and analyzing viewers' polls. It was in New York that he had met the Reverend Paul Isaiah.

Isaiah was a third-year student at Union Theological Seminary, only then his name was Barry Barrows. The two men had met through a common friend, Sara Oden. She had left her secretarial position with the same television network where R.G. had worked to take a position in the finance department of the seminary. She introduced the two at a birthday party held in her apartment. R.G. was immediately taken with the charismatic divinity student. They became fast friends, each admiring qualities in the other that they missed in themselves.

While both brilliant and confident, R.G. lacked charm. He was uncomfortable around most people, preferring to be alone. When he did seek company, he was awkward and ill at ease. He didn't know how to make small talk or ask questions that would lead people to open up. At parties he stood in the corner and watched others mingle and laugh. When he was forced into conversation, he tended to be staid and formal. These unfortunate habits led others to assume that he was aloof and arrogant. This had been true all his life and slowly became a self-fulfilling prophecy: R.G. could be arrogant and self-centered. He was, after all, brighter than everyone he knew. He could accumulate, store, and use information that others thought useless or obscure.

Isaiah was the opposite: outgoing, gregarious, and garrulous. He was not an attractive man physically; his gray eyes made him look ominous, and his short, squat body made him unimpressive—until he opened his mouth. When he spoke, his cadence, inflection, timbre, and delivery could be spellbinding. When he told a story or even a joke, others stopped speaking. He could bring men to tears with a sad tale, or make a prude laugh at a bawdy joke. He oozed a passion for life that trapped all who knew him in its sticky sweetness. Yet, despite his profound people skills, he lacked the rudiments of organization. His life was cluttered and his thoughts often in disarray.

They were as much a match intellectually as they were a mismatch physically, fitting together like the two center pieces of a jigsaw puzzle. Their friendship was sown at that party and blossomed in the years that followed. R.G. was Isaiah's best friend and Isaiah was R.G.'s only friend. Jointly they strengthened each other's weaknesses and, sadly, misdirected each other's characters.

"You been watching the news of late, R.G.?" Every word spoke of Isaiah's North Carolina upbringing.

"Sure. I bet you're interested in all that hospital stuff." R.G.'s voice had a nasal quality that most found annoying; Isaiah, however, had learned to overlook it.

"You sound skeptical."

"You're the religious man. I'm just a simple administrator."

"There's nothing simple about you, R.G." Isaiah said smiling. "If it weren't for you, this organization wouldn't exist and neither would its ministries. No, there's nothing simple about you, sir. If there were, you wouldn't be earning six figures."

R.G. grinned. "I never was very good at humility."

"Perhaps. But no one can hold a candle to you when it comes to marketing. That's what I want to talk to you about. I think I know how we can increase revenues."

R.G. opened the notebook he had brought with him. "I'm for anything that makes money."

Isaiah punched the intercom button. "Christie, honey, would you bring in some coffee and see if you can scrape up some lunch for R.G. and me? Oh, yeah, hold all the calls."

"For how long, sir?"

"For the rest of the afternoon. I'm going to be very busy."

## Monday, March 23; 4 P.M.

Adam was no stranger to libraries. He had often described himself as a bibliophile. He found books a comfort to be around. His love for books had begun as a child. Smaller than most of the neighborhood children, and possessing no innate talent for sports, he was often teased. With few friends, Adam made friends with books; he had found them far more faithful. As Adam grew older, he learned to deal with people and his own poor self-image. He developed both a keen mind and great personal confidence. He no longer needed books for his friends, but he kept them his friends anyway.

The elevator took him to the third floor of the downtown library. Down the hall was a room with a sign over the door that read Newspapers. At the information desk he asked for copies of the *San Diego Union* for the last three weeks. The librarian brought a stack of papers on a cart and pushed them toward Adam. Taking the stack to an empty table, Adam began a systematic perusal, confining himself to the national and local sections. The headlines reminded him of just how much he had missed recently. There had been another near miss of a commercial airliner and a private plane over Lindberg Field. A new glitch had developed in U.S./China relations. Adam resisted the urge to read all the articles and forced himself to concentrate on his search.

It hadn't been long before Adam found what he was looking for. There had been two other healings during the time Adam was in

137

for treatment. He made a copy of the article and returned the papers. Then on a whim he asked, "Is there a way to find articles that have been written on similar subjects, but in different newspapers throughout the nation?"

"Yes," replied the librarian. "You simply use the Subject Index." She pointed to a computer screen at the end of the counter. "What's your subject?" she asked as she walked to the computer.

Adam felt a sense of embarrassment. "Well, I'm trying to find more information on healings that have taken place at Kingston Memorial Hospital. I was wondering if similar reports had been made elsewhere."

"You're the second person to ask for that information."

"Second?"

"Yes. Another man came in earlier this afternoon, worked for a couple of hours at the microfiche machine, and then left. In fact, he left this piece of scratch paper with references to articles."

Adam took the paper and looked at it. "May I have this?"

"I don't see any harm in it. The microfiche machines are over there. Articles less than a month old won't be in there. You'll have to look through our back issues. We have most of the major papers."

Adam spent the next hour and a half feeding the microfiche film into the machine which projected the image onto a screen to be read. With a punch of a button Adam could have photostat copies of whatever appeared on the screen. What he found amazed him and, to his surprise, frightened him too. Gathering his notes and copies, he returned the boxes of film and walked quickly from the room. His mind struggled with the newfound information.

"It can't be," he said quietly to himself. "It simply cannot be."

# Fifteen

## Monday, March 23; 6 P.M.

Adam's private sanctuary was a bedroom that he had converted to a home office. It was an unusual blend of the old and the contemporary. Books, their jackets worn from use and the passage of time, lined the shelves that covered three of his walls. In a corner an acrylic stand held a tattered edition of *Webster's Unabridged Dictionary.*

Spread before him on an old, scarred desk were the copies he had made of the newspaper articles. He had read each of them three times. Only one of them was of substantial length. The rest were short, pithy articles sequestered away in the back sections of the papers. Short as the articles were, their substance bothered him. He had considered calling Rachel Tremaine, but decided against it. Since they were meeting in a couple of hours, he could tell her in person.

Leaning back in his chair, he rubbed his tired eyes. He wondered why he had pushed getting together. He could have asked his questions over the phone. Was it the act of a single man on the prowl? Adam was single, but he didn't consider himself on the prowl. In fact, he hadn't had a date since his engagement broke up three years before. Adam considered himself unlucky with women. He had been engaged twice. The first engagement began and ended in college. He thought he had found his true love. She was a bright history major he had met in class. They shared many of the same interests: old movies, baseball, and education. They spent every day together, studying, eating in the school cafeteria, and walking around campus. They were the perfect couple—everyone said so and Adam agreed. They became engaged at the beginning of their junior year. Six months later, she transferred to a school in the East and left behind her memories and her affection for Adam. He never heard from her again.

The second engagement was to a woman in the church. She was gregarious and captivating in manner and appearance. Her long blond hair and fine features turned the heads of many men; Adam had been no different. Much to the delight of the congregation, they started dating; six months later they were engaged; four months after that Adam discovered her infidelity. He was broken and she unrepentant. Adam explained the breakup and her absence by simply saying, "Things didn't work out." Twice rejected, Adam focused on his work and doubted that he would ever marry.

His meeting with Rachel certainly wasn't a date, and yet he had to admit that she was attractive. True, she was caustic and remote, with little in her personality to commend her to anyone. She was unlike any woman Adam had ever known. And yet, he found himself looking forward to their meeting.

Two hours. He wondered how to spend the time. Glancing at his answering machine, he saw the light was flashing. He chose to ignore it. He had turned the ringers of his telephone off so that he would not be disturbed. After all, it was his day off, and any emergency could be handled by one of his deacons.

Adam rose and removed an old Bible from the shelf. It was the one he had used in college and seminary. Its corners were bent and worn, its pages soiled and covered with notes scribbled by his own hand. This Bible had become a special friend to him. Moving from the desk to an overstuffed easy chair, Adam opened the Bible at random and began to read.

At 8:10 p.m. Adam parked his blue Volkswagen Rabbit in front of the coffee shop and saw Rachel waiting near the entrance. As he opened the restaurant door, she said curtly, "You're late."

"I'm on church time."

"What is church time?"

"It's an old saying around the church—if you're ten minutes late, then you're five minutes early."

"Sounds like an excuse for irresponsibility."

"You're probably right." Adam had purposed not to be baited.

The coffee shop was small but popular with medical people. The hostess led them to a small booth in a corner. After perusing the menus, Rachel ordered a pasta plate and Adam a hamburger from a friendly waiter.

Although he knew he was being almost too direct, Adam asked the question that had been on his mind for hours. "What happened to David?"

"I'm not free to discuss that. The patient-doctor relationship is confidential."

"I'm his minister. I was there shortly after he was healed. All I want from you is your medical opinion about what happened to him and how it happened."

"I wish I knew. The truth of the matter is that nobody knows."

"Is it your job to find out?"

"Yes."

"You don't seem to be pleased with the task."

"You're very observant."

"I'm in the people business. So why don't you like it?"

"Because I'm a surgeon, not a private investigator. I spend my life healing, not chasing mystery men around."

"Have you ever seen anything like this before?"

"No. Just what has happened at the hospital."

"What about the other healings?"

"What other healings?"

Adam reached into his pocket, pulled out several sheets of paper, and handed them to Rachel. She looked at the photocopied newspaper articles briefly and then handed them back.

"So?" she asked.

"What can you tell me about these? What happened to the Langfords? What happened to Lisa Halley?"

"I don't know."

"Don't you think the answer may rest with them?"

"No more than the answer rests with the Loraynes," she said tersely.

Adam realized he had been pushing a little too hard. "I'm sorry. I must be more frustrated by this than I realized."

The conversation paused when the waiter appeared with their food.

"Why does this bother you so much?" Rachel asked.

"I'm not sure. And I don't know if the word *bothered* is the right term for it. *Concern* is more like it."

"I would think Mr. Lorayne's sudden recovery would please you."

"It does. It's just that things don't fit. It's not the healing that concerns me; it's the way it took place. A man boldly enters and leaves the ICU unnoticed and David is healed—not just from an anesthesia-induced coma, but even of his surgery. Prior to that a severely burned girl wakes up with new skin. Again no one knows how. Bill Langford was healed of inoperable cancer. And then there are the occurrences at the other hospitals."

Rachel stopped mid-bite. "What other hospitals?"

Adam reached into his coat pocket, this time removing several more sheets of paper. "I wondered if you knew about these. I did a little research at the library today, and here's what I came up with." He handed her the paper. "As you can see, there have been reports of similar events in San Francisco, Fresno, and Los Angeles. It forms a pattern. Our mystery man has been working his way south for the last two years."

"Why haven't we heard about it before?"

"Simple. Look at the press coverage. There aren't more than ten paragraphs for the whole time. It appears that no one took the reports seriously."

Rachel looked at the copies of the articles and then ran her eyes down the handwritten list that Adam had prepared. The paper was divided into columns, one each for date, place, the newspaper that carried the article, hospital, name of patient and ailment from which they recovered unexpectedly. She was puzzled. Why would Adam pursue this information with such fervor? Could Dr. Morgan be right? Was Adam Bridger the Healer? The thought made her uncomfortable.

"So, what do you think?" he asked, as if a child searching for praise.

"Well done. But what does it mean?"

"It means we have more avenues to pursue."

"We?"

"Why not? We can help each other. You want to find this guy because you have to. I have my own reason for wanting to know what's going on."

"And just what are your reasons?" Rachel tried to hide the skepticism in her voice. "What motivates you?"

"That's hard to say. Making the pieces fit, I suppose."

"What pieces?"

"Nothing fits. Okay, suppose there is someone who is endowed with a special ability, or maybe heretofore-unknown treatment. Why keep it secret? Why not do as many have done in the past—develop a following? A following that would provide support. Why does this person slip in and out unnoticed? What's his goal? What's his message?"

"Message? Who says he has to have a message?"

"History. Recent history and biblical history. In every case of healing in the Bible, there was been an accompanying message. In the Old Testament, it was to authenticate the messenger, to distinguish him from the others who might pretend to speak for God. Jesus healed out of love, but also to authenticate His claim of messiahship. The disciples worked miracles that authenticated their message. So, why is it there is no message?"

Rachel thought about what Adam had said, then asked, "What makes you think these occurrences have any spiritual connection? From my perspective, our Healer could have walked off a flying saucer somewhere to bring peace and health to mankind. Or, perhaps he's some medical genius who is too shy to accept credit. Or, perhaps . . ."

"Okay, I get the idea." Adam interrupted. "I'll admit my intellectual bias. But then again, you have some pretty strong biases yourself."

Rachel responded by silently taking another bite of pasta. *If Adam is our Healer,* she thought, *he also has mental trouble. Is he trying to guide me or mislead me?*

They ate in silence for a few moments. Adam struggled with Rachel's comment. It was true that he was approaching this mystery with a biblical bias, but was that wrong?

The Bible was the sole authority for life. He had found its teachings true and sound—indeed, life-changing. The miraculous was a primary principle of biblical history and, as a student of the Bible, he would naturally apply it to this situation as he did with all others.

Adam broke the silence. "I assume you have interviewed the other families who have had similar events."

"You mean the Langfords and the Halleys?"

Adam nodded.

"Actually, I haven't talked to them."

"I would think that would be one of the first things you'd do."

"They've disappeared—all gone on vacation or something."

"Let me get this right. Both the Langfords and the Halleys have left town?"

"Well, they're never home. Their neighbors haven't seen them. Other family members don't know where they are. Both have had their houses broken into. That Priscilla Simms woman almost got herself killed. In fact, her boss did get killed. Didn't you hear about it on the news?"

Adam felt the pit drop out of his stomach; his anxiety registered on his face.

"What's the matter," Rachel asked. "You don't look very well." Then a moment later, "You're not thinking that..."

"Excuse me," Adam said, as he rose quickly from the table. "I've got to find a phone."

Within three minutes he had returned. "Come on," he said. "We're leaving."

# Sixteen

## Monday, March 23; 9:10 P.M.

"Will you please tell me what's going on?" It was a command, not a request.

Adam eased the car into traffic and accelerated. The VW Rabbit's small engine responded quickly.

"After you told me that the Langford and Halley homes had been broken into, it occurred to me that it might not be a coincidence. So, I called the Loraynes'. There was no answer. Then I called Larry Lorayne—they were preparing a party for them—he told me they never showed. They've been trying to reach me all day." Adam felt guilty about ignoring his answering machine. "The police want to talk to me."

"So where are we going?"

"Larry Lorayne's house. He's going to notify the police that we are on the way."

"Curiouser and curiouser," Rachel said.

"Excuse me?"

"It's a quote from *Alice in Wonderland*. My father used to read it to me. The more I know about this problem, the less I understand."

Larry Lorayne was looking out the living room window when Adam and Rachel arrived. He reached the car before they had unbuckled their seat belts.

"Where have you been, Pastor?" Larry asked excitedly. "I've been trying to reach you for hours."

"I'm here now, Larry," Adam said soothingly. "Do you know Dr. Tremaine?"

"No." Larry was still agitated.

"That's right, you weren't at the hospital when David was released."

"No, I was here fixing barbecue for the family. We were going to celebrate."

"Dr. Tremaine performed the surgery on David," Adam said, choosing not to mention her role as investigator for the hospital.

"Pleased to meet you," he said absently.

"Is your wife in the house?" Adam asked, wanting to move the conversation inside.

"Yeah. Come on in."

Eva was sitting on the couch. Adam could see her eyes were red from crying. "Hello, Pastor," she said weakly. "Can I get you some coffee or a soda?"

"No, thank you." Adam sat on a love seat and motioned for Rachel to join him. "This is Dr. Tremaine," Adam said to Eva. "She performed the surgery on David."

"Hello," Eva said. "Would you like something to drink?"

"No, thank you."

Larry began to pace.

"Larry, why don't you sit down and tell me what happened?" Adam inquired.

"Well, it's like this," Larry said, sitting in a chair opposite Adam. "They were going to come over after they left the hospital. David said he wanted some real food and there was no longer any reason why he couldn't have some. Well, I had been watering the grass out front while I was waiting for the coals to get hot, and I went out to check the sprinkler when I saw them coming down the street. Living on a cul-de-sac like we do, there's only one direction for them to come from. Anyway, I looked down the street and saw their car. I turned to shout to Eva that they were here when I heard tires squealing. A car had come out of the driveway about ten houses down. I didn't hear a crash like an accident or anything, so I figured it was a near miss. Then I saw this tall guy get out of the car and walk over to David's car. A couple of minutes later the car that came out of the driveway headed out, and then David's car pulled a U-turn and followed it. I yelled at 'em to come back, but they were too far away. And that's it, no call, nothing. Then the police called."

"The police?" Adam felt his stomach tighten.

"Yeah, they called about two hours later saying that they found David's car abandoned about three miles from here."

"How did the police know to call you?" Adam asked.

"Because I gave them my number when I called them."

"Where did they find it?"

"There's a small elementary school nearby that's not used anymore. They found the car in the parking lot." Adam watched as blood drained from Larry's face. "That's not all—they found blood on the car."

The news shocked Adam. "Were you able to give a description of the other car to the police?" Adam asked softly.

"Just that it was a blue sedan. I couldn't see the license number."

"I just don't understand, Pastor," Eva said quietly. "How can this happen? After such a good thing like David being healed, how could such an evil thing happen?"

"I don't know," Adam said shaking his head. "There's little we can do but wait and pray. I know that's not what you want to hear, but unfortunately that's the way it is. You know I'm here if you need me."

Adam asked that they join hands so that they might pray. Eva eagerly reached over from her place on the couch and took Adam's hand. Larry moved from the chair to the couch to sit next to his wife and took her hand. Without thinking, Adam reached over for Rachel's hand and then led them in prayer. For Rachel, it was the first time she had bowed her head in prayer since she was a child. Had it not been such an emotionally charged moment, she would have objected.

Adam's prayer didn't contain flowery phrases or insincere platitudes, but just the simple words of a man concerned about a friend.

The prayer touched Rachel. Adam was sincere and open, expressing fear, anxiety, and hope. She did not need her medical degree to know that the prayer had a relaxing effect on Larry and Eva.

The doorbell rang as Adam finished. A man who identified himself as a police detective was asked in.

"Hello, Detective McGinnes," Larry said, motioning him in. "This is Pastor Adam Bridger and Dr . . ."

"Tremaine," Rachel said.

"I'm glad we found you, Pastor," McGinnes stated. "I've got some questions for you."

McGinnes was a pale-complexioned, thin man with dark eyes and a hairline that receded at the part. His slight build seemed incongruous with his profession.

"I'll be happy to be of any help I can," Adam replied.

"Of course," McGinnes said.

"Would anyone like coffee?" Eva interrupted.

"Yes, thank you," McGinnes replied and watched as Eva left the room. "Pastor, I understand you were one of the last ones to see David Lorayne and his family. Is that correct?"

"I was with them shortly before they left the hospital, as was Dr. Tremaine."

"So you both saw them leave the hospital?"

"Correct." Adam replied.

"Dr. Tremaine, just what is your involvement with the Loraynes? Are you the family doctor?"

"No," Rachel replied. "I'm a surgeon at Kingston Memorial and I performed his surgery. I'm also doing some research for the hospital."

"What kind of research?"

"I'm not sure you'd understand."

McGinnes looked at Adam who only shrugged. "Try me."

Rachel seemed recalcitrant to answer, but then stated matter-of-factly, "I'm investigating the recent events that have occurred at the hospital."

"Events?" McGinnes asked.

"The healings," offered Adam.

McGinnes nodded knowingly. "Yes, there's quite a ruckus over there—people jammed into the lobby like they are. I almost didn't make it through."

Eva brought a serving tray and set it on the coffee table.

"Did either of you walk out of the hospital with the family?"

"No." Both Rachel and Adam answered simultaneously.

"What did you do after they left?"

"I had some questions for Reverend Bridger," Rachel replied, "so we went to the doctors' lounge and talked."

"How long did the meeting last?"

"Less than twenty minutes," Rachel said.

McGinnes sighed. "I had hoped that you might have seen or heard something useful." He took his coffee and drank it in almost one swallow. Setting his cup down, he continued, "I'd like to have your home number, Dr. Tremaine, in case I have more questions. I already have the Pastor's here—he was listed in the phone book."

Rachel hesitated, then recited her number.

"Are you aware of the burglaries?" Adam asked.

"What burglaries?"

"There have been two burglaries that may be related to this case," Adam replied, "At the homes of the Langfords and the Halleys. Both had members of their families in Kingston Memorial when they were healed."

"How did you find out about that?" McGinnes asked.

"Actually, Dr. Tremaine discovered it."

McGinnes turned his attention to Rachel and said, "Well?"

"As I said," Rachel began, "I've been assigned to research the special events that have happened at the hospital. I attempted to interview the Langfords and the Halleys at home. They were never there. I had heard about the shooting at the Langfords' on the news, a neighbor of the Halleys told me about the break-in at their house."

"I hadn't made the connection," McGinnes said. "I'll look into it."

"I hear you've found the car," Adam said.

"That's correct. We found it in the parking lot of a nearby school," McGinnes said.

"Did you find anything else?" Adam asked.

"These folks have probably told you about the blood."

"Only that you found some."

"Not much—just a little around the driver's door and on the hood of the car. It looks like someone, probably the driver, resisted the abductors."

"That would be Michael," Larry said. "He was a scrapper as a kid."

"We're pretty sure it was Michael too," McGinnes said. "The nurse who walked them to the car said that David and his wife got in the backseat. Besides, David would be in no shape to struggle anyway—with his stitches and all."

No one bothered to tell McGinnes that David no longer had stitches.

"But there wasn't enough blood to indicate..." Adam paused and searched for the right words.

"Murder? Oh, no. The blood we found could be accounted for by a good-sized scrape or cut."

"That's a relief," Larry said.

"They're not out of danger yet," McGinnes said. "Has anyone called about them? Asked for ransom or anything like that?"

"No," Larry said, shaking his head, "but then neither David nor I have much money. I live off my Navy retirement and David's retired from General Dynamics. We have enough to get us by, but not much more."

"If anyone does call, then let me know. We'll set up a phone tap and trace the calls."

"I have a question," Rachel said. "Larry tells us that a car pulled in front of the Loraynes and stopped them, and then the Loraynes followed the car. Why would they do that?"

"Who knows?" McGinnes replied. "They either tricked them or threatened them. Whatever the case, the Loraynes felt compelled to go along."

Adam had another question. "You say you talked to one of the nurses. Why didn't you talk to Dr. Tremaine while you were at the hospital?"

"We tried, but she wasn't there."

Adam looked at Rachel for a moment. She had told him that she wasn't free until 8 that night and he assumed that she would be working at the hospital.

"I was doing research on spontaneous healing at the UCSD library,"

Rachel said. "Not that there was much to find."

"Well," McGinnes said, standing and placing the notebook he had been using into the side pocket of his suit coat, "I should be going." Larry stood to show him to the door.

As McGinnes was leaving, he handed Adam and Rachel business cards and said, "I would appreciate any help I can get on this."

After McGinnes left, Adam did his best to encourage Larry and Eva. He wanted to tell them that everything would be fine, and that their loved ones would soon be home safe and sound. But he couldn't. He knew they understood that they might never see David, Ann, and Michael alive again. "I know this is hard on you," Adam said. "The unknown is always frightening. What's important now is that we remain at our best and not jump to conclusions."

"And that we keep praying," Eva said, as a tear ran down her check.

"And keep praying," Adam agreed. "It's also important for you two to draw strength from one another. You can weather this together. God will help you, I will help you, and the church will help you."

"I appreciate that," Larry said, "but we're not part of your church. Truth is, we don't go to church much. We can't expect any help."

Adam smiled. "I know, but that doesn't matter. I'm adopting you. If you need anything, then don't hesitate to call." Then, remembering the flashing red light on his answering machine, Adam's smile was replaced with chagrin. "I'll even pick up my messages more frequently."

"Look," Larry said. "I'm sorry if I came on a little strong about that. It's just that I was concerned, and I tend to be a little quick on the trigger."

"No need to apologize," Adam said. "Considering all that's going on, you have a right to be on edge."

Larry looked at Eva and then took her hand. "Thanks for coming over, Pastor. David said you were the best, and now I know what he means. You've been a big help."

"I wish there was more that I could do," Adam said quietly. "I really do."

"We know, Pastor," Eva said. "But we do appreciate what you've done."

Adam stood and hugged Eva and then Larry.

"Please, keep me posted," Adam said as he stood on the front stoop. "I'll check with you tomorrow."

Adam and Rachel drove in silence, each lost in their own thoughts. Rachel was mystified. Why hadn't she made the connection about the break-ins like Adam did? Perhaps she didn't care enough to ask the right questions. One thing was for certain—she didn't possess the caring attitude that Adam did. She had watched him closely tonight. His love and concern, coupled with his self-possession, intrigued her. There was more to this man than she had first realized.

Pulling into the hospital parking lot, Adam drove behind to a parking area secured with a card-operated gate. They sat in silence for a moment, then Adam spoke.

"I appreciate the time you've given me tonight."

"I'll admit," she replied, "that I've never had an evening like it."

Before she closed her door, she paused thoughtfully, and then asked, "We can assume that the Langfords and the Halleys have met the same fate as the Loraynes. Do you agree?"

Adam reluctantly nodded his head and said, "Yes, I do."

"Why would anyone want to abduct recently healed people?"

"I don't know," Adam admitted. "There's a lot I don't know about this, but I intend to find out."

"This could be dangerous, you know."

"Yes, I know. And not just for us, but for the next person healed."

Rachel thought about that for a second. "What makes you think there'll be another healing?"

"I'm not certain, but I think this is just the beginning."

"The beginning of what?"

"I wish I knew. At least, I think I wish I knew."

Rachel nodded her agreement and then shut the car door, turned, and walked across the parking lot.

# Seventeen

## Monday, March 23; 8:30 P.M.

"Are you sure you feel up to this?" Reedly asked as he seated Priscilla Simms.

"Yes, thank you."

"It's not that I'm not pleased. But considering all that you've been through lately, I thought you might like to be left alone. I mean, with the death of Irwin and all."

"Sitting around solves nothing. I'd rather be out than hanging around the house all alone."

"Perhaps you're right." Reedly opened his menu. "May I order for you?"

Priscilla was amazed at the irony that was Thomas Reedly. The brusque-looking man was compact, not standing more than five-foot-eight. His short stature coupled with a ruddy complexion made him look like a commercial fisherman. Yet, despite his rough exterior, he was a gentle and surprisingly cultured man.

"Sure," she replied. "But nothing too spicy."

Reedly gave his order in Spanish to the Hispanic waiter.

"Well," Priscilla said, "I'm suitably impressed."

"The Spanish? It helps in my work."

"How long have you been a police officer?" she asked.

"Seventeen years."

"Long years?" she asked, blowing blue smoke toward the ceiling.

"No. For the most part I enjoy my work. There's a certain satisfaction in it."

"Not to mention the occasional thrill."

Reedly smiled at her insight. "Not to mention the occasional thrill."

Perceptive as Priscilla was, there was much about Thomas Lloyd Reedly she didn't know. In many ways he seemed an anomaly. Those who saw his stocky and rugged appearance might assume him to be ponderously slow. Those who knew him knew otherwise. In some ways Reedly was what he appeared: strong, forceful, and determined. But he had a smooth side that had been cultivated over the years. His was a keen mind that hungered for both knowledge and pleasure. He was as much at home watching science programs like "Nova" on the local Public Broadcasting station as he was watching the Chargers play football. He read widely, preferring novels of depth and current nonfiction to shallow mystery paperbacks, although he would admit to a fondness for Stephen King and Dean Koontz.

Like all men, Reedly was the product of his home and education. Both his father and mother taught in the local middle school and instilled a love of learning in him from his earliest years. He had gone off to college and majored in English, graduated and, to satiate a patriotic hunger, had entered the military. As an Army officer he served two tours of duty in Vietnam as a medic and was decorated twice for heroism. Reedly found no pleasure or comfort in the medals. What others called heroism, he considered duty.

When the Army released him from his duty, Reedly returned to school to pursue a master's degree. With the help of GI benefits, he continued his studies in English and set his mind on teaching. It was while in graduate school at San Diego State that he encountered his first significant disillusionment. Vietnam had divided the U.S., with those who favored a stand against communism in Indochina squaring off against those who rallied for peace at any price. The disparity of opinion didn't bother him, but the way the disparity was handled did. Students shouted obscenities and threw stones at the police. This violence against those sworn to protect the lives of those abusing them touched something in the heart of Reedly. He looked at the men in uniform as soldiers who fought a battle against a different enemy, a criminal enemy that often had more rights than the police themselves. He had fought on a foreign land for people he did not know; they fought on their own soil for people they did know.

He felt a kindred connection with the men in the beige uniforms he saw at that protest. He felt that they were contributing something rather that just taking from society. And like him, they received no thanks for it. Reedly understood what the police must have felt when some of the citizens they were sworn to protect turned and assailed them with vile verbal abuse. He admired their courage and strength. Six months after his discharge, he was patrolling the streets of San Diego.

Now he was forty-seven years old and still patrolling the streets. Many of those in his academy class had been promoted to detective or higher and were administrating different departments. Reedly turned down those promotions. He liked street work. He liked uniform work. When he retired, he would retire a uniformed officer.

The waiter brought a bottle of red wine to the table. After opening the bottle, the waiter offered the cork to Reedly who gave it a perfunctory sniff and nodded his approval.

After the waiter left, Priscilla asked, "Has he been identified?"

Reedly knew that *he* was the assailant who had killed Irwin Baker a few days before and would have killed Priscilla, had he not been shot by a bullet from Reedly's service revolver. Priscilla stared at the glass of wine in her hand. It was a painful question for her to ask.

"Yes. He was a small-time crook who did mostly first-story burglaries. Private residences and small businesses mostly. Nothing very complicated."

"Does anyone know why he was at the Halleys'?"

"Simple burglary, I suppose. Several other houses had been hit recently. There's been a rash of break-ins throughout the county."

Priscilla shook her head. "Too big a coincidence. Remember, the Langfords' home was robbed too."

"So?"

"So?" Priscilla sounded shocked. "Both the Halleys and the Langfords had a family member healed at Kingston Memorial. Something is going on, and I want to know what it is."

"All right, suppose you're correct. What devious plan is afoot?"

"That's the question, isn't it? I don't know, but something is up."

"Well, I'm afraid there's not much I can tell you. Every room in the house was ransacked. Your assailant wasn't very tidy."

"When he came out of the house, his hands were empty. Wasn't there anything in the house worth taking?"

"Plenty. But maybe you surprised him before he could lift anything."

"Not likely. If so, then he would have left behind a carrying bag. Or, if he was stealing televisions and stereos, then those appliances would have been unplugged and moved away from the wall."

"How do you know they weren't?"

"Because if they had been, you'd have told me." She peered seductively over her glass. "Wouldn't you?"

Reedly laughed out loud. "You are clever, I'll give you that. All right, it's true. It appears that he was looking for something specific. Just what, no one knows."

The waiter brought their deep-fried beef flautas smothered in sour cream and guacamole.

"Boy, this is going to be hard on the diet," Priscilla said.

"With your level of activity, I don't think you have anything to worry about." With that, Reedly lifted his glass and toasted, "To health."

"To truth." Priscilla countered.


## Monday, March 23; 9:30 P.M.

"It's all set," R.G. said, handing a handwritten note across the desk.

Isaiah quickly read the note. "You don't think this is too soon?"

"Ya gotta make hay while the sun shines, my daddy used to say."

"But this happens Thursday night." Isaiah shifted uneasily in his chair.

"That is the beauty of it. You'll be in San Diego for a crusade anyway. After that just hold on to your hat."

"You think they'll buy it?"

"Hook, line, and sinker. Before the end of the week, you'll be the most sought-after man in the nation."

"For a price," Isaiah said.

"For a big price," R.G. corrected.

## Monday, March 23; 6:15 P.M.

In Los Angeles the Milt Phillips after-show party was underway with its usual imported wines, select cheeses, and exotic hors d'oeuvres. The parties had such a reputation that few guests ever left early. Tonight everyone who had appeared on the show had stayed—including Dr. Charles Cruden, astrophysicist, novelist, lecturer, and popularizer of science.

"Well, Dr. Cruden," said Milt Phillips, "I see you have again added more admiring souls to your fan club."

"Stars and starlets still seem such strange company for a scientist. But, I must admit that I completely enjoy it."

Phillips studied Cruden. His physical appearance would have served him well in show business. He had just the right amount of gray at the temples, and just the right build, the right height and weight to be the leading man in most movies. He also had one of the finest minds in the nation. As a Nobel prize winner in astronomy, he was cast into stardom by his best-selling novel, *Orion and Me*, which was loosely based on his life. Since then he had been a frequent guest on "The Milt Phillips Show," a late evening talk program that featured the hottest stars and newest comedians. Cruden's smooth voice and quick wit carried well over the air waves.

"Apparently they enjoy you," Phillips said. Then, changing his tone, he continued seriously, "You said some pretty harsh things tonight."

"You mean about the reported hospital healings in San Diego?"

"Yep. I bet you have made a lot of people mad."

"I was only responding to your questions. Besides, no one can stay popular forever. It's that kind of hysteria and mumbo jumbo that will catapult our society back to the Dark Ages."

"You don't believe that it's even remotely possible?"

"What? That people with terminal illness are being miraculously healed? Not a chance. I don't know exactly what's going on down there, but I do know this—it's no miracle."

"Well, I'm not the one to defend the plausibility of miracles, but I do have an idea. How about a special program with you and a couple of people from San Diego—people who are close to the situation—going head to head on the issue? If your schedule will permit."

"I'll see that it does," Cruden said sardonically.

## Tuesday, March 24; 8:45 A.M.

"You look like death warmed over," Fannie Meyers said.

"It's nice to see you too," Adam replied, as he picked up his mail from Fannie's desk. "Any calls?"

"Nothing for you. It's been pretty quiet actually."

"Good. I've got a busy day."

Fannie stared at Adam for a moment. "Are you feeling all right? You look beat." She wanted to ask if he had any news on the Loraynes, but she already knew the response—no news and no answers. He was blaming himself, she knew that, but nothing she could say would release him from his self-*inflicted* guilt. It was a malady that touched many ministers—adopting responsibility for others. Indeed, some left the ministry because the emotional burden became too heavy.

"I'm fine, thanks. I just didn't sleep well." In truth, the dream had returned—the crooked boy pleading for help, and Adam unable to even offer words of comfort.

"How about some coffee?"

"That would be nice." Adam walked through the door that joined his office with Fannie's. Inside he opened his briefcase and brought out a notepad. He stared at the blank sheet of paper on which he would begin the outline of his sermon. Pulling a Greek New Testament from the bookshelves that lined two of his walls, he immersed himself in the process he had honed over the years: exegesis from the ancient Koine Greek text, formation of an outline, review of commentaries, and finally the sermon's composition. The process took the better part of two days. Deep in concentration, Adam failed to notice Fannie as she brought the coffee he had requested.

Later Fannie entered the office again. "There's a Dr. Tremaine on the line. She insisted on talking to you now."

Adam smiled. *Insistent* was a good word for Rachel. "Thank you, Fannie." After she left, Adam picked up the phone.

"I hope nothing's wrong," Adam said.

"It's happened again." Her voice was tense. "I thought you would want to know."

"You mean another healing?" Adam's pulse quickened.

"Exactly."

"What happened?"

"Not over the phone. If you can make it to the hospital tonight, I'll explain everything."

"I'll be there. What time?"

"Eight."

Adam wondered at her economy of conversation; she was almost monosyllabic.

"Eight it is."

The line went dead. Adam listened to the dial tone for a moment and then placed the receiver back in its cradle.


"Very well done, Dr. Tremaine," Dr. Morgan said, rising from his chair. "Very well done, indeed. Now all that remains is to see if the Reverend Bridger is our man."

"I don't feel good about this," Rachel said tersely.

"What is there not to feel good about? You are simply trying to help the hospital solve a problem."

"It's the lying that bothers me."

"Why, Dr. Tremaine, how quaint! Please remember that we have 600 patients here, and it's our responsibility to protect them."

*Protect them from what?* Rachel wondered.

# Eighteen

## Tuesday, March 24; 4 P.M.

Paul Isaiah glanced around the dimly lit interior of the San Diego Sports Arena. In the center of the court area that had served many sporting events was a prefabricated stage, its support structure hidden behind a valance of deep-blue fabric. An acrylic pulpit dominated the center of the stage. Around him was row upon row of vinyl-covered seats in which thousands of people would tomorrow sit and listen to him preach his customized version of the Gospel.

"Up here, Reverend." Isaiah turned to find the source of the distant voice. In the weak light he saw a figure waving. "Wait there; I'm coming down." The figure began to make its way down the concrete steps.

"R.G., I thought that might be you. Everything okay?"

"Perfect as always," R.G. replied glibly. "How about you? Are you going to be your usual captivating self?"

"There shouldn't be any complaints," he said with a grin. The two men walked up the stage and stood behind the pulpit. "How long have we been doing this now? Nine years?"

"Almost."

"I still can't get used to it. Thousands of people will gather here to hear me." Isaiah gazed around the cavernous structure. "It's a long way from those tent revivals we did in the South."

"I can't argue with that."

"Tell me, R.G., what are a couple of old southern boys doing with an office in L.A. and traveling all over the world?"

R.G. shrugged his narrow shoulders, "Making money, of course."

Isaiah thought silently about that. While he knew that R.G. was the practical one of the two, the unbridled frankness bothered him. Isaiah had not started off to be a charlatan and didn't consider himself one now. He had entered seminary with the goal of pastoring a small country church somewhere. When had he changed?

Perhaps it was the specter image of three coffins that haunted him. One coffin so tiny, so incongruous. Three coffins that visited his mind daily, that robbed him of any spontaneous joy.

"Paul!" A rough hand shook him. "You're doing it again. Come on, man, snap out of it."

"Sorry R.G. I . . . I was thinking."

"Are you taking your medication?"

"Of course. But enough of that, we've got work to do. Tell me about the press coverage."

As the two men walked through the dimly lit hall, R.G. spoke of the press coverage, the music program, the timing, and the expected monetary results.

## Tuesday, March 24; 7:50 P.M.

At 7:50 P.M. Adam pulled his car into the hospital's back parking lot. He told himself that he had chosen the rear emergency room entrance because parking was easier, and he didn't mind the longer walk, but he wondered if his real motivation wasn't to avoid the mass of the ill camped at the front entrance. He especially feared seeing the crooked little boy. Once again he felt ashamed.

Entering the hospital, Adam decided to walk up to the fourth floor office wing. Since Rachel hadn't told him where to meet her, he thought that might be a good place to start.

Adam had just turned down the office corridor when he noticed a large piece of paper with his name in red letters taped to a door: "Adam, please meet me in room 602. If I'm not there, wait for me. Rachel."

Adam knew the sixth floor was reserved for cancer patients. Returning to the stairway, Adam climbed the additional two floors. Pausing outside the hospital room, Adam looked at his watch: it was exactly 8. Thinking that Rachel might be waiting inside for him, he quietly entered the room. There was only one patient in the small cubicle but no sign of Rachel.

Adam felt uncomfortable. Although he had been in hospital rooms hundreds of times, it was always to visit members of his church. Here he was alone with a man he had never met who was suffering from some form of cancer.

Adam drew closer and noticed that one of the IV bags contained a solution of morphine. Adam couldn't help but feel that the man was dying. Minutes passed like hours as Adam watched the slow, shallow breathing of the man.

Feeling compelled to do something, Adam stepped closer to the figure on the bed. His minister's compassion welled up within him. The sight of the patient's thin frame and shallow breathing tugged at his soul. Adam often admired doctors: at least they could do something—medicate, operate, treat. They could immediately see the results of their efforts—even if the results were bad. All Adam could do was speak encouraging words and pray.

To be sure, prayer was important, but it often seemed so passive. At times he envied those who believed in faith healing. Often he wished he could simply lay hands on the sick as Jesus and the apostles had done and see the disease evaporate. He had even fantasized about the lame walking and the blind seeing as a result of his prayers. It wasn't that Adam lacked faith; there was no doubt that God could heal. It was that Adam had never seen it occur at the request of a person.

*Perhaps I'm just afraid,* Adam thought, *afraid that if I prayed for a miraculous healing and it didn't happen I would feel embarrassed—embarrassed for me and for God.*

But he was alone now. What would it hurt to try? After all, he had seen David Lorayne not only come back from a coma but be miraculously healed of his illness and surgery. Maybe God was doing something new now. Maybe Adam had been drawn into this because God Himself was beginning a new work in Adam's life.

Moving closer to the patient, Adam laid his right hand on the man's forehead and took one of the man's hands in his own left hand. The patient did not respond to the touch. Closing his eyes, Adam began to clear his thoughts. He imagined himself standing before a huge throne on which God sat. In hushed tones, he began to pray, "My Heavenly Father, I acknowledge that You are the God of the universe, and that nothing is beyond Your reach. I come before You praying for this man whose name I do not know, but I do know that he needs You. Grant now this miracle."

Opening his eyes slowly, Adam gazed down at the figure on the bed. His stomach churning with emotion he said in a soft, rhythmic tone, "In the name of the risen Lord and Savior Jesus Christ, be heal..."

Suddenly the room was filled with the bright light from the hallway. A silhouetted figure stood in the doorway.

"Will you please come with me, Reverend Bridger?" The voice was polite but unmistakably resolute.

"Who are you?" Adam's heart was racing.

"My name is Mr. Sanchez, Reverend. I'm in charge of hospital security. Our hospital administrator is very interested in speaking to you." The door had closed behind Sanchez allowing Adam a clearer view of him. What Adam saw was a Hispanic man who was one or two inches taller than he. He had wavy, brown hair and a neatly trimmed mustache. It was difficult to be sure, but Adam suspected that under the three-piece suit was a well-muscled body.

"I was to meet Dr. Rachel Tremaine here." Adam said, wondering what to do next.

"She is waiting for you too." Sanchez moved over to Adam's side and took his left arm in a firm grip. "Now, if you'll please come with me."

"I'm afraid I don't understand."

"I'm sure your questions will be answered if you'll just accompany me." Obediently, Adam released the patient's hand and let Sanchez lead him from the room.

# Tuesday, March 24; 8:15 P.M.

"I don't believe this!" Adam spat out his words bitterly. "You mean to tell me that you set me up? That this was all a scheme so that you could watch me?"

Dr. Evan Morgan studied the irate minister. "If you will sit down, this time together will proceed much more smoothly."

Seated around the conference table with Dr. Morgan were Bill Sanchez and Rachel Tremaine who sat quietly and stared at the table.

"How much do you have to do with this, Rachel?" Adam asked, sounding more hurt than angry. Rachel didn't respond.

"She was doing as I asked, Reverend," Morgan said firmly. "Now, please sit down."

Adam raised his hands in resignation and seated himself. "I would very much appreciate some answers," he said, holding his anger in check.

Morgan blew a cloud of blue smoke into the air.

"I'm glad to hear that, Reverend," Morgan said smiling. "That means we have something in common. You see, we want some answers too. For example, why are you here tonight?"

"You know the answer to that as well as I. I'm here at the invitation of Dr. Tremaine."

"Is that the only reason?"

"Yes." Adam had decided to phrase his answer carefully. He was already at a disadvantage and he knew it. They had succeeded in angering him and his anger was clouding his mind. There were things he wanted to know, and to get that information he'd have to calm down.

"You've come to our hospital on other occasions, haven't you?" Morgan continued.

"Ministers often visit their members when those members are hospitalized." Adam's voice was now controlled.

"I think there's more. In fact, I think there's more to you than meets the eye. Wouldn't you like to tell us about it?"

"I don't know what you mean."

"I think you do," Morgan said coldly.

"Then you're wrong."

Morgan set his pipe down and then folded his hands behind his head. "Reverend Bridger, we here at the hospital have had a difficult time of late. Some unusual events have happened, events that have been inaccurately reported in the media. I think you have a key role in these events. In fact, I think you are at the hub of our troubles. I would appreciate it if you would give us more than short, glib answers."

Adam felt his anger swell again but determined that he would not lose control. "Let's have an understanding here. I must be quick to remind you that I am here at my own sufferance. You have no authority to hold me or, for that matter, to question me. I must also remind you that you do not constitute a court of law. I will answer only those questions I choose to, and I will answer them as copiously or as briefly as I wish."

Rachel looked up in astonishment. She had not thought Adam capable of such strong statements.

"Very well, then," Morgan said. "Let me summarize. You, of course, are correct. You were set up. We've been watching you since you drove into the parking lot. Like most hospitals, ours is equipped with video surveillance of all the areas surrounding the hospital. A very useful capability, since several times a year someone attempts to help himself to our pharmacy. In addition to an outside surveillance system, we have a partial interior system as well. We even had a specially installed camera in the hospital room where you were a few minutes ago."

"So?"

Morgan sighed and leaned forward. "We believe that you are the so-called Healer."

Adam's mind raced back to the patient in the room. He remembered his own hesitancy about praying for the healing of the unknown man, thought of his own struggles to believe in miraculous healing, then laughed out loud—a hard and deep and resonant laugh. The unexpected laughter stunned the others.

Morgan's face reddened. "I see no humor in all this."

"I'm sure you don't," Adam said, wiping a tear from his eye. "I can assure you that I am not your man."

Morgan stood and began to pace behind the conference table.

"Isn't it true that you parked in the rear lot?"

"Yes. Where did *you* park?" Adam retorted.

"That's different," Morgan said angrily. "All staff park in the rear lot."

"I parked there so that I wouldn't have to pass through the mass of people camped in your lobby." Adam saw no reason to bring up the haunting, crooked little boy.

"Isn't it also true that you entered through the emergency room and avoided the elevators by using the stairs instead?"

"True, and for the same reason that I've already given."

"And when you were alone with the cancer patient, didn't you stand over him? Didn't you touch him?"

"Guilty as charged, Dr. Morgan," Adam said sarcastically. "I confess to praying. But please don't tell the other ministers. I might not be asked to the next luncheon." Adam laughed out loud again.

"Your sarcasm doesn't help."

"Oh, doesn't it? I find it very helpful. And I find this laughable."

"Laughable?"

"Certainly. You and your amateur investigators have accused me of being your Healer, and your only evidence is that I parked in the wrong lot, took the stairs instead of the elevator, and prayed for a dying man. I hope you are better at medicine than detective work."

Rising from his seat, Adam walked to the door. Turning to face the others, he said, "Dr. Morgan, Mr. Sanchez, I want to thank you for the entertaining evening, but I do want you to understand something, and I want you to understand it very clearly. You may think that because I'm a minister I can be used as a doormat. Well, understand this—if you ever attempt to pull a stunt like this with me again, I will make sure that the family of the man in room 602, the AMA, and any medical review board I can think of will hear of this breach of ethics. And I'll make sure the news media hears of it."

Dr. Morgan spun on his heals and spat, "Do you think you can threaten me ..."

"I just did."

Morgan's jaw stiffened and his face turned crimson. Sanchez remained seated but cast a vicious stare at Adam.

Turning to Rachel, Adam said in a much more somber tone that conveyed his hurt, "I'm sorry I wasn't worthy your trust."

As Adam left, Rachel felt tears well up in her eyes.

# Nineteen

## Tuesday, March 24; 8:45 P.M.

"How could she?" Adam said to his car. He squeezed the steering wheel until his knuckles turned white. Imaginary dialogues filled his mind. In each one he masterfully told off the pompous doctors who had attempted to trap him.

By the time Adam pulled the car into his driveway, he knew he must do something with his anger. The only thing it would do would be to destroy his logic and force him into poor decisions. Yet, denying the emotion was useless.

Adam felt the need for physical exertion, but it was too soon after his surgery. He would have to settle for something more pedestrian—a simple walk. Entering the apartment, he changed into sneakers and a blue jogging suit.

Adam stepped from the apartment into the night air and saw a full moon in a clear sky surrounded by stars. There was something therapeutic about a night sky, the Milky Way casting its band of speckled lights across the heavens. What was it the astronomers said—a billion galaxies, each with a billion stars? Somehow the vastness of space made his problems seem less significant.

But the problems weren't insignificant. The Loraynes were still missing, kidnapped by people with unknown but probably violent motives. He wondered if the Loraynes could see the stars tonight from wherever they were.

Adam's adrenaline-laced anger soon gave way as he walked. At first his mind churned with the events of the last few days, but with each step he gained more perspective and grew calmer. Forcing back the emotion-induced haze, Adam began to think as he had taught himself to think: systematically.

He asked himself what he really felt. He discovered not a simple answer, but one that was layered like a cake. He felt fear for the Loraynes, and he felt frustration at not being able to help. But he also felt something else, something powerful and nagging. He knew it had to do with what had just happened at the hospital. They had treated him improperly, attempting to trap him. They had also been condescending. At his very core, Adam was a humble man, but he had a professional pride in his education and his vocation. Yet, because of his vocation, others had made the mistake of assuming he was a superstitious fanatic. Those outside church life often thought that a spiritual mind could not be a reasoning mind. They did not realize that some of the finest minds of the ages were filled with belief and faith. Isaac Newton wrote more about religious matters than scientific. Pasteur, Pascal, and others revered as intellectuals possessed an abiding Christian belief.

Adam walked without direction or destination until he found himself at the back gate to the play yard of the elementary school. The gate was chained in such a fashion that it could be opened part way.

Slipping through the opening, Adam made his way into the play yard. He could hear the breeze rustle through the leaves of a nearby fruitless mulberry tree. In the distance he heard a car horn honk, and the sound of a television program drifted through the air from one of the nearby homes.

Walking to the large swing set, Adam sat down on one of the plastic seats and looked out over the empty schoolyard. It had a lonely, haunted feeling, a sensation with which Adam could relate. He too felt lonely and haunted. Just as the schoolyard was missing children, he was missing something. As a minister, he had held many counseling sessions with those who sought his advice. Often, married couples would come to him for help. Invariably, one or the other would ask if marriage was worth the trouble it took to stay together. Adam gazed at the dust on his sneakers and knew inside that, compared to the loneliness of a solitary life, companionship was worth it.

Adam counseled himself that night as he had counseled scores of others who came into his office. He asked what the real source of the problem was. In what were the negative emotions rooted? The answer came quickly. The problem was not only the way he had been set up—he had a right to be angry about that—but the one who helped set him up—Rachel. He knew he had no right to expect anything of her. As a doctor her first loyalty was to a hospital embroiled in an impossible situation. And yet, he felt deeply disappointed that she would have gone along with Morgan and Sanchez in such a ridiculous scheme. He was hurt, and that's what was eating him. That and the ever-present sense of helplessness. The question remained: What could be done?

"Okay," Adam said to himself, "enough of this pity party." With that, he rose from the swing and began to pace around the play yard. He walked in a large circle that took him from the swing set past the monkey bars, onto the paved basketball courts, along the chain-link fence and back to the swing set. He had no idea how many times he made the circuit; he just walked and talked with himself. Interspersed in his self-dialogue he prayed. The prayers were short like Post-it Notes stuck to the door of heaven in which he asked God questions about himself, about the future, and about what to do.

When Adam finally returned home, his feet hurt, and his body was weary, but his mind was now clear. He now knew what he must do, and it would begin tomorrow with a phone call to Dr. Rachel Tremaine.

Rachel was furious: furious with Dr. Morgan for suggesting such a juvenile ploy to trap a man who was so clearly innocent, and furious with herself for acquiescing to the scheme. She had participated in an unethical activity. Adam Bridger would be well within his rights to file a complaint with the hospital board of directors and license review board.

After Adam had left the conference room, the three conspirators sat in stunned silence. None had anticipated his reaction. They had expected him to either confess to being the Healer or, at best, make a meager attempt to explain his actions. Instead, he had dominated the meeting, refusing to be manipulated or verbally abused. Instead of catching Adam in a compromising situation, he had caught them. As they sat staring at the door through which Adam had just exited, Rachel gathered her things and walked toward the door.

"Wait a minute," Dr. Morgan said. "I think we had better talk about this." Rachel ignored him and exited the room. It took less than four minutes for her to walk to the elevators, descend to the first floor, leave the building, and get in her car. Two minutes later she was on the freeway headed home. Except she didn't go home.

As Rachel pulled onto her street, she thought of her home. Inside it she would be warm, cozy, and absolutely alone. Except she didn't want to be alone—not now. But she didn't want to talk to anyone either. What she needed was a crowded place where she could get lost. She realized the oxymoronic nature of her thoughts: it was ridiculous to want to be alone in a crowd. From her medical training she knew the root of the compulsion: she wanted a relationship with people, but didn't want the responsibility or the risk that relationships could bring. That's why she had no close friends and was cordially estranged from family. While she enjoyed living alone, she had moments when she desired, even hungered for, the warmth of other people. Now was such a time.

The impersonal crowd Rachel was looking for was found in a Mission Valley movie theater. At the ticket window she asked when the next show started but not the name of the movie. She purchased a ticket to *Bully*, a new comedy starring Michael Keaton as a self-serving, womanizing vice-president who suddenly becomes President of the United States, and becomes a better person through the advice and intervention of the ghost of Teddy Roosevelt, played by a horribly miscast Mel Gibson.

The movie was of no consequence to Rachel; she just wanted to be some place other than home or the hospital. At the snack bar she bought a large popcorn, two boxes of bon-bons, and a diet cola. In the darkened theater she sat in the back row and munched the popcorn furiously in a subconscious effort to release pent-up anxiety. The scene at the hospital replayed itself repeatedly in her mind, and every time it did, she filled her mouth with popcorn. Halfway through the movie and the second box of bon-bons, Rachel felt more composed and watched the movie with growing interest. It didn't take long for her to understand the writer's point: people can change. In the movie, the ghost of Teddy Roosevelt was encouraging the reluctant new President to seize control of his life and his destiny, and in the process find out that there was more to life than he had ever experienced.

*That's what I need,* Rachel thought, *someone to keep me from making a fool of myself.* By the end of the show, Rachel was still angry, but her ire was controlled. The movie had given her time to distance herself from the day's events. It had also given her a new perspective. Maybe she could make changes in her life. *It's a shame there's not a friendly ghost to guide me.*

Twenty minutes later, Rachel was home—with a stomachache.

## Wednesday, March 25; 8 A.M.

She had attempted to apologize, when he had called at 8 the next morning, but Adam wouldn't allow it. It was clear that she was sincere when she said, "I'm sorry." After some coaxing he had been able to convince her to meet him.

"Just trust me," he had said. "There's someone I want you to meet. He may help us both solve our problems."

"Who is he and what can he do about finding our mysterious Healer?" Her voice revealed her weariness.

"If I told you, you wouldn't believe me. Just show up at the address I gave you. I promise, you won't be disappointed."

"When?"

"Ten o'clock this morning."

"What if I have rounds this morning?"

"Do you?"

"No."

"Good. I'll see you there." Adam hung up and smiled.

## Wednesday, March 25; 10 A.M.

"Incredible," Rachel said, her eyes wide in amazement. Before her was the largest house she had ever seen. From the La Jolla address Adam had given, she had guessed that they would be meeting at an expensive home, but this was more than she could have imagined. The house, its copper roof weathered to an emerald green, was an architect's dream. Thin, fixed windows, tinted against the sun, provided a panoramic view on the manicured landscape and the blue Pacific ocean. Cedar siding graced the walls, and sculptured Egyptian dogs lined the long driveway and walkway.

"It takes your breath away, doesn't it?" Adam took Rachel by the arm and ushered her up the winding sidewalk. He pushed the doorbell next to two massive oak doors. The doorbell chimed several bars of Vivaldi's *Four Seasons*, causing Rachel to look at Adam and roll her eyes. A moment later one of the doors swung open.

"Martin," Adam said jovially, "it's good to see that you still open your own doors."

"Come in, Adam. I've been expecting you."

As they entered the foyer, Adam said, "Martin, I want you to meet a friend of mine, Dr. Rachel Tremaine. Rachel, this is Martin St. James, our host."

"I'm pleased to meet you, Dr. Tremaine. May I fix you anything to drink?"

Rachel studied the man for a moment. He had a thin, blond beard; his face was narrow and drawn, punctuated with bright blue eyes. He reminded Rachel of the stereotypical nerd.

"Coffee would be nice," she responded.

"Anna," he called, "will get you some coffee? How about you, Adam?"

"No thanks. I had a late breakfast."

Martin nodded. "Please, let's go into the living room."

Martin led them from the foyer into a massive room dominated by a circular fireplace and a spectacular view of the ocean and shoreline known as Black's Beach. The room could only be described as opulent. French impressionist art hung on any wall that was not windowed. One wall was a tinted window from the floor to the ceiling which towered twenty feet above them. Several Persian rugs were strategically placed on the floor. Martin led them to a white leather divan that was situated to allow the best view of the ocean.

"Your home is," Rachel paused for the right word, "remarkable."

"Thank you," Martin responded with a slight grin. "It's all Anna's doing. She really has a knack for decorating. I don't have a head for such things. Speaking of Anna, I think I'll go see if I can find her." Turning to Adam he asked, "Sure I can't get you anything?"

"Positive, but thanks anyway." Martin nodded and exited the room.

"If you don't mind me saying so," Adam said, "you look positively shell-shocked."

"This place is incredible." Rather than sitting down, Rachel wandered from painting to painting. "I don't believe it."

"What don't you believe?"

"This painting. It's ... it's a Monet."

"I'm afraid I don't know much about art."

"You'd have to be an idiot not to know Monet."

"If the shoe fits."

"I'm sorry," Rachel said softly, joining Adam on the couch. "That's twice I've apologized today."

"That's okay, pastors develop thick skins early in their ministries."

"It's just that that painting must be worth thousands, maybe even millions."

"I don't doubt it. I'm sure he could afford several more."

"Several more?"

"When a man makes $150 million in one year, he can afford many things."

Rachel's eyes widened. "What does he do to make that much money? He can't be more than thirty years old."

"Twenty-eight actually; and the best way to describe what he does to make all that money is to say that he's a problem-solver."

A quizzical look shadowed Rachel's face. "He solves other people's problems? What kind of problems?"

"Many kinds. He has solved problems for computer designers, electrical engineers, and even medical researchers. You see, he is a bona fide genius in certain fields. He has this magnificent capacity to take complicated problems and reduce them to simple terms—simple for him, anyway—and find solutions. When a research organization or technical business comes across a problem their people can't handle, they call on Martin."

"And he can solve any kind of problem?"

"No. He'd be the first to admit that he's not omniscient. He is, however, very good with electrical/mechanical problems. He has a true photographic memory. If he sees, hears, or reads something, then it is forever locked away in his brain."

"He must be an incredible scientist," Rachel said.

"Actually, I'm not a scientist at all." Adam and Rachel turned to see Martin enter the room accompanied by a heavyset woman with a thin mouth, puffy eyes, and dark, tightly curled hair. She was carrying a serving tray with a crystal pot and several china cups. "I'm really an artist of sorts. Or, a technician if you prefer. You see, a scientist is one who adds to the body of humankind's knowledge. Artists and technicians use the available knowledge to achieve some end. Just like doctors. Most medical doctors are not scientists."

"I don't wish to be rude," Rachel commented coolly, "but I'm not sure I can agree with that."

"All right," Martin's blue eyes sparkled. "Adam tells me that you are a surgeon. Is that correct?"

"Yes."

"And you think you are a scientist?" Martin continued.

"Yes, again."

"Do you agree with me that the purpose of science is to increase humankind's knowledge about the world around it?"

Rachel nodded.

"Does your daily professional work add to medicine's body of knowledge?"

"Well," Rachel said tentatively, "I spend a great deal of time reviewing medical journals and papers. I also attend conferences to increase my knowledge of surgical procedures. In addition I . . ."

"Excuse me," Martin interrupted. "But how is that science?"

"It's science because I've increased the body of knowledge," Rachel responded pointedly.

"You've increased *your* personal knowledge, but you've added nothing to knowledge as a whole. Actually, all you've done is master what others have discovered."

Rachel desperately tried to think of something to bolster her argument, but came up empty-handed.

"You see, most medical doctors are technicians—highly skilled and highly trained, of course—but technicians, nonetheless. I don't say this to demean your profession; on the contrary, I owe a great deal to your vocation."

Rachel looked at Adam who sat silently smiling.

"If you're done torturing our guest with your logic," Anna St. James said, speaking for the first time, "I would like to introduce myself." Turning to Rachel she extended her hand. "I'm Anna, Martin's sister. Please don't mind Martin; all of this is a game to him."

"Perhaps your brother should consider a career in law," Rachel said.

"Actually, several lawyers have utilized Martin's gift," Anna said, handing a cup of coffee to Rachel. "Cream and sugar?" she asked. Rachel shook her head no.

"Anna runs the house," Martin said. "As I've said, I have no head for such things."

"God created your head for loftier things, Martin," Anna said as she poured three cups of coffee.

"Perhaps," Martin replied. "But Adam and Rachel did not come here to talk about me." Turning to Adam he said, "On the phone you said that you needed my help with a problem. I will do whatever I can to aid you."

"Thank you," Adam replied, his tone turning serious. He began to relate all that he knew about the unknown Healer of Kingston Memorial Hospital, David Lorayne's healing and kidnapping, and Rachel's involvement with the hospital. He also told Martin of the other hospitals that had had similar occurrences. He read from the paper on which he had compiled the information from the newspaper reports. With eyes closed, Martin listened intently.

When Adam had finished, no one spoke. Martin, eyes still

closed, sat motionless. Rachel watched him carefully, wondering if he were asleep. After several minutes Martin broke the silence.

"Dr. Tremaine, do you have anything to offer?"

Rachel felt ill at ease. At first she had convinced herself that she would not offer any information, but being confronted with a direct question, she realized that she had nothing to render. In many ways Adam knew more than she. She had the medical charts, but they revealed nothing of substance—only that very sick people were now very well.

"No," she replied simply.

"Does that mean you have nothing of worth to offer," Martin asked pointedly, "or that you have information you wish to harbor?"

Rachel wanted to hate him. Not only was he forcing her to realize her ignorance, but to admit it publicly as well.

"I have nothing additional to offer." It was the best answer she could give.

"I don't wish to be a rude host," Martin said suddenly as he jumped from the couch. "But this situation presents some interesting challenges, and I wish to give it my fullest attention. Anna will take care of you. It was a pleasure meeting you, Dr. Tremaine. I'll let you know when I have something for you. Stop by again, Adam, and we'll play chess; maybe I can win one for a change."

Without another word, Martin turned and quickly exited the room.

"Would you like to stay for lunch?" Anna asked. "I can fix some salads."

"Do you think you can actually get Martin to eat?" Adam asked, laughing. "You're always complaining that when he has his mind on something he doesn't eat properly."

"He doesn't," Anna said scowling. "It's horrible. I've seen him go three days without touching a morsel of food." A smile came to Anna's face. "But I've finally found a way to make him eat."

"This I've got to hear." Adam leaned forward on the couch.

"Well, it's really quite simple. I'm surprised that I hadn't thought of it before. All I do is turn on every television and radio in the house. The noise drives him crazy. He figures it's worth sacrificing a little time to eat rather than have to put up with all that ruckus."

"What are you going to do when he finds a way of turning all those things off from his think tank?"

"Think tank?" Rachel asked.

"It's where Martin goes to work on a project," Adam responded. "I've been in there only once. It's a small room with only a desk
and an easy chair. In there he can shut out the world and give full
attention to the problem he's trying to solve."

"I would have thought it would be filled with computers,"
Rachel commented.

"Martin has computers, but he doesn't use them often," Anna
said. "He says they're terribly slow."

They drank their coffee and made small talk until Adam arose.
"If you'll excuse me," he said, "I need to find the little preacher's room."

"Do you remember where it is?" Anna asked.

"Sure."

After Adam had left the room, Rachel and Anna chatted
about Rachel's work, and about the lovely view out the window. The
conversation died for a few moments as they watched a man float
by suspended from his brightly colored delta-wing hang glider.

"They fly by all the time," Anna said. "The Torrey Pines glider
port isn't far from here."

"Do you ever tire of looking at the ocean?" Rachel asked.

"No, never. We're not from a rich family. Actually things had been
pretty tight for us until Pastor Bridger came along. He's responsible for all this."

"Adam?" Rachel was bewildered. "I don't understand."

"Oh, he hasn't told you about what he did for us? Of course not.
He's too humble." Anna poured more coffee into Rachel's cup. "We're
indebted to the pastor. If it weren't for him, things would be a lot
different for us."

"How so?" Rachel asked.

"I'm twenty years older than Martin and I've taken care of him
since our mother died. The funeral home asked us who our minister was and we were at a loss. Ours was not a religious family. I had
been to church only a few times with friends; Martin had never been.
In fact, Martin has still never been to church." Anna smiled, then
said, "You can keep him in your prayers."

Although Rachel felt like saying that she kept no prayers, she held her tongue and asked instead, "You're not members of Adam's church?"

"Oh, I am now, but not Martin. He doesn't see much use for church. He's a pure pragmatist, but we haven't given up hope."

This struck Rachel as odd. She had assumed that Adam would be interested only in those who shared his own religious views. Yet here he was a friend to someone who was antagonistic to those beliefs.

"Anyway," Anna said, "the funeral director recommended Adam. We said fine. Adam called on the phone that night. I was still pretty upset. I mean, I had to take care of Martin, and the only income I had came from waiting on tables at a local Denny's. He listened as I told him all my woes. I told him about Martin who had just decided he was quitting school. He said he only went to school to make Mom happy and now she was gone. The next day, Adam came by to visit and ask us some questions. You know, questions about what we wanted in the funeral service. He also wanted to see how we were doing. We were living in North Park back then, in an apartment. Adam took a liking to Martin right away, and that wasn't easy to do. You may have noticed how blunt Martin is. Back then he refused to talk to most people, and when he did talk, he often said cruel things.

"You see, we thought Martin was a slow learner—you know, retarded." Anna laughed. "He was always in trouble at school for refusing to pay attention or do his work. We just didn't think he was capable of schoolwork. Martin had always stayed to himself. He didn't speak until he was nearly six years old, and then it was another three months before he made a complete sentence. He never played with other kids, but would just sit in a chair and stare out the window. Now we know that his mind was thinking great things. Back then, however, we just thought he was slow."

"Didn't your parents have him tested by the school psychologist?" Rachel asked.

"Yes, but the results were confusing. His teachers would promote him each year, probably so that they wouldn't have him back again. Anyway, Pastor Adam was sitting on our couch talking to Martin and me just like you're sitting there now. Only Adam saw something in Martin, something no one else had seen. And I think that

Martin saw something in the pastor. The pastor looked Martin right in the eye and said, 'You play chess, don't you?'

"I declare, Doctor, to this day I don't know how Pastor Adam knew that. You see, Martin had been playing chess since he was five. Our daddy taught him. Within two weeks, Martin could beat my dad. They used to play every day until Dad died. Martin was only six when Dad died." Anna walked to the mantle over the fireplace and picked up a black and white photo in a plain wood frame and brought it over to Rachel. "This is a picture of my father and Martin, taken while they were playing chess. No one could beat Martin. Not that he had many people to play with. But when he did play at school, or when Mom and Dad had friends over, Martin would always win."

"What did Martin do when Adam asked about the chess?"

"Oh, it was something. Adam said, 'You play chess, don't you?' And Martin said back, 'Yup.' That's all, just, 'Yup.'" Anna laughed and then continued. "Then Adam leaned back in the chair, scratched his chin, and said, 'I can beat you.' Then…" Anna laughed again and Rachel couldn't help offering a sympathetic smile. "Then Martin laughed. Doctor, I had never seen Martin laugh before. When he was done laughing, Martin said, 'No one ever beats me.' Then the pastor leaned forward and said, 'I can beat you. In fact, I can beat you almost every time we play. I'll even put a bet on it.'

"Well," Anna continued, "that got Martin's goat. Martin asked, 'What kind of bet?' Then the pastor leaned back, scratched his chin some more, and then said, 'If you win, then I have to do whatever you ask. But if I win, then you have to do whatever I ask.'"

"What did Martin do with that?"

Anna smiled again. "Martin may lack many things in life, but pride isn't one of them; since he was just sixteen years old at the time, he was full of teenager pride. He couldn't turn Adam down. So they played. And do you know what? Adam beat him in thirty minutes. It infuriated Martin, but Adam held him to the bet."

"What did Adam ask Martin to do?"

"I can answer that." Anna and Rachel turned to see Adam enter the room. "You shouldn't be telling this story, Anna."

"Oh, why not?" Anna said. "You're just too humble."

"Still, it makes me sound like too much of a hero. I was just doing what I could."

"Excuse me," Rachel broke in. "Will someone tell me what the bet was?"

Anna looked at Adam who just shrugged. Anna spoke first, "He made Martin promise to give his best effort at school for the next thirty days."

"Martin was a man of his word," Adam said. "He went back to school, gave it his best, and amazed his teachers. They had assumed what everyone else had assumed—that Martin was learning disabled. I called the school and spoke to the principal and Martin's teachers. I asked them to give him something really hard to do. When they did, he felt challenged. The rest is history."

"There's more than that," Anna said. "Martin's ability to learn accelerated. He graduated high school one year later, and college two years after that. But as smart as Martin is, he doesn't fit well in society. He would never be able to hold down a nine-to-five job. So Pastor made some calls and people started calling Martin for help— and paying too."

Rachel looked at Adam with a puzzled expression.

"At the time we had an engineering consultant in the church," Adam said, in response to Rachel's unspoken question. "He consulted with various aerospace companies. He complained that he was having trouble solving a problem for one of his clients. I asked how much the problem was costing and he told me thousands of dollars a day in delayed production. I suggested he contact Martin. He was leery at first, so I suggested that he retain him based on Martin's ability to solve the problem. If he couldn't solve it, then Martin would get nothing. If he did come up with a solution, then Martin would be paid 10 percent of the money saved during the first month. Martin solved the problem in fifteen hours and a business was born. Two years later he made his first million."

"Incredible," Rachel said. "So that's why he's willing to help you."

"I like to think it's because we're friends," Adam said.

"And that's what it is," Anna said. "That's exactly the reason." Then to Adam she asked, "Will you stay for lunch?"

"Actually, no," Adam replied. "There's a little restaurant I want Dr. Tremaine to see. But thank you." Adam stood to leave.

"It was a pleasure meeting you, Dr. Tremaine," Anna said as she escorted them to the front door. "I hope you will come and visit us again. Good-bye, Pastor."

# Twenty

## Wednesday, March 26; 11:15 A.M.

"This was the place you wanted me to see?" Rachel asked, as she looked at the hot dog covered with chili that Adam had handed her.

"No finer food around." Adam took a large bite.

"Where I come from, a restaurant is far more than a hot dog stand at the beach."

"My dear Dr. Tremaine," Adam said feigning shock, "look around you. Here we stand at La Jolla Cove, the prettiest spot in all of San Diego. We have an azure sky for our ceiling, the deep blue of the Pacific Ocean for atmosphere, and the cry of gulls for our music. No dark and dismal restaurant interior for us. Besides, you can get extra onions here."

"Oh, you do wax poetic." Rachel took a bite of her hot dog. She found it surprisingly good, although she wouldn't admit it. She also wouldn't admit that Adam was right; it was a beautiful day. The blue waves, topped with a fringe of white, rhythmically crashed on shore. The gulls overhead reminded her of the fantasy she often used to relax after a difficult day's work. Mentally, she walked on the beach often, but physically almost never. "If I ate that many onions, then birds would fall from the sky every time I exhaled."

"Hmm. There's a mental picture."

They left the hot dog stand and began to stroll along the concrete walkway that paralleled the shore. "So," she said between bites.

"So, what?"

"So, why are we here? I assume you brought me out here for some reason."

"This is where I come to think," Adam said reflectively. "It's my place to ponder."

"This thing is really eating you, isn't it?" she asked.

"I'm afraid so. I can't get it off my mind. I want the Loraynes back. Somehow, I feel responsible."

"Responsible? Why would you feel responsible? You didn't kidnap them."

"I know. Unfortunately, reason and emotion don't always mix." Adam tossed the hot dog wrapper in one of the waste receptacles that punctuated the meandering walk and clasped his hands behind his back. "Logically, I know that I'm not responsible, yet the feeling is there. It's a psychological phenomenon that affects many ministers. They see their church members as extended family. They feel responsible to God for the people given to their care."

"Sounds to me that you're feeling guilty over something you can't control. Guilt makes a lousy motivation."

"It's not really guilt that bothers me, it's powerlessness. There is so little that I can do. Oh, I can pray, and that's good. But my heart wants to do more."

Rachel looked at him. He was a confusing man to her. Physically he wasn't much to look at, with his thick glasses, square jaw, and receding black hair. Hardly every girl's dream. Yet, there was something about him. He was self-possessed. He emitted a confidence without being arrogant. He was kind, gentlemanly, intelligent, caring and, as she saw last night in the hospital conference room, he could be quite forceful. His concern was genuine, honest, almost childlike. *He would have made an excellent doctor*, she thought.

"Look, Adam," Rachel said quietly. "I'm not much good at comforting, and I'm even worse at counseling. But I think you're being too hard on yourself. You've done more than most people would in your place, even more than other ministers. You've worked with the police. You've comforted the family. You have even helped me with my work, and I certainly haven't helped you. You've asked your genius friend, odd as he is, to do what he can. What else can you do?"

Rachel deposited her hot dog wrapper in a nearby waste bin and then they walked on in silence. A few moments later Adam stopped and turned toward Rachel.

"I have brought you out here for a reason. There's something I want to say." He stared unblinkingly at her face. "It is very important for you to believe that I am not the Healer. I need to find the Healer as much as you. He is the key to the Loraynes. I know that if we can find him, we will have the information we need to find the Loraynes."

"How can you be so sure?" Rachel said stiffly. "You make it sound like a statement of fact."

"Not fact; faith." Adam said grinning. "And I need your help."

Rachel wasn't sure what to answer. How could she be of help? Actually, it was Adam who had made all the headway. But somehow, she couldn't turn him down.

"I'll do what I can."

"Great," Adam said jubilantly. Turning, they continued their walk. Without comment, Adam took Rachel by the hand. Her first impulse was to pull away, but she didn't. His hand was warm and firm, and it made her feel wanted. She felt like a schoolgirl who was walking hand-in-hand for the first time.

"It would be helpful if you would tell me who you are." Priscilla cradled the telephone's handset between her ear and shoulder and looked under the piles of papers on her desk for a note pad.

"I can't," the anonymous woman caller said. "I don't want to lose my job."

"It is against station policy to respond to anonymous calls." That was a lie, but Priscilla found an artfully used lie very helpful at times.

"Fine. I'll call another station," the caller replied tersely.

"No, wait. All right, you win. Let's hear it." Priscilla would have to find out more about her caller in other ways.

"Well, you know that Reverend Paul Isaiah will be in town this weekend and that he is holding a press conference this afternoon at 2:30."

"Paul Isaiah," Priscilla said thoughtfully. "You mean the name-it-and-claim-it preacher. Isn't he the one they call 'the Reverend of Riches?' "

"Reverend Isaiah is a wonderful man," the voice snapped. "I'll not listen to him being spoken of disrespectfully."

"I didn't mean to offend." *So,* Priscilla thought to herself, *my mystery caller is a friend of Paul Isaiah.* "Please, go on."

"I shouldn't be telling you this, and the only reason that I am is because Reverend Isaiah is too modest to tell you himself."

"What shouldn't you be telling me?"

There was a short pause. "He's the one."

"The one what?"

"The one you're looking for. He's the Healer. He's the one who's been healing people in Kingston Memorial Hospital."

Priscilla felt her pulse quicken. "How do you know that?"

"That's not important. What is important is how you can know."

"And how is that?"

"Come to the press conference and ask him. He won't offer the information but, if confronted, he can't deny it."

Priscilla looked across the crowded newsroom, cluttered with desks and office equipment, at a white dry marker board. The board was used for field assignments and listed the event to be covered and the reporter assigned the task. Squinting, she was able to see that the event had been delegated, but she couldn't make out the reporter's name.

"Someone will be there," she said.

"It would be better if you were there," the voice said, and then the line went dead.

## Friday, March 26; 2:30 P.M.

It was a small gathering; two reporters from local newspapers, three from radio stations, and Priscilla who also brought along a station cameraman. Priscilla was not surprised by the low turnout. It was a heavy news day; an eighty-acre brush fire burned out of control near the Wild Animal Park in Escondido, an F-14 Tomcat fighter jet crashed on a runway at Miramar Naval Air Station, and the San Diego Police SWAT team was negotiating for the lives of hostages being held by a disgruntled employee of an electronics firm in Kearny Mesa.

"This had better be good," she said to her cameraman, as she sat on a metal folding chair in the back row. She had had to pull a lot of strings with Pham Ho to get him to change the field assignment and allow her to attend this meeting. Pham was going to make a great news director. He was already giving her a bad time about her role at the station. Give Pham time to settle into Irwin's old job and she might never get her way again.

The press conference was being held in one of the large rooms of the Radisson Hotel in Mission Valley. A small dark wood podium with the hotel's logo was in front of the room. Priscilla counted fifty chairs. *A little optimistic*, she thought.

A young woman with long straight blond hair and carrying a stack of manila envelopes entered the room. She looked at the six reporters and scowled. She seemed clearly disappointed at the turnout. The woman stepped behind the podium.

"Good afternoon," the blond said with mock cheerfulness. "We will be starting soon. I have been asked to apologize for our late start, but Reverend Isaiah had an emergency counseling call." Priscilla looked at her watch; the conference should have started ten minutes earlier.

"In the meantime," the woman continued, "I will hand out these packets of information. They contain some things you may find helpful."

When Priscilla opened her packet, she found the usual press kit information: a one-page biography, various sizes of black and white photos of Paul Isaiah, and a brief article about the upcoming "Feel Good about Yourself" campaign in San Diego.

A moment later a short, stout man with piercing gray eyes entered the room. Priscilla recognized him from the publicity photos. He wore a dark blue suit with a yellow silk tie and matching yellow handkerchief in his breast pocket.

"You are certainly gracious people to take time from your busy schedules to attend this conference." His voice was clear and pleasant. Each word was enunciated in a way that captivated Priscilla's attention. If it weren't for his deep Southern drawl, he would have made a great anchorman on any news program. "I know professionals like you are pressed for time, so first allow me to apologize for my tardiness, but a man said he would kill himself if I didn't talk to him—and we couldn't have that, could we? Oh, before you ask, I am happy to inform you that he is doing fine."

Priscilla stood up and spoke; as she did the cameraman turned on his camera light and intense white light filled the room: "Reverend Isaiah, may I ask a question before we begin?"

"Certainly, Ms. Simms," he replied.

"Are you the one who is responsible for the unusual healings taking place at the Kingston Memorial Hospital?"

Isaiah's bright and ready smile dissolved from his face. His gray eyes turned cold and hard. "I would really prefer to talk about our upcoming crusade."

"I have a tip that you may be the Healer," she persisted. "Is that true?"

The other reporters shifted nervously, but remained in stunned silence.

"There have been those who have come to our meetings who report physical healings," Isaiah said coolly.

"Excuse me, Reverend Isaiah," she interrupted. "My question deals specifically with the Kingston Memorial Hospital."

Isaiah began to fidget behind the podium. "I really don't want to confirm that kind of rumor."

"Very well, sir." Priscilla decided to press the point. "If you will not confirm the suspicion, then will you deny it?"

"I think it best that I neither confirm nor deny suspicions."

"Perhaps you could tell us why you are being so evasive?"

"Discretion is the better part of valor," Isaiah replied, smiling weakly.

"It could also be misunderstood as deceit."

Isaiah looked deep into Priscilla's eyes with near hypnotic

effectiveness, then asked in a quiet tone, "Do you think I am deceit-ful, Ms. Simms?"

Priscilla had been a journalist too long to fall into the trap of pub-lic slander. If she answered yes, Isaiah might have grounds to sue her and her station.

"I'm not a judge, only a reporter," she replied coyly.

"Perhaps then we can let the matter drop."

Not wanting to let the matter drop, Priscilla asked, "So then you deny being the Healer?"

Isaiah stood statue-still behind the rostrum, his face stern, his mouth a tight slit. After a moment of uncomfortable silence, he asked, "Does anyone else have a question?"

A young man in a pullover sweater stood and said, "I do. I'm Ralph Lews from the *San Diego Union.*"

"Welcome, Mr. Lews," Isaiah said, and a new smile graced his face. "What is your question?"

"Are you the Healer?" Lews asked, and then sat down.

Isaiah's new smile evaporated. "This press conference was called to talk about the upcoming 'Feel Good about Yourself' campaign, not idle rumor. Does anyone have any questions about the campaign?"

No one said anything.

"I see," Isaiah said. Priscilla noticed that he looked like a scold-ed puppy. "The information you've been handed has the pertinent details on the upcoming crusade. Many lives will be changed during that time. You could've had a great part in that, but you let distraction get the best of you." Isaiah quickly turned and marched from the room.

"Got it?" Priscilla asked the cameraman.

"Every drop of sweat," he replied. "You really put it to him."

"It's simple," she said smugly. "If he weren't our man, then all he would have to do is simply deny it. But, if he is the Healer and he didn't want us to know about it, then he has a problem. His Christian ethic won't let him lie and say that he's not the Healer, so the only thing left is to neither confirm nor deny his involvement."

The other reporters had gathered around Priscilla, pummeling her with questions to which she would reply, "Sorry, you'll have to get your own story."

## Friday, March 26; 3 P.M.

"Well?" Isaiah sat down in the overstuffed chair of the hotel room.

"You were magnificent, as usual," R.G. said exuberantly, as he poured Chivas Regal into two glasses. "Worthy of an academy award."

"Did I look nervous enough?"

"Positively petrified."

"So you think they bought it?" Isaiah took the glass of Scotch from his friend.

"I guarantee that tomorrow night the Sports Arena will be packed to the rafters, to see not only Paul Isaiah but also the Healer." Then, raising his own glass, he said, "Till tomorrow night."

"Till tomorrow night." They drained their glasses.

# Twenty-One

## Friday, March 26; 11:20 P.M.

"Did you see it?" Even over the phone Rachel's voice carried a restrained excitement.

"You mean Priscilla Simms' report on the 11 o'clock news?" Adam asked, using the remote to turn down the volume of his television.

"Yes. I know it's late, but I wanted to know what you thought."

The hour was no problem for Adam who seldom went to bed before midnight. "Truthfully, I'm not sure what to think. It's all well and good for a news report to imply that Paul Isaiah is the Healer; after all, it makes good news. But it's quite another thing to prove it."

"You don't believe he's our Healer then?" Rachel seemed disappointed.

"Well, I can't say that he's not, any more than I can say that he is. But something just doesn't sit well with me."

"Like what?"

"I'm not sure. Maybe it's the way Isaiah handled the press conference. If he is the Healer, then why not admit it? He has never turned down publicity before, so why now?"

"I don't know how you preachers think. You tell me." Adam could tell that Rachel was exasperated.

"Look," Adam said soothingly, "I know you want to have this whole thing over with. So do I, but we can't assume that the first guy to stand up and say 'I'm the Healer' will be the one we're looking for. We must be careful. We're dealing with more than a mysterious Healer who walks pell-mell through a hospital and heals folks of diseases. Members of my church are missing as a result of this, and two other families have disappeared."

"Are you saying this guy isn't worth investigating?"

"Not at all. I think he should be investigated."

"Good," Rachel said. "I am planning to attend Reverend Isaiah's show tomorrow."

"Service," Adam said matter-of-factly.

"What?"

"It's called a service or meeting, not a show." Adam said. "The more I think about it, though, maybe *show* is the better term."

"Why?"

"Isaiah doesn't have a very good reputation with most ministers and churches. You see, he's not orthodox."

"I don't get it. Do you mean that he's not orthodox because he doesn't belong to the same church as you?"

"Not at all. Let me see if I can explain. As you know there are a lot of different Christian denominations, and these denominations differ from one another in areas of worship technique, government, and some areas of doctrine. For example, if you could visit several different denominations on any given Sunday, you might see the different modes of baptism. The Roman Catholics sprinkle babies, the Greek Orthodox church immerses infants three times, Baptists immerse only those who are able to understand and tell of a conversion experience. So where Roman Catholics insist on infant baptism, Baptists refuse it. In that way, they are very different. But, in many ways they are the same, that is, they hold to the same basic beliefs. Again, for example, you might visit a Presbyterian, Episcopalian, Catholic, and Baptist church and find in each worship service the minister preaching on the death, burial, and resurrection of Christ. Or, you might hear them preach a message about man's sinful nature."

"What you're saying then is that there are certain basic beliefs common to all orthodox churches."

"Exactly. Churches that base their belief and authority in the Bible will hold certain truths as dogma. These beliefs would include Christ's deity; the Trinity—that God the Father, God the Son, and God the Holy Spirit are one God with three distinct personalities; Christ's death on the cross and His bodily resurrection. There are more of these cardinal beliefs, but you get the idea."

"And Paul Isaiah doesn't hold these beliefs?"

"If he does, he sure keeps them quiet. Some he flatly denounces. He preaches a message of wealth. It is his belief that God has intended everyone to be rich. If they're not rich, then it's because they choose not to be. He never preaches about personal responsibility to man or God. He never mentions sin and seldom mentions Christ. His services are more pep rallies than worship experiences."

"Sounds like sour grapes to me," Rachel said coolly. "From where I sit, his message is as good as anyone's, and these other preachers are just envious of his fame."

Adam was silent for a moment. He couldn't help wondering about her antagonism toward ministers. He wanted to ask her about it, but decided that was not the kind of discussion to be held over the phone, especially at nearly 11:30 in the evening. "I can assure you," he said breaking the silence, "that is not the case. Perhaps when we have more time, I can explain it a little more clearly."

"Why don't you come with me tomorrow and you can explain it then. It starts at 7, so maybe we can have an early dinner together."

Adam was taken aback. He was having trouble understanding Rachel. At times she was hostile to him and his profession. At other times she seemed to be genuinely friendly.

"That will be fine," he said somewhat meekly. "I'll be in my office all day tomorrow, in case you need to get hold of me."

"You work on Saturdays?"

"That's the best time to finish my sermon in peace and quiet. Besides, I've missed a lot of office work because of my surgery and all the running around I've been doing. Shall I pick you up?"

"Nope," Rachel said forcefully. "This one's on me. I'll pick you up at your office at 4:30."

"Let me tell you how to get there from the hospital." Adam gave detailed instructions. "Do you think you can find it?"

"I'll find it."

"That will be fine," Adam said and hung up the phone.

## Saturday, March 27; 4:40 P.M.

Adam clenched his folded hands in his lap until his knuckles turned white. The small and agile '56 Thunderbird in which he rode darted in and out of traffic along Friars Road in Mission Valley.

"You're not nervous, are you?" Rachel asked. "You know there have actually been those who think that I lack a certain amount of driving etiquette. Can you believe that?" Rachel brought her car up tightly behind a car in the left lane and then sharply veered into the right-hand lane. A car behind her honked its horn; Adam closed his eyes.

"They may have a point, you know," Adam replied, as he slowly opened his eyes.

"I feel at my best behind the wheel of this car. My dad gave it to me when I graduated medical school. It gives me a sense of purpose and self-determination, a feeling of self-control." Rachel leaned back in the bucket seat and accelerated. "A psychiatrist friend of mine says it's because I have so little power in my personal life. You're a man of wise counsel; what do you think?"

"I think dropping to within twenty miles of the speed limit would be good a idea." Adam said tensely.

"Why, I believe you're scared, Reverend Bridger." Rachel laughed.

"I prefer to think of it as cautious and expedient."

"Expedient? How so?"

"There's a Highway Patrol car just a few cars ahead of you."

Rachel decelerated quickly until the car's speed matched the flow of traffic.

"Thanks," she said. "The last thing I need is another ticket. My insurance would cancel me."

"I must admit," Adam said, thankful for the police car ahead of them, "this is a side of you I never imagined."

"We all have our quirks, Adam. This is one way I release stress.

When I'm in my car, I am the absolute ruler of my life. There are no phones in here, no hospital administrators, no uncooperative patients; just me and my thoughts."

"I imagine your life is fairly stressful dealing with disease on a daily basis," Adam said sympathetically.

"It's not disease that bothers me," Rachel said stoically. "Disease is never malevolent. It doesn't choose its victims; it simply follows nature's plan. A virus doesn't say, 'Aha, here comes a likely host for me to live in.' It infects and grows because that's what it's designed to do; that's how it lives. People are another matter entirely."

"How so?"

"Unlike disease, people can be vicious." Rachel spit her words out. "They can be dishonest and unscrupulous—plotting and planning the demise of others. Odd as it sounds, Adam, I don't much like people."

"Why not?"

Rachel did not respond but gazed steadily in front of her, her hands alternating squeezing and relaxing on the steering wheel.

"Something you want to talk about?" Adam asked quietly.

"Please don't play psychologist with me; leave that to the professionals," Rachel said curtly. For the next few minutes they rode in silence. Rachel broke the stillness, "That was uncalled for. I didn't mean to imply that you weren't a professional. I'm sure you're very good at what you do, it's just that...that I'm a very private person."

"I understand," Adam said calmly. "I didn't mean to pry."

"Well, enough about me," Rachel said with mock cheerfulness. "What about you? How do you deal with your stress? Or, are ministers exempt from stress?"

Adam laughed loudly. "That is one of the two great myths people believe about ministers. The first is that ministers work only on Sunday, and second, that we are free from the normal stresses of life. The truth of the matter is that many ministers work far more than forty hours a week, and face more stress than many believe. Some researchers have placed the ministerial profession in the top five of stress-causing occupations."

"What could be so stressful about a minister's life?"

Adam paused and gathered his thoughts. "It's not an easy thing to explain. First, you have to understand what a minister believes about himself. The typical clergyman believes that God has called him to be a minister. That is, God, for whatever reason, has specifically picked him to serve Christ's church. That alone is enough to cause stress. To think that God has chosen you for a task is…well, for lack of a better term, frightening. Of course, the young minister enters his first church after four years of college and three years of seminary, believing that he is going to change the world for Jesus. Two years later, after struggling with personalities and finances, he realizes how tough a job it is."

Adam gazed out the side window. "The ministry has changed over the last few decades. Twenty or thirty years ago ministers were considered pillars in the community. Their presence was valued and their counsel sought. Today, many view the minister as a perpetrator of superstition, and an interloper in the private lives of people. Actually, all a minister wants to do is improve the lives of those around him and to serve God; to bring faith into the lives of the faithless, not for personal gain, but because he knows it makes a difference."

As Adam spoke, Rachel directed the car onto a freeway off-ramp, down a frontage street, and then adroitly parked the car near the entrance to the Great Wall, a popular Chinese restaurant. The parking lot was nearly empty; the general Saturday night crowd wouldn't arrive for another hour.

"I didn't mean to sound bitter," Adam continued. "Actually, the ministry has great challenge. I wouldn't consider changing careers."

"Are you trying to convince me or yourself?" Rachel asked. "Come on, let's eat."

The restaurant was decorated in the typical Chinese-American style with an abundance of red and gold on the walls. Large plastic dragons hung everywhere. A large gold relief of the Great Wall of China dominated in the entrance foyer. An uncommonly tall Chinese waiter led them to a corner table. Only four other people were in the room.

"Allow me to order," Rachel said taking the menu. "If I mention anything you don't like, just say so." Without looking at the menu, she ordered several dishes—cashew chicken, Mongolian beef, sweet and sour pork—and a large bowl of won-ton soup. She also requested two pairs of chopsticks. "You do know how to use chopsticks, don't you?" she asked.

"I think I can manage," Adam replied.

"Good. Somehow Chinese food just doesn't seem like Chinese food without chopsticks."

"I have some news you might be interested in," Rachel continued. "You remember that list you gave me of hospitals that had similar experiences with healings?" Adam nodded. "Well, I must admit that at first I was embarrassed that you found out about them before I did."

"I was lucky."

"No, you weren't. Don't play humble with me—you were just plain smart. Anyway, I've been doing some calling, and have found out a few things."

"Like what?" Adam was obviously interested.

"Well," Rachel said, pulling a small packet of papers from her purse, "the first thing I discovered is that no one wants to talk about this. I had to really bend some arms. Most gave in when they found out that I was from Kingston Memorial Hospital. I guess they're glad it's our hospital with this problem and not theirs. Anyway, here it is." She handed Adam the folded papers.

"As you can see," she continued, "the only pattern is the cities in which the healings occur: San Francisco, Fresno, Los Angeles and now here. Of course, all that means is that our Healer is moving south."

"What about the people healed?" Adam asked.

"No pattern. Only one healing in each city. In San Francisco, a woman was healed of severe psoriasis, a skin disease; in Fresno, a child with leukemia was suddenly well; and in Los Angeles, the most dramatic case occurred: a young man who had been in a motorcycle accident was found sitting up in his ICU bed, which is a remarkable feat considering his pelvis was fractured and his spinal cord severed at the neck."

"Did anyone see him? The Healer I mean."

"No. The patients were either asleep or unconscious. None of the hospital staff saw anything either."

So the only sighting we have is from Lois Langford and what little information David Lorayne had to offer."

"Correct. And as you know, she's missing along with her husband, the Halleys and the Loraynes." Rachel saw Adam grimace at being reminded about his missing members. "Any word from the police?"

"None. I call them at least twice a day, but the response is always the same—nothing new. There just isn't much for them to go on."

The conversation stopped as the waiter brought the soup. They watched as he dished the soup into their bowls. The soup had a wonderful aroma and looked like a Chinese stew with shrimp, vegetables, beef, and pork floating in a clear broth.

"What about these other people?" Adam continued. "Are any of them missing?"

"I asked that, and the answer was always no. It appears that the disappearances are exclusively our problem. I suppose we could drive up and talk to some of them."

"I don't think it would do any good. As you've said, none of them saw anything. For some reason things seemed to have changed in the Healer's usual method of operation."

"How so?"

"Well, so far we have had three healings; the other cities each had one—or at least one reported. Here there has been more publicity."

"That may not have been intentional," Rachel remarked. "It could be that the other hospitals were able to keep it quiet."

"You're probably right," Adam conceded. "That's another reason I don't think Paul Isaiah is the Healer; he's far too public. I've got a feeling that the real Healer is still out there, and if he is, we'll find him."

"Assuming, of course, that whoever is kidnapping those who have been healed and their families don't find him first."

# Twenty-Two

## Saturday, March 27; 6:45 P.M.

It took less than twenty minutes for Rachel and Adam to navigate the busy roads from the restaurant west on Interstate 8 and take the Midway Drive turnoff to Sports Arena Boulevard. The parking lot was filling rapidly with a stream of cars. Rachel and Adam had to wait in a line of cars while a police officer directed traffic.

"I hope you don't mind walking," Rachel said. "I like to park away from the rest of the cars. Keeps the Bozos from dinging my doors."

"I think I can handle it," Adam replied.

Rachel parked the car at the far end of the west lot and the two of them began the long walk to the arena.

The Sports Arena was a large concrete structure that served as home for San Diego's soccer team, the Sockers, and the IHL hockey team, the Gulls.

"Amazing," Rachel said. "Simply amazing."

"What's amazing?" Adam asked.

"The crowds. There's got to be thousands of people here. And all to see this preacher."

"There have been those who have drawn bigger crowds. What's

astounding is that Isaiah usually doesn't get crowds this big. Oh, he gets six or seven thousand, but nothing like this. I guess his press conference really did the job."

As they were walking toward the arena, they were passed by two white vans, each with a satellite dish mounted to the top.

"The television news is here in force," Rachel said. "It looks like every station with a news program has shown up."

Several vans and cars, each with the call letters of their station painted on the side, were lined up near the entrance. Two cameramen, apparently from competing stations, were situated at the entrance doors taping the long line of people as they entered the building.

Adam was amazed at the conglomeration of people; there were young and old, children who held tightly to the hands of parents or grandparents. But, the most poignant of all were the ill. They had come in droves: wheelchair-bound paraplegics wheeled themselves forward or were pushed along by hopeful family members; the blind, led by friends, walked eagerly to the building that housed their hope; and the bent, misshapen, crippled, and diseased moved forward in unison, driven by a dream born of despair. Some struggled alone, others had help, and all had the same goal: new health. It was as if all the hospitals had been emptied of their infirm. Fathers carried children too weak to walk, and husbands held wives decimated by disease. Adam watched as one old woman, hunched over and unable to stand erect, labored to make her way up the stairs. Four men carried another man on a stretcher, each looking very somber; the man on the stretcher moved his lips in silent prayer.

Compassion welled up in Adam. He could feel the tears filling his eyes. These people had come because this was their last hope. Here, they thought, was a chance to be whole, to be normal. It infuriated Adam, because he knew that Isaiah could not deliver that hope. They would leave as they came, crippled and ill, and they would blame God for it.

He looked at Rachel, her face was stoic as she averted her eyes. *We each deal with the pain of others differently,* Adam thought. Rachel simply blocked it out.

Adam started to say something, but his words died in his mouth. In the line, just about to enter the building, was the one who haunted the halls of his mind day and night—the crooked little boy. He held the hand of a tall woman with long, blond hair. It looked as though she had not eaten or bathed in days. She stared unblinkingly forward through hollow eyes. The little boy, his spine contorted, waddled as he walked. Just before the boy entered the building, he turned and saw Adam. Seeing a face he knew, the boy smiled weakly. All of Adam's haunted dreams came back in flash-flood fashion. Adam knew the boy would pervade his dreams again—maybe forever.

Inside the arena, seating was filling fast. Rachel and Adam had to sit in the upper level. From there they could see the whole staging area. A large pulpit dominated the raised platform. Flowers were everywhere, with the brightest ones surrounding the pulpit. A grand piano was on the stage as well as a large organ, a harp, and several electronic keyboards. Overhead was a large screen on which the enlarged image of the stage area was projected so that those seated in the back rows could see everything that happened in colorful detail.

A few moments after Adam and Rachel were seated, a tall, stately man with dazzling white hair stepped up to the podium and the musicians took their places.

"Welcome," the man said in a loud and deeply resonant voice. "Take your brochures that you received when you came in and look on the back page." The sound of thousands of rustling papers filled the auditorium. "There you will find the words to the songs we are about to sing." The musicians began to play softly in the background. "Let's begin this time of glorious worship by singing praises to God. Stand with me, and sing until the rafters shake."

Almost in unison 14,000 people stood and began to sing, each joining his or her voice to the magnificent basso voice of the man in the pulpit. Those who could not stand sang just as loudly. The singing continued, song after song, for thirty minutes. Adam noticed that the choice of songs were all old and familiar hymns that dealt with the might and power of God: "Great Is Thy Faithfulness," "A Mighty Fortress Is Our God," "Joyful, Joyful," and others. With each song the crowd became more involved and intense. Many sang with eyes closed and hands lifted in the air; some swayed back and forth as they sang; and others simply wept.

After the singing, the audience was seated. A young woman, tall, slender, with bright blond hair, stepped into the pulpit and began to speak. She told of her life before coming to a Paul Isaiah meeting, her broken marriage and her addiction to drugs. She also told of her life as an abused child and resulting resentments.

"But now I'm free," she shouted. "Now I'm free and you can be free too. Reverend Isaiah has given me new life, Hallelujah." The crowd thunderously applauded. "Would you like to have new life?" she asked. "Then let me introduce you to the man who can show you the secrets of happiness, fullness, joy, and success—the Reverend Paul Isaiah."

The audience stood to its feet and applauded as the stage musicians began playing an up-tempo song. A small, balding man bounded quickly to the front of the platform but did not stand behind the pulpit. He was clapping his hands together in time with the music, encouraging the audience to join him. Soon everyone was clapping to the music and continued to do so until the music stopped nearly ten minutes later.

"Amen!" Isaiah shouted, in his high-pitched Southern drawl. "Amen! Isn't sheee wonderful? Isn't sheee beautiful? What a testimony! And you know what? You can have a testimony just like hers, because God loves you and has all the best planned for you. If you believe that, say, 'Amen!'"

The crowd responded with a loud, "Amen."

"If you believe God loves you, say 'Amen!'" Isaiah said powerfully. The crowd responded thunderously.

"If you believe God will help you, then say 'Amen!'" Isaiah was now shouting and the crowd was shouting back. "Glory, glory, glory; lift your hands in praise to God." Immediately thousands of hands were raised and waved back and forth.

Adam watched with an analytical detachment. In a matter of moments Isaiah had, through a well-formulated procedure, worked most of the crowd into a near frenzy. Adam also noticed that Isaiah had fallen into a "folk preaching" cadence which was popular in some areas of the deep South. He did this by adding an "uh" sound at the end of every phrase.

Isaiah continued, "I know why you've come-uh. I know why you're here-uh. You're hurting-uh, you're discouraged-uh, your life lacks meaning-uh, so you need help-uh. Well, you've found it tonight-uh. Right now-uh. You can have peace-uh. You can have joy-uh. Right now-uh. Do you believe-uh?"

"Yes," the crowd shouted.

"It's yours to claim-uh. Do you believe-uh?"

"Yes!"

"God-uh wants you to be happy-uh. Do you believe-uh?"

"Yes!"

"Are you ready to be released-uh?"

"Yes!"

"Are you ready to be free-uh?"

"Yes!"

"Are you ready now-uh?"

"Yes!"

The noise hurt Adam's ears. He looked at Rachel, expecting to see her laughing at the little man on the stage; instead, she was transfixed.

Isaiah began his sermon, pacing continuously across the stage. Although there was very little Bible quoted, and still less any real application, Adam had to admit that Isaiah was an exceptional speaker. Every eye was fixed on him as he pranced up and down the stage, swinging his arms in near windmill fashion and occasionally punching the air with his fist to make a point.

Isaiah talked of personal peace and prosperity. He proclaimed with great enthusiasm that all could be wealthy and healthy, and that God desired all of His children to thrive. Among orthodox clergy this was often referred to as a "blab-it-and-grab-it" gospel.

Isaiah proclaimed his message forcefully and with great authority: "If it's in your heart-uh, you can have it-uh. If you believe it-uh, then it will be so. It all rests in your faith-uh, your belief-uh, and your willingness-uh to step out in confidence."

After the sermon, Isaiah began the healing portion of the service, in the fashion so popular with some television evangelists, describing in vague terms a disease or physical affliction and then asking the person who fit the description to come forward. Other times he would call people forward by describing their physical ills in great detail.

An elderly man in a wheelchair was wheeled onto the stage and positioned to the right of the pulpit. His frail image appeared on the large monitors overhead. Isaiah approached and crouched down in front of him.

"What is your name, brother?" Isaiah asked in a kind and hushed tone, holding a microphone near the man's mouth.

"George Wilbur," the man replied, his voice wavering.

"Have you come for healing today, Brother George?" The camera that fed the overhead monitors zoomed in for a tight shot of Isaiah and George.

"Yes."

"The problem is in your back, isn't it, George?"

"Yes."

"How long have you had this problem?" Isaiah asked kindly.

"Twelve years."

Suddenly Isaiah popped up from his crouched position. "Twelve years!" he shouted. "Did you hear that? Twelve years! Twelve years of pain. Twelve years of frustration. Twelve years of not being able to walk. And now he wants to be healed. If you think he can be healed, then say, 'Amen!'"

The crowd responded loudly.

"I said if you think God can heal Brother George, then say, 'Amen!'"

The response was almost painfully loud and followed by peals of applause. Immediately Isaiah held up his hand and quieted the crowd, taking them from exuberance to stark quiet.

Then in hushed, reverent tones he said, "But I am just a man; a human like you. There's nothing special about Reverend Isaiah. I am frail and powerless." He paused and slowly let his eyes scan the crowd. It was as though he was drinking in the silence, appreciating his control of the crowd.

"I am frail and powerless," he repeated and bowed his head. The camera slowly tightened its shot until Isaiah's head filled the overhead monitors. Slowly, Isaiah raised his head, revealing tears streaming down his cheeks. His lower lip quavered. Another camera relayed the image of the wheelchair-bound man who had now buried his face in his hands. Then slowly, almost imperceptibly at first, Isaiah began to nod his head.

"I am not special," he said, as a broad smile spread across his face. His next words erupted explosively, "But God is! God is powerful. God is true. God is here." On cue the band began playing, and Isaiah began skipping across the stage clapping his hands in time to the music and shouting, "God is here! God is here! God is here!"

Moments later the crowd was on its feet clapping and shouting with Isaiah, "God is here." Some danced in the aisles, others waved their hands in the air. On the monitor Brother George was clapping his ancient hands and beaming.

The pandemonium continued for five minutes and ended only after Isaiah had stopped dancing. Pulling a large handkerchief from his coat pocket, he began to dab at his sweat-covered face and bald head as he slowly moved over to face the man in the wheelchair.

"Are you ready, Brother George?" Isaiah asked in a hoarse and winded voice. "Are you ready to receive the grace of God?"

"Oh, yes," George replied. Tears filled his eyes and he raised his thin hands into the air.

"Are you ready to praise God-uh?"

"Yes, I praise God. I praise God."

"Then Brother George," Isaiah said loudly, as he placed a hand on George's head, "then in the name of Jesus, I command that demon in your back to come out. Come out demon! Come out-uh in the name of Jeeeesus-uh!" Isaiah was rocking the man's head back and forth as the man shook in an epileptic-like fit. "Release this man-uh. I command it-uh!"

Slowly the man, with Isaiah's hand still coupled to his head, began to rise as if Isaiah were lifting him up by his gray hair. They stood together before the transfixed eyes of the crowd, as spotlights from the back of the building illuminated the strange pair.

Then with volcanic force Isaiah bellowed, "Be releeeeassssed-uh!" As he did, he released the man who staggered for a moment, then slowly took one step forward, then another. A moment later the man was walking. The band began to play, and Isaiah once again began skipping across the stage shouting, "God is here. God is here."

George, now free, began pushing his wheelchair around the stage, dancing with it in rhythm to the music. The crowd jumped to its feet and pandemonium once again descended on the arena.

"I have a word of knowledge," Isaiah shouted, his shrill voice amplified by the public address system piercing the arena.

"What's that mean?" Rachel asked in a voice just loud enough to be heard over the noise of the crowd.

"Basically, it means that God has just revealed some hidden information to him," Adam replied.

"There is someone here—someone with a sight problem. No, that's not quite right." Isaiah paused and put two fingers to his forehead and then continued, "The person is blind. It's a man who has suffered for years. He is in this section over here." Isaiah pointed to a large group just to his left. "Is there a man, a man by the name . . ." He paused for a moment and placed the fingers to his head again. "A man named Woody? No, wait. His name is Wood. Is there a blind man named Wood in this section?"

"Yes!" came a shout. A man who appeared to be in his forties was making his way forward with the help of a woman.

"Come, my brother," Isaiah said with arms lifted out. "Come to the healing that God has for you." Two ushers helped the man and woman onto the stage area.

Isaiah, microphone in hand, met the man on stage and placed an arm on his shoulders. Silence fell over the crowd.

"Tell the people your name, Brother." Isaiah said, placing the microphone to the man's face.

"Wood. Gerald T. Wood," the man replied.

"How long have you been afflicted?"

"Eleven years," Wood said meekly. "I haven't been able to see for eleven years."

"What do the doctors say?" Isaiah prodded.

"Hopeless. They say I'll always be blind."

Isaiah turned to the crowd and thundered, "When the doctors give up, God gets going." Several people shouted, "Amen." "You see, doctors don't have faith. They live off the faithless, and when they can't fix you with all their expensive medications, they say, 'Tough luck.' But not so with God. Not so with God."

Turning back to the man, he asked, "Do you want to be healed today?" The man nodded his head. "Do you believe that God can heal you?"

"Yes."

"Louder," Isaiah commanded.

"Yes," the man shouted.

"I say, do you believe that God can heal you?"

"Yes!" the man screamed. Adam could see on the arena monitors that the man was shaking.

Isaiah handed the microphone to a nearby assistant and quickly laid his hands on the head of the man and shouted, "Be healed in the holy name of our God. Be healed. I rebuke this devil of blindness; I rebuke it in the Lord's name. Open your eyes, Brother Wood, open your eyes and see God's world."

Adam watched the image on the monitor intently. Slowly the man opened his eyes and blinked a few times. Then he started laughing and jumping. "I can see. I can see!"

"What do you see, Brother Wood?" Isaiah asked.

"I see you. I see everything," he said excitedly.

"Tell the people what's on my head." Isaiah said playfully.

The man looked at Isaiah's bald head and replied, "Not much."

Isaiah and the crowd laughed heartily.

Isaiah started skipping again crying out, "Glory, glory, glory, glory!"

The scene was repeated again and again. One who came suffered pain because one leg was shorter than the other. Another came complaining of migraine headaches. Still another shared how she had been emotionally abused as a child and couldn't love. All were healed and each healing brought deafening applause.

Suddenly, Adam's attention was riveted to two people making their way down the aisle. One was tall, the other pitifully short: the crooked little boy was waddling alongside this mother. Adam leaned forward in his seat, oblivious to all around him, his eyes fixed on the two out of 14,000. What would Isaiah do with these two? How would he handle such an obvious deformity?

This boy could not be a plant. His disease was not psychosomatic. *If Isaiah heals this lad*, Adam thought, *then I'll believe that Paul Isaiah is God's man.*

As the two approached the stage area, two burly men stopped them. Adam watched closely as one of the two men shook his head. The mother seemed insistent, but was making no headway. Adam wanted to rush to her side; to stand up for her and her crippled child, but he was too far removed. He watched helplessly as the two men led the child and his mother around the stage and out of sight. Adam knew that tonight's service was over for them. They would leave disappointed again, their sorrow unresolved and their sadness compounded. For the first time in his life, Adam felt like cursing.

A beeping sound redirected Adam's attention.

"We've got to go," Rachel said hurriedly. "Come on, you can help me find a phone." They located a pay phone in the entrance foyer.

Rachel dialed the hospital. After identifying herself to the switchboard operator, she listened for a moment and then said, "All right, I'm on my way."

"I'm afraid I can't take you home directly," Rachel said. "I have to get to the hospital."

"Why? What's up?" Adam asked, obviously confused. "I thought you were off regular rounds."

"I am," she said coldly. "It appears you were right about the Reverend Paul Isaiah; he isn't the Healer."

"What makes you say that?"

"Because there has been another healing at the hospital, and this one is as unbelievable as the rest."

# Twenty-Three

## Saturday, March 27; 8:45 P.M.

Although the drive to Kingston Memorial Hospital was less than twenty minutes long, it seemed like hours to Adam for two reasons. First, he wanted to quiz Rachel about the telephone conversation, but knew, because of the short time she spent on the phone, that there was very little to tell; the second was Rachel's driving style. On the way to dinner, Adam discovered the "thrill" of riding with Rachel, but then she had been playful; now she drove with a tense compulsion, weaving in and out of traffic, accelerating where she could and slowing abruptly when she had to. He wanted to say, "If you're not careful, we'll be sitting in the lobby of your hospital asking people if they're the Healer," but thought better of it.

The tires squealed on the macadam as Rachel abruptly brought the car to a stop in the physician's parking lot. Rachel exited the car quickly and walked determinedly toward the hospital. Adam had to run a few steps to catch up with her. They entered the hospital through the back entrance and immediately went to the staff elevator. Adam wondered if the lobby was still packed with the infirm, or if they all had gone to Paul Isaiah's service.

Adam looked at Rachel. Her face was marred with a frown, her jaw set tight, and her eyes fixed. She was obviously deep in thought.

"A penny for your thoughts," Adam said, hoping to lighten the moment.

"I'm not in the mood for clichés," Rachel replied brusquely.

When the elevator reached the third floor, Adam and Rachel quickly stepped into the long pale white corridor. Rachel led the way in a quick and determined march through a passageway and into a doughnut-shaped corridor with the nursing station and supply rooms in the middle. Rachel stopped at room 314. Looking inside, Adam could see several white-coated doctors and Dr. Evan Morgan. *Ah, the Grand Inquisitor*, Adam thought.

Rachel and Adam stepped into the room. As they entered, Dr. Morgan shot Adam a disapproving glance but said nothing.

"I got here as soon as I could," Rachel said.

"I would like to introduce you to Michele Gowan," Morgan said. "Michele has the whole hospital excited, don't you Michele?"

Michele, who was seated on the edge of her bed, responded with a smile. Her face was radiant with joy and she would occasionally giggle.

"You know Dr. Patton and Dr. Levine, don't you?" Morgan asked.

"We've met at a few meetings," Rachel replied.

"Dr. Patton is Michele's neurologist, and Dr. Levine works in the ER." Rachel exchanged handshakes. "Let me fill you in, Dr. Tremaine," Morgan said, and began to read from a chart. "Dr. Patton, you'll let me know if I get any of this wrong, won't you?"

"Of course," Patton said. Adam wondered whom Morgan was trying to impress with the display of social niceties.

Morgan read mechanically from the chart: "Michele Gowan is a twenty-three-year-old white female whose major medical difficulties have involved her advanced state of cerebral palsy which she developed at birth for unspecified reasons. She was admitted to the hospital through the emergency room this evening at 6:30 with a head injury she received when her mechanized wheelchair tipped over on the drive of her parents' home. Michele hit her head on the bumper of her parents' car. She presented with an eight-cen-timeter laceration that was treated in the ER. X-rays revealed a slight fracture of the left parietal skull bone. She was admitted overnight for observation."

Adam was dumbfounded. The description Morgan was reading couldn't be the young woman on the bed. Adam had seen several individuals with cerebral palsy and knew that they were able to exercise only minimal control over their bodies. Only through great concentration and patience could some of the lesser afflicted feed themselves or pick up a book. This woman showed no signs of brain damage.

"For twenty-three years," Morgan continued, "Michele has lacked sufficient neural-muscular control to feed herself, dress herself, or communicate verbally. She has spent most of her life in a wheelchair. As you can see, something has happened to Michele."

"Something wonderful," Michele said jubilantly.

"Dr. Patton," Morgan said, "if you would, please."

Patton was an unlikely looking doctor; his hair was brown and shoulder length, making him look more like a 1970s college student. "As can be readily seen, Michele no longer exhibits the phenotypic characteristics of cerebral palsy. Let me demonstrate." Patton reached into his doctor's smock and brought out a small notepad. Without saying anything, he tossed it to Michele, who adroitly caught it and then playfully threw it back. Patton missed his catch. "As you can see, her eye-hand coordination is normal. Apparently better than mine." Then he addressed Michele, "Would you stand for us, please."

Michele obediently slid off the bed. Once on her feet she paced up and down the room effortlessly and then struck a model's pose. She was obviously relishing her newfound freedom. No longer was she an active, healthy mind trapped in a disobedient body. She was truly free, a freedom that only one like her could appreciate.

"Michele," Rachel said, as Michele took her place on the bed, "how do you explain what's happened to you?"

"I don't know," Michele said sweetly. "All I know is that I fell asleep—probably from the pain killer—and when I awoke, I was like this."

"You don't remember anything or anyone?" Rachel asked.

"No. But I do remember feeling very warm right before I woke up." Michele smiled again. "But I'm okay now."

Rachel was exasperated. "You mean to say that you went to sleep with cerebral palsy and woke up normal?"

"Exactly. And look, Doctor," Michele said, pointing to the left side of her head, "the place where I hit my head is all healed up."

Rachel stepped closer and examined the spot where Dr. Levine treated the wound. There was no sign of a gash, scar, or even stitches. There was absolutely no evidence that there had ever been a wound.

Morgan turned to Dr. Levine, a short, dark-skinned man known as one of the best trauma doctors in the field. "Dr. Levine, do you have anything further to add?"

"Actually, no." Levine looked shaken. "To tell the truth, I'm still having trouble believing this is the woman I worked on a few hours ago. Not only has she gained motor control, but her muscles which had atrophied over the years are full and firm. In the emergency room, she couldn't speak clearly enough for me to understand what she was saying. Now, if it weren't for the shaved spot on her head, I'd say that someone was playing a trick on me."

"Has anyone called my parents?" Michele asked. "I'd really like to see them."

"As a matter of fact, we called them just a short while ago," Morgan said smiling. "They'll be here soon, I'm sure."

Turning to the others, Morgan asked, "What now?"

"I would like to run some tests—actually, a whole lot of tests," Patton said. "I want to compare the results with tests I've run on her earlier. I've got to tell you, this is one for the books."

"Do you think anyone will believe it?" Morgan asked.

"Right now, Dr. Morgan," Patton said, "I'm not sure I believe it."

"When will I be able to go home?" Michele asked.

"I'll schedule the tests for tomorrow, Michele," Patton said. "I don't see why you can't go home after that."

"No!" Adam interjected.

"Excuse me?" Patton said. Morgan stared angrily at Adam.

"Listen," Adam said. "If I could have a word with you privately, I can explain."

"Well," Morgan said, "we've bothered this young lady all we need

212

to. Her parents will be here soon, and I'm sure they will have a lot to talk about."

Dr. Morgan led the group into the corridor and over to the nurses station. "Gloria," he said to a nurse as she rose from her desk to meet him, "the patient in room 314 is not to be disturbed. I want you to notify all your nurses that you are the only one to go into that room with the exception of Dr. Patton, Dr. Tremaine, myself, and her parents. Is that clear?"

"Yes, Doctor," she replied timidly.

"I also don't want anyone talking about this, understood? Whoever leaks this to the outside, especially the media, had better have another job waiting."

"Yes, Doctor, I'll see to it."

Adam was amazed at Morgan's Jeckle-and-Hyde transformation. In Michele's room he was the epitome of decorum; outside the room he was a martinet.

Morgan led the group to the elevators which took them to his office on the eighth floor. Once inside, Morgan turned quickly on Dr. Tremaine.

"What's he doing here?" he demanded, indicating Adam with a motion of his head.

"I saw a news report that implied that Reverend Paul Isaiah, who was speaking at the Sports Arena, was the Healer." Rachel was unshaken by Morgan's tone. Adam found himself admiring her composure. "I thought it worthy of investigation. Since church and theology are far from my forte, I asked Reverend Bridger to be my consultant. We were at the meeting when I was paged."

"All right, Bridger," Morgan said, spitting out his words. "Let's hear what you've got to say. Just why shouldn't we release that girl?"

"Because if word gets out that she has been healed, then she very well may be kidnapped, like the others," Adam said forcefully.

"Kidnapped?" Morgan said.

"It was in my report to you," Rachel said. "The Langfords, the Halleys, and the Loraynes are all missing—not only the person healed, but the entire immediate family. I'm afraid Reverend Bridger is right."

"But she is in danger only if word gets out," Morgan remarked. "Word won't get out."

"How can you be so sure?" Adam asked. "Word got out about the others. The news media is already snooping around, and if anyone can find someone to talk, they will. We're not dealing with hospital gossip here; we're dealing with a woman who has been healed in an unmistakable way. Word is going to get out."

"I can't be responsible for everything that goes on outside this hospital." Morgan was indignant.

"No, but you can be responsible for Michele," Adam said. "Just do your best to keep her here or secretly transferred somewhere else. You can provide security for her."

Morgan thought for a moment then said to Patton, "Is there any medical reason to keep her here after you run your tests?"

"Only if the tests reveal a problem," Patton responded. "But from the looks of her, I doubt they will."

"Then," Morgan said sternly, "release her whenever she wants to go. I doubt that we have any legal grounds for holding her." Turning to Adam, he said, "I'm sorry, Reverend, but that is the way it will be. Now I think we all have plenty of work to do—especially you, Dr. Tremaine. I want some answers and I want them soon."

With his anger barely under control, Adam left Morgan's office. Rachel followed close behind.

"What are you going to do now?" Rachel asked.

"I don't know," Adam said with vehemence. "I've never met such a cold-hearted man. He doesn't care about the people in the hospital, just the hospital."

"I won't argue with that," Rachel said. "But doing something foolish won't help. Why don't you let me buy you some coffee and drive you home?"

"All right," Adam replied with a grin. "But you have to promise not to keep me out too late. After all, I do have a sermon to preach tomorrow."

The two exited the hospital in silence, their minds on the events of the night. A short distance away, hidden by the dim light, a man sat in a car and watched as Adam and Rachel drove away. After making a notation in a small notebook, he dropped his car into gear and drove out of the parking lot.

# Twenty-Four

## Saturday, March 27; 9:50 P.M.

The bright light illuminated the night, causing many in the crowd to instinctively close their eyes. One woman, her bright-red hair shining under the rays of the small artificial sun, stared at the three-inch glass lens just under the beam.

"This is Priscilla Simms speaking to you live. I'm standing just outside the Sports Arena where a short while ago the Reverend Paul Isaiah finished an animated service. Over 14,000 people attended tonight's service, many of them hoping for a healing. Just yesterday at a press conference, Reverend Isaiah refused to deny persistent rumors that he is the mysterious Healer who has haunted the corridors of Kingston Memorial Hospital, leaving in his wake several incredible stories.

"Take, for example, the events surrounding David Lorayne—an event that many are describing as miraculous. Mr. Lorayne lay in his hospital bed in a deep coma. Many believed he would die. Then, inexplicably, an unidentified individual entered his ICU room. When he left, David Lorayne was well.

"Or consider Lisa Halley, a seventeen-year-old high school

student whose third-degree burns left her barely clinging to life. Lisa Halley went to sleep horribly scarred and awoke completely healed.

"Our investigation has shown that prior to these events, a Bill Langford was healed of terminal cancer. Instead of dying, he was made whole.

"But, as if these events were not strange enough, each of these people and their immediate families have disappeared. Police are investigating but state they have little evidence to go on.

"You, our faithful viewers, may recall how KGOT-TV's own news director, Irwin Baker, was cruelly gunned down outside the Halleys' home. Police are still investigating.

"Despite the disappearances and Irwin Baker's murder, the baffling and miraculous healings have led many of San Diego's ill to leave their hospitals and homes to wait for the Healer's return to Kingston Memorial Hospital. Because of the hospital's limited vacancies, many have begun sleeping in the hospital's lobby and corridors. Tonight, many of them are here."

The camera began to slowly pan across the crowd around Priscilla; the pathetic, pleading faces of crippled and diseased children were carried via satellite link to tens of thousands of homes in San Diego County. The camera paused on one particularly poignant group composed of several teenagers in wheelchairs or on crutches. Many in the crowd began tearful pleas for the Healer.

"They came tonight hoping for a miracle—a miracle that didn't happen. They came with their palsies, their pains, and their fears. Now they leave just as they came.

"At this point no one can say for certain whether Paul Isaiah is the Healer. If he is, then one must ask, where is he now?

"This is Priscilla Simms for KGOT-TV at the San Diego Sports Arena."

The cameraman clicked off his spotlight. It took a moment for Priscilla's eyes to adjust to the night.

"You were kind of hard on him, weren't you?" the cameraman asked.

"I was hard," she replied angrily, her words short. "He led me to believe that he was the Healer. I went on the air and stated as much. People believed me. I wasn't nearly as hard as I wanted to be."

"I thought you were concerned about these poor folks," he said, motioning to the crowd.

"Don't turn into a moralist on me, Frank. The best thing I can do for these people is report the truth." Priscilla walked over to the white KGOT equipment van and sat down in the front passenger seat. "Come on, I want to get out of here."

## Saturday, March 27; 11:45 P.M.

"So?" Rachel asked.

"So, what?" Adam responded.

"You've been staring out that window ever since we got in the car. I want to know what you're thinking."

Adam grinned sheepishly. "I'm sorry. I tend to do that when I have a lot on my mind. I was just wondering what to do about Michele Gowan."

"What can you do?" Rachel said pragmatically. "You've already called the police and informed them that she may be in danger. Other than that, there's nothing more to do."

Adam said nothing and turned his gaze out the window again.

"You are an enigma," Rachel said. "I don't think I've ever met someone so full of contradictions."

"Contradictions?" Adam replied, puzzled.

"Well, maybe contradictions is too strong a term. What I mean to say is that you are full of life. You're fun, intelligent, and tender; qualities that are too often missing in men. Yet, you're so intense. Adam, you can't save the world. There will always be people who get hurt by other people. Unfortunately, these things have happened to those for whom you feel somehow responsible, but driving yourself to emotional exhaustion isn't going to help; and neither is taking on a whole new set of worries about Michele Gowan."

"Do I detect a small chink in that stoic medical persona?" Adam asked, grinning.

"I'm just concerned, Adam."

Adam stared with appreciative eyes at Rachel. By most standards, she might be considered plain. Her intelligence might have frightened some men, but Adam found it exhilarating. It hadn't taken him long to see past the critical and hard shell she used to shield herself from something—a past hurt or a present fear. Strip away the artificial veneer, and a woman of true beauty and rare substance would emerge like a butterfly from a cocoon.

"Adam," Rachel repeated. "Are you listening to me?"

"What? Oh, sorry. I was daydreaming."

"At 11:45 at night? What could you possibly be daydreaming about?"

"You," Adam said softly. Rachel cut her eyes away. "I'm sorry, I've embarrassed you."

"Don't be silly," Rachel responded quickly. "Doctors don't get embarrassed."

Adam wanted to tell her what he felt. He wanted to share his attraction, his appreciation. Somehow, he couldn't, not yet. Especially since he wasn't quite sure what he felt himself. And most of all, he was aware of her lack of faith. He could pursue nothing between them as long as she refused to consider her need of Christ as her Lord.

"Well, I may be embarrassed if I don't get some sleep. I have to preach tomorrow. It's one thing when the congregation falls asleep in the middle of the sermon; it's quite another thing for the preacher. It detracts from my credibility."

The idea of Adam bent over and sleeping in the pulpit caused Rachel to laugh aloud.

"I don't think I've ever heard you laugh before, Rachel; it becomes you."

Rachel felt a warmth within her; a strange and unfamiliar emotion. Uncertain how to respond, she chose to ignore it.

"How about coming to church tomorrow?" Adam asked.

Rachel shook her head. "Sorry, I'm not ready for that." There was a decisiveness in her tone that made Adam drop the subject. They had pulled into his driveway, and he wished her a good rest before getting out of the car.

## Sunday, March 28; 7 A.M.

The alarm went off at 7 A.M., and Adam began his Sunday morning routine. Since he had arrived home late last night or, more accurately, early that morning, he had not been able to review his sermon notes, and this added to his always present anxiety.

He was tired; his sleep had been frequently disrupted by the reoccurring vision of the crooked little boy; his mind was besieged by competing thoughts of the Loraynes, the Healer, and Rachel. Struggling to free his mind of its weariness, he began to prepare for the day with a hot shower and a strong cup of coffee. Fifty minutes later he was on his way to church.

The church was packed with regular attenders as well as those who came only sporadically. Adam circulated among the crowd prior to the service as he always did. When he first entered the ministry, he would enter the sanctuary with the choir at the front of the church and then take his place in the padded oak chair just to the left of the pulpit. This, however, felt too formal. Adam felt separated from the people, like an actor in a play. It wasn't long before Adam made it a habit to be in the sanctuary when the congregation arrived and spend time talking with as many as he could before the start of the service.

Each person he talked to today questioned him about the Loraynes or asked him his opinion on all the strange goings-on at the hospital—no one had to mention which hospital. Although those who asked about the Loraynes were truly interested, each time it was mentioned, Adam felt pierced.

When the organ began to play, Adam made his way down the aisle and took his usual place in the pastor's chair. From here he could see the faces of the congregation. Unconsciously, he estimated the attendance, something he did every service. Today it was easy—standing-room only. Adam felt good about what he saw, especially since last Sunday had been so abysmal. People were smiling, and there were many faces he had not seen in a long time. Despite the anxiety that he felt every Sunday morning, Adam had missed worshiping with these people during his illness.

The service went well. The singing was spirited and the message well received. During the invitation time, when the congregation was given an opportunity to "walk the aisle" to ask for prayer, request church membership, or make other spiritual commitments, several came forward.

Following the service, Adam stood in the foyer to greet those who had worshiped there that day. People filed by, shaking his hand and reiterating their joy at having him back in the pulpit. The last person in line was Fannie Meyers.

"Did you go through the mail, Pastor?" she asked.

"Ever the faithful secretary, aren't you?" Adam said. "No, I haven't looked at the mail since Friday. Why?"

"There's a registered letter for you from a television station in Los Angeles. They let me sign for you. I thought it might be important."

"And you're just a wee bit curious," Adam said smiling. "Well, all right, let's go see what it says."

In the office, Fannie rifled through the stack of unread mail. "Here it is," she said, handing Adam the envelope. The return address was printed in blue ink and read: KLLA-TV.

Adam sat down in his desk chair and read silently. Fannie watched as his eyes quickly moved down the page.

"Well?" Fannie asked.

"They want me to appear on the 'Milt Phillips Show,'" he replied.

"That's great!"

"I'm not so sure. They want me to be on a show about modern-day miracles. Although they don't say it, I'd wager it's the Healer they have on their mind. To make matters worse, one of their guests is going to be Dr. Charles Cruden."

"The astronomer?" The excitement faded from her voice. "As I recall, he doesn't think too highly of religious people."

"That's putting it mildly. Actually, he's downright hostile." Adam leaned back in his chair and closed his eyes. "Why me? There are hundreds of ministers between here and L.A. I wonder how they got my name?"

"Perhaps from the news reports or possibly from someone at the hospital. Are you going to do it?"

"I don't know. It means a trip to Los Angeles, and I don't know that I have the time. Besides, they're taping this Wednesday; I wouldn't have much time to prepare, and I doubt I could get back in time for prayer meeting."

"It might be good for the church," Fannie prodded. "Dick Slay can handle the prayer meeting."

"Although Dick would do a fine job, I doubt my appearing on the 'Milt Phillips Show' would help our church or anyone in it." Adam abruptly sat up. "Wait a minute. Maybe I can use it to help someone."

"Who?"

"The Loraynes and the other missing families." Adam pulled a yellow notepad from his desk. "Here's what I want you to do first thing tomorrow." He began to write quickly on the paper and then handed it to Fannie.

"Do you think they'll let you do it?" Fannie asked looking up from the paper.

"Insist on it."

# Twenty-Five

## Monday, March 29; 10 A.M.

The crowd in Michele Gowan's small hospital room made it seem all the more cramped. Michele reclined on top of the covers of her bed, wearing a pink robe with tiny roses embroidered on it. She was nearly unrecognizable to those who had known her before. Her thin, gaunt appearance had been replaced by a full and robust body. She had curled her brown hair and put on makeup, something she had never been able to do before.

Standing near the head of her bed were her mother and father. Pat and Katherine Gowan had recovered quickly from their initial shock. After the hospital had called and asked them to come down, they had expected the worst. Instead, they were greeted with a daughter they had never known—a daughter without cerebral palsy. Katherine's scream had echoed in the halls, bringing doctors and nurses scrambling. When she regained her composure, she wept with tears of joy and unbelief at the miracle that was her daughter.

Pat Gowan responded somewhat stoically, at least outwardly, but his mind raced and his heart pounded. He had stood silently watching his wife and daughter weep in each other's arms. Then, slowly, he raised a trembling hand and brushed back the hair from Michele's forehead, tears rolling silently down his cheeks.

Also in the room and standing at the foot of the bed was Dr. Patton, with a stack of reports from the medical tests he had run. Standing next to him was Detective Art McGinnes of the San Diego Police Department. Rachel was near the door. A black man in a dark pin-striped suit and dark tie was speaking:

"I believe you folks know everyone here but me." His voice was deep and resonant. "I'm Special Agent Norman Greene of the FBI. You are already aware of the other missing people who have had experiences like yours. Technically, only the Lorayne family disappearance can be officially described as a kidnapping. The others are still classified as missing persons, and Detective McGinnes is handling those as well as helping us on the Lorayne case."

"So you're here to offer us protection," Pat Gowan said.

"Actually, no." Greene shifted uncomfortably on his feet. "Manpower consideration prohibits us from doing that. McGinnes tells me that the best the SDPD can offer is to increase patrols in the area."

"That's the *best* you can do?" Gowan asked angrily. "At least the hospital provided guards outside the door."

"Mr. Gowan," the agent said, "we are aware of the problem. It is extremely unlikely that the kidnappers would attempt to abduct your family. So far, they have acted very discreetly. I doubt that they would be so unwise as to make another attempt."

"That's not much comfort," Katherine said. "I want some protection for my family."

"Is there someplace outside the city you could go?" Greene asked. "Perhaps stay with some family members, or rent a home out of town? Maybe even take a trip?"

"I have a business to run," Pat said bitterly. "I have employees and clients who depend on me. I'll not run away."

"I thought you might say that." Greene handed them a card. "Here is my card. I've written my home phone number on the front. Also, on the back I've written the number of On Guard Security. It's a private security firm that we've worked with before. They're the best in the city. If you want, they'll send out a couple of guards to watch the house."

Pat Gowan took the card without comment.

"If I can be of any help," McGinnes said, speaking for the first time, "feel free to call me. I work out of the downtown station. If I'm not there, they'll know how to find me."

"Anything else we should know?" Mr. Gowan asked gruffly.

"Just be on the lookout for anything unusual," Greene said.

McGinnes and Greene excused themselves and left the room.

"Well, Doc," Pat said, "any reason my baby can't come home?"

"No medical reason," Dr. Patton said. "I've run every appropriate test I can think of, and there is no reason for Michele to be kept here. I've got to tell you, I'm still having trouble believing all of this."

Michele smiled. "Me too."

"Well then," Dr. Patton said, "I have other patients to see—although the rest of the day is sure to be boring after this. If you'll excuse me."

"Any last words, Dr. Tremaine?" Pat's voice softened as it usually did when he spoke to women.

"Just that if you think of anything that might help me figure out what's going on, please let me know." Rachel handed her card to him. "My pager number is on there. Call if you remember anything, anything at all."

"We'll do that," Pat said. Then turning to his daughter, "You ready to go home, Honey?"

Michele leapt from the bed. "I've been ready for a long time. Say," she said with a wide grin, "how about letting me drive the van home?"

"Not until you have had some lessons," Katherine said with maternal authority.

As Rachel entered the corridor outside Michele's room, she heard her name called. A Filipino nurse was walking toward her.

"Yes, what is it?" Rachel replied.

"We just got a call at the nursing station from Dr. Morgan's office. He'd like to see you as soon as possible."

"Thank you, Nurse. Will you please call his office and tell them that I am on my way up?"

"Sure." The nurse turned quickly and left the way she came.

In the staff elevator Rachel wondered what awaited her. She had grown to dislike Dr. Morgan more and more. In fact, she resented him—resented his taking her off surgery to play detective, his often condescending attitude, his self-centeredness, and his treatment of Adam.

Rachel paused at the last thought. She really did resent Dr. Morgan's treatment of Adam. Rachel wondered at her attraction to a man with whom she had so little in common.

The elevator stopped at the eighth floor and Rachel stepped into the large reception area and then to the opulent office of Mary Rivers, Dr. Morgan's administrative assistant.

Mary Rivers rose from behind her desk. "It's good to see you again, Dr. Tremaine. Dr. Morgan is waiting for you." Mary stepped over to the door that joined her office with her boss' and opened it.

"Dr. Tremaine is here to see you, Dr. Morgan." Mary stated.

Morgan was standing with his hands clasped behind his back staring out the window at the ever-present mass of ill camped at the hospital. "Thank you, Mary. That will be all," he said without turning around. Rachel walked over to a chair opposite the desk but did not sit down.

"They keep coming," he said quietly. "They come in a steady stream from who knows where. They fill our lobbies, restrooms, and our corridors. Many are sleeping outside. Some refuse to leave or even to eat. The Salvation Army is feeding and clothing some of them. There's no place for them here, and still they come."

As he spoke, another car pulled to the curbside in front of the lobby. An elderly woman helped from the car by a young man began to slowly make her way along the crowded walk.

"Some are terribly ill," he continued. "We've already treated nearly two dozen people in our emergency room—diabetics without insulin, people with fevers, and worse. Thankfully, none have died—yet. There's no way to get them to leave. No way at all." Morgan sighed and rubbed his temples. Without seeing his face, Rachel could tell he was very weary. "If I force them to leave, the media will flay me alive. If I let them stay and one of them dies on our doorstep, then the media will have me again. It's a lose-lose situation."

Turning, he faced Rachel; she could see anger in his eyes. "And it's all because of this Healer, whoever or whatever he is. They sit out there on the slim hope that this miracle worker will show up; and when he does show up, he walks right by them, heals one person in a hospital room, and then leaves."

Morgan began to pace nervously around his office. "I've got questions, mind-boggling questions, and I'm not getting any answers. I'm not getting answers from you; I'm not getting answers from security; all I'm getting is pressure from the hospital's board of directors, and a hundred calls a day from the media. What's going on?"

"I'm afraid I don't know, sir," Rachel said.

"You don't know. You don't know." Rachel could see the fury in Morgan's face. "Well, I appointed you to find out. This could have been good for you. This was your chance to separate yourself from the other doctors and rise to the top. I trusted you with a very sensitive project—one that may have dire effects on this hospital—and I get nothing from you. You have been dragging your feet on this, Rachel, and I don't like it."

"I've done what I can, Dr. Morgan." Rachel could feel her own anger rising. "If you will recall, I didn't ask for this project."

"I don't care what you asked for," Morgan's words were fierce and loud. Rachel wondered if they could be heard in the reception area. "I gave you a job to do. You may be a surgeon, but you're a surgeon at *this* hospital. If you ever want to step into one of our surgical rooms, or any surgical room in Southern California, you had better straighten up your attitude!"

Rachel clenched her teeth. She felt like a teenager being scolded by a parent. How dare he speak to her in this way. She felt the urge to unleash her pent-up emotions but kept them in check. She would show him her superiority by not playing his game.

"Doctors." Mary Rivers had entered the room.

Dr. Morgan ignored her and continued, "If you're not careful, Doctor Tremaine, I'll have your job."

"Doctors," Mary repeated.

"If an egocentric Neanderthal like you can have my job, then I don't want it!" Rachel exploded.

"Doctors!" Mary yelled, stepping between them. Silence flooded the room. Tears streamed down Rachel's cheeks, Morgan's face was beet red. Both had fists clenched as though ready to come to blows.

"Excuse me," Mary said calmly, "but Dr. Morgan has a call on line one."

"I don't want to take any calls," he said bitterly.

"It's the chairman of the board," Mary stated.

Morgan took several deep breaths. "All right, thank you, Mary, you can go now." Then, looking at Rachel he said, "Get out!"

"Gladly." Rachel spun on her heels and quickly left the office. As she walked, she kept her eyes straight ahead. She wanted to avoid any eye contact with Mary or others in the reception area. Marching over to the elevator, she fiercely punched the down button. Fortunately, the elevator arrived quickly.

## Monday, March 29; 1:15 P.M.

Pham Ho sat on the edge of the desk and listened to the one-sided conversation:

"We didn't mean to cause you any trouble, and we'll take special precautions this time." Priscilla held the phone to her ear with her left hand and massaged her temples with her right. "But this is an important story and you're a key…Of course, I understand your position…Yes, I know that you have a family to support, but… if you'd just let me stop by and…well, I'm sure that security has put pressure on you, but we can…no, if you would just let me finish…no, don't hang up…Hello? Hello?" Priscilla sighed aloud and gently set the receiver back on the phone.

"That sounded like fun," Pham said sarcastically.

"Like a root canal." Priscilla leaned back in her chair and resumed massaging her head. "I've got such a headache." Pham reached into his pocket and pulled out a small yellow tin of aspirin.

"Still trying to get information out of the hospital?"

"Yeah, but I'm definitely a persona non grata. They must have really brought the hammer down over there. I can't get anyone to talk to me. No one in administration is returning my calls."

"Not even Carl Fuller, their PR guy?"

"Especially Carl Fuller. And our sources have dried up. I've called Dr. Robert Ailes and Nurse Karen Hobbs—they were the ones that clued us in on Lisa Halley—and they're not there. At least, I've been told they're not there. I finally tracked Karen Hobbs down, and she not only won't talk to me, but blames me for nearly costing her her job. I even tried popping in on them but was met by a gorilla in a guard uniform who ushered me to their head of security, a guy named Sanchez."

"What happened?"

"He read me the riot act," Priscilla replied, and pulled a cigarette from her purse. "He accused me of causing the problem at the hospital, encouraging patients to leave other hospitals with false hopes, and endangering the lives of patients."

"Don't light that," Pham said grimacing. "It's a state law, remember? No smoking in enclosed areas. What did you say to him."

Priscilla looked longingly at the cigarette and then tossed it on the table. "Nothing. He was furious. He threatened half a dozen law suits. Then before I could say anything, he had me ushered out."

"Well, that explains it," Pham said casually.

"Explains what?"

"Our attorneys just received a restraining order on your behalf. The court orders you to stay away from the hospital. The attorneys say the hospital is trying to get the court to ban everyone on our staff, but could only get you—at least so far."

"Oh, great." Priscilla was exasperated. "So how do I do my job?"

"From a distance, I suppose," Pham said. "Besides, you have another problem."

Priscilla looked at the man sitting on the edge of her desk, "Like what?"

"The Reverend Paul Isaiah is suing you, me, and the station for last Saturday's broadcast. You were pretty rough on him."

"Not half as rough as I wanted to be," Priscilla said acerbically. "He deserved worse than I gave him."

"Perhaps, but his lawyers don't think so."

"Well, that's what lawyers do—sue people. That's why this station retains several good barristers."

"You're right, of course. Stations like ours get sued occasionally, and usually win. We'll probably win this one too. Nonetheless, you're to stay away from the hospital and Paul Isaiah."

"It's not right!" Priscilla exclaimed, and hopped out of her chair. "It's just not right."

"Agreed, but that's the way it is."

Priscilla retrieved her purse and the cigarette from her desk. "I need some fresh air." Quickly she turned and left her office. A moment later she returned. "I'll find a way to get to the bottom of this. I'll be a player in this mystery; maybe only a small player, but I'll definitely do something!"

# Twenty-Six

## Monday, March 29; 3 P.M.

"You understand why we must ask," Greene said, as he sat in one of the chairs near Isaiah's desk.

"Of course," Isaiah said cheerfully. "I want to help in any way I can. I'm only sorry that a Special Agent of the FBI had to drive from San Diego to Los Angeles. Couldn't we have done this over the phone?"

"These things are best handled in person, Reverend." Greene pulled a notebook from his pocket and simultaneously turned on a small pocket recorder. He used the recorder as an electronic memory to supplement his poor note-taking ability. He had found that leaving the recorder in his pocket made the one being interviewed less nervous.

"We attempted to contact you after your service Saturday night," Greene continued, "but you got away too fast."

"I'm sorry about that. So many people want to talk to me after a service that I have to plan a..." Isaiah searched for the right word "...well, an escape route. It's not that I don't care for the people, you understand, but when they press on me and...well...someone could get hurt."

Greene didn't comment, but looked into the deep, gray eyes of Isaiah. The captivating charisma that was so dominant at last Saturday night's service was now absent. One-on-one, Isaiah was quiet and reserved, almost embarrassingly shy.

*What kind of man am I dealing with?* Greene wondered. *Is Isaiah a charlatan, preying on the hurts of others? Or, is he really a man of God— a prophet with mystical powers? Or, is he just crazy—perhaps a psychotic with a messiah complex?* After eighteen years in the FBI, Greene felt he had seen it all. Isaiah, however, baffled him. Greene had run the usual wants and warrants check on Isaiah, but found nothing. Isaiah was squeaky-clean.

Greene's thoughts were interrupted by the opening of Isaiah's office door. A tall, thin man with curly hair entered the room.

"Come in, R.G., come in," Isaiah said, springing to his feet. "There's someone I want you to meet. R.G., this is Special Agent Norman Greene of the FBI. Agent Greene, this is R.G., the real brains around this place."

Greene stood to his feet and shook R.G.'s hand. His hand was moist, an indication to Greene of anxiety. Both sat down and faced Isaiah.

"I'm afraid I don't understand," R.G. said timidly. "Is there something wrong?"

"That's what I'm here to find out." Greene's voice took on a serious, professional manner. "Are you aware of the recent events at Kingston Memorial Hospital?"

"We are," Isaiah said matter-of-factly. "At my press conference a woman reporter asked some confusing questions, I thought she might be a troublemaker—we get them from time to time—so I thought it best not to give her a direct answer."

"Your answer implied that you were responsible for the healings." Greene watched Isaiah's eyes closely. He watched for unusually frequent blinking, or a telltale breaking of eye contact that would indicate Isaiah was lying.

"Actually, my answer was meant to reveal nothing."

"Why be so evasive?" Greene asked, hoping to apply a little pressure.

"Mr. Greene," Isaiah said slowly, "I have been in this ministry a good number of years. I have learned over those years that the news media can, and frequently does, report inaccurately or edit a story to have greater appeal. For example, when the Pope came to the United States, a reporter, trying to make a name for himself, decided to trick him. When the Pope stepped from the plane in New York, the reporter asked, 'Are you going to see the go-go girls here in New York?' Well, the Pope was stuck. If he said yes, it would imply that he was immoral; but if he said no, it would imply that he had no compassion for lost souls. So the Pope answered the best he could. He answered with a question. He asked, 'Are there go-go girls in New York?' You know, he was acting naive. Pretty smart really, but the reporter got him. Front page headlines the next day read: Pope's First Question, 'Are There Go-Go Girls in New York?' "

Greene laughed in spite of himself.

"Do you see what I mean?" Isaiah continued. "With some newspeople even the truth can get you into trouble."

"So then," Greene said, "you deny being the Healer?"

"I deny nothing. I've simply explained to you why I didn't answer that reporter's question. I felt she was leading me."

"Are you the Healer of Kingston Memorial Hospital?" Greene decided to turn up the heat by asking pointed questions.

Isaiah smiled. "Has this Healer committed a crime?"

"Actually, no. But there have been some crimes that may be related to the Healer's activities."

"But the Healer is not wanted—legally, I mean?"

"Only for questioning." Greene realized that Isaiah had turned the tables on him. He cursed silently.

"Since the Healer is not wanted for any crime and I assume you are not here with a warrant, then all I can say at this time is that I know of nothing that will help you with any crime you may be investigating. R.G., do you know of anything?"

R.G. shook his head silently.

"Well then," Isaiah said, "if there's nothing more, I'll ask my secretary, Miss Harper, to show you out." Isaiah pressed a button on his intercom as he and R.G. stood to their feet; Greene remained seated.

"Perhaps you don't understand, Reverend Isaiah," Greene said tersely. "So far, two men are dead, one a killer, the other a TV news executive who happened to be in the wrong place at the wrong time. In addition to that, three families are missing, one of them certainly by kidnapping. We believe the others may have been abducted also. If you are the Healer, then take care; whoever is doing this may come after you."

Christine Harper stepped through the door in response to the electronic summons. "You called for me, sir?"

Greene stood to his feet. "If you think of anything that might help me, please call. The last thing we want is to see anyone else get killed—especially an entire family."

R.G. cringed. Taking Greene by the arm, he quickly led him to the door.

"Take care, Reverend Isaiah," Greene said from the door, "and thank you for your time. We may be seeing one another again."

Isaiah didn't reply. He had heard the last few sentences, and his mind now filled with other thoughts—images of three coffins, three ever-present coffins.

Shedding her clothes quickly and throwing them on the bed, Rachel stepped into the shower and turned the water on, letting it run hot and hard. Facing the multiple streams of water, she allowed the steam to circle her head; then, leaning back against the shower stall, she slid down the wall until she was seated on the floor. The water pounded on her face and streamed down her body.

Angrily, she rehearsed the events of the last few weeks. What was going on? Not long ago she was an up-and-coming surgeon, one of the best in the hospital; now she wasn't even sure she was employed. She could see Evan Morgan's red face and hear his venomous words. The scene kept replaying itself in her mind.

Tears came to her eyes and, covering her face with her hands, she began to sob. She hated it when she cried, but she couldn't help herself. All the pent-up emotion of the last few weeks—the healings, the frustrating investigation, her uncertain feelings for Adam, and now her confrontation with Morgan—welled up with volcanic proportions. She was glad that there was no one to see her cry.

After a few moments the warm water began to do its therapeutic work, and she began to unwind. After a few minutes more she was able to block out any meaningful conscious thought and listen to the sound of water spraying against her body. Reality intruded on her world when she realized she had used all the hot water. As she stepped from the shower, Rachel quickly dried and put on a terry cloth robe.

As she continued to dry her hair, she thought about Adam. *What do we have in common? I am a woman of science; he is a man of faith. I am in the community of medical professionals; he is part of the clergy. I look to no one but myself for strength; he looks to God. There is no hope for any kind of relationship.*

*What is there about him? Most women would not consider him handsome, but I am not like most women. I enjoy his quick wit, his sense of caring, his gentle intelligence.*

Placing the towel on the rack, she picked up her hair dryer and turned it on high. A few moments later, she looked at her reflection in the mirror. *Could Adam ever be interested in me?* she asked herself. She paused as she took a long look at the woman in the mirror.

"In all honesty, Dr. Tremaine," she said aloud to herself. "Adam may not be every girl's dream, but then again you are not every man's fantasy. Mirrors are great for removing self-deception."

With Adam's face still clearly etched in her mind she thought, *Maybe, just maybe, something worthwhile may come of all this Healer nonsense.*

## Tuesday, March 30; 6 A.M.

Morning came early for Rachel. She had spent a restless night dreaming various scenarios of her confrontation with Dr. Morgan. Arising at 6 o'clock, she prepared a light breakfast. Still uncertain about her position at the hospital, she struggled with her next course of action. If she was about to be fired, then she had some decisions to make.

After breakfast she took several three-by-five cards and began to write all her possible options. *Option 1: Go into private practice.* Under that she began two columns. Column one she titled "positives," column two "negatives." Under each she began listing all the pluses and minuses of private practice: initial cost of office equipment, greater malpractice insurance, and years of building a patient base.

On another card she wrote, *Option 2: Join an established medical firm*. Again, she listed positive and negative considerations.

Rachel took note of her now detached attitude. Emotion would not solve her problem, but cold rational logic would. She would simply do as she had always done: analytically consider all the available options. This was the way she chose both the college and medical school she had attended. She even chose to accept residency at Kingston Memorial Hospital by this same method.

She continued this exercise for another hour. Stacking the cards, she wrapped a rubber band around them and left them on the kitchen table. The kitchen clock read 7:45—time to leave for the hospital.

The engine of the '56 T-Bird came to life as Rachel pulled out of her drive and made her way over the surface streets to Interstate 805. The heavy freeway traffic moved smoothly but slowly. Rachel didn't care—she wasn't looking forward to seeing Morgan again.

Through her rearview mirror Rachel noticed a dark sedan weaving across the lanes of traffic. The car was noticeable, not only because of its erratic course, but because a large dent that creased the right front fender. The right front headlight was also missing. Rachel wondered how it felt to have a brand-new car damaged, knowing that you still had five years to pay on it. "I guess that's what insurance is for," she said aloud.

Taking the Genesee Street turnoff she pulled from the freeway, the mystery car followed. Rachel drove slowly over the side street as she tried to push her anxiety about Morgan from her mind. She had decided that a direct, yet nonconfrontational, approach would be the best course of action. If he didn't want her around, she would leave without another word.

A movement in the rearview mirror caught her eye. It was the dark sedan. The driver was tailgating dangerously close to Rachel's car.

"Idiot!" she said aloud. "What's the matter, the dent you've got isn't big enough?" Rachel accelerated and watched as the car fell behind. Immediately the sedan sped up.

"I don't need this," she said. At the first opportunity she turned right. "If you want the road that bad, then you can have it."

The car followed. Rachel's heart began to beat faster. "What is this? I'm in no mood for games." Again she accelerated, and again the car did the same. Rachel took the next possible right and the car followed. Her pulse raced and her mind filled with frightening thoughts: A drive-by shooting? An abduction? Suddenly, Rachel remembered the Loraynes, Halleys, and Langfords. Was someone after her now?

"All right," she said to herself, "think this through. First, let's see if he really is following me." Rachel took a sharp left turn, the car followed. Then she took another turn, but this time the sedan drove past the intersection.

Rachel slowly drove through several more intersections to see if the pursuer would double back and begin the chase again. After each intersection she expected to see the damaged sedan, but it never returned.

"Rachel," she said aloud, "much more of this paranoia and you'll need professional help." After a moment she laughed nervously. "You're even talking to yourself."

Rachel parked in the far end of the doctor's lot and walked to the rear entrance of the hospital. Once inside, she went directly to her office and, suppressing her anxiety, called Morgan's extension. She was connected with Mary Rivers.

"Good morning, Dr. Tremaine," Mary said cheerfully.

"Good morning. Is Dr. Morgan in, please?"

"I'm sorry, Dr. Tremaine, but he hasn't arrived yet. May I take a message?"

"I'm in the hospital and need to speak to him for a moment. When he has time, would you page me?"

"Certainly. Anything else?"

"No." Rachel hung up the phone and looked around her tiny office. There was little for her to do now but wait. Her anxiety over seeing Dr. Morgan again filled her with nervous energy; the last thing she wanted to do was sit around the office. But, what to do?

After a moment's thought Rachel decided to wait in the surgical theater. The observation area had recently been renovated. It looked very much like it had before, with its three rows of padded movie theater seats and its glass wall overlooking the operating room. However, a new video system had been installed that allowed the observers to see in far more detail than previously possible.

Rachel was lucky—a surgery was in progress. Two other doctors were in the room watching the video monitors suspended from the ceiling. It took only a moment for Rachel to realize what was going on. In the operating room several people stood around the chest of the patient, each with his head bowed, intent on what he was doing. Rachel took a seat in the last row and watched the monitor as the lead surgeon slowly removed the patient's heart from his chest cavity and set it in a stainless steel bowl. Rachel had never seen a heart transplant before; all transplant surgeries were sent to hospitals that specialized in the field, usually in the San Francisco area. She wished for a moment that she had chosen cardiology as her specialty. Rachel watched in awe at the surgeon's easy and fluid movements. He seemed nonchalant at having just removed a person's heart.

Once again Rachel was filled with the thrill of surgery: the precision, the technology, the very thought of repairing the biological machine called the body. She realized how much she had missed surgery over the last few weeks.

# Twenty-Seven

## Tuesday, March 30; 11 A.M.

The buzzing of the intercom startled Adam. He was trying to prepare himself for the "Milt Phillips Show." He wasn't sure what they expected of him, so meaningful study was difficult; Adam knew the show could go in many directions. The topic of modern-day miracles was just a starting point; the show would probably deviate from there. Milt Phillips prided himself in playing the instigator—a role he played very well.

"Yes, Fannie?" he said into the intercom.

"A Mr. Martin St. James is on the phone for you."

"Thanks." Picking up the receiver, Adam said, "Martin, I was hoping I'd hear from you soon."

"Well, I've been busy, but I've got something you might be interested in."

"Great. What is it?" Adam asked enthusiastically.

"Can't say over the phone." Martin's tone was serious. "When can you stop by?"

"Is today okay? I've got to be in the L.A. area tomorrow."

"The sooner the better. Bring Dr. Tremaine too."

Adam looked at his Daytimer notebook. "My calendar is free all afternoon. How about 2:00?"

"I'll be here."

Adam had an uneasy feeling as he hung up the phone. What had Martin found? Looking at his watch, he saw that it was 11 o'clock. Maybe he could catch Rachel at the hospital, take her to lunch, and then to Martin's. Dialing the hospital, he asked for Rachel.

"She's not in her office," the receptionist said. "Shall I page her?"

"No," said Adam. "I'll just stop by. If you talk to her though, would you please tell her that Adam Bridger is on his way over?" The hospital operator said she would, and Adam hung up.

"Fannie," Adam said as he walked through the door that joined their offices. "I'm going to be gone for the afternoon."

"That must have been an important call," Fannie said.

"I don't know how important, yet."

"Martin St. James," Fannie said quizzically. "Is he related to Anna St. James?"

"The very one."

"Why haven't I seen him at church?" Fannie asked.

"Lord willing, you will someday."

"Oh, you mean he's not a believer? That's too bad. If he's related to Anna, you'd think that he would be a church person."

Adam smiled at Fannie. "I'm sure Anna would appreciate your prayers for him."

"I thought I might find you here."

Rachel jumped. She had been so engrossed in the heart surgery going on in the OR below her that she had not noticed Dr. Morgan enter the observation deck and sit next to her. "I didn't mean to frighten you."

"I'm sorry, I guess I was more entranced than I realized." Morgan's unexpected arrival made Rachel's heart race.

"And well you should be," Morgan said casually. "That's Dr. Yuri Sarlov down there."

"*The* Dr. Sarlov?" Rachel said with amazement. "Of Boston General?"

"The very one." Morgan smiled. "He came on staff here last week.

239

He's been working with our cardiac department for months, flying in every few weeks. He's setting up a heart transplant team here."

"I hadn't heard." Rachel was still amazed. A pioneer in the field, Dr. Sarlov was considered the most successful and brilliant heart surgeon in the world.

"We've been keeping it under wraps. We weren't sure we would be able to get him. He was well established in Boston. You can't get a man like that with money."

"So how did you get him to come here?" Rachel's eyes were fixed on the video monitor.

"I don't want to reveal too many secrets," Morgan said. "But I can tell you this: we offered him a free hand in setting up the program, and as much research time as he wants. We also have to share him with the UCSD medical school. That's where his lab is." Morgan sounded like a proud father. "I don't mind telling you this whole thing is costing a bundle."

"I can imagine."

"We almost lost him when this Healer thing began." Rachel turned and looked at Morgan. In the dim light he looked weary. "He said he didn't want to be associated with a hospital that had 'mystic' overtones. I was able to convince him that the matter would be cleared up soon."

One of the other doctors in the observation deck turned and said pointedly, "Do you mind? We're trying to concentrate. If you want to talk, then ..." The doctor stopped mid-sentence when he recognized Dr. Morgan. "Oh, sorry, Dr. Morgan, I didn't know it was you."

"Actually you're right, Doctor." Then to Rachel he said, "Let's go where we won't be so distracting."

Exiting the observation deck, they walked slowly down the hall. "Did you want to go to your office?" Rachel asked.

"No. The last place I want to be is my office. Let's just walk."

After a moment's silence Morgan continued, "This is not easy for me to say, Dr. Tremaine, so I would appreciate it if you'd allow me to finish without interruption."

Rachel felt her stomach tighten. It sounded like one of those things employers say to employees just before they fire them.

"Certainly," Rachel said, attempting to sound confident.

"Our last meeting was neither productive, nor professional. Such confrontations should not be allowed to go on in a hospital. As you've probably noticed I value team effort very highly. That team effort has not been present in our investigation."

Morgan paused as they passed a nurses station. Once out of hearing range he resumed: "This problem of ours, and by that I mean the mysterious healings, must be solved soon. The number of people in our lobby is increasing daily. There's no more room for them. Many are refusing to eat unless we admit them. We've hired extra security, put up additional surveillance equipment, and still the Healer slips by us. The media is hounding us day in and day out. One station even sent a reporter to spend the night in the lobby, to see how we are treating the unadmitted ill. Other hospitals are losing money and blaming us. The editorial pages of the city's newspapers are filled with opinions. Our board of directors is pressuring me to solve the problem, but not one of them can suggest a means of doing so."

Morgan paused again as two nurses walked by them. Rachel had not realized the pressure Morgan was under.

"Our in-patients are giving us trouble now as well," Morgan continued. "Several have put up impassioned signs on their doors begging the Healer to pick them. Many are refusing medications that make them sleepy, because they're afraid the Healer won't stop by if they're asleep. The more paranoid patients are afraid that if we catch him, we will hide him somewhere so that we won't lose money."

Morgan ran his fingers through his silver hair. Then, stopping by some windows that overlooked Interstate 805, he turned and faced Rachel.

"That's why I'm glad I found you today, and why I need to say what I'm about to say."

*Here it comes,* thought Rachel.

Taking a deep breath, Morgan said, "I'm sorry for the scene I made in my office yesterday. I let the pressure get to me. What I said was uncalled for, and certainly unprofessional. I hope you will forgive me. I also hope that you will stay on staff here. It would be a great loss to lose a surgeon of your skill and dedication."

Rachel felt her jaw drop; receiving an apology instead of being dismissed left her dumbfounded.

"Are you all right, Dr. Tremaine?" Morgan asked with concern.

"Yes." Rachel said clearing her throat. "Yes, of course. And I too want to apologize."

"Good," Morgan said smiling broadly. "Now that that is taken care of, let's get back to work, shall we?"

"Absolutely," Rachel said, shaking Dr. Morgan's hand. "Absolutely."

Adam blinked in disbelief at the sight before him. Standing with his back to the information desk, Adam estimated that 300 people were crammed into the lobby. The hospital had set up one corner of the lobby as a makeshift hospital wing. Gurneys served as beds. Two nurses roamed the lobby treating patients the best they could. Many refused treatment in hopes that the Healer would be especially moved by their plight.

The lobby chairs were filled with those whose illness did not confine them to bed. Many others lay on the floor. One man, thin and frail looking, held a hand-lettered sign that simply read, "PLEASE."

A pathway through the crowds had been cordoned off. The unadmitted ill were required to stay behind the nylon ropes in order to allow foot traffic through.

"She's on the phone now, sir," the woman behind the information desk said. Adam had Rachel paged when he couldn't reach her on her office phone.

Taking the phone, Adam said, "Rachel? Good. Martin has called and he wants to see us. I thought we might catch a bite to eat and then head over to his place."

"What kind of information does he have?" Rachel asked.

"He wouldn't say. He just asked us to come over."

"Do you think it's important?"

"If I know Martin, it is. How about it?"

"All right," Rachel said. "Meet me at the second floor doctor's lounge; you can get some coffee there. I'll be with you in a few minutes."

The doctor's lounge was the same one where Adam had met Rachel, when she questioned him about David Lorayne. That event seemed like months ago, when in reality it had only been days. The lounge was empty, but a dirty ashtray and coffee stains on the Formica-topped table indicated that someone had been there recently. The smell of cigarette smoke permeated the air. Adam wondered about the paradox of doctors who smoked.

Twenty minutes passed before Rachel appeared.

"Sorry to be late," she said. "I was asked to help with a problem patient."

"A problem patient?" Adam asked.

"Yes," she said with disgust. "She's with some religious group that doesn't believe in medical treatment. Jehovah's Witness, I think."

"Are you wanting to give her blood?"

"That's right." Rachel replied. "How would you know?"

"It's one of their beliefs. It has something to do with a verse in Leviticus about not eating meat with the blood still in it, because the life is in the blood. From that they have determined that blood transfusions are sinful. They're even willing to die, if need be."

"Well, not only is this woman going to die, but so is the baby she's carrying."

"She's pregnant?" Adam sounded shocked.

"That's why she needs the transfusion. She's suffering from placenta previa." Adam looked puzzled so she continued. "That means that the placenta is located too low in the uterus and causes hemorrhaging. With prompt treatment the bleeding can be stopped, but she's refusing treatment. She began to hemorrhage hours ago and has lost a dangerous amount of blood. If she doesn't let us treat her soon, both she and the baby will be in real trouble."

"Are there others with her?" Adam asked.

"Three of them. They stand around her bed guarding her. They're polite enough, but they encourage the mother to refuse the needed blood."

"So what are you going to do?"

"There's nothing I can do," Rachel said. "She's not even my patient. I was called in because they thought a female doctor might help. Unfortunately, it didn't. Her regular doctor is helpless. The only thing he could do is declare her mentally incompetent. Unfortunately, she's very competent."

"Why not let me try?" Adam said. "It can't hurt."

Rachel looked at Adam. "Are you serious?"

"Sure, why not?"

"I don't know if that's wise," Rachel said reluctantly.

"Rachel," Adam's voice was serious, "we're dealing with a life here, maybe two. Even if the mother survives, she'll live the rest of her life knowing that she let her unborn baby die."

"I'd have to clear it with her doctor." Rachel paused and thought for a moment. "Okay, I'll ask. Let's go, maybe we can still catch him at the room."

Going to the maternity ward and then walking quickly through the corridors, they arrived at room 288. As they did, a chubby, balding man in a white smock stepped from the room.

"Dr. Abrams," Rachel said, "do you have a moment?"

"A moment," he replied. His face, drawn and creased with a frown, revealed his weariness.

Rachel took him by the elbow and led him out of voice range from the room.

"I want you to meet someone," she said. "He might be able to help. This is Reverend Adam Bridger and he's asked for a chance to speak to your patient in 288."

Dr. Abrams peered at Adam as though analyzing every feature of his face. "Just what do you have in mind?"

"Just a simple conversation with the woman alone," Adam said.

"And what do you hope to accomplish by speaking with my patient?"

"I hope to save her life and her baby's life," Adam said matter-of-factly.

"What kind of minister are you?" Abrams asked.

"I pastor a community church not too far from here."

"You're aware that she's a Jehovah's Witness?"

"I am," Adam stated.

Abrams took a deep breath, then let it out slowly. "I don't suppose it would hurt. Go ahead. Her name is Angela Pierce. I'll be waiting at the nursing station. You said, however, that you'd like to speak to her alone. I'm afraid her friends may make that a little difficult." Abrams turned and walked away.

"Do you mind if I watch?" Rachel asked.

"Not at all."

"What are you going to do?"

Adam shrugged and said slowly, "I don't really know."

Adam entered the room, followed closely by Rachel. Inside, he was greeted with the stares of three individuals: two middle-aged women and an elderly man.

"Hello," Adam said cheerfully, as a broad smile crossed his face. The smile was not returned. The only acknowledgment was a slight nod by the man. Looking at the patient, Adam saw a pale, slim, and very young, pregnant woman.

"You must be Angela," Adam said. He moved to the edge of the bed and gently took her hand. "I hear you're not doing so well."

"Are you another doctor?" Angela asked softly. Adam could see fear in her eyes. He wondered how committed she was to refusing treatment.

"Me? No. I'm just here doing what I do best, visiting people like you. People who want someone to respect them and care for them."

Looking past Adam, Angela said, "I know her. She was here earlier."

"Dr. Tremaine?" Adam said. "She's a good friend of mine. We were just about to go to lunch, but I wanted to stop by and see you first."

"Why?"

"Because you are special and because your life is about to change."

"What do you mean?"

"Well, I'm not sure I can explain it." Adam didn't want to pursue that thought yet, so he changed the subject. "I hear you're a religious person. Is that true?"

"I'm a Jehovah's Witness," she replied firmly.

"How long have you been with them?"

"Two years."

"Is your husband a Jehovah's Witness?" Adam continued to hold Angela's hand, even though she made no pretense of holding his.

"No," she said averting her eyes.

"Angela," Adam said softly. "Where is your husband now?"

A solitary tear rolled down her face. "He's very angry with me. He thinks I should have the blood transfusion."

"But you don't think you should, do you?"

Angela shook her head. "I must have faith. If I take the blood, Jehovah will think I don't have faith. Besides, the Bible says not to."

"Does it?"

"Yes, it does," said a stern voice behind Adam. Adam turned toward the man who looked to be near seventy. He had a dignified air about him. "The Bible says that the life is in the blood, and we are not to take the life. We are not to eat meat with the blood still in it."

Adam smiled nonchalantly. "Thank you. I've read the Book of Leviticus too." Returning his attention to Angela, Adam continued, "Do you like reading the Bible, Angela?"

"Yes, very much."

"And you believe the Bible is the authority for your life?"

"Of course," she said. "So long as it is properly interpreted."

Adam had heard that line many times before. It was usually used by those who felt certain portions of the Bible might be contrary to their thinking. The best way to deal with those passages was to declare them improperly interpreted.

"I love the Bible myself," Adam said. "It's been my companion for a long time. Tell me, Angela, what's your favorite part of the Bible?"

Angela thought for a moment. "I have so many favorites it's hard to choose. I like the Old Testament a lot. I like the story of Joseph."

Adam smiled. "That's a favorite of mine too. What part of Joseph's story do you like best?"

Angela perked up, thankful to have something to distract her from her troubles. "I like the part where he's sold into Egypt and rises in power because of his hard work and dedication to Jehovah."

"He was a faithful man, wasn't he?"

"Oh, yes. Because of that, Jehovah could use him."

"All right, Angela, how about a trivia question? How did God use Joseph's captivity in Egypt?"

"Lots of ways, I guess. One of the most important things was to save the Egyptians and his own family from the famine that was to come."

"Did it work?"

"Oh, yes. Jehovah revealed that a famine was to come to the land, and so Joseph commanded that all the people bring in a portion of their crops to be saved for later. Because of that all the people, including Joseph's family, were saved from starvation."

Adam knew that there was more to the story than what Angela was telling, but that didn't matter. She was describing the portion he had hoped she would.

"I have always loved that story," Adam said. "I'd like to ask you something about it."

Angela looked at him suspiciously. "What?"

"Well," Adam said, "why did God use Joseph to save the people from starvation? Why didn't God just stop the famine?"

"Because that was Jehovah's choice. He could have stopped the famine, but He chose to work His will through Joseph."

"You mean that Jehovah God sometimes works His will through people?"

"Yes, of course."

"Do you know what I think, Angela?" Adam said quietly. "I think your unborn baby and you are just like the Egyptians, and Dr. Abrams is your Joseph. I also believe that Jehovah God can work His will through people like Dr. Abrams."

"Now just a minute here, Mister," the old man said. "I don't think you know what you're talking about." The two ladies began to talk simultaneously. The room was filled with chatter. Adam never took his eyes from Angela.

"I think it would be better if you left, sir," one of the ladies said coldly. "You're not going to change her mind."

"Angela," Adam said kindly, "I have a story to tell you; a joke actually, but if you want me to leave, I will."

Angela paused for a moment and stared at Adam. Then she gently squeezed his hand. Adam's smile broadened.

"There was this man who lived in a small town. One day a big storm came through. It rained so hard that the dam overflowed and the town was flooded. The man escaped the rising water by climbing onto the roof of his house. Pretty soon the water had risen all the way to the eaves and he was trapped. Then a man in a small boat came by and said, 'Hop in and I'll take you to safety.' But the man refused, saying, 'God will save me.' Despite the pleas of the boat owner, the man would not come off the roof and the waters continued to rise. A little while later another man came by in a rubber raft. He

said, 'I've got room for one more; get in and I'll take you to safety.'
But the man refused, saying, 'I have great faith. God will save me.'
The waters continued to rise. Finally, a helicopter hovered overhead and a man with a bullhorn shouted down, 'I'll lower a rope.
Tie it around you and we will save you.' But again the man refused
and waved the helicopter off, shouting at the top of his lungs, 'God
will save me.' So, do you know what happened next?"

Angela shook her head.

"Well, the waters kept right on rising and the man drowned.
Suddenly, he was standing before God and he was upset. He said,
'I don't understand, God. I had faith that You would save me.
Why didn't You save me from drowning?' God answered, 'I tried—
three times!' "

Angela laughed, and Adam laughed with her. A moment later
and in a solemn tone, Adam said, "Angela, you and your baby are
on the roof and the water is rising. When you stand before God and
He asks you why you let your baby die, what will you say? If you ask,
'Why didn't You save me,' God will reply, 'I tried, but you refused
My help.' "

Angela's eyes filled with tears.

"Angela," Adam said. "Letting the doctors help you is not a sin.
You need to be like Joseph in Egypt; let God pick how He will perform His miracles."

The three began to object again, but Adam held up his free hand.
"And you three—what will you tell your God when He asks why
you encouraged someone to die?"

"It is our faith," the man said. "I don't expect you to understand."

Adam ignored him, and returned his attention to Angela.
"Angela, you won't be alone. If these folks leave you, then I'll be
here. I'll visit you every day that you're in the hospital. You won't
be abandoned, not by me. Angela, there is no reason for you and
your baby to die. Choose life, Angela; choose life."

Nodding her head in agreement, Angela burst into tears of
relief. The three visitors silently left the room. Adam leaned over
the bed and took the sobbing young woman in his arms and held
her while she wept. Rachel stepped from the room and raced
down the hall to find Dr. Abrams.

Rachel and Abrams returned a few moments later. Seeing Dr. Abrams enter the room, Angela wiped the tears from her eyes and said, "I'm ready, Doctor. But please call my husband."

Stepping away from the bed, Adam said, "I'll check in on you tomorrow."

Abrams patted Adam on the back and said, "Someday I want to hear all about how you did this."

"It was nothing really," Adam whispered. "All I did was tell a joke."

"You're amazing," Rachel said, as she and Adam stepped into the empty elevator.

"Oh, not really," Adam said with genuine modesty. "When I first looked into her eyes, I could tell that she was scared. I don't think she really believed she was doing the right thing. All I did was help her understand that it was all right to accept help."

"Well, you did what none of the rest of us could do."

"I'm glad I could help. Now how about some lunch, and then off to Martin's."

Rachel and Adam stepped from the elevator into the lobby. Once again the swelling crowds shocked him. Without looking at the crowd around her, Rachel said, "Let's get going." Quickly she turned and, with her sight fixed to the ground, she walked out the lobby doors with Adam close behind.

Once outside, Adam said, "They make you uncomfortable, don't they?"

"Who?" Rachel asked evasively.

"The people in the lobby. The sick."

"Yes, I suppose they do." Rachel seemed slightly embarrassed. "I suppose you think it's silly for a doctor to be so ill at ease with sick people, but there's nothing in our training to prepare us for such an onslaught. Oh, the hospital has some training for emergency care after an earthquake, or some other disaster, but this is different."

"Well, if it's any comfort," Adam said, "they make me feel uncomfortable too, and helpless. I even dream about them." Suddenly it occurred to Adam that he had not seen the crooked little boy. Had he just overlooked him, or had his mother given up and taken him home?

# Twenty-Eight

## Tuesday, March 30; 2 P.M.

Anna St. James greeted Adam and Rachel as they entered the spacious house. Rachel was still taken aback by the captivating view of the Pacific Ocean. She couldn't help but wonder about the eccentric genius in whose grand house she stood.

"Come in," Anna said cheerfully. "Martin is expecting you."

Adam gave Anna a friendly hug. "You remember Dr. Tremaine, don't you?"

"Of course. Who could forget a pretty face like hers?"

Rachel felt herself begin to blush.

"Where is Martin?" Adam asked.

"In his study. He wants you to go on down." Anna led them to a narrow staircase. "Go ahead. I'll bring something cool to drink."

As Rachel and Adam started down the stairway, Adam remarked, "This is an honor. He doesn't let just anyone come down here. It's his sanctuary."

"How many times have you been here?" Rachel asked.

"This is only my second time, even though I've been to his house dozens of times."

At the end of the stairway was a corridor lit by bare fluorescent bulbs. The walls were a plain white. It was obvious that Anna's decorative skills were confined to the living quarters above. There were two doors in the corridor; one of them swung open.

"Adam, come in," Martin said, "and bring Dr. Tremaine with you. I have something to show you."

"I don't mean to be critical," Adam said, "but wouldn't it be a lot more pleasant if you had a few windows?"

"I come here to work," Martin said, "not to gaze out windows. Now, let me show you what I've come up with." Stepping over to the desk, Martin unfolded a small folder filled with paper. "I haven't been able to do much to find your Healer. I traced his movements the best I could, but came up with little more than you already had. So, I directed my attention elsewhere—to the kidnappings. First, I compiled the dates of each kidnapping and then correlated those with the dates of the healings. Best I can tell so far, the kidnappings are confined to San Diego. Police records from the other cities fail to show any missing persons whose disappearance coordinates with any healings.

"I checked the police records here," Martin continued, "but to no avail. I'm sorry to say this, Adam, but San Diego's finest are as baffled as anyone else."

"Wait a minute," Rachel interjected. "You mean the police actually let you look at their records?"

"No," Martin replied simply.

Rachel paused before asking, "Do I want to know how you were able to obtain official police records?"

"No," Martin replied again. "I don't think you want to know, and I know Pastor Adam doesn't."

Rachel looked to Adam for a response and saw a brief look of concern.

"So, where are we?" Martin asked rhetorically. "We know that the kidnappings are directly related to the healings; that much is obvious. Since the kidnappings occur only in the San Diego area, we may surmise that the kidnapper resides here or near here; this too is obvious. We can also surmise that the kidnapper has hospital connections. Someone in your hospital, Dr. Tremaine, is aiding the kidnappers, or is the kidnapper."

"That's a pretty big leap in logic," Rachel said defensively.

"Not at all," Martin said matter-of-factly. "First, we should note that each abduction occurred in a home or near a home."

"So?" Rachel said.

"So, it means that the kidnapper knew the address of each family abducted."

"But," Adam interrupted, "the Lorayne family wasn't abducted at home."

"No," Martin agreed. "They were abducted on the way home."

"And from this," Rachel said, "you assume that someone on the hospital staff is responsible for these people disappearing?"

"Exactly. Or, at the very least, helping the kidnapper. After a little creative research, I can say not only that there is a hospital connection, but also tell you the most likely suspect."

Martin paused. He was obviously enjoying his lecture.

"Who?" Rachel asked anxiously.

"Not yet, my dear Doctor," Martin said firmly. "Not yet. First, we must finish the foundation before we build the house." Pulling another stack of papers from his desk, he said, "Feeling confident that the hospital had an inside person involved in all this unpleasantness, I did a little more research. I checked the bank statements of all the significant employees."

"You what?" Rachel interjected. "Are you telling me that you copied private bank information?"

"Of course." Martin was taken aback by Rachel's outburst.

"Whose bank records?" Rachel asked.

"Anyone who might have access to personal information on those who were healed."

"Including me?" Rachel asked.

"Certainly," Martin replied. "But don't worry, you're clean. Which is more than I can say for one of your coworkers."

"What gives you the right to pry into my private affairs?" Rachel asked angrily.

"Not what," Martin replied evenly, "but who. You gave me the right."

"I did no such thing!"

"Did you not come to my home and ask for my help?" Martin asked.

"Yes, but I …"

"And was it not your concern to gather information on the mysterious happenings at your hospital?"

"Yes, but again, I don't see how that gives you the right to …"

"When you and Adam came to me to ask my help, you made no restrictions on my activities. You wanted information. I'm attempting to give that to you."

"But what you've done is illegal," Rachel objected.

"Technically, yes. But let me pose a question for you, Dr. Tremaine. If these families—these eight people—are alive, then shouldn't we do all we can to rescue them?"

"Well, yes. But …"

"And while I don't approve of electronic burglary, I don't approve of leaving people in captivity when it may be in my power to aid their release." Martin accentuated his message by pointing a bony index finger in staccato fashion. "Am I to understand, Dr. Tremaine, that you would prefer that we allow those hapless people to remain imprisoned—especially considering the great danger they're in—while we waste days trying to find a more legal avenue?"

"No, I guess not." Rachel felt confused and angry. Her privacy had been invaded; yet, it had been done for a noble effort. Turning to Adam she said, "Surely you don't approve of this."

Adam didn't reply at first, but after a moment's silence he said to Martin: "You know that I can't approve of illegal information gathering."

"I know. But then again, I didn't ask for your approval, did I?" Martin's words were firm but respectful.

"Well, no." Adam replied.

"You didn't break the law, Adam; I did. The real question is: Are you going to turn your back on this information and on those who can benefit from it?"

Adam was silent for a moment. He was caught in an ethical conundrum. As a Christian and a pastor, he was spiritually bound to be ethical in all his dealings; but here right and wrong melded into an indistinct whole. He looked at Rachel who merely shrugged her shoulders.

"I suppose," Adam said, "that I can refuse the information and feel guilty for not acting, or I can use the information and feel guilty about its acquisition. I'll go with the greater good." Then turning to Martin, he said, "You mentioned danger."

"Sure, Adam, think about it. Why would anyone kidnap several families whose only commonality is that they have experienced a miraculous healing?"

Adam shook his head, unable to come up with an answer. He looked to Rachel whose eyes widened in understanding. She raised a hand to her mouth and closed her eyes and, without opening them, quietly said, "Someone is probably using them for guinea pigs."

Adam's mind was suddenly filled with grotesque images of David Lorayne strapped to a table, while an unseen man with a rusty scalpel slowly cut open his chest.

"Who is the hospital contact?" Adam asked bluntly.

"My best guess is the man who has added $300,000 to his checking account since the first healing—Bill Sanchez."

"Bill Sanchez?" Rachel was nonplused. "Do you mean Bill Sanchez of security?"

"The very one."

Rachel was surprised. She had not considered the possibility of an "inside" man. The fact that he was the head of security disturbed her all the more.

"Anything else?" Adam asked.

"No," Martin replied. "I'll keep working on finding your Healer, but, to be honest, I don't have a great deal of information to work with."

"Thanks, Martin." Adam shook his hand and then, to Rachel, said, "I think we had better be going."

"Oh, no," Anna said as she appeared in the door. "I've just made some refreshments. Please stay and visit a while. We so seldom have friends in our home."

Rachel thanked her and numbly ascended the stairs.

"Now what?" Rachel asked Adam as they drove away from the St. James home two hours, four cups of coffee, and half a cake later. "Should we go to the police?"

Adam took Ardath Road to the I-52 on-ramp. "Perhaps, but I don't think it would do much good. The only evidence we have is that someone has been paying him large amounts of money. The police can question him, but without evidence of his involvement in a crime, they can't hold him. Let's not forget what you've said, that he's a former police officer himself—wounded in the line of duty at that. How about confronting Dr. Morgan with the information?"

"I don't know," Rachel said reluctantly. "He can be pretty irascible. Besides, Sanchez isn't the one we're after. We want the guy who's paying him. Still, we need to tell someone. What's that FBI agent's name?"

"Special Agent Norman Greene."

"Let's go to my place and call him. I'm sure he could do something."

"Okay, but then I have to go." Adam said. "I've got a big day on television tomorrow."

Adam felt uncomfortable being alone in Rachel's home. He had long ago established a policy of never being alone in a woman's quarters. Not so much because he feared temptation, but that he feared misunderstanding. Churches often attract hurting people who sometimes transfer affection to a kind authority figure like a pastor. Adam knew of several ministers whose careers had been hampered or even destroyed by unfounded allegations.

However, Adam trusted Rachel. She displayed no neurosis that might make a visit to her home professionally dangerous. After all, he was there only to make a phone call.

The interior of Rachel's apartment was far different than Adam expected. What it lacked in furniture, it made up for in plants. There were scores of them throughout the unit. Some hung from the ceiling, others sat on shelves, or on the floor.

Noticing Adam's distraction with the plants, Rachel said, "Plants make the perfect companions: they don't talk too much, eat too much, or get their feelings hurt."

"Do you mean I need to sprout roots to be your friend?"

"Not at all," Rachel said smiling. "You're different. You're not like anyone else I've ever known. There's a quality about you that I find … attractive."

"Please, you're making me blush."

"I'm serious." Rachel sat on the couch and motioned for Adam to sit next to her. "Not only are you intelligent, but you seem genuinely to care for those around you. Take that Jehovah's Witness woman today. We doctors tried everything we could to change her mind. You managed it in less than fifteen minutes. You really amaze me."

"Thanks for the kudos, but shouldn't we be making a phone call?" Adam was beginning to feel uncomfortable.

"In a minute," Rachel said. "I wanted to say first that, well, I'm sorry for blowing up at Martin's house. He was doing what he thought was right, and I shouldn't have spoken to him that way."

"Your privacy had been invaded. Anyone would have felt the same way; I know I would have."

"Perhaps, but I'd like to apologize anyway."

Adam looked at the woman on the couch with him. Each time he saw her he was more attracted to her. He suspected that he was falling in love. For most people that would be good news; for Adam it presented a problem. It wasn't that he feared a relationship with a woman—he had very nearly married twice—but Rachel was different. She was outside the faith. He was attracted to her, but she was an unbeliever; his life was dedicated to belief and those who believe. Yet, he couldn't dismiss her, for she had touched his soul. The bottom line was that Adam was confused. He needed time to think. And pray.

Slowly, almost imperceptibly at first, Rachel moved closer. Magnetically they brought their lips together. They kissed, slowly and gently. Adam's heart throbbed so hard he was sure it was audible to Rachel.

Breaking the embrace, Rachel stood and said, "The phone is on the end table. I'll be back in a few moments."

Numb from the unexpected kiss, Adam merely nodded his head. Pulling Agent Greene's card from his wallet, Adam dialed the number. After identifying himself to a receptionist, his call was forwarded. Adam glanced at his watch: it was 4:50.

"This is Agent Greene," a resonant voice said over the phone. "What can I do for you, Reverend?"

"I have some information that you may find interesting. However, I'm a little embarrassed to say that I can't tell you how I obtained the information."

"Well, let's hear it."

Adam repeated the information about Sanchez's bank account and the correlation between his deposits and the abductions.

"That's a pretty incredible accusation, Reverend. I'm not supposed to ask you how you got it?"

"That's right," Adam said. "I'm trying to protect a friend who may, for a noble purpose, have bent the rules a little."

"A little!" Greene laughed. "I didn't know you preachers were such a sneaky lot."

"We're full of surprises." Adam returned the laughter.

"All right, I'll check into it. Unlike your friend, I'll need a court order to look at his bank records, but that shouldn't be a problem. One other thing, Reverend; don't talk to anyone else about this. Sanchez may have other hospital people involved. You've done your part, now let me do mine."

"Agreed. You will keep me posted, won't you?"

"Of course." Greene abruptly hung up.

"Nothing to do now but wait." Adam heard Rachel's voice behind him.

"I guess so," Adam said, as he turned and looked over his shoulder. What he saw caught him completely off guard. He leaped from the couch. Standing before him was Rachel, in an elegant gossamer nightgown that set off her fair skin and dark hair to perfection. Adam attempted to speak, but only managed to stutter.

"My dear Adam," Rachel said seductively, "you look like you've seen a ghost. Do you like it?" Slowly, Rachel walked toward him.

# Twenty-Nine

## Tuesday, March 30; 5:05 P.M.

"Out!" Rachel screamed. "Get out!"

"Rachel, listen." Adam said softly.

"I want you out, right now!" Rachel's face was bright red.

Adam stood his ground. Grabbing her firmly by the shoulders he said, "I'll leave, but first you must listen to me. It is important that you understand."

Saying nothing, Rachel, glared through angry and embarrassed eyes at the man who had just spurned her.

"I am not rejecting you," Adam spoke softly. "There is no problem with you. You are very attractive—very alluring. God knows it is taking every bit of discipline I have to say no, but I must."

Tears rolled freely down Rachel's cheeks.

Adam continued, "I am flattered, but I still must say no. Not because I don't care for you, but because I do. Rachel, I am a minister; if I give in now, everything I've studied for, everything I believe will be wasted. Tomorrow I will be racked with guilt, and then what will our relationship be like? I know it sounds puritanical to you, but I cannot make love to you now, because it will ruin our friendship."

Rachel pulled away from him and hid her face in her hands.

"Rachel, I have feelings for you—strong feelings. Feelings I never expected. I am drawn to you. You occupy my thoughts day and night. Rachel, I honestly believe I'm falling in love with you, but I need time."

"I wanted to please you," Rachel said, fighting back the rising flood of tears. "I have never done this before in my life. You are the only man I have ever been attracted to, and oddly enough, I never wanted to be attracted to you. I should have known better than to become involved with an archaic Bible-thumper. This is the twentieth century, Adam. Wake up, or perhaps I should say, grow up."

"It was never my intention to hurt you."

"Well, you did!" Rachel snapped. "I feel like a fool!"

"I wish I knew what to do to make you understand," Adam said meekly.

"I'll tell you what to do, Adam. Leave now!" Rachel's tone had turned cold and hard.

Adam's heart skipped a beat. Without a word he turned and left.

Rachel walked to her bathroom, turned on the faucet, and splashed cold water on her face.

"I will not cry," she told herself. "He isn't worth it." A moment later she fell to her knees and sobbed uncontrollably.

Within fifteen minutes after Adam left, Rachel had washed her face and changed from the gown into a pair of jeans and blue sweatshirt with a Yale insignia. Five minutes after that she was careening down the freeway, releasing her anger in aggressive driving. Only San Diego's massive freeway system and understaffed Highway Patrol kept her from being stopped for reckless driving. Within ten minutes she slowed to the speed limit, moved to the right lane of I-8 and took the I-805 north turnoff.

*He's not worth getting killed over*, she thought. *After all, he's just a man.* She let that thought marinate in her mind. Was he just a man? Or was he something more to her? If she wasn't attracted to him, then why did she act like such an imbecile? And if she felt nothing for him, then why was she so upset?

"It's time for a long conversation with yourself," Rachel said aloud. "There are a few things we need to get worked out." Without thought of where she was going, Rachel continued up the I-805 to I-52. Before she was conscious of the fact, she found herself driving the narrow streets of La Jolla headed for La Jolla Cove, the place where she shared a hot dog with Adam.

In what many San Diegans would consider fortune just short of a miracle, she found a parking place right in front of the park next to La Jolla Cove. Several people strolling along the green grass gawked at the antique T-Bird she drove. Taking the parking place as an omen, Rachel left the car and began walking the serpentine concrete walk, pausing from time to time to gaze at the ocean as it cast its churning waves onto the shore. The cool salt air and setting sun proved a natural sedative. With hands behind her back she walked along the walk, then through the grass and back to the beginning of the walk again. She circled the small park four times while she thought about herself and Adam.

At first she was angry with Adam for spurning her. She reminded herself of what Shakespeare had said, "Hell hath no fury like a woman scorned." She smiled at that thought. Then she was angry with herself for being so foolish to begin with. *What was I thinking?* she asked. *Did I really think that I could seduce a preacher? And why was I so angry when he rejected me—no, he didn't reject me, he . . . he . . .* she paused to search for the right phrase. . . *he did what was right. Of course, what else could I expect?*

Rachel thought about the man named Adam Bridger. At first he had seemed a superstitious cleric who clutched onto God because the world was too difficult to face. But now she knew that he was a man with a keen intellect and a heart for people. He proved that several times, but never more than the kind, yet firm, way he dealt with that Jehovah's Witness woman. Now he has shown himself to be a man of both character and conviction. *Just how many men like that are there in the world? And how many of them would be interested in an opinionated, quick-tempered doctor?*

There was a great deal to Adam that she didn't understand. He carried himself with a confidence and assurance that few possessed, and that she didn't possess despite her usual intense manner. There seemed to be a well of strength and wisdom. Somehow she knew that well must be connected to Adam's God. Rachel had never had any use for religion and she knew very little about it. Her father's atheism was a source of pride for him, and something he attempted to instill in his daughter. Her mother, who spent her entire married life cowering in the shadow of Rachel's father, offered no opinion on the matter, or any other subject. Rachel loved her mother, but despised her servant role in the home and determined at an early age to be nobody's second. As much as she loved her father, she hated his domineering personality, always saying what was on his mind regardless of whose feelings it hurt. Yet she still admired the man who created in her a love for medicine as he loved medicine. It was that admiration for her father's strength and a fear of her mother's meekness that made Rachel who she was: strong, forceful, and quick to share what was on her mind. In many ways she had become her father, and she both hated and appreciated that.

God was never spoken of in her home except to list reasons why He did not exist. Rachel took such pronouncements from her father as fact, without supplying any of her own thoughts to the matter. Now she was attracted to a man who saw all of life through eyes of faith and belief. Adam was a man whose beliefs were easily seen and not just heard. Rachel came to understand that without faith there would be no Adam, at least not the Adam she knew.

*What if Adam is right and my father wrong?* she asked herself. *What if all that Adam believes is true?* The thought proved sobering for Rachel—sobering and frightening. She didn't know how to answer the question because she knew nothing about God or faith. She knew only medicine and that had proved incapable of making her a better person or a happy one.

The sun was beginning its slow slide into the ocean, leaving the sky scarlet with streaks of red. Looking back down the walk, Rachel saw the hot dog stand where Adam had taken her for "dinner." The owner of the stand was packing away the condiments as Rachel approached him.

"Is it too late to buy a hot dog?" she asked.

"Almost, but for you I'll stay open a little longer," the vendor said. He was a large, olive-skinned man in a red-and-white checkered apron. "What'll it be?"

Rachel thought for a second then said, "A chili dog with extra onions."

"Food of the gods," the man said.

"A friend recommends it," Rachel said through a big smile. It was neither the hot dog nor the man that made her smile; it was the remembrance of the last time she ate a chili dog here, and the recollection of the man who bought it for her. She knew now what she would do: she would eat her hot dog while walking around the park one more time, then go home, call Adam, apologize profusely, and ask to see him again. And when she did see him, she would be open to anything—spiritual or otherwise—that he had to say. For the first time in Rachel's memory she felt good—really, really good.

"Excuse me," a voice said behind her, "aren't you Dr. Rachel Tremaine?"

Turning, she saw a man with a goatee. "Yes, who are you?"

"That'll be $2.50," the vendor said.

"Please allow me," the goateed man said, pulling a wad of bills from his pocket, peeling off a five and handing it to the man in the checked apron. "Keep the change." Then, taking Rachel by the elbow, he began to lead her to a dark sedan parked alongside a red curb reserved for emergency vehicles. "It's important that I talk to you," he said. "It's about Reverend Adam Bridger."

"Adam?"

"Yes. He needs to speak to you right away."

"Who are you?" Rachel asked again.

Looking over his shoulder, the stranger saw that they had walked about twenty feet away from the hot dog cart. "Please get in the car," he said forcefully.

"I don't think I want to do that," Rachel said, making no attempt to hide her annoyance. "And what is this about Adam?"

"Just get in the car and don't make a fuss."

"Forget it," Rachel said, pulling herself free. "I don't know who you think you are ..." She stopped mid-sentence. She knew who they were: the abductors, and the car at the curb was the one that had followed her a day before. The man with the goatee pulled his coat back, revealing a revolver. Rachel knew nothing about guns but did know that her life was in danger. She suddenly felt helpless and alone. She didn't know what to do, so she acted on impulse: she screamed.

Her captor acted quickly, reaching out and seizing her sweatshirt. Then with incredible strength and agility, he dragged her the remaining few feet to the dark sedan and threw her in the open back door, stepping in behind her.

"Hey," the vendor cried out, but too late. In just a few seconds the goateed man had snatched Rachel from the sidewalk and thrust her into the car which sped away with tires squealing. All that remained of Rachel's stroll at the beach was a hot dog with its topping of chili streaking the sidewalk.

## Wednesday, March 31; 7:15 A.M.

Adam drove slowly, not because he was punctilious about traffic laws, but because he had much to think about.

After a restless night, Adam had risen early to review his notes for the "Milt Phillips' Show." Yet, he found it difficult to concentrate on anything but Rachel and last night's incident. He replayed the scene over and over in his mind. He knew he was right in refusing her advances, but he wondered if he could have done so in a better, less hurtful way. How could doing right feel so wrong? He could still see the shock on her face when he said no; the hot stream of tears running down her face. Adam was as miserable as he had ever been.

"This seat taken?" a jovial voice asked.

"It's good to see you, Dick," Adam said, motioning to the empty bench seat on the opposite side of the table. Adam had asked Dick to meet him at the local Denny's restaurant.

"Well, it sounded important." Dick turned toward the waitress, raised one finger and silently mouthed the word "coffee." The waitress nodded.

"I hope I'm not making you late for work," Adam said quietly.

"I own the trucking firm," Dick said with a broad grin. "I can be late anytime I want."

The waitress brought the coffee and a menu to Dick who waved it off and quickly ordered bacon and eggs, the same breakfast he ate nearly every day. Adam declined breakfast saying he would just have coffee. "I hope you have good news about the Loraynes."

Adam shook his head. "I wish I did, but the police have discovered nothing, and we're no closer to understanding the Healer thing than when it all started. I have to admit it's starting to weigh on me."

"I know," Dick said, taking a sip of his coffee. "Some of us at the church are worried about you."

"I'm okay, but I could use a little . . . advice." Adam's words came out haltingly.

"About the Loraynes?" Dick asked.

"Uh, no."

"If it's about this television show you're doing today, then I'm afraid I can't be of much use."

"No, it's not that at all."

Dick could clearly see that his pastor was uncomfortable. He also knew that asking for advice, even from a close friend, was a difficult thing for Adam to do.

"It's . . . it's of a personal nature," Adam said.

"Look," Dick said, "why don't you just spit it out? We're friends. I'll stand by you and do whatever I can."

Adam took a long, deep breath and said: "It's about Rachel Tremaine."

"Wait, I know that name."

"Dr. Rachel Tremaine—she performed my surgery."

"Oh, yes, now I remember." Dick said smiling, "You told me she gave you a pretty bad time about being a preacher."

"That's the one, but I've discovered that there's a lot more to her."

"Oh?" Dick replied, leaning back in the booth and raising an eyebrow.

"Let me start from the beginning." Adam relayed the events of the last few days. He spoke of the investigation, the walk at La Jolla Cove, and Rachel's offer last night. As Adam finished, the waitress brought Dick's breakfast. Dick closed his eyes and rubbed the bridge of his nose. Adam couldn't tell if he was thinking or marshaling his concentration to stifle his urge to laugh.

"Let me get this right," Dick said. "You go into her home to use the phone, you kiss for a moment, and then while you're making your call, she comes out in a nightgown."

"That's right," Adam said, looking down into his coffee cup to avoid eye contact.

Dick said nothing for a moment. Then with a broad grin he said, "My pastor—the lady-killer. Don't let Mrs. Bachelder hear of this."

"She won't hear it from me."

"She won't hear from this side of the table either." Dick grinned again. "I'm sorry, Pastor, it's just not every day that a man hears that women try to seduce their preacher."

"This is the first time, and I hope it's the last," Adam said defensively.

"Well, for what it's worth, I think you did the right thing and showed more strength than most men could—preacher or not."

"I don't feel strong; I just feel confused."

"It sounds like you have feelings for this woman," Dick said.

Adam sat quietly and turned his empty coffee cup on the table. "Yes, I think I do. That brings about a whole new set of problems, doesn't it?"

"What do you mean?" Dick asked.

"Well, she's not a believer. In fact, I think she may be an atheist."

"And so you think that a relationship between you two wouldn't work out."

"That's what I've been teaching our church, especially our youth. We should avoid being unequally yoked."

"Talk to her."

Adam looked puzzled, "Talk to her?"

"Sure. Look, how do you know that God didn't put her in your path to solve two problems: companionship for you and salvation for her? For all you know, you're supposed to fall in love."

Adam blinked hard. "But I don't see how . . . I mean . . ."

"You amaze me, Pastor. How can you be so talented and not see that talent yourself? Talk to her. If anyone can show her the truth, you can. Do you remember that time we were downtown and we came across the police attempting to stop a suicide? You identified yourself as a minister and offered to help. Do you remember that?"

"Of course. The man's wife had left him and took the kids with her. He had a gun to his head and was standing in the middle of Broadway."

"And what did you do?" Dick asked pointedly.

"The police let me talk to him and he gave up his gun."

"Exactly. But not only did you convince him not to kill himself, but you even had him laughing. It was incredible, you and this guy standing in the street surrounded by the police, and you're telling jokes—and he's laughing."

"Well, that was different."

Dick chuckled. "No, it wasn't. Adam, you're the most persuasive man I know. You can do things with words that are unbelievable. You're blessed in that way, and that's not just my opinion. I could bring dozens of people from the church in here and they'd tell you the same thing."

"So, what's your point?"

"My point is this: stop feeling guilty for being attracted to a woman. Talk to her. Tell her the truth about your beliefs, and your feelings, and then let God do the rest."

"It seems too simple."

"It is, and that's why you're overlooking it. You've been through a lot lately and maybe the simple things are getting by you. Trust me, just talk to her. She'll see the light, and if she doesn't, then at least you'll know where you stand."

"But after last night, she may not want to talk to me," Adam said with concern.

"She will, and if she doesn't, then make her want to talk to you."

Adam leaned back and thought. Could it be that simple? It sounded exactly like advice he had given others in similar situations over the years. Apparently, he was too close to the situation to see the obvious.

"Thanks, Dick," Adam said smiling. "I think I'll do just that. As soon as I get back from L.A., I'll call her and we'll have that talk. I appreciate your help."

"Do you appreciate it enough to pay for my breakfast?" Dick asked and then laughed.

Adam joined the laughter.

It took just over two hours for Adam to arrive in L.A. It took another thirty minutes to find the studio where the show would be taped. Identifying himself to a young security guard, he was directed to the guest parking. From there it was a short walk to the studio's reception area where a young man led him to the makeup room.

A matronly woman dabbed powder on his face and combed his hair. Adam noticed that he was the only one in the room.

"Am I the first here?" Adam asked.

"Oh, no," the woman said. "The rest have already been through. You're the last."

"I'm not late, am I?" Adam was suddenly concerned that he had misunderstood the time he was to be there.

"No. They don't start taping until 1. Mr. Phillips wanted to meet with a couple of the guests beforehand."

Adam wondered why he had been excluded, but then decided he was being paranoid. A short time later Adam was led to the set.

The set was different than the one normally used by the "Milt Phillips' Show." Instead of the typical setup with a large desk and several chairs in a row, there were four chairs set in a semicircle around a large glass coffee table. Adam was shown where to sit on the stage.

"The director and Mr. Phillips will be here shortly," his escort said.

For twenty minutes Adam sat alone on the set feeling rather conspicuous. Cameramen and technicians began arriving and positioning equipment.

"You must be Reverend Bridger," a loud voice said from nowhere.

Adam looked around to see who had spoken but saw no one nearby. The cameramen continued to ignore him as they went about their duties.

"I'm in the control booth, Reverend," the voice said. "Look up and to your left."

Adam did as he was told. On the next floor above and behind a glass wall stood a man waving. The man wore a headset.

"Go ahead and speak," the man said. "The set is wired for sound."

"Yes, I'm Adam Bridger," he said, feeling a little self-conscious at speaking to the empty room.

"Good. I'm Jerry Williams, the director. Margo, the floor director, and the rest of the folks should be with you in a minute, so just make yourself comfortable. Can I get you some coffee?"

"No thanks. I'm fine."

"Great. We'll be starting soon. Margo will get your mike and whatever else you need."

True to the director's word, a side door opened and a line of people entered the set. Adam recognized two of them—Milt Phillips and Dr. Charles Cruden. Three others entered whom Adam did not recognize: an extremely tall, thin woman with blond hair; another woman wearing jeans and a T-shirt, and a squat man in a three-piece suit. The five of them walked directly to the set.

"Reverend Bridger?"

"Yes, Mr. Phillips," Adam said cordially. "I'm pleased to meet you."

"And I you." Phillips shook Adam's hand. "Let me make some introductions. This is Dr. Charles Cruden, our astrophysicist for the program. This lovely young lady," he said, motioning to the tall woman, "is Amelia Larsons. She teaches New Age philosophy. Over here is Dr. Robert Jennings, a local psychiatrist. Finally, let me introduce Margo, our floor director. Let's have a seat and talk about today's show."

Adam took the seat he had been assigned and watched as the others did the same. Adam thought the seating arrangement had been established with some purpose in mind. He could only guess as to the reasons. Phillips sat in the center. To his left was Dr. Cruden, and to Dr. Cruden's left Jennings. Adam sat to the immediate right of Phillips, and Amelia to Adam's right.

"As you all know, our show deals with modern-day miracles," Phillips said. As he spoke, Margo scurried about clipping lapel microphones to everyone. "The program will be an open forum with dialogue being shared by you folks. I will ask some questions to get us started and will moderate the show. During the last portion of the show, we will take questions from the audience. I hope you will all feel free to say what's on your mind. Any questions?"

"Audience?" Adam hadn't thought about an audience being present.

"Yes," Phillips said. "They're being seated now." Adam looked up and saw that a small crowd was being ushered into the studio.

"Any other questions?"

"Yes," Adam said. "When will I be able to make my appeal?"

"Oh, yes," Phillips said. "You made that a contingency, didn't you? Well, we'll save some time for you at the end of the program."

"Three minutes to taping," the director said from overhead.

Everyone waited in silence for the cue from the floor director. Suddenly, Margo held up five fingers that signaled five seconds left before the taping began. The show's theme song filled the room. With each passing second she brought one finger down until only one remained with which she abruptly pointed at Phillips.

"Good evening," Phillips said, smiling. "Tonight, we are doing something different on our show: we are having an open discussion on modern-day miracles. Recently, our newspapers have been filled with fantastic stories of miraculous healings in the San Diego area. Stories of burn victims, cancer patients, and others, suddenly being returned to health.

"To help us in our discussion," Phillips continued, "is the eminent astrophysicist Dr. Charles Cruden of the Jet Propulsion Laboratories in Pasadena; Dr. Robert Jennings, a psychiatrist in private practice and author of *Real World Living*; Reverend Adam Bridger of the Maple Street Community Church in San Diego and pastor to one of the individuals allegedly healed. Also with us today is writer and New Age teacher Amelia Larsons."

Monitors mounted out of camera range allowed Adam to see what was being recorded. As each individual was introduced, a closeup of their face appeared on the monitor.

"Reverend Bridger," Phillips said, turning to face Adam, "you are close to the events at Kingston Memorial Hospital, and I understand that you're helping in the investigation. Just what's going on down there?"

Adam cleared his throat nervously. "Actually, I'm not an official part of any investigation. I'm involved because one of my members was healed and later mysteriously disappeared."

"Tell us what happened to your church member—a Mr. Lorayne, isn't it?"

"Yes," Adam said. "David Lorayne was admitted to the hospital for surgery. Although the surgery went well, David slipped into a deep coma. He began to quickly waste away; his heartbeat became very irregular and his breathing labored. The doctors had doubts that he would live through the night."

"Then what happened?" Phillips prodded.

"I was in the hospital to visit with the family. I had just been in the room with David and his wife, but had left to talk to the rest of the family. When I returned, David was sitting up in bed talking."

"So, he just woke up?" Phillips asked.

"Actually, there's more to it than that. Had he just awakened, we would have said that he simply came out of the coma. However, there was something else that took us all aback."

"What was that?"

"As I said earlier, he had gone in for surgery. After his sudden awakening, the doctors examined him. What shocked them the most was that his surgical incision was gone."

Several in the audience gasped.

"Gone?" Phillips asked.

"Yes. I was there. There was no sign that an incision had ever been made."

"And you expect us to believe all this?" Cruden said sarcastically.

Since Adam was aware of Cruden's acerbic nature, he wasn't surprised by the sudden sarcasm. "Actually," Adam said smoothly, "I have no expectation of you at all. I was asked to tell what happened and I have done so. What you believe or don't believe is entirely up to you."

"I, for one, choose not to believe this fairy tale," Cruden remarked coldly.

"Why?" Phillips asked.

"Because surgical scars simply don't disappear. It is impossible."

"Why is it impossible?" Phillips prodded.

"Because it defies known laws of nature. It is too much to believe."

"How would you explain it, then?" Phillips asked.

"Without a reliable investigation, it would be hard to say, but it could be many things: a promotional gimmick, hysteria, a mix-up in hospital records."

"Each of your suggestions is equally unbelievable," Adam interjected. "The nurses had changed his dressing several times and each time they saw the surgical incision. And let's not forget his wife who was with David immediately before his surgery, and with him continually after. No, in the case of David Lorayne, something supernatural happened."

"A miracle?" Cruden's sarcasm was evident to all. "I'm afraid I don't believe in miracles, Reverend Bridger. I don't believe in your God, or anyone else's God. I am an empiricist. I believe only in that which is tangible."

A few in the audience applauded. Someone shouted, "Right on!"

"In other words," Adam said, his voice even and controlled, "you only believe in what can be perceived through the five senses."

"Exactly. All things are rational and measurable."

"Well," Adam said smiling, "I don't think you really believe that. In fact, I think you believe in many intangibles."

"Such as?"

"Such as emotion," Adam said matter-of-factly. "You see, Dr. Cruden, not all things are measurable. Take love, for example. Not even the most ardent empiricist would deny that love exists, yet it defies measurement. Can one have a quart of love? Or, a pound of anger? Could you, for example, amass fifty yards of joy? Of course not, yet each of us has experienced these qualities."

Many in the audience laughed. Dr. Cruden's face turned crimson red.

"Wait a minute," Dr. Cruden said pointedly. "I can measure anger. When a person becomes angry their heart rate increases, the amount of adrenaline in their system increases and, if they're angry enough, their face may become red as the capillaries expand and raise the skin's surface temperature."

"But you've not measured anger," Adam countered. "You've described only the physical results of anger, and that is the true role of experimental science, describing results. Really, all that science does through its observations and experimentation is to describe the fingerprints of God."

"But I've already told you that I don't believe in God."

"What you believe is immaterial to truth. Disbelief does not change reality. You and I may drive down the road in my car and, at great speed, head directly for a large tree. Now you and I could sit in that car as it speeds toward the tree and say that we don't believe we will get hurt; but the truth of the matter is that when we slam into the tree, we will probably die. At which point your belief in God will be of particular importance."

A few in the audience applauded again.

"Before we go on," Phillips said, turning to the camera, "we need to take a commercial break." The red light on the camera went off. "Excellent, people, excellent. Keep up this intensity, and we will have an exceptional show."

Cruden said nothing. He had underestimated this preacher. Adam was proving a worthy intellectual opponent, something on which he had not planned. Cruden decided that he would have to be very careful. He didn't want to be shown up.

"Ten seconds to air time," Margo said. Ten seconds later one of the camera's red lights came on.

"We're back with a fascinating discussion on miracles," Phillips said to the camera. "In a few moments, we will be going into the audience to hear what they have to say; but for now, let's return to our panel. Reverend Bridger, perhaps you could tell us exactly what a miracle is."

"I suppose there are many definitions that could be used, but a good definition would be something like this: A miracle is a supernatural event that achieves some useful purpose and reveals the presence and power of God."

"So there is purpose to a miracle?" Phillips asked.

"Yes. Take the miracles of Jesus. The Bible records thirty-five miracles that Jesus performed. This is not to say that Jesus performed only thirty-five miracles, but that of the miracles He performed, thirty-five were recorded. Of those recorded miracles, nine showed power over nature: walking on the water, turning water into wine in the city of Cana, stilling a storm on the Sea of Galilee, and so on. He also performed six exorcisms, and three times He raised the dead. The vast majority of Jesus' miracles dealt with healings. Seventeen times it is said that Jesus healed. Almost all of Jesus' miracles dealt with human suffering."

Cruden remarked, "I'm sure you know that many of the miracles in the Bible have been shown to be impossible."

"They're all impossible," Adam said. "That's why we call them miracles."

The audience roared with laughter.

"What I'm saying, Reverend Bridger, is that certain miracles can scientifically be shown to have never occurred."

"I'd like to hear this," Phillips said.

Cruden continued, "Take, for example, the story of Joshua's prayer that the sun would stand still in the sky so that he might carry on a battle. As we all know, it is the earth's spin on its axis that makes the sun appear to rise and set. So, for the sun to stop in the sky, the earth must cease its rotation."

Cruden was speaking as though he were lecturing a class of freshmen in basic astronomy, a class he taught while in graduate school.

"Suppose that this God of yours decides to help Joshua out by stopping the earth's rotation. What would we find? Well, first of all, since the earth spins at 66,600 miles per hour, if the earth were to stop its spinning suddenly, then all those things not securely attached would fly off at the same 66,600 miles an hour. We call that inertia. Your Joshua and everyone else on the planet would go careening into trees, mountains and the like. Also, things like cave stalagmites and stalactites, many of which date past the age of Joshua, would be broken off in their caves; but when we visit the caves of the world, we find those geological formations resting comfortably in their places."

Cruden continued. "But that's not all. We can show through mathematics and physics that if the earth stopped spinning on its axis, it would generate enough heat to boil water. No one could live through such temperatures."

Phillips turned to Adam. "Well, Reverend Bridger, what do you make of that? Do you dispute Dr. Cruden's conclusions?"

"No." Adam said flatly.

Phillips was surprised. "So you agree that such a miracle could not have taken place?"

"Not at all. It is not his conclusions that are at fault, but, rather, his initial assumption." Adam turned his attention to Cruden. "You see, Dr. Cruden, you began your discussion with the assumption that there was a God who was powerful enough to stop the earth's spin, and that that same God was motivated to do so. Is that not true?"

"Yes," Cruden said tentatively.

"I'm afraid you don't give that God much credit. If God is capable of doing such a great feat, and reasonable enough to want to do so, then doesn't it also follow that God would take into account the problems such an act would have? You see, the Joshua miracle is more than one miracle. God not only stopped the earth's spin, but also allowed for the results of such an act and accounted for them. The God of the Bible would not stop the earth from spinning and then snap His fingers and say, 'Oops' when people began crashing into trees and hills. If you allow a God powerful enough and intelligent enough to be able to perform such a feat, then you also must allow for a God who is intelligent enough to compensate for difficulties caused by His act of power."

The stage was silent. A moment later Phillips said, "We'll be right back after these messages."

Phillips directed questions to the psychiatrist, Dr. Robert Jennings, who spoke of the mind's ability to make one well or ill, and insinuated that the healings were a result of psychological processes. Phillips asked how so many occurrences could happen in the same hospital and at about the same time. Jennings had no answer. Phillips further asked how surgical scars and scorched flesh could be simply willed away, and again Jennings had no answer.

Adam had to agree with Phillips. "We're not dealing with psychosomatic illnesses. The people healed have had dramatic reversals of illness and trauma."

"The mind is a powerful thing, Reverend Bridger," Jennings said. "Certain Eastern mystics are able to control their breathing and heart rate in an incredible fashion. I have personally witnessed a practitioner of Eastern meditation enter a three-foot-square acrylic box, place himself in a hypnotic suspended animation, and then have the box anchored and submerged in a swimming pool for nearly half an hour. When brought back to the surface, he slowly climbed out of the cube and was none the worse for wear. Now, those who lack training might assume that the man worked a miracle."

"I'll agree that the mind is a wonderful and powerful thing," Adam replied. "I also agree that we have much to learn about its operation and powers, but all your mystic did was control certain biological functions—granted to a marvelous degree—but he did not exchange scorched flesh for whole. He did not turn a body rendered nearly useless by cerebral palsy into a normally functioning one as we have seen recently. No, we are not dealing with psychosomatic workings; we are seeing a genuine miracle. These are miracles I can't explain, but they are miracles."

"That's superstitious hogwash," Cruden snapped. "And if I weren't on television and in the presence of ladies, I would describe in more colorful terms."

Amelia Larsons spoke for the first time: "Don't restrain yourself on my account. Not only could I endure your colorful language, I might even be able to use enough of my own to put a tinge of red in your checks." The crowd laughed uproariously. Adam had to work at not laughing out loud himself.

"Tell us, Ms. Larsons," Phillips said, "just what is your take on all of this?"

Smiling, Amelia responded, "Well, I have to agree with Reverend Bridger: miracles can and do happen. You see, the universe is filled with energy, and each of us can tap into that energy. By learning some of the ancient principles taught to us by spiritual people of eons ago, plus what we learn new every day, we can harness the healing force of the universe. It hinges on getting in touch with ourselves and our past selves—I mean our former lives. The people in San Diego have learned to let the tides of the universe flow through them: ebb and flow and flow and ebb. Perhaps this is the dawning of a new and enlightened age."

Her comment was greeted with silence and stunned silence. After a moment Phillips said to Adam, "So you and Amelia are in basic agreement?"

Adam looked at Amelia, then at Phillips. He then looked at Dr. Cruden who surrendered a small smile. Adam blinked several times trying to make sense of Amelia's statements, then said, "I don't think we are in agreement. We both believe in miracles, but my belief is in biblical miracles: God using His power to achieve a holy end. The source of the miracle is not an impersonal force to be tapped into like someone harvesting syrup from a maple tree. Besides, these people who have been healed were healed unexpectedly. Two were unconscious at the time and the other two were awakened from a sleep and saw a man standing over them. No, someone is the Healer."

Cruden spoke up, "It all sounds like nonsense to me. It's all basically the same mumbo jumbo."

"We are all spiritual beings," Amelia said. "Reverend Bridger's views may be a little narrow and biased, but he is right when he says that miracles happen."

Adam looked at Amelia for a moment. She gave him a quick smile and a knowing wink. He knew she was trying to be helpful and to divide the panel into "those wooden-headed scientists" against "we enlightened spiritual leaders," but he didn't want his words and beliefs confused with hers. To some they must have seemed very much alike, when they couldn't have been any further apart.

Phillips stepped into the audience for questions and comments. The crowd seemed evenly divided between rationalists and believers. One man accused Adam of propagating myth and preying on the weak-minded for pecuniary gain; he was booed into silence.

Several questions were directed to the other guests, but center stage clearly belonged to Adam and Dr. Cruden, with Cruden dominating the taping with rapid-fire questions and a fountain of facts. Fifty minutes and six commercial breaks later, Phillips turned to face the camera: "Reverend Bridger has asked for a few moments at the end of the program to deliver a very special message. We now allow him that time."

Adam looked directly into the camera and spoke in even, somber tones.

"Regardless of the various views put forth here, one fact remains concerning the healings at Kingston Memorial Hospital: someone is abducting patients who have been healed. My statement today is short and very simple. If the abductor of these innocent people is listening, I plead with you; please release them.

"By now, I'm sure you are aware that they can tell you nothing of value. Their healings are as mysterious to them as they are to the rest of us. I don't know what it is you want, but surely these people can be of no service to you. Please, I beg of you, release the hostages.

If need be, you can contact me at Maple Street Community Church in San Diego. I will do whatever I can to obtain the release of those you hold. Call me. You can trust me."

Adam sat back in his chair signaling the end of his speech. The set was quiet for a moment. Then Phillips spoke. "I think we all can say 'Amen,' to that, Reverend." Then, to the camera, "This has been the 'Milt Phillips Show.' Thank you for joining us."

The show's theme began to play in the background. A moment later the red light on the camera blinked out.

"That's it, folks," Margo shouted to the workers. "Let's wrap it up."

Dr. Cruden walked over to Adam and shook his hand.

"Well, Reverend, you have made a worthy opponent. It is obvious that we have some serious disagreements, but those notwithstanding, I hope you get your people back." Despite Cruden's kind words, it was obvious that he was angry.

"Thank you," Adam replied simply.

The others gathered around to offer support and best wishes. Then, one by one, they left to go back to their own worlds. Adam wondered if all of this had done any good. Alone, he left the stage and the studio and began the two-hour drive home.

# Thirty

## Wednesday, March 31; 4 P.M.

Adam arrived home shortly after 4 that afternoon. The taping of the "Milt Phillips Show" was done earlier than usual, allowing Adam to start home while the other guests attended a post-show party. Adam had been in no mood to party. He had taken his time driving back, allowing his mind to mull over the events of recent days. Wearied from his trip to Los Angeles and still depressed over the exchange with Rachel the night before, Adam desired only a quiet evening and a good night's sleep.

Entering his home, he was greeted with a flashing light on his answering machine. He sighed and punched the button.

"Pastor, this is Fannie," the recorded voice said. "Call me as soon as you get in. It's urgent. I'll be leaving the office at 3, so call me at home."

For a moment, Adam considered ignoring the request, but decided that weariness was easier to endure than guilt. Fannie wouldn't have said it was urgent unless it was a matter of importance. He dialed her home number.

"Oh, I'm so glad you called, Pastor," Fannie said. "A man from the police station has called several times today. I told him I didn't know what time you'd be back. He was very insistent."

"Do you remember his name?" Adam asked.

"Yes. Detective Art McGinnes."

"Did he say what he wanted?"

"No, only that you should call him as soon as you got back."

"All right. Give me the number."

Fannie recited the number and then said, "I hope nothing's wrong. Maybe they've found the Loraynes."

"We'll soon know," Adam said. "I'll see you in the office tomorrow."

Adam dialed the number he had been given. A man answered the phone.

"Homicide. Detective Alan speaking."

"This is Adam Bridger. May I speak to Detective McGinnes, please?"

"He's not here. Can I take a mess . . . Wait a minute. What did you say your name was?"

"Adam Bridger."

"Reverend Bridger?"

"Yes."

"Hold on, I've got a message for you."

Over the phone, Adam could hear papers rustling.

"Here it is. Are you in San Diego now?"

"Yes. I just arrived."

"Detective McGinnes wants to see you right away. Do you know where Grossmont Hill is?"

"I've been there a couple of times."

"Good. McGinnes wants you to meet him there. You got a piece of paper?"

"Yes, go ahead."

The detective recited an address. Adam recognized it as being in a well-to-do neighborhood of the Grossmont district which overlooked much of San Diego.

"You leaving right now?" the detective asked.

"Yes, in a few minutes."

"Good. I'll radio McGinnes that you are on your way."

"Do you know what all this is about?" Adam asked.

"All I know, Reverend, is that someone has been killed. I don't know who."

Adam slowly hung up the phone. His stomach twisted within him. Had they found the Loraynes—dead? Or had someone else been killed? There was only one way of finding out.

It took twenty-five minutes for Adam to work his way through traffic to the address he had been given. Once there, he saw several police cars parked by the curb and uniformed officers standing nearby. A yellow plastic ribbon was stretched on stands across the front yard. Words in large black letters, Crime Scene—Do Not Cross—SDPD, were repeated for the entire length of the band. A crowd milled next to the barricade under the scrutiny of several uniformed officers. Adam noticed several television vans parked nearby.

Walking up to one of the uniformed officers, Adam asked to be led to Detective McGinnes.

"Are you with the press?" the officer asked.

"No. McGinnes asked to see me."

Satisfied, the officer walked under the barricade and into the house. From the opulent exterior Adam could tell the house was expensive. The white stucco, two-story home had a Spanish design.

A moment later, McGinnes stepped through the door and motioned for Adam to come in.

"I've been trying to reach you all afternoon," McGinnes said.

"I've been in the Los Angeles area taping a television show."

"You gonna become one of those TV evangelists?"

Adam chuckled. "Hardly. I was asked to be a guest on the "Milt Phillips Show." He's doing a special on the healings and miracles in general."

"I wish I could have seen it," McGinnes said.

"You still can," Adam replied. "It doesn't air until tonight."

"I'm afraid I'm going to be busy most of the night." Motioning with his head, McGinnes said, "I want you to see something."

Stepping through the foyer and into an expansive living room, Adam suddenly retched with nausea. On the white walls were sprays of blood. On the floor was the tape outline of a body; near the head, a large, dark, moist spot stained the powder-blue carpet. Another taped figure portrayed a man on the floor leaning against the wall. The wall behind the figure was bathed in brownish red. Police technicians milled around gathering evidence and taking photos.

"Do you know whose house this is, Reverend?"

Adam shook his head, afraid that if he spoke he would lose control of his stomach.

"It's the Gowans. You remember them, don't you?"

"Yes, of course," Adam said quietly. "I met them at the hospital. Who are the . . . the . . ." Adam pointed at the outline figures.

"Victims? Two security guards that the Gowans had hired. It's not exactly clear what happened, but it looks like the one on the floor was shot in the back of the head, and the one next to the wall was shot while trying to stop the abduction. We found his gun in the corner where he must have thrown it when he was shot. Poor guy, he took two shots in the throat and three in the abdomen before he died. We won't know for sure until the reports are in, but it looks like they used automatic weapons, AK-47's or maybe an Uzi, no doubt illegally modified to fire as a full automatic. Sure made a mess."

"Can we go outside?" Adam's nausea was growing.

"Oh, sure. Sorry, Reverend, I didn't realize. I get kinda' used to these things. I remember my first murder scene; I turned the same shade of white as you."

Adam wiped the beads of perspiration from his forehead with the sleeve of his shirt. "Any word on the Gowans?"

"Nothing. The good news is that their bodies are not in the house; they must still be alive."

"Abducted like the others?"

"Most likely." When the color had returned to the minister's face, he continued, "I wanted you to see this for a reason. You and your doctor friend have been playing detective with this Healer thing, and you need to know that this is big league."

"I don't understand."

"You're in over your head here, Reverend. People are getting killed as well as kidnapped. I want you to stay out of it. You may be in danger."

"I'm not what they're looking for," Adam said matter-of-factly. "I don't see how I can be threatened."

"Just keep alert and out of the way. Go on vacation or something."

Vacation sounded good to Adam. He was emotionally and physically exhausted. His work at the church was suffering. But somehow, he just couldn't let go, couldn't release the Loraynes, or the mystery.

"I'll be careful," Adam said.

A uniformed officer walked over and said to McGinnes, "The station wants you to call. They have some information for you."

McGinnes went back into the house. A few moments later he returned, his face hard and somber.

"What is it?" Adam asked softly. "Word about the Gowans?"

The detective slowly shook his head and said solemnly, "It's Dr. Tremaine. She was abducted at La Jolla Cove. An elderly couple saw the abduction and several others witnessed the event, but didn't see enough to be of much help. There was one good eyewitness though: a man operating a hot dog stand. She was buying a hot dog when a man approached her and led her away."

"How can they be sure it's Rachel?" Adam asked.

"The hot dog vendor heard one of the men call her by name."

Adam said nothing. His stomach churned, his pulse raced, and his knees were shaky. He felt like weeping and screaming in anger all at once. Instead, he walked slowly to his car and drove away. Preoccupied as he was with his thoughts, Adam didn't see the man in the crowd, the only one in the crowd who watched him instead of the police; a man with eyes filled with concern and sorrow; a man who arrived too late to help or to heal.

Adam sat alone in his office. He had kept the mini blinds shut, blocking out the outside world. The silence of his office was a balm to his active mind and overwrought emotions. The whole thing was inconceivable to him. Most of his life had gone along smoothly with only the occasional bump in the road. To be sure, those bumps had been significant at the time—two broken engagements, the death of his parents; but compared to what he had been exposed to the last few weeks, they all appeared minor.

Abductions, miraculous healings, murders, crowds of hurting people searching for a mystery man, deformed children asking for the

Healer—it was beyond comprehension.

Images of the Gowans' blood-splattered home overlapped with mental pictures of Rachel. Tears welled up in Adam's eyes.

"There must be something that can be done, God," Adam prayed aloud. "There must be something, but what? How can we find these people?"

Leaping from his chair with nervous energy, Adam paced his office floor, alternately praying and thinking.

"I've got to calm down and think," he said to himself. "Organize my thoughts. Reason. Concentrate. Analyze." Walking to the stereo on one of his bookshelves, he placed a tape in the player.

A chorus of male voices sang Gregorian chants in rhythmic Latin. Although he was teased by a few people for listening to "monk music," it was Adam's favorite. He had found the slow, rhythmic tempo conducive to thinking and often played the tape when he had a difficult problem to face.

Still pacing, Adam had listened to the Easter litany and Christmas litany three times when he stopped mid-step.

Smiling, he turned his face heavenward and mouthed the words, "Thank You." A moment later he paged Detective McGinnes.

"McGinnes? I would like to see you right away and also your friend from the FBI."

"Not possible. I am kinda' busy, you know."

"It's imperative you be here. I don't want to do what I have to do alone."

"What are you planning?" McGinnes asked suspiciously. Adam never heard the question. He hung up the phone, flipped the cassette over and began pacing again.


"You are out of your mind!" McGinnes said. "There is no way I can sanction this. I don't know what Greene thinks, but it's clear to me that you've slipped a cog."

"It's the only way," Adam said with quiet assurance. "Besides, the mechanism is already started. I've placed a call to Milt Phillips and his group. They've agreed to help me."

"You're nuts," McGinnes continued, leaping from his chair. "You could disappear like the others, or worse yet, get killed.

You've seen what these crazies can do, and there's nothing to say that they won't do it to you too."

Special Agent Greene sat in silence listening to the exchange between the two men.

"You just gonna sit there, Greene?" McGinnes asked bitterly. "Don't tell me you're gonna help this crazy preacher."

Greene slowly rubbed his eyes, revealing his weariness. "Frankly, I don't see how we can stop him."

McGinnes stood silently staring at Greene and then exploded, "I'll have nothing to do with it—nothing!" Spinning on his heels, he turned and exited Adam's office. Greene and Adam stared silently at each other.

"I hope you know what you're doing," Greene said, breaking the silence.

"Sometimes, we must walk by faith and not by sight." Adam was stoic.

"I find sight more comfortable," Greene said.

"And I find faith more dependable," Adam countered.

"I appreciate your help," Adam said, sitting in the studio chair. "Without your cooperation this wouldn't work."

"Are you kidding?" Priscilla Simms said. "When this breaks, it's going to be one of the year's biggest stories. When Milt Phillips called and asked to use the news studio, Pham Ho was glad to oblige, providing that a reporter be present. I'm the reporter."

"So, you're here for the story, even though you don't know when you can broadcast it?"

"Well, not just for the story," Priscilla answered quietly. "I have a more pressing reason."

"Care to tell me about it?"

"Not much to tell, really." Priscilla straightened the lapel microphone on Adam's sport coat. It was a needless gesture, but it gave her something to do with her hands while her mind recalled the event that haunted her nights. "These people you're after killed a friend of mine. I promised him I'd find out who did it."

An uneasy silence filled the next few moments.

Priscilla smiled slightly and said, "So much for detached journalism."

"I think I can understand," Adam said, taking her hand and looking into her soft blue eyes. "These people have hurt those I care for, and I want them stopped."

"I wish I could do more," she said.

"You can pray for me."

Priscilla laughed lightly. "I haven't prayed since I was a child. I may need to be reintroduced to God."

"I'm sure He remembers you."

For a long moment, Priscilla gazed at this unusual man before her. His confidence was genuine, not the false bravado of a man trying to impress those around him. He possessed a quiet assurance that spoke of inner strength and certainty. He was not the hero type; his thick glasses reflected the studio lights and the deep lines around his eyes revealed years of intense reading and study. He certainly didn't seem like a man about to place himself in the midst of a lethal unknown.

"I didn't expect to see you again so soon," Milt Phillips said, stepping onto the set. "You know you really upset Dr. Cruden. I don't think I've ever seen the man so angry."

"That wasn't my intention," Adam said, rising and shaking Phillip's hand.

"I know, but it makes great television," Phillips said, laughing.

"Mr. Phillips," Adam said, "I'd like you to meet Priscilla Simms. She's the news anchor for the station."

"Yes, I recognize her. I'm pleased to meet you."

"I watch your show all the time," Priscilla lied. "You have a lot of fans in San Diego."

"Well, if they're all as good-looking as you, I may just move my show down here permanently." Then to Adam he said, "I thought you might like to know that we have arranged a direct feed to L.A. We'll record here and electronically send it back to our own station. What we tape this afternoon will be broadcast this evening in place of what we taped earlier today."

"So everyone will think that it's a normal program?"

"Well, since you're the only guest, it will seem a little unusual, but I'll state at the beginning of the show that this is a special interview. Sorta' like a news scoop. In addition to that, we've notified all the key news stations as well as the papers. If our kidnappers don't watch my show, then they're sure to catch it on the news."

Adam nodded. "When do we begin?"

"In about five minutes. Think you'll be ready by then?"

"Yes, but I need a few minutes to myself."

"Certainly," Phillips said and stepped from the set.

Priscilla hesitated a moment and then said, "Good luck and Godspeed."

Adam leaned back in the studio chair and, closing his eyes, silently prayed.

From a darkened corner of the studio, Agent Greene watched Adam's still figure and wondered if he too shouldn't pray.

# Thirty-One

## Wednesday, April 1; 6:15 P.M.

The ninety-minute taping passed quickly with a minimum of retakes. Adam played his part well, acting reserved and cautious when needed. Milt Phillips proved to be a consummate actor, prying deeply into each comment Adam made and appearing both amazed and skeptical.

The premise of the program was simple. Adam Bridger, pastor and counselor, was the Healer, revealing himself now to stop the kidnappings. Without rehearsal, Adam was able to answer every question Phillips presented to him. Each answer was convincing and captivating. When the show ended, tens of thousands of viewers believed that Adam Bridger was indeed the mystery Healer of Kingston Memorial Hospital.

"I must admit," Phillips said, rising from his chair, "that you almost had me persuaded. And if you can do that, then the people out there will believe it."

"I just hope the right people believe it," Adam said somberly.

"Why shouldn't they?"

Adam didn't answer. His thoughts were shrouded in fear.

Priscilla made her way from behind the cameras to the set. "If you ever give up preaching, you can make a career in television." Adam responded with a smile. "I hope everything works out for you," she continued. "You're a very brave man, Adam."

"Not brave, Ms. Simms, just desperate."

"If you're ready," Agent Greene said, stepping onto the lighted set, "I have several things to discuss with you."

"Certainly," Adam said. "If you'll excuse me, Ms. Simms."

"Priscilla," she said. "Please call me Priscilla." Stepping toward Adam, she leaned forward and kissed his cheek. "Take care, Reverend. Remember, you promised me a story."

Adam blushed. "Thank you."

Turning, he followed Greene through a crowded newsroom filled with people preparing for the 5 o'clock news.

"We've allowed this station to 'leak' the story during their news broadcasts," Greene said somberly. "The other stations will run it after the 'Milt Phillips Show.'"

Once inside the dressing room, Greene turned and locked the door. Reaching inside his suit coat pocket, he pulled out a small, gray box and two small, tightly rolled coils of wire.

"This is your wire," Greene said. "You're to wear it at all times. And I mean *all* times. I want to be able to hear you snore, eat corn flakes, and burp. There will be two cars with agents at your place twenty-four hours a day until this thing is over," Greene continued. "When you go for a drive, those cars will follow you."

"Discreetly, I hope," Adam said, removing his shirt and tie.

"You won't even know they're there."

"How will I be able to tell the good guys from the bad?"

"You won't." Greene taped the small transmitter to Adam's undershirt. Then, running one wire under Adam's arm, he taped a small microphone to his chest. "This last wire that I'm taping to your back is the antenna."

Greene finished affixing the microphone and transmitter and handed Adam his shirt.

"Now what?" Adam asked.

"Now we wait," Greene said stoically. "You go about your usual business as best you can, and we will be close by. When and if they nab you, we follow the signal of your transmitter, and we bag 'em."

"Best I can?" Adam was puzzled. "What do you mean, 'Go about my business as best I can?' "

"You don't think the only people watching the show are the kid-nappers, do you?" Greene shook his head in disbelief. "When that program airs in a few hours, thousands of people will believe that you can heal every disease known to man. Do you really think your life will ever be the same?"

Adam's mind began to fill with images of the hospital lobby. Hundreds of people waiting for an unknown Healer. What would they do now that they had a name? He had been too absorbed in his plan to think of that. In an attempt to help a few, did he cold-ly and falsely build up the hopes of the many? Hopes that could never be realized? A face filled Adam's mind: the small, haunting face of a crooked little boy.

## Wednesday, April 1; 11:45 P.M.

No more than ten minutes had passed after the program aired when it happened. The flood-gates of anxious, hurting people burst forth into Adam's life. Telephone call after telephone call came; calls which Adam knew he could never answer. The phone would ring eight, nine, ten times and then stop only to start ringing again. The sound of the ringing echoed off the walls and through his tender soul, and with each ringing, Adam's stomach tightened.

"What have I done?" he asked the empty room. "I can't talk to these people. I can't help them. Dear God, I've built them up only to dash their hopes again. They'll think I'm a sadistic fiend." The phone began to ring again. Adam turned the ringer off, so that he at least didn't have to hear it. For the first time ever, he wished he had an unlisted number.

In the new silence Adam stood—alone, his sensitive emotions bleeding within him. His stomach, encouraged by unbridled feel-ings, rebelled, sending searing pains through his abdomen and back. Stepping into his bathroom, he pulled a small, brown plas-tic medicine bottle down and removed one yellow and pink cap-sule. Throwing the capsule to the back of his throat, he swallowed hard. The doctor had prescribed Axid once for an ulcer; now he was glad that he kept a supply on hand.

*I'm committed now*, he thought. *All I can do is follow through with the plan.* Adam felt exhausted. "Sleep," he said aloud. "I need sleep."

The days and nights of the last few weeks had taken their toll. Adam's mind was sluggish and his emotions raw. He desired nothing more than to close his eyes in long, quiet slumber that would take away his troubles. Perhaps when he awoke, he would find his world normal once again . . . a world with no kidnappings and murders; no mysterious Healers and crooked little boys. Adam leaned against the bathroom wall and slowly slid down until he sat on the tile floor. A moment later he dozed.

A banging on the door startled Adam. Had he imagined the sound? The banging continued, followed by a muffled voice. Could this be it? Could it be the kidnappers outside his door? He reminded himself that these kidnappers were also killers; he had to be careful. Slowly he approached the door and listened. He could hear a woman's voice, "Please, Healer; you've got to help me!"

Adam wondered how a stranger could find him at home. Then he remembered—in the new phone book he had included his home address as well as the church. If one person had found him, then others would also. The thought shook him to the bone.

Another voice filtered through the door. "I was here first; go away!" the first voice shrieked. It was the woman's voice.

"No, you don't understand," said the second voice in raspy tones. "I simply must see the Healer." Adam guessed the second one was an elderly man.

"I don't care. I was here first."

"Please, it's a matter of life and death. My death."

"My daughter needs him more than you do."

Adam listened as the two argued. All he had wanted to do was help, to have Rachel and the others returned safely. Now, he questioned his actions. Outside his door stood the pitiful and the pained, those for whom hope was a word used by those who could not understand their anguish.

"Is this the Healer's place?" A new voice sifted through the door.

"I've got to see him. Is he in?"

"Wait your turn," the elderly voice shouted bitterly. "We were here first."

The pounding and yelling continued. For Adam, the minutes passed like epochs of guilt, fear, and pain. New voices arrived, some heavy with accent, others young and pitiful.

Adam's imagination, vivid from weariness and raw emotion, ran wild. Slowly he raised himself up and peered out the peephole. There the lame and infirm were pushing, shouting, trying to reach a man who had lied to them—a man who could give them nothing more than despair. Adam watched as a woman raised one red and dilated eye to the peephole and tried to peer into the apartment. Adam pulled back quickly, his heart thundering.

Being a good minister required a sensitive spirit, a tender heart that allowed for true empathy. That tender heart and sensitive spirit now betrayed Adam. It squeezed and crushed him. Every cry, every knock on the door, every overheard argument echoed in his brain and reverberated in his heart. Every plea impacted his brain like a fiery arrow, and burned through his soul. He tried to ease his flood of guilt, to quiet his searing conviction, but to no avail. Slowly, Adam crouched on the floor alone and wept, deep and bitter sobs. Hot tears came unbidden to his eyes. Then Adam wished the unforgivable: he wished for his own death.

A minute later, or an hour, Adam didn't know, the cacophony ended. Had they gone? Once again, Adam placed his ear to the door and heard a voice outside. It was the small, innocent voice of a child sounding like a lone trumpet in the darkness.

"Will the Healer make me well, Mommy? Will he make the pain stop? Will I be able to run with the other children? Will I be able to play ball? I want to be able to run in the park."

Adam did not hear the answer. Stifling the scream that welled up in him with volcanic force, he ran to the back of the apartment and out the back door. In the darkness Adam did not see the man who slept on his back landing. His foot caught the man's reclined body, and Adam fell hard to the ground. He felt the air leave his lungs and the stony ground scrape away the flesh from his palms. Stunned, Adam stood, shook his head, and gasped for air.

"It's him!" someone shouted. "It must be him!"

Adam sprinted for the back fence and scaled it quickly, his raw hands injured all the more by the rough wood wall.

"He's running away. Wait, please come back. Don't go. I need you."

Tears raced down Adam's face as he ran blindly through his neighbor's backyard, past the house and into the street. Behind him, he could hear voices calling out to him, pleading with him to return. But Adam continued to run, not knowing where he was going. He just knew that he had to get away.

Lost in his torment, Adam didn't notice the dark sedan following behind. A mile later he collapsed in the street, lost in the tumultuous sea of guilt. He lay quietly on the still, warm asphalt.

The car behind him stopped. Two men, one with a black goatee, the other short and fat, got out and walked over to the prone figure in the street.

"Turn him over so I can see his face," the man with the goatee said.

The other man rolled Adam onto his back.

"Please," Adam said deliriously, "I can't help you. I want to, but I can't. Don't you understand? I just can't."

"Recognize him?"

"Yeah," the short man said. "It's him, all right."

"What's the matter with him?"

"Dunno. Nuts I guess."

"Well, at least he saved us the trouble of breaking into his house. That woulda' been hard, with all those people."

"Yeah. Mohammed came to the mountain this time."

"Well, we better make sure he stays quiet for awhile."

Crouching over Adam, the bearded man raised a fist high above his head and let it hover for a moment. Adam opened his eyes just in time to see the plummeting fist. Instinctively, he moved his head to the side. His assailant's fist slammed into the asphalt street with bone-cracking force.

Screaming in pain, the man bolted upright, gazed at his bleeding hand, then in uncontrolled rage began kicking Adam. With each kick Adam recoiled in pain. One kick landed just under the ribs, paralyzing his diaphragm and leaving him desperately gasping for air. Another kick landed just under his left temple and darkness filled Adam's mind.

The kicking lasted another minute; then the goateed man, holding his broken and bloody hand, stopped and gazed at the unmoving form on the ground. Slowly, he reached down and touched Adam's neck, feeling for a sign of life. "He still has a pulse," he said. "Get him into the car."

The fat man hoisted Adam over his shoulder and threw him in the backseat of the sedan. Then the man paused and looked puzzled.

"Hurry it up, will ya'," The other man said. "My hand's killing me."

"What's this?"

"What's what?"

"This." The fat man patted Adam's chest, feeling the microphone. Then with a jerk he ripped open Adam's shirt and gazed down at the electronics taped to Adam's undershirt. "He's wired for sound."

"Get rid of it quick, and let's get out of here."

The fat man grabbed the tape and yanked. The tape held, the shirt ripped. A moment later the car sped off.


"Unbelievable." Greene uttered under his breath.

Special Agent Norman Greene walked through the rubble that had been Adam Bridger's furniture and personal belongings. The room had been ransacked, not by thieves but by a mass of people intent on finding one man. Police were milling in and around the apartment. They had been called to break up the crowds and now they stood around in bewilderment, trying to make sense of the situation.

"They really did a number on the place, didn't they?"

Greene looked coldly at the young agent who spoke. "Where were you when all this was going on?"

The question caught him off guard. This had been his first real assignment since coming to the FBI. Now he felt responsible for losing the one he had been assigned to protect. "Agent Baker and I were monitoring his transmissions. We didn't realize that he had left until we heard him gasping for air and then the struggle."

Patrick Morris had already given Greene the pertinent facts ... the gathering crowds, Adam's weeping, and finally his desperate attempt to flee the pitiful people outside his door who would give him no peace.

For Adam, a man trained to care for and hurt with others, it must have been sheer torment to listen to the constant cries for help.

"We were ordered not to interfere until Reverend Bridger was abducted," Morris continued. "We were only doing as we were told."

"I know," Greene said solemnly. "I was a fool to let myself get talked into this. The question now is: Where is Adam Bridger?"

"We lost the signal soon after he left his home. One of our people found the transmitter in the middle of a nearby street."

There was an uneasy silence. Then Morris voiced what was already common knowledge, "They've got him, and we don't know where he is."

A gentle hand stroked Adam's hair, slowly and tenderly moving from forehead to ear. The hand was joined by another hand, and then another. The tender strokes changed, moving from caressing to tugging, pulling, vicious hands. Soon there were ten hands, then a hundred, then a thousand disembodied hands pulling, grabbing, reaching through the darkness.

Adam attempted to run into the duskiness that engulfed him, but the hands were everywhere pulling at his clothes and limbs. The hands began to scratch his face and clutch his throat. Several clawed at the skin of his chest and back.

"You forgot me," said a childish voice. "You forgot all about me, didn't you? You're supposed to help people, but you forgot me— left me."

"Who are you?" Adam shouted, covering his eyes from the probing hands.

"The forgotten," the voice said sadly. "One of the forgotten who needed you. You should have cared. Isn't that what you teach your people . . . to care?"

Suddenly, a figure appeared in the black distance, a tiny figure surrounded by a small light, but too distant for Adam to identify. Adam tried to cover his eyes again, but the other hands viciously pulled them away.

"Look at me," the infantile voice commanded. "Why didn't you help me? Why did you leave me?"

The illuminated figure grew larger as it approached until a misshapen child stood before him. "Why did you forget me?"

"I ... I didn't," Adam cried. "There was nothing I could do. I wanted to help but I couldn't. It's not my fault."

"But you forgot me."

"No, I didn't. I'm helpless. I'm not who you think I am."

"You forgot me," the crooked boy repeated. "Forgot. Forgot. Forgot." The boy chanted in a taunting rhythm. Soon thousands of others chanted in a crescendoing cacophony of voices, "Forgot, forgot ..."

"It's not my fault," Adam screamed. "It's not my fault."

Adam bolted upright, eyes wide in terror, his dream still vivid and echoing in his mind. A second later he noticed the searing pain in his side and the pounding of his head.

"Easy, Adam," a familiar voice said. "You're not in any shape to be doing sit-ups. I think you were dreaming."

Turning to face the voice, he saw Rachel. They were sitting on the floor. Blood stained her Yale sweatshirt and jeans—his blood. It occurred to Adam that Rachel had been cradling his head while he was unconscious. She must have been stroking his hair.

"Thank God you're alive," he said painfully.

"You'd better lie down again," she said tenderly. "I'm afraid they messed you up badly. You have at least two broken ribs and a broken nose. I don't think there are internal injuries, but I can't be sure. For a while, I was afraid you were going to slip into a coma."

Rather than lying down, Adam struggled to his feet. His side and head protested. He was having trouble seeing. Touching his face, he discovered his left eye was swollen shut and his right eye was filled with tears. He blinked away the bleariness in his good eye and looked around.

There were other people in the room. Willing himself to concentrate, his vision cleared, and he saw the concerned faces of David and Ann Lorayne. Adam smiled weakly and, in a false show of bravado, said, "I've come to see why you haven't been in church lately."

Continuing to scan the room, he saw another elderly couple. "Mr. and Mrs. Langford, I presume." They nodded.

A man stood and approached Adam. "My name's Halley, John

Halley. This is my wife, Judy, and my daughter, Lisa. I take it you're not with the police?"

Adam shook his head slowly. In a corner of the room, Adam recognized the Gowan family. Seeing them brought back the ghastly scene in their home.

"Where are we?" he asked quietly.

Rachel got up from her place on the floor. "We're on a boat headed out to sea."

Adam paused as he digested the information. He was still groggy from his beating. Adam had noticed the swaying of the floor and the low droning sound from beneath them, but had attributed it to his injuries.

"A boat?" he asked.

"They put us on it after they brought you here. They had been keeping us in one of the old tuna canneries on the wharf."

The room was especially large for a boat, but the rocking of the floor gave undeniable credence to the statement. There was a window on one wall but the glass had been painted opaque. "How long was I out?"

"About an hour," Rachel said. "You really scared me." She threw her arms around his neck. "I'm sorry for what I said. I'm sorry for what I did. And I'm sorry that you're trapped here with us."

Adam winced in pain as he embraced her.

"Oh, I'm sorry," she cried and immediately released him. "I guess I'm not much of a doctor."

"You're wonderful," he said reassuringly. As Adam struggled to clear his foggy mind, he remembered the crowd outside his door, his emotional turmoil that resulted in his fleeing his home and, most of all, the beating.

Suddenly, Adam remembered the tiny transmitter taped to his back. Reaching behind him, he found, to his horror, that it was gone.

"I'm afraid I've made things worse," Adam said.

"What do you mean?" Rachel asked.

"I was carrying a small transmitter. It was supposed to lead the authorities here, but it appears that our captors found it."

"You mean you purposely allowed yourself to be captured?" David Lorayne asked incredulously.

"That was the idea," Adam replied. "Unfortunately, it didn't quite work out the way I planned." Adam felt an overwhelming sense of embarrassment. If he hadn't lost his emotional control, then things might be different now. He hadn't planned on an onslaught of ill and dying people.

"What do we do now?" Rachel asked anxiously. "I think they plan to kill us."

"That we do," said a voice behind them.

Turning to face the door, Adam saw a man he had seen before. "So you're the Healer? I have waited a long time to meet you. I have big plans for you. Very big plans, indeed."

# Thirty-Two

## Thursday, April 1; 7 A.M.

Adam faced the three men who had entered the room. The one in the center, a tall, curly-haired man with deep green eyes, slowly surveyed the occupants of the room and then grinned sardonically.

"Do you know me?" The man asked in a deep Southern drawl.

Adam said nothing.

"No? Well then, introductions are due. You've already met Mr. Bill Sanchez, formerly head of security at Kingston Memorial Hospital."

"Sanchez!" Rachel exclaimed as she turned toward him. "So Martin was right."

"Who's Martin?" Sanchez asked gruffly.

"I think a better question is why you are mixed up in this." Rachel said.

"The money's good, and people like R.G. need protection too."

"But you had a good position at the hospital," Rachel said.

"I had a barely adequate position. The money I received from the police department for my injury combined with my hospital

298

paycheck just wasn't enough. Besides, I've developed a rather expensive habit."

"Habit?" Rachel was perplexed.

Sanchez didn't respond, but R.G. did. "A drug habit, Doctor. Something that began with a need to ease the pain of his injured arm."

"I'm not proud of it," Sanchez said, "but being in a hospital and surrounded by so many drugs, well, I just couldn't help myself. It was only a matter of time before someone caught me stealing narcotics."

"Enough about Mr. Sanchez," R.G. said. "I also want you to meet Mr. T.J. Haman. He does odd jobs for me. You may recall, Reverend Bridger, you two met last night."

"I recall," Adam said, as he stared at the goateed man with a bandaged right hand. "I'm also familiar with his work."

"I do owe you an apology," R.G. said with mock courtesy. "Mr. Haman does have a tendency to be a little overzealous about his work, but it really is your own fault; if you hadn't moved, Mr. Haman wouldn't have hurt his hand and wouldn't have felt compelled to express himself with further action."

"You still haven't told me your name."

"Oh, of course. Most just call me R.G."

"Why do you look so familiar?"

"My employer is a rather public person, not unlike yourself. Perhaps you've heard of him—Reverend Paul Isaiah? Although I try to stay out of the limelight, I occasionally appear on television with him."

"You mean he's behind all of this?" Adam asked truculently.

R.G. guffawed. "Absolutely not. Paul Isaiah is spineless and neurotic. To be sure, he is not scrupulously honest, but he lacks the imagination and courage to be really great. For those things, he turns to me. All he is good for is to bring in the crowds with his promises of healing and riches."

"You mentioned plans," Adam said. "What plans?"

"Living rich," R.G. said cryptically.

"Living rich?"

"Yes. First, you are going to help me live. Second, you are going to make me, I mean us, rich."

"I'm afraid I don't understand."

"Of course, you don't. Let me explain. First, you need to know that I'm dying. That may come as good news to you, but I find it distressing. You see, I have a form of lymphatic cancer. It's under control now, but I know that it will shorten my life appreciably. But, if you are who you say you are, then you know this already. So the first step in our plan is for you to heal me of my disease; then you'll heal Mr. Sanchez of his painful arm and drug addiction. After that, I'll manage your public appearances. We'll have huge crusades and tens of thousands will come and be healed and gratefully pay."

"And if I refuse?" Adam said defiantly.

"Refuse? Oh, you won't do that. But just in case you feel compelled to resist, we may have to motivate you." Walking over to Lisa Halley, R.G. began to gently stroke her hair. "You see, Reverend Bridger, men like you have this noble habit of caring for those around you. I'd be willing to bet that you would rather die yourself than see any harm come to these innocent people." Lisa closed her eyes as he leaned over and kissed her forehead.

John Halley sprang to his feet with volcanic rage, hands reaching for the throat of the man who dared touch his daughter. With catlike speed Haman leaped forward and brought his leg up in a swift and brutal kick; the toe of his shoe struck Halley solidly in the stomach, doubling him over. Haman delivered another kick to his face and Halley fell backward, unconscious, his head making a sickening thud as it struck the deck.

"Dad!" Lisa tore away from R.G.

"Such heroics are useless," R.G. said coldly. "In fact, any further attempts to defy me will be answered swiftly and painfully."

Rachel left Adam's side and knelt near the fallen man. Quickly, she checked his breathing and then ran her fingers down the back of his neck. Each vertebrae was in place; his neck was not broken.

"I trust he'll live?" R.G. asked with mock concern.

"He'll live," Rachel replied curtly. "No thanks to your monkey there."

Haman began to move forward, but R.G. waved him off.

"It wouldn't do to antagonize him, Doctor," R.G. said. "He's fiercely loyal, but there is a limit to his patience. I would so hate to see him destroy you before I have made full use of you."

"What use do you have for them, now that you have me?" Adam said, hoping to redirect their captor's attention to himself.

"Insurance, my dear Reverend, insurance." R.G. gazed silently at the sobbing Lisa as she held her unconscious father's head. "Since I brought you here against your will, and since I have entertained your friends against their will, I felt you might be...well, resistant to helping me. So, I keep them as motivational help."

Adam was puzzled. "I don't understand."

"Why, you surprise me. It's really quite simple. If you don't help me, I'll kill them."

Adam had seen the death this man had left behind; but hearing it spoken so coldly chilled him.

"In fact," R.G. continued, "while we waited for you, we constructed a little something to help us." He snapped his fingers, and Sanchez left the room only to return a few seconds later struggling with a concrete-filled plastic pail that hung from a length of chain. "This, my dear Adam—you don't mind me calling you Adam, do you?—this simple little device is an anchor. We have one for each of you."

Adam's mind filled with the awful thought of the Langfords, Halleys, Loraynes, and Rachel rapidly descending through the cold Pacific, struggling for breath that would never come. A chill ran down his spine.

"Oh, don't look so despondent," R.G. said laughing. "I hear that drowning is a rather pleasant way to die. We are presently cruising a mile out from the Scripps Institute of Oceanography. Some of the ocean's deepest waters lie beneath our hull. In all probability, you would be crushed by the water pressure before you actually drown."

"Some comfort," Rachel said sarcastically.

R.G. ignored her and kept his attention riveted to Adam. "You will do as I ask, or I will begin dropping your friends overboard one at a time." Adam said nothing, his mind frozen with fear. "But for now, I will leave you. I'm sure you and your friends have much to talk about. So, gather your strength, because when I return, you will do exactly what I ask."

Special Agent Greene sat in the small corner room of the San Diego FBI office and watched as the blanket of high clouds of a Pacific

301

marine layer slowly surrendered to the morning sun.

Sunrise came as it always had. People filled the freeways with their cars as they always had, but this day was different for Greene. Somewhere out there, in this city or the next, was Adam Bridger, abducted, and Greene felt responsible. *It was a stupid move,* he reminded himself again. *The whole plan was ill advised and against policy.* While it was true that he had not originated the idea, and was, for all practical purposes, helpless to prevent Adam from following through with his intentions, Greene's supervisor was going to be indignant.

The door to his office opened. Greene looked up expectantly at the young agent who entered.

"Sorry," Patrick Morris said, interpreting the expression on Greene's face. "No word yet. The police have an APB out and our forensics people are going over the apartment and the street where we found the blood and transmitter."

The image of the transmitter filled Greene's mind. It had been crushed; ground into the asphalt road. "Anything else?"

"No, but I hear that Clark is on his way down."

Greene grimaced. The thought of his supervisor driving in from L.A. chilled him. An otherwise perfect career was about to receive a huge black mark.

"Anything I can do for you?" Morris asked. "How about a cup of coffee?"

"No, thanks. I've had at least a dozen cups since sunrise."

"I know what you mean." Morris turned to leave, then paused and said, "We'll find him. I know it and you know it. We'll find Adam Bridger and all the rest."

Greene was staring out the window again. "The question is," he said slowly, "will we find them in time?"


Greene passed the next two hours with paperwork and phone calls. There was little more he could do but wait for lab and field reports. *Rapport can be a horrible thing,* he thought to himself. He had handled dozens of kidnappings before, but they were always strangers to him. Unfortunately, a rapport, an instantaneous rapport, had sprung up between he and Adam. It was not an unknown man mysteriously snatched from his home; it was someone he knew and even admired.

Morris entered the room again. "There's someone here to see you."

"Is it important?"

"I think you better see him."

"Why?" Greene said, trying to interpret Morris' tone.

"He won't speak, but he gave me this note."

Greene took the folded piece of paper and opened it. The words were written with precision block letters: I KNOW WHO THE HEALER IS. I KNOW HOW TO FIND HIM. WILL YOU HELP?

"Show him in," Greene said.

Greene stood as Morris escorted the man into the office. Stepping around his desk, Greene extended his hand. "I'm Special Agent Norman Greene." The man shook hands. "Please sit down." The man did so. Returning to his place behind his desk, Greene quickly looked his guest over. He was five-foot-eight or so and slender in build. His head was bald on top; what hair he had was light brown and formed a semicircular band from ear to ear. His eyes were a radiant blue that demanded trust and his face plain—neither handsome nor homely. The thing that distinguished him most to Greene was his confident air. Most civilians who came into his office appeared overwhelmed, but this man sat quietly and comfortably as though he were in his own living room.

"I'm sorry," Greene said cordially, "I didn't catch your name."

The man reached slowly into the breast pocket of his white sport shirt and pulled out a card. What he read caused Greene to stare at the man for a few long, disbelieving moments. After a moment's reflection Greene handed the card to Morris and said, "See what you can do about this."

John Halley groaned as he slowly regained consciousness. Rachel wanted to do more for him, but without medical supplies there was little she could do.

"What now?" Pat Gowan asked gruffly. "Are you going to do what he asks?" The question was clearly pointed at Adam.

"I wish I could," Adam replied soberly.

"What do you mean you 'wish' you could?'" Gowan asked tersely. "You can't let them kill us."

"You don't understand."

"No, *you* don't understand," Gowan was shouting. "I'm not gonna let my wife and daughter be tossed overboard because of you. Do what he asks. I have seen what kind of people these are. You should see what they did in my house."

Turning slowly, Adam faced the distraught man. Gowan had been through a great deal in recent weeks: his daughter's cerebral palsy and the accident that led to her hospitalization, her miraculous healing, and the massacre in his home. "I have seen," Adam spoke softly. "I was there with the police."

"Then you know that you must do what he asks." Gowan's face had turned red with rage; his clenched fist hung stiffly at his side.

"Honey," Katherine Gowan pleaded, "please don't. It will only make things worse." She had seen his temper before. Although a good man, Pat Gowan could lose his temper quickly. "I need you now," she said. "I need you beside me, not fighting, but beside me."

He looked at his wife. In her tender and pleading eyes he found the sedative to calm him. "You're right, dear. But he needs to do what they ask."

"I can't," Adam remarked to no one in particular. "I'm not who they think I am."

"What do you mean?" Bill Langford asked.

"I'm an FBI plant. I'm not the Healer. It was all a ruse to flush out the abductors. I was wired with a transmitter. The FBI was to follow the signal after I was abducted."

"Then the FBI is on its way?" Adam couldn't help but notice the hopefulness in Langford's voice.

"No. I think these guys discovered the transmitter too soon." Adam looked at the faces in the room. For a very brief moment, they had held a glimmer of hope. "I'm afraid we're on our own."

A young woman was ushered into Greene's office and hasty introductions were made.

"Thank you for coming, Ms. Lolly," Greene said, shaking her hand. "I know that it was short notice."

"I hope I can be of some help," she replied nervously. "I'm afraid I'm a little uneasy."

"That's to be expected, but I assure you there's nothing to worry about. All we need is someone to interpret for us." Motioning with his head toward the man seated across from his desk, Greene continued, "This gentleman is your client."

Turning, she made a few quick gestures with her hands. The man responded with similar gestures.

"Would you please ask him his name?" Greene sat down in his chair.

"Actually," she replied, "it would be better if you asked the questions and I will sign your words. Just pretend I'm not here and speak directly to him."

Feeling a little uneasy, Greene began slowly, "Thank you for coming. Would you mind telling me your name?"

The quiet, bald man instantly signed with his hands.

"My name," Lolly said, giving voice to the silent man, "is not important. I have come to help you find the man pretending to be me—pretending to be the Healer."

"Are you saying that you are the one responsible for the healings in Kingston Memorial Hospital?"

"Yes," was his short reply.

"Nonetheless," Greene insisted, "your name would be most help..."

"The man pretending to be me is in very great danger," Lolly's voice interrupted Greene. "We have very little time to waste. I can take you to him, but we must hurry."

The quick hand motions revealed the Healer's anxiety.

"But, how do I know what you say is true?" Greene asked, wondering if his suspicion would be translated as well.

"Because I have told you it is so."

"I still need more information before I can do anything."

The man's face clearly revealed his frustration. Greene had no doubt that the man believed what he was saying.

"What information do you need?" the man asked.

"Your name for starters," Greene said firmly.

"If I give you my name, will you let me show you where to find the missing people?"

"It will speed things along."

Reaching into his back pocket, the man pulled a worn wallet and, extracting his driver's license, handed it to Greene. Greene took it and cast an expert eye over it. It appeared to be valid. An address was listed in Riverside, California. The name listed was Charles Gregory. Greene quickly memorized the information.

"Thank you, Mr. Gregory," Greene said, handing the license back. "Now, how is it that you know what we in the FBI don't know?"

"The same way I knew you were the agent I needed to speak to. The same way I know who needs to be healed. The same way I know your man needs help."

"And what way is that?"

Gregory paused before answering, then signed, "God tells me."

"God tells you?" Greene was uncertain whether to feel incredulous or to believe Gregory. Although not a man given to belief in the supernatural, he did have to acknowledge that many unexplained things were happening.

Gregory continued signing, "I must remind you again that time is short. If you do not act now, many will die."

Greene leaned back in his chair and glanced at Morris who was standing silently near the door. Morris shrugged. Greene had to make a decision. If Gregory was the Healer, then he just might know where Adam and the others were; if he was a crazed impostor, then precious time could be wasted on a wild-goose chase.

"Where is he?" Greene asked.

"On a boat. I can lead you there."

Greene fell silent again. A boat could be anywhere: out to sea, or in one of the many marinas. Without a specific location and description, it could take days to find the right craft.

"How can you lead us there?" Greene asked.

"I can't explain; I just know. Please, let's not waste any more time." Gregory's signs were augmented by a pleading expression on his face. Greene quickly calculated his options, then decided to believe the slim, bald man.

"Morris, get a car and call the Coast Guard," Greene said, jumping to his feet. Turning to Lolly, he asked, "Would you come along? It would save us a lot of time."

"Of course," Lolly said.

"Then let's go."

# Thirty-Three

## Thursday, April 1; 8:50 A.M.

"I've been more than patient," R.G. said. He, Haman, and Sanchez had entered the room, Sanchez with an Uzi machine gun in his crooked arm. "You have had thirty minutes to think over my proposition and now it is time for an answer. Do we have a bargain, or do I start dropping your friends into the ocean?"

"How do I know you won't do that anyway?" Adam asked with feigned bravado.

"Frankly, you don't," R.G. replied. "But I offer you my word."

Rachel laughed in spite of herself. Haman began to move toward her, but R.G. once again waved him off.

"I have warned you, Dr. Tremaine," R.G. said tersely, "not to presume on Mr. Haman's or my patience. One more act of rudeness and I may leave you to Mr. Haman's devices."

Something in Haman's eyes struck terror in Rachel's heart. His eyes were coal black and seemed never to blink. He was a man who enjoyed his anger and hatred. He was a man to stay far away from—very far away.

"I'm the one you're interested in," Adam said, redirecting attention to himself. "What makes you think I can do what you ask? It must be obvious that the healings have been selective. After all, I didn't heal everyone in the hospital."

"Yes, I noticed that, and I must admit that the reason for that intrigues me. Perhaps when we have more time and a better working relationship, you can tell me the logic behind your actions. For now, the only thing I'm concerned with is what you can do for me. Will you heal me or not?"

Heavy silence hung in the room. Adam could hear the ocean lapping at the sides of the boat, and feel the slow rhythmic rocking as the craft rolled in the easy swells on the surface. Adam knew there was no response to give. If he attempted to heal R.G., he would surely fail; and if he refused, then they would all have the breath and life crushed out of them in the deep and cold Pacific. Their bodies would never be found. The thought of twelve bodies anchored with concrete, floating upright from the dark ocean floor like individual stalks of wheat, made him shudder.

"Am I to take your silence as a no?"

Adam shrugged, "I don't know what to tell you."

R.G.'s face slowly turned a fierce red. Barely under control, he said in a voice just above a whisper, "Then I'll have to motivate you." He nodded to Haman who stepped from the room only to return a few seconds later. He carried a roll of three-inch silver duct tape in his hand. Motioning to Sanchez, the two walked over to Bill Langford who stood next to his wife at the far corner of the room. Haman grabbed Langford by his hair and, in one swift, savage motion, pulled him face down onto the deck.

"Bill!" Lois charged forward to help her husband, but stopped short when she saw Sanchez place the barrel of the small Uzi machine gun in Bill's ear. The message was clear: any attempt to interfere would mean certain death. Haman adroitly taped Bill's wrists together behind his back with the duct tape. Even the strongest man would have been helpless to release himself.

"Tell them," Lois shouted, hot tears streaming down her face, "tell them the truth." Stepping toward Adam, she pleaded, heartbroken and terrified; her anguish multiplied by her helplessness. "You must tell them the truth. It's the only way."

"And what truth is that?" R.G. asked coldly.

Adam realized he had nothing else to do. If he remained silent, then they all would die. If he told the truth, they still all would die. The truth couldn't hurt.

"I'm not the Healer," Adam said softly, as he gazed at the helpless Bill Langford.

"I beg your pardon?" R.G. said.

Turning to face his abductor, he uttered the words again, "I'm not who you think I am. I am not the Healer. It was only a ruse to flush you out, a ruse that didn't work."

R.G.'s laughter caught Adam off guard.

"What's so funny?" Adam asked angrily.

"Why, you, my dear Reverend," R.G. replied between spasms of laughter. "You are the source of my laughter."

"I don't understand."

"Surely you must. Oh, I think it is very noble that you should sacrifice your morals enough to lie on the odd chance that it might save your friends. Very noble, indeed. Unfortunately, you are not a very convincing liar."

"But it's true," Lois Langford shouted.

The laughter continued. "Is this the best you could do? Oh, I have overestimated you."

Anger welled up in Adam: anger of desperation and frustration. R.G. did not believe him. It was clear to Adam that nothing would convince this man that he was not the Healer.

"I hope you rot in the deepest, darkest corner of hell," Adam said, spilling his helpless frustration.

The laughter stopped. "Hell? Hell, you say?" R.G.'s expression turned cold. "I don't believe in your hell or your heaven. For that matter, I don't believe in your God. Don't try to manipulate me with your ancient myths. I'm not one of your mental midgets who dutifully come to church each Sunday to see what God wants them to do. I've played that game, and I've played it productively and profitably, so don't try your guilt and fear tactics on me."

Adam stood in a silent rage. For the first time in his life, he wanted to harm another person. He wanted to reach his fingers around the arrogant captor's throat and squeeze and squeeze until he could squeeze no more.

R.G. continued coldly and analytically, "I may not know the source of your power, but I certainly don't attribute it to your God."

"The day will come when you will know just how wrong you are."

"Unless you do as I say, that day will come a lot sooner for you than for me."

"Perhaps, but our deaths will be relatively quick, while yours will slowly sap your life away until you're an invalid at the mercy of others."

Adam's words hit a chord; R.G. leaped forward and brought a crashing backhand to Adam's face. Adam recoiled in pain. Instinctively, he ran his tongue along his right cheek: two teeth were loose.

"Bind them all!" R.G. screamed. "Bind them and bring them topside."

The bright sunlight assaulted Adam's eyes, and the salt air invaded his lungs. One by one they had been brought from the lower cabin and made to kneel near the stern of the boat. In the distance, he could see the small wooden pier owned by the Scripps Institute of Oceanography. A light fog was moving in from the ocean toward the shore.

"You amaze me, Reverend Bridger," R.G. said. "After going through so many pains to heal these people here, you are now willing to let them drown? Just what kind of man are you?"

"And just what kind of man are you?" Adam replied.

"I am the kind of man who knows what he wants and doesn't mind pursuing it. Unlike you, I am not encumbered by artificial sentimentality. I simply want life and the best of what life has to offer." R.G. laughed again. "You, of course, think I'm a Beelzebub in the flesh. Or, perhaps you think the devil owns me. Is that it, dear Pastor? Do you think I'm possessed?"

"I think you're sick," Adam spat his words out.

Lois Langford, her hands taped behind her back, began to weep.

"Don't give them the satisfaction, honey," her husband said soothingly. "If we're going to die, then let's do so with dignity." Lois bit her quivering lip. Then, looking in her eyes and communicating what only a couple of long years can communicate, he said, "At least we're together."

"How noble," R.G. said sarcastically. Then to Adam he said, "What shall it be? Do as I say and we all will live and prosper."

"Do you really expect me to believe that you'll let the others go?"

"Forget the others," R.G. replied. "I can make you rich. I can make you more famous than the Pope or the President. Just say the word."

"There is nothing I can do for you."

"You're stoic now, but we will see." Turning to Haman, he said, "Bring the good doctor to the railing." Without hesitation, Haman approached Rachel and, grabbing her arm, brutally yanked her to her feet.

"It's me you want," Adam shouted. "Leave her alone."

"You know what you must do," R.G. replied coldly.

"Don't you understand? I *can't* do what you ask. It is not within my power."

"I see." R.G. nodded at Haman who carried one of the large concrete-filled plastic buckets and set it at Rachel's feet. The crude anchor had one end of a six-foot length of chain embedded in it.

"So I am to die?" Rachel asked calmly.

"Apparently," R.G. replied with a sigh. Haman bent to one knee and prepared to wrap the chain around her feet.

"Then I have nothing to lose," she said evenly and in a quick motion and with a force that belied her size, she kicked with all her might. Her heavily soled athletic shoe caught Haman square on the nose. Blood splattered the deck. She had hoped to drive the bridge of his nose into her executioner's brain, killing him, but all she succeeded in doing was breaking his nose and enraging him.

Wordlessly, Haman stood upright and wiped the blood from his face. Without warning, he punched her in the abdomen, doubling her over. Then, grabbing her by the hair, he straightened her up and brought another fist to the side of her jaw. Rachel fell to the deck in a heap, blood trickling from her mouth.

"NO!" Deep inside Adam's soul an explosion occurred: an explosion fueled by fear, frustration, and unbridled rage. Bolting to his feet, hands still taped behind his back, Adam screamed and charged Haman in an adrenaline-powered rush. Haman spun on his heels but was too late. Head down like an enraged bull, Adam slammed into Haman's stomach, propelling both of them over the boat's railing.

Haman broke the surface of the water with his back, Adam's head still pressed into his stomach. The force of the fall pushed both men below the surface. His reason and logic gone, Adam began kicking with all his strength. He knew only one thing: he had to keep the animal Haman away from Rachel and the others. So, he kicked, pushing deeper and deeper into the ocean. If Adam had it in his power, he'd push the madman to the very bottom of the dark sea where he could never again torture the innocent.

The cold water quickly revived the stunned Haman. Realizing what had happened, he reached for Adam's throat, but could grab only with his unbandaged hand. In one quick move, he yanked Adam's head up and began to squeeze his throat.

Adam jerked his head back in an attempt to free himself, but Haman was too strong. Without the use of his hands, Adam resorted to the only weapon he had left. Although not a muscular man, Adam, filled with rage and strengthened by the adrenaline that coursed through his veins, wrapped his legs around Haman and interlocked his feet, squeezing with all the power his muscles would provide. He felt one of Haman's ribs break, but Haman refused to let go. Adam could feel his trachea being pinched shut and knew the carotid arteries that carried blood to his brain were closed in the vise grip of Haman's hand. Adam squeezed his legs together again. Through the murky green water Adam could see the white teeth of Haman grimacing; air bubbles streamed from his mouth and nose.

The moments seemed like ages as the two struggled desperately, Adam driven by desperation and Haman by rage. Even though the salt water blurred Adam's vision, he could still see the anger in Haman's face. Haman tightened his grip with a monumental effort. Adam's oxygen-starved brain struggled to remain conscious, but the soft blur of the ocean's green faded into black. Adam's body went limp. The struggle was over.

"What was that?" R.G. asked, redirecting his attention from the spot where Adam and Haman had plunged into the ocean.

"What was what?" Sanchez asked puzzled.

"That sound."

Sanchez listened to a low hum reverberating across the surface of the water. "Sounds like a boat motor."

Both men turned simultaneously to see the white and orange painted hull of a Coast Guard clipper bearing down on their port side. Another sound caught their attention, a low, rhythmic chopping sound that came from overhead.

"Helicopter," Sanchez shouted.

"Get us underway," R.G. ordered and snatched the Uzi machine gun from Sanchez's hand.

"We can't outrun a helicopter."

"I'll take care of the helicopter, you start the engines."

Sanchez sprang forward toward the bridge of the ship as the orange and white helicopter descended.

"This is the U.S. Coast Guard. Drop your weapons and prepare to be boarded," a voice commanded from above.

R.G. swung the Uzi in the direction of the helicopter and fired a burst of bullets, the rounds piercing the metal hull. A crewman immediately returned fire with his M-16 and R.G. fell to the deck, two bullets piercing his heart.

"Cut your engines and prepare to be boarded," the voice commanded. Sanchez stared at the limp body in an expanding circle of blood, then switched off the engines and, placing his hands on his head, walked out of the cabin onto the deck.

A few moments later the Coast Guard clipper pulled alongside and bobbed on the ocean swells. The seasoned crew of the cutter deftly lowered a twenty-two-foot RHI Zodiac into the water. Greene and several armed crewmen boarded the small boat and quickly made their way to the drifting cruiser. Minutes later they were on deck.

"Are there others aboard?" Greene asked, his regulation .38 in hand.

"No," Rachel said groggily, struggling to her feet. "But Adam went over the side with one of them." Each word sent pain piercing through her jaw.

"Where?" Greene asked.

Rachel, her hands still bound behind her, nodded over the side where Haman and Adam fell, then screamed, "Adam!"

A short distance away the limp body of Adam was floating facedown, rising and falling with the ocean swells. Greene stripped himself of his jacket and shoes, and handing his pistol to one of the crewmen, leaped into the ocean; two Coast Guard crewmen followed him into the water. A few moments later, with the help of the others, the body of Adam Bridger lay on the deck of the boat. His face was blue and deep purple marks circled his neck.

Even to the untrained eye, it was obvious that Adam was not breathing.

"Cut me free!" she shouted. "Hurry!"

A crewman produced a knife and cut the duct tape binding Rachel's hands. Oblivious to the pain, she ripped the tape from her wrists and threw it to the deck. Racing to Adam's side she quickly checked for a pulse but found none. Her instincts as a doctor took over as she administered CPR. Another Coast Guard crewman joined her, tilting Adam's head back and blowing air into his lungs.

"Come on, Adam," she said, as she compressed his chest with her hands. "Don't leave me." Tears rolled off her cheeks and fell on the still form beneath her. After a minute of compression, she felt for a pulse. She resumed the procedure knowing that she was attempting the impossible. He had been gone too long, but she had to try and bring life back to the only man she had ever loved.

"It's over," Greene said quietly. "There's nothing more you can do."

Rachel continued compressing Adam's chest.

"Rachel, it's hopeless. I know it hurts, but you've got to face it— Adam is dead."

She stared down at the lifeless eyes that gazed at the blue sky above. The life of Adam Bridger was gone. Unashamedly she began sobbing. David and Ann Lorayne wept in silence as they stared at the lifeless form that had been their pastor.

Quietly, almost imperceptibly, a man in a white sport shirt stepped through the crowd and gazed at Adam's body through tear-filled eyes. Then, kneeling on the deck, the man extended a hand and gently laid it on Adam's unmoving chest. At first, Rachel felt compelled to tell him not to touch Adam. Yet, somehow she knew she must refrain.

Silence cloaked the ship, even sea gulls overhead seemed to know that this was a moment to be still. The only sound in the air was the soft slapping of the ocean against the hull and the resonant thumping of the helicopter.

The man closed his eyes and a faint blue aura surrounded his hand. Then, before the astounded eyes of all, the purple bruises on Adam's neck began to lighten until they disappeared altogether. A moment later, Adam's body went rigid, jerked in spasms, and he coughed. Rachel leaped to her feet and covered her mouth with her hands, stifling a scream.

# Epilogue

## Thursday, April 8; 7 P.M.

The large room at the rear of DaVinci's Restaurant was filled with those who only a few days before had stood together on the deck of R.G.'s boat, preparing to die. Now, they and the others caught up in the events surrounding the Healer sat at a long table eating and laughing.

Adam took a bite of lasagna and shook his head. "I don't remember a thing after passing out. Last thing I remember was seeing Haman's ugly face; the next thing I remember seeing was Rachel's face, which I thought was a considerable improvement."

"I should hope so," Rachel said, smiling. "What do you suppose happened to Haman?"

"Drowned, probably," Greene said, twirling spaghetti on his fork. "We were too far out for him to swim back. The Coast Guard expects his body to wash up sometime."

"Can we talk about something other than floating bodies?" Priscilla Simms asked.

"Sorry," Greene replied.

"And what about the Healer?" Priscilla asked, taking another bite of her antipasto salad.

"Gone," Greene said. "He quit talking, or signing should I say, as soon as he did whatever he did to Adam. When we got back to port, he disappeared in all the excitement. I sure had a lot of questions for him. We checked the address on his driver's license. It turned out to be an apartment building, but he hadn't lived there for six months, and no one knew anything about him." He shook his head in disbelief. "It appears that our Healer has become invisible again."

"A deaf and mute Healer," Art McGinnes said. "Now that's irony for you."

"It also explains why there was no message," Adam said.

"Message?" Priscilla was puzzled.

"Adam believes that miracles are always accompanied by a message from God," Rachel replied for Adam. "It's driving him crazy."

Adam looked deep into Rachel's eyes. They had spent the day together, strolling along the walk at La Jolla Cove and drinking cappuccino at a nearby coffee house. As they walked, Adam shared his heart with Rachel. He spoke of his feelings for her and also of spiritual things. He talked of the hope of his faith; and for the first time, Rachel listened without interruption. Occasionally she asked questions and spoke of her attraction to him. Adam was as honest as a man could be. When he told her that he loved her, he also told her of the conundrum his affection caused. She understood the difficulty.

"You know of my faith, and I know of your firm atheism," Adam had said stoically.

"Not so firm," Rachel had said.

"I don't understand," Adam replied.

"My atheism isn't so firm," she said taking his hand. "I've seen things that cannot be explained. I don't know for certain that God is the cause of it all, but I can no longer dismiss that possibility." She had reached up, put her hand behind his head and pulled his lips to hers in a gentle, warm kiss. "I don't know if all that you say is true, but much of it makes sense. I promise you this, Adam: I will consider what you've said, and I will remain open to your God." She was surprised as Adam removed his glasses and wiped away a stray tear.

"Well, maybe this will help," Greene said. His words brought Adam back to the present. Greene extracted an envelope from his suit coat pocket. "The Healer paid some kid off the street to bring it to me and asked that I give it to you."

Adam opened the plain envelope and pulled out a small hand-written note addressed to him. He read the note aloud, "I'm sorry that I couldn't stay. I imagine we have much in common, but my task is immense. I'm sure you have many questions. I assure you that those questions will be answered soon. Wait for the others who are to come, and listen to what they have to say. They have the message. Malachi 4:5."

"Malachi 4:5—what's that?" Priscilla asked in true reportorial fashion.

Adam thought for a moment and then recited, "Behold, I will send you Elijah the prophet before the great and terrible day of the Lord."

"What's that mean?" Rachel asked.

"I think he means to say that one greater than he will be coming, and then . . ." Adam broke off mid-sentence.

"And then the end?" Greene asked reluctantly.

"The beginning," Adam replied.

The silence was broken by a beeping sound.

"My pager," Rachel explained. "I'll be back in a minute." Sgt. Reedly, Priscilla's date for the evening, moved away from the table to give her enough room to get out.

The conversation continued after she left.

"What's going to happen to Paul Isaiah?" Adam asked.

"Well, his ministry is finished, that's for sure," Greene replied. "But I don't think he'll do any hard time. He didn't have anything to do with the abductions—that was all R.G.'s doing—although he did admit he was a charlatan, at least part of the time."

"Part of the time?" Adam asked.

"Yeah," Greene continued. "He's a real case for the psychiatrists. It seems that he lost his wife and two kids in an auto accident. He was a young preacher then, and the accident made his mind snap. He blamed God for taking them. He couldn't understand how God could do that to him when he was preaching His message. So he decided to get even, but since he couldn't attack God directly, he decided to do it through His people. The odd thing is that there were times when he thought he was doing God a favor. At times he would be working against God, at other times working for Him. That's where R.G. came in. R.G. simply took control. He was able to play Isaiah like a fiddle, saying just the right things to swing Isaiah's fragile mind whichever way he wanted."

"That's sad," Priscilla said.

"His lawyer is going to argue diminished capability," Greene said. "The worst that will happen is that Isaiah will be ordered to get professional help."

Rachel walked back into the room. "I'm sorry, but I have to go. There's been another healing."

"Healing?" Adam said. "I thought the Healer had left."

"Well, if he did, he left us something to think about. Anyway, I've got to go. The hospital wants me there right away."

"I'm coming with you," Adam said to Rachel.

The long table at DaVinci's emptied with astonishing speed. Adam, Reedly, and several others hastily threw money on the table to pay the bill and then raced from the restaurant. Priscilla was already on her cellular phone by the time Reedly opened the car door for her. Adam and Rachel were the first out of the parking lot and the first to arrive at the hospital. A moment later they stood in the hospital lobby. Neither spoke, for what they saw astonished them. The lobby, formerly the habitat of the hurting and ill, was in joyous tumult. The crippled were dancing, the blind were looking at magazines, and the dying were leaping for joy. Some sang aloud, others wept. Families embraced and doctors stood dumbfounded.

Adam looked around the room in disbelief. Along the walls were the tangled masses of walkers, wheelchairs and oxygen bottles, the wreckage of lives formally devoid of hope. As they stared in stunned silence, a movement caught Adam's eye. Looking down he saw the child whose formally sinuous spine was now straight and normal. He walked over to Adam and said cheerfully, "Hi, Mister." Then he hugged Adam's leg.

Tears rolled from Adam's eyes. Across the lobby the boy's mother stood with hands clasped together and pressed to her mouth. She wept with a joy born of great affliction. Adam understood.

Placing his hand on the boy's head, Adam said, "Hi, Buddy." The boy smiled, then giggled an infectious little boy's giggle. And then he giggled some more. Soon Adam giggled, then laughed. His laughter was joined by the boy's mother, then Rachel, and soon the lobby echoed with peals of thunderous joy.

Somehow Adam knew that neither he, nor the world, would ever be the same.